ANNE RICE

INTERVIEW
WITH THE
VAMPIRE
Claudia's Story

ART AND ADAPTATION BY
ASHLEY MARIE WITTER

Yen Press

Interview with the Vampire: Claudia's Story

Art and Adaptation: Ashley Marie Witter

Text copyright © 2012 Anne O'Brien Rice and The Stanley Travis Rice, Jr. Testamentary Trust
Illustrations © 2012 Hachette Book Group, Inc.

Yen Press
Hachette Book Group
237 Park Avenue, New York, NY 10017

www.HachetteBookGroup.com
www.YenPress.com

Yen Press is an imprint of Hachette Book Group, Inc.
The Yen Press name and logo are trademarks of Hachette Book Group, Inc.

First Edition: November 2012

ISBN: 978-0-316-17636-1

10 9 8 7 6 5 4 3 2 1

WOR
Printed in the United States of America

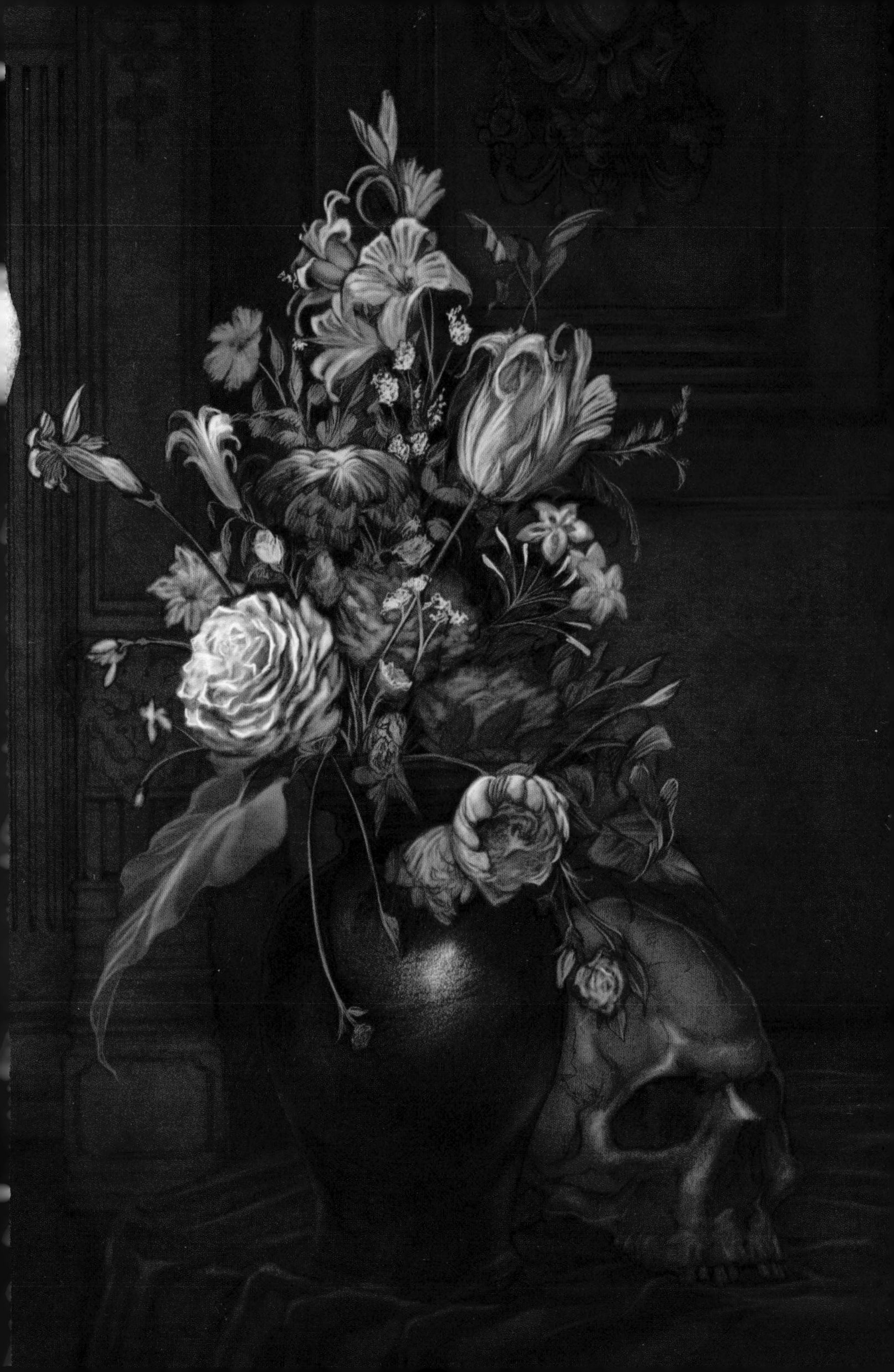

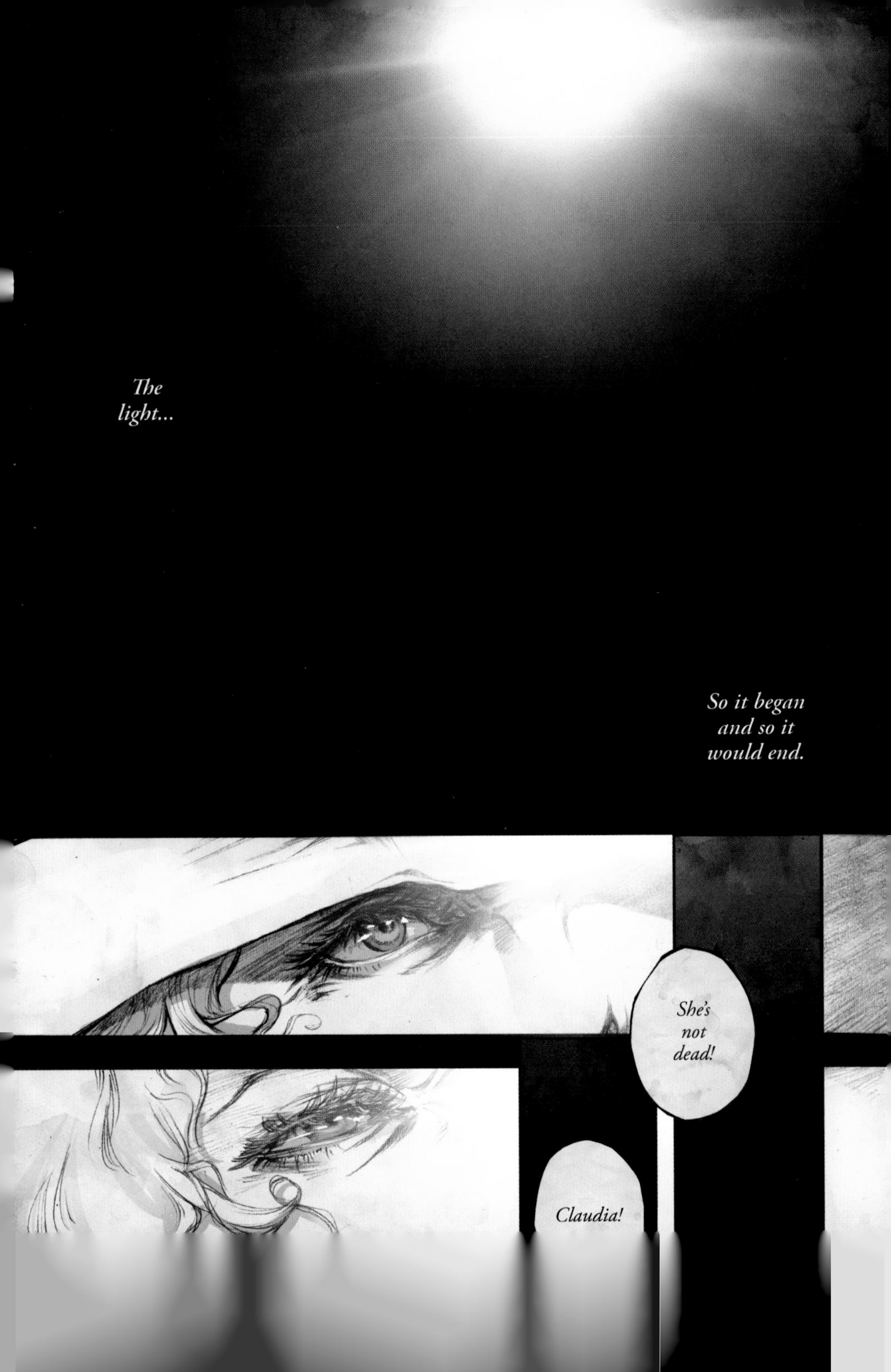
The light...
So it began and so it would end.
She's not dead!
Claudia!

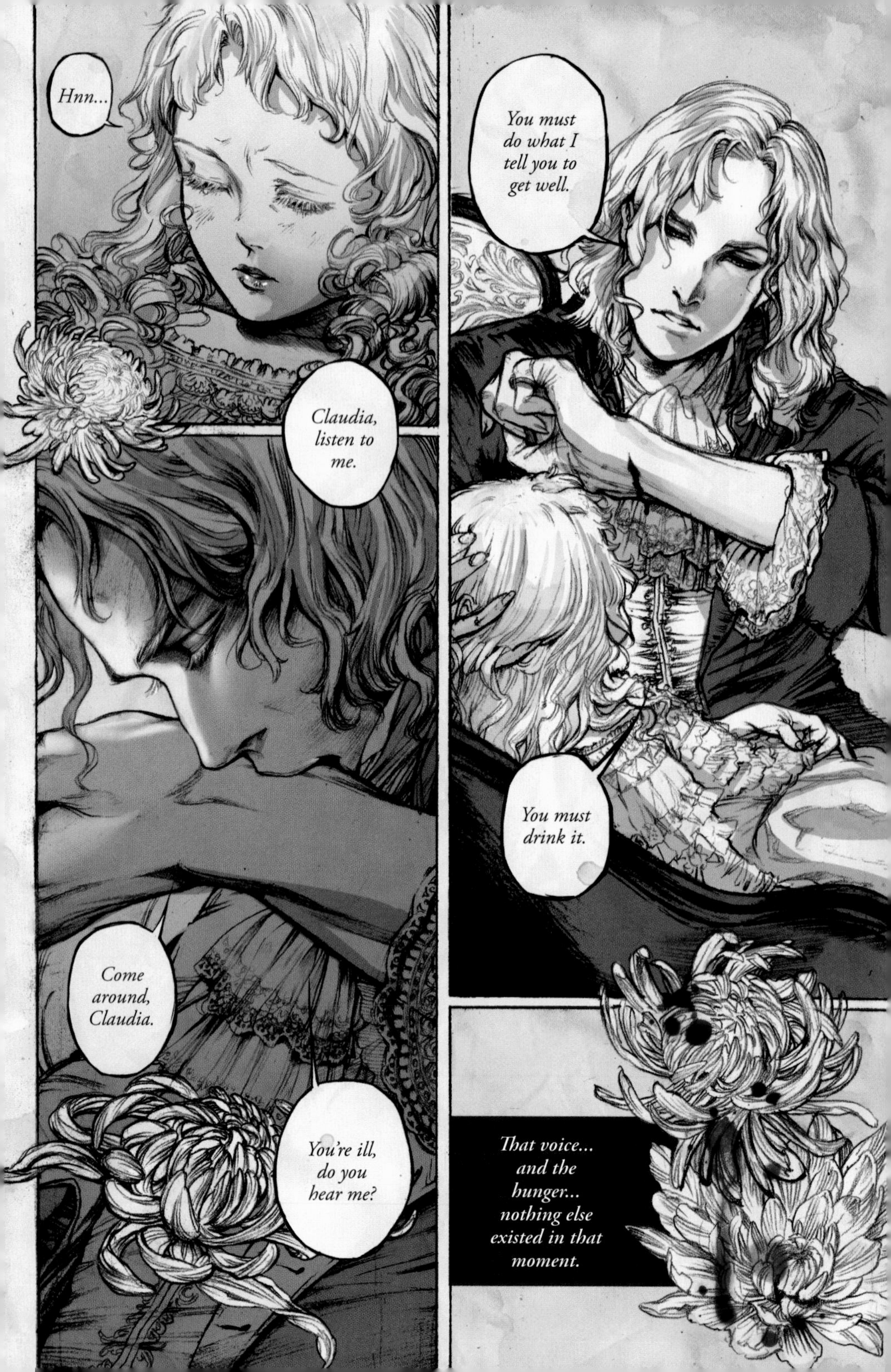
Hnn...
Claudia, listen to me.
Come around, Claudia.
You're ill, do you hear me?
You must do what I tell you to get well.
You must drink it.
That voice... and the hunger... nothing else existed in that moment.

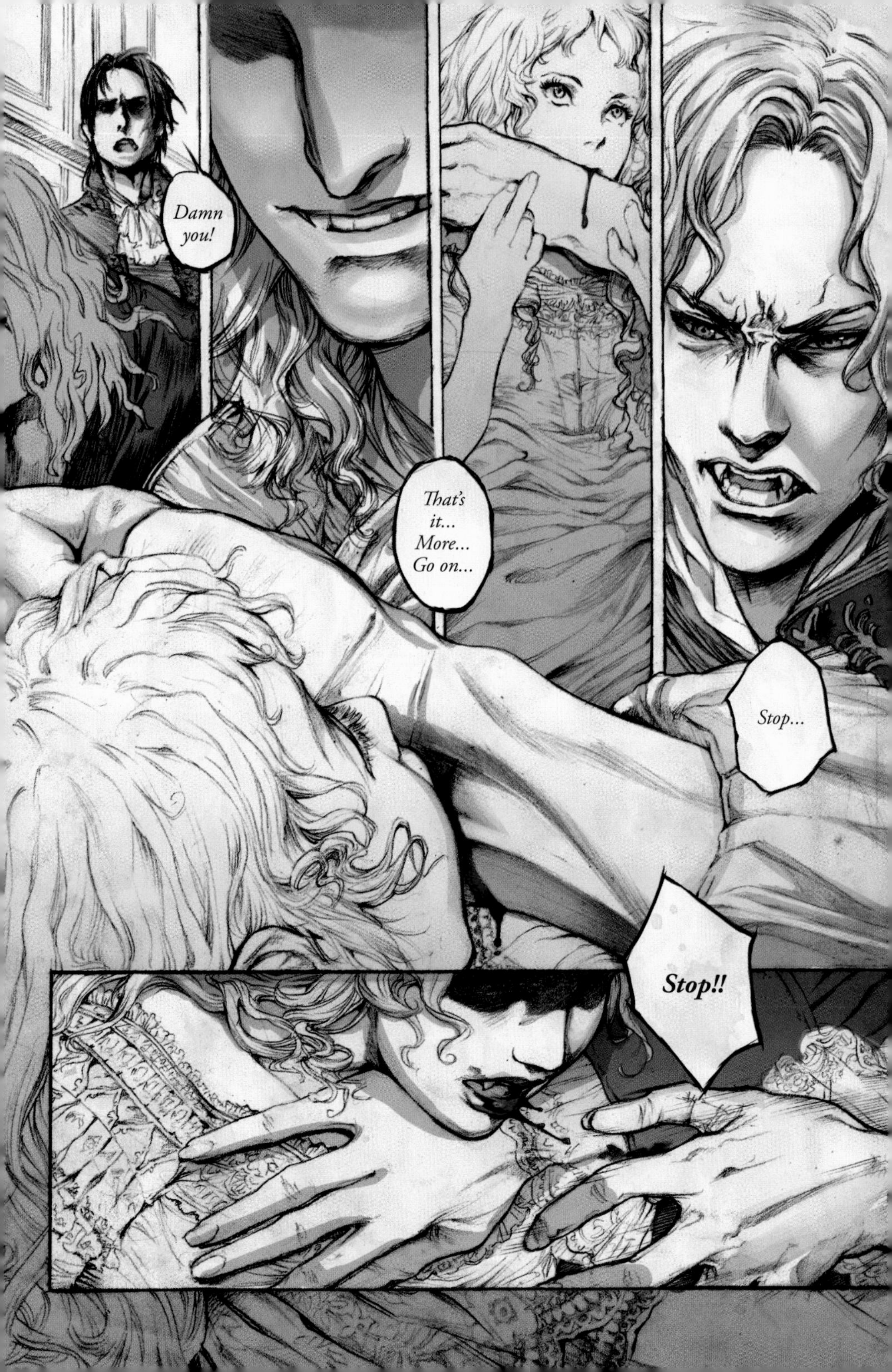

Damn you!
That's it... More... Go on...
Stop...
Stop!!

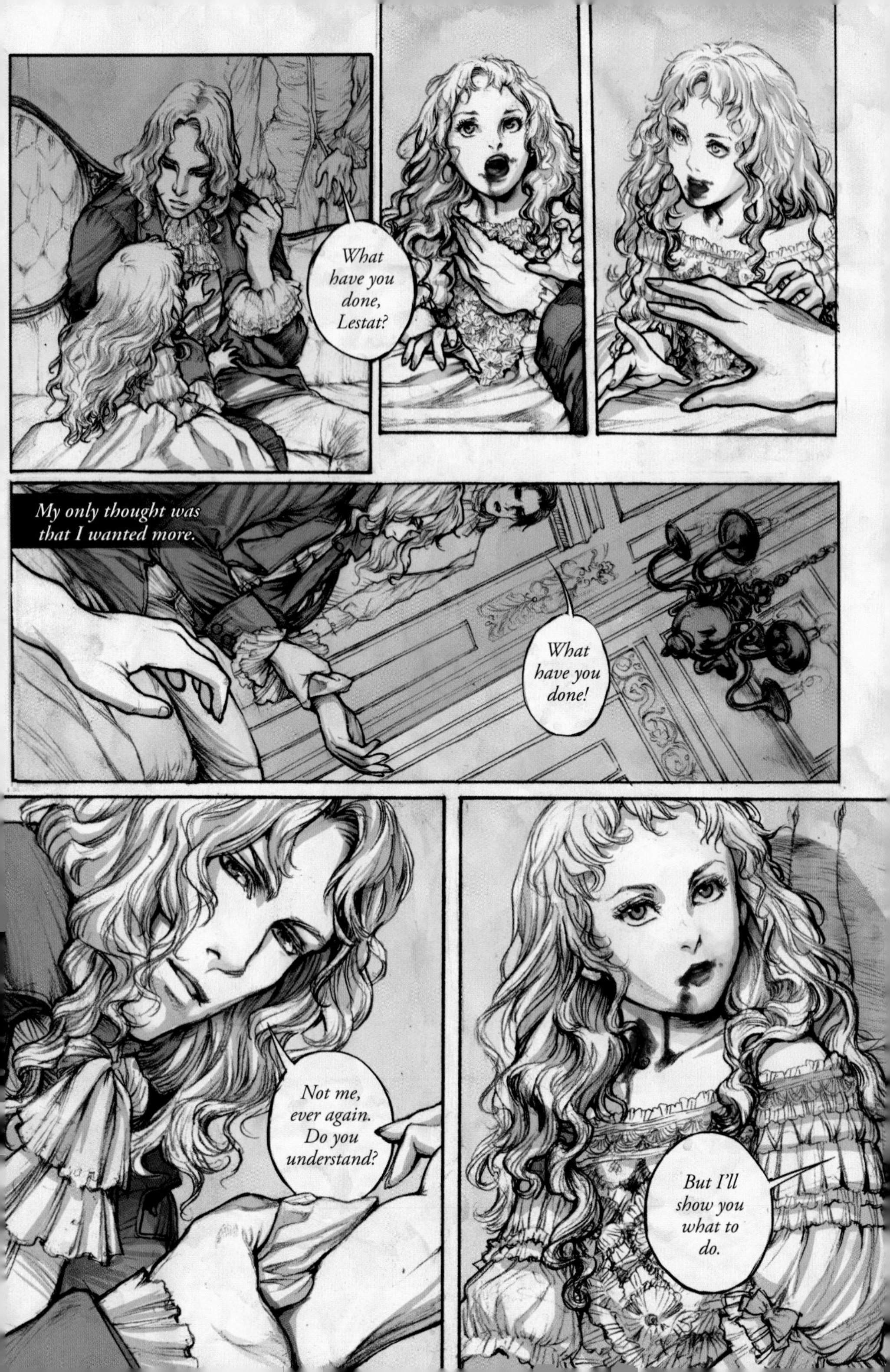
What have you done, Lestat?
My only thought was that I wanted more.
What have you done!
Not me, ever again. Do you understand?
But I'll show you what to do.

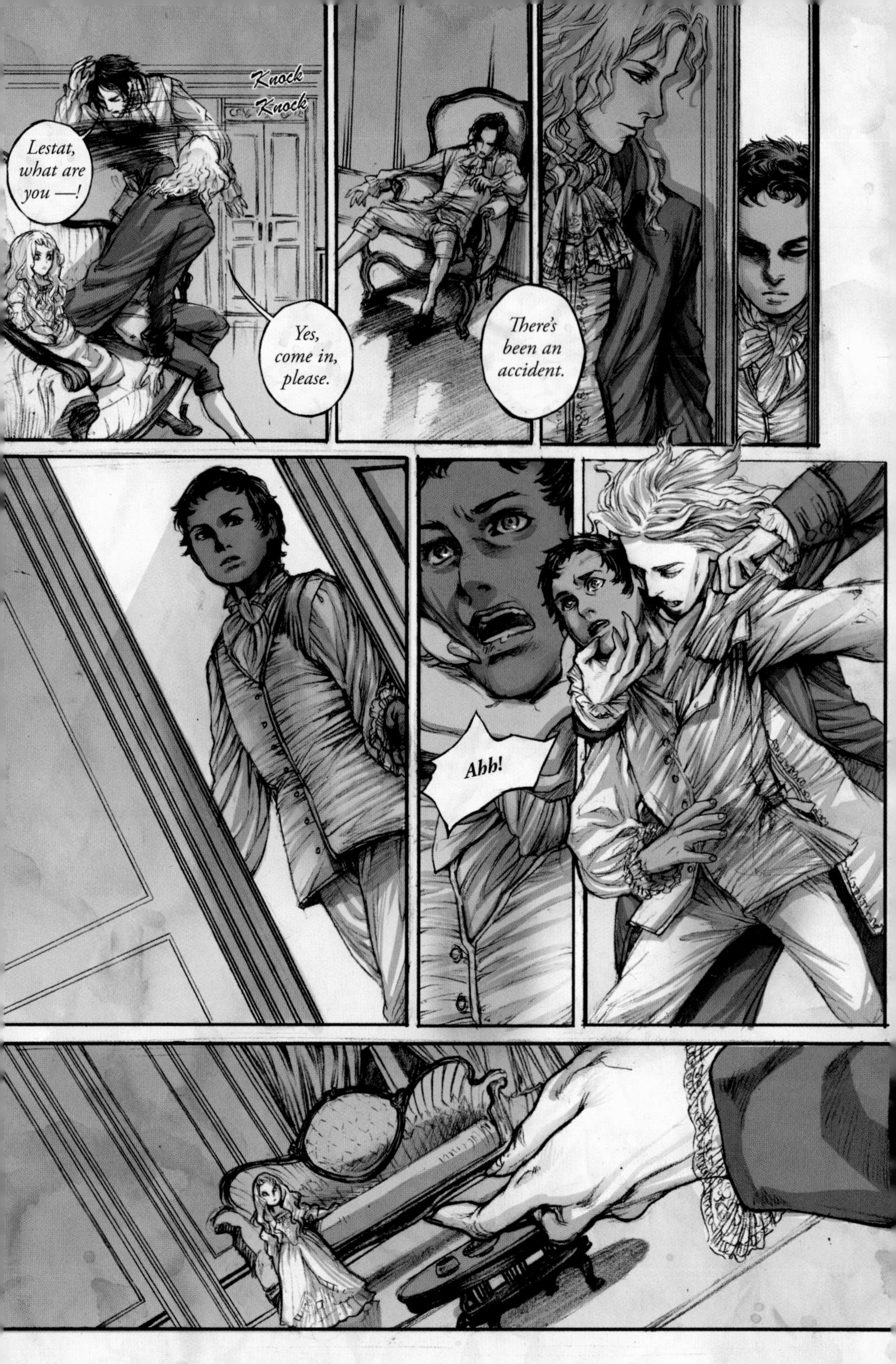
Knock
Knock
Lestat, what are you —!
Yes, come in, please.
There's been an accident.
Ahh!

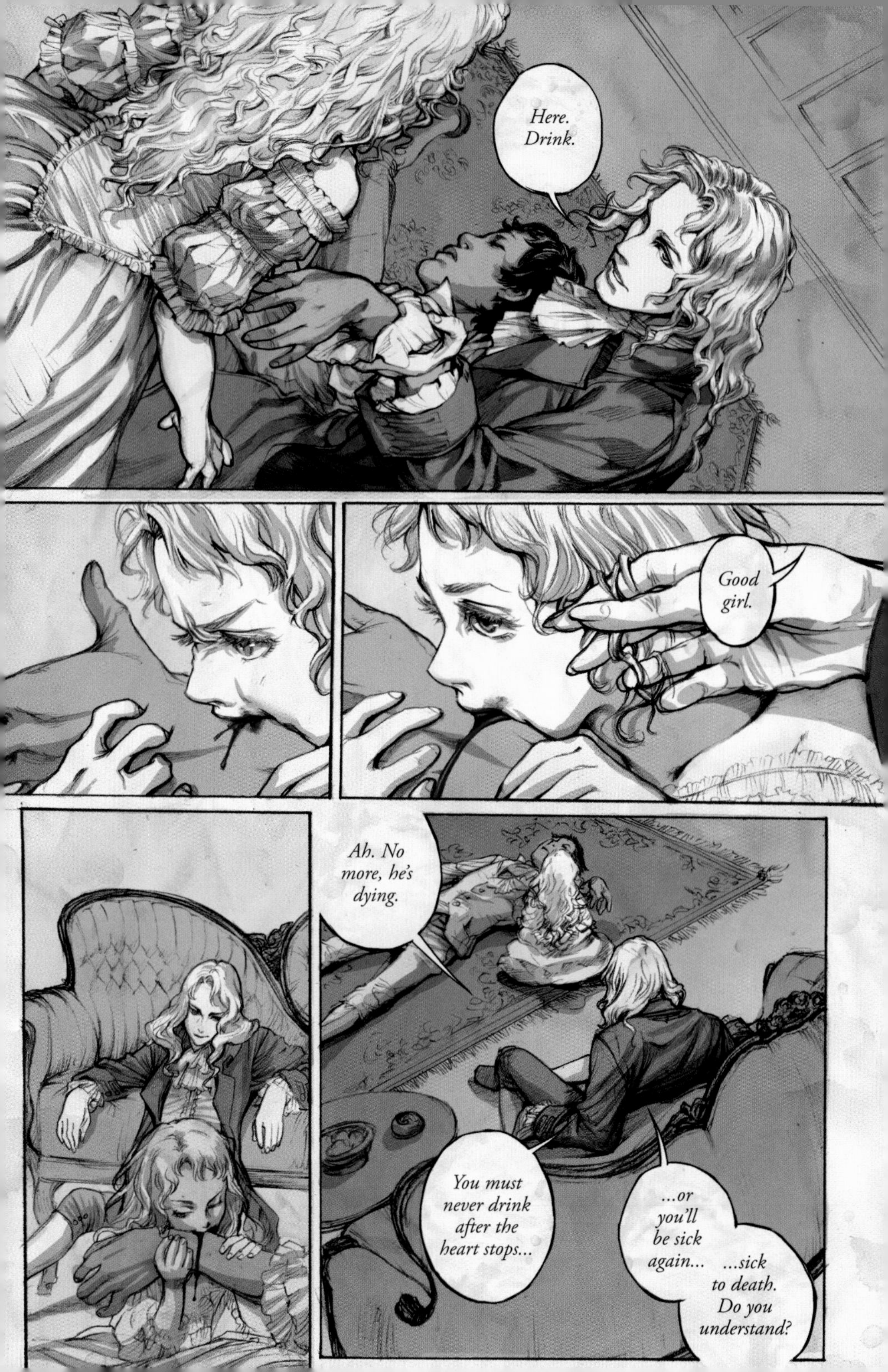

Here. Drink.
Good girl.
Ah. No more, he's dying.
You must never drink after the heart stops...
...or you'll be sick again...
...sick to death. Do you understand?

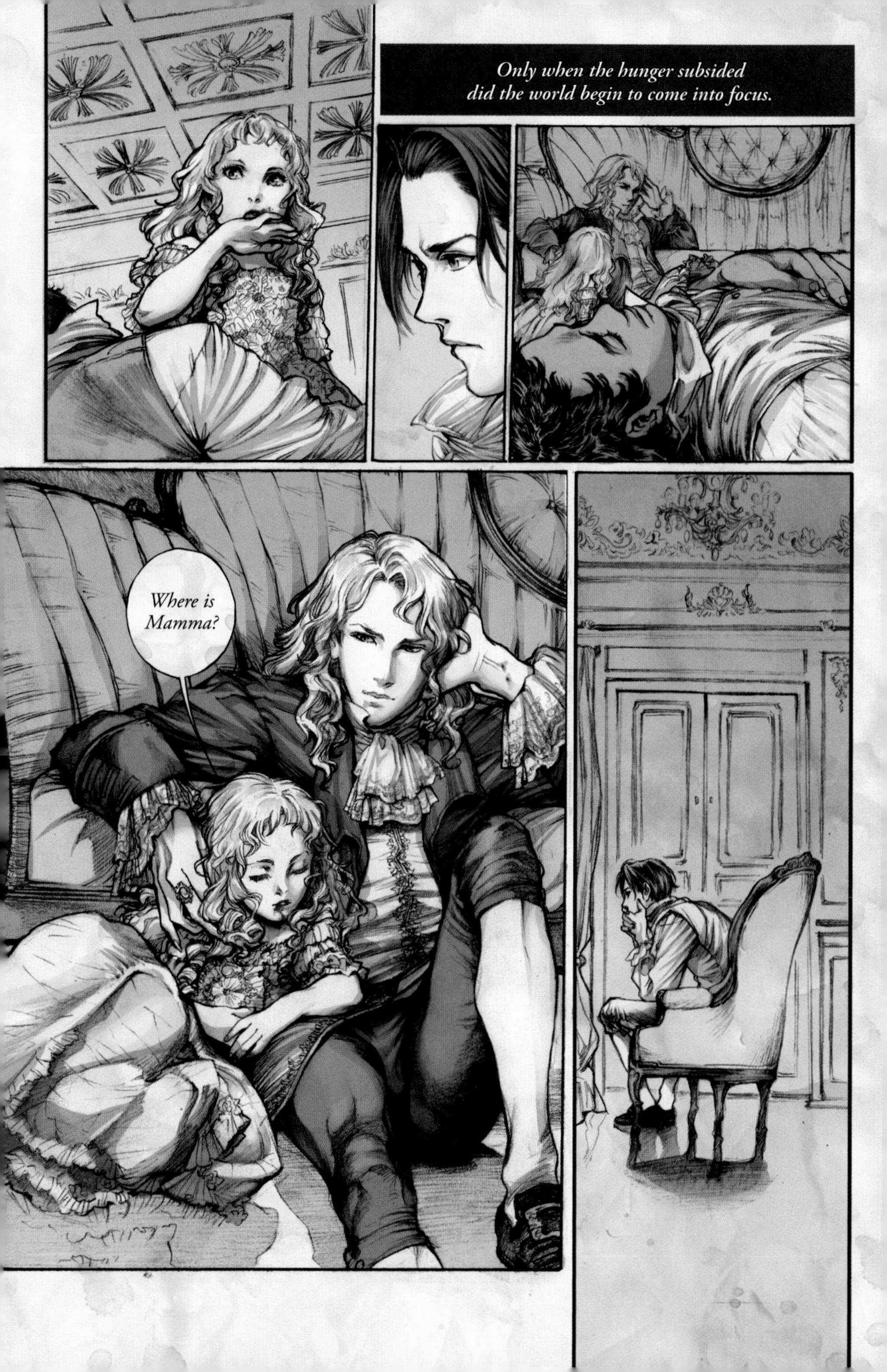
Only when the hunger subsided did the world begin to come into focus.
Where is Mamma?

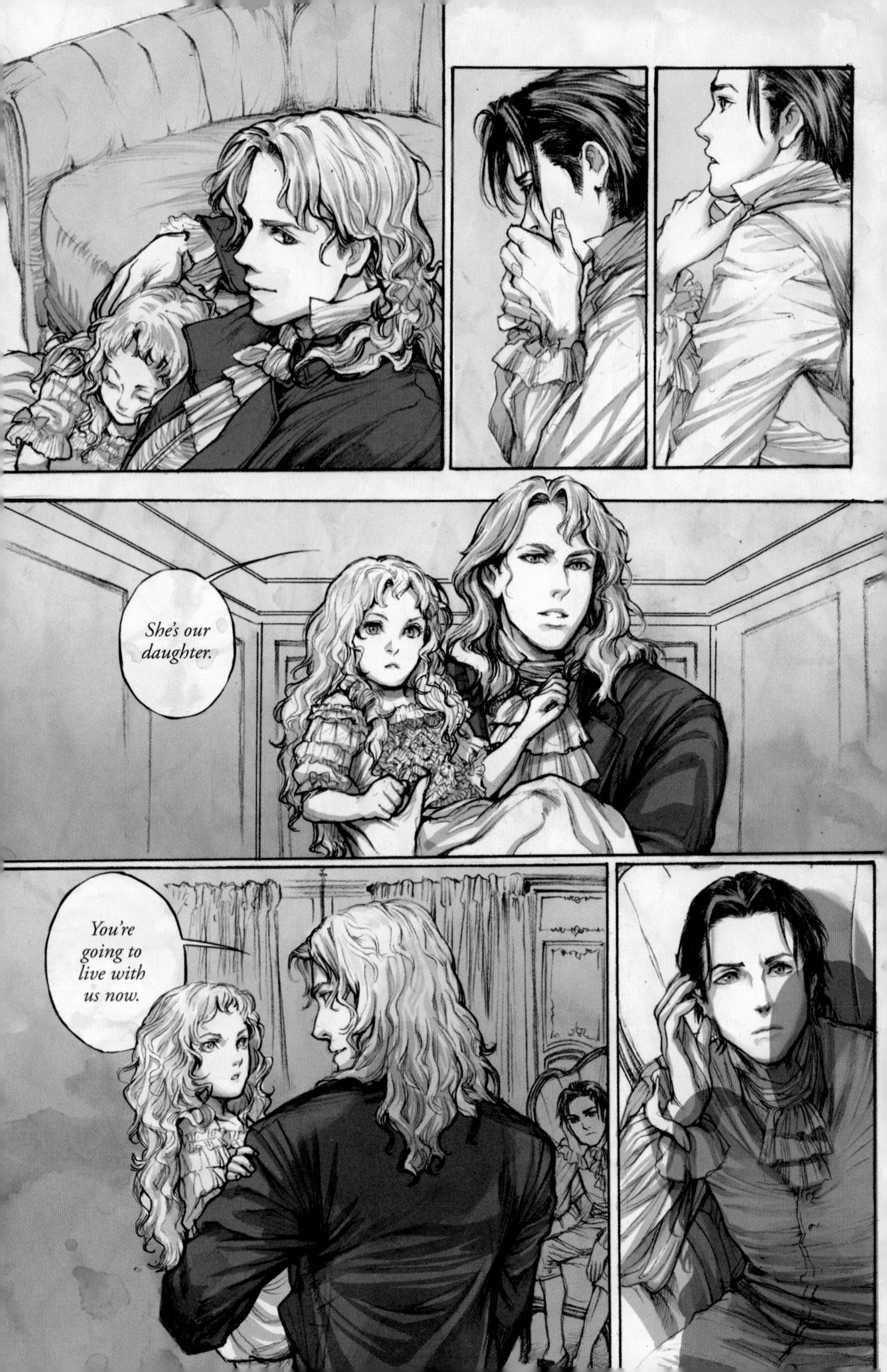
She's our daughter.
You're going to live with us now.

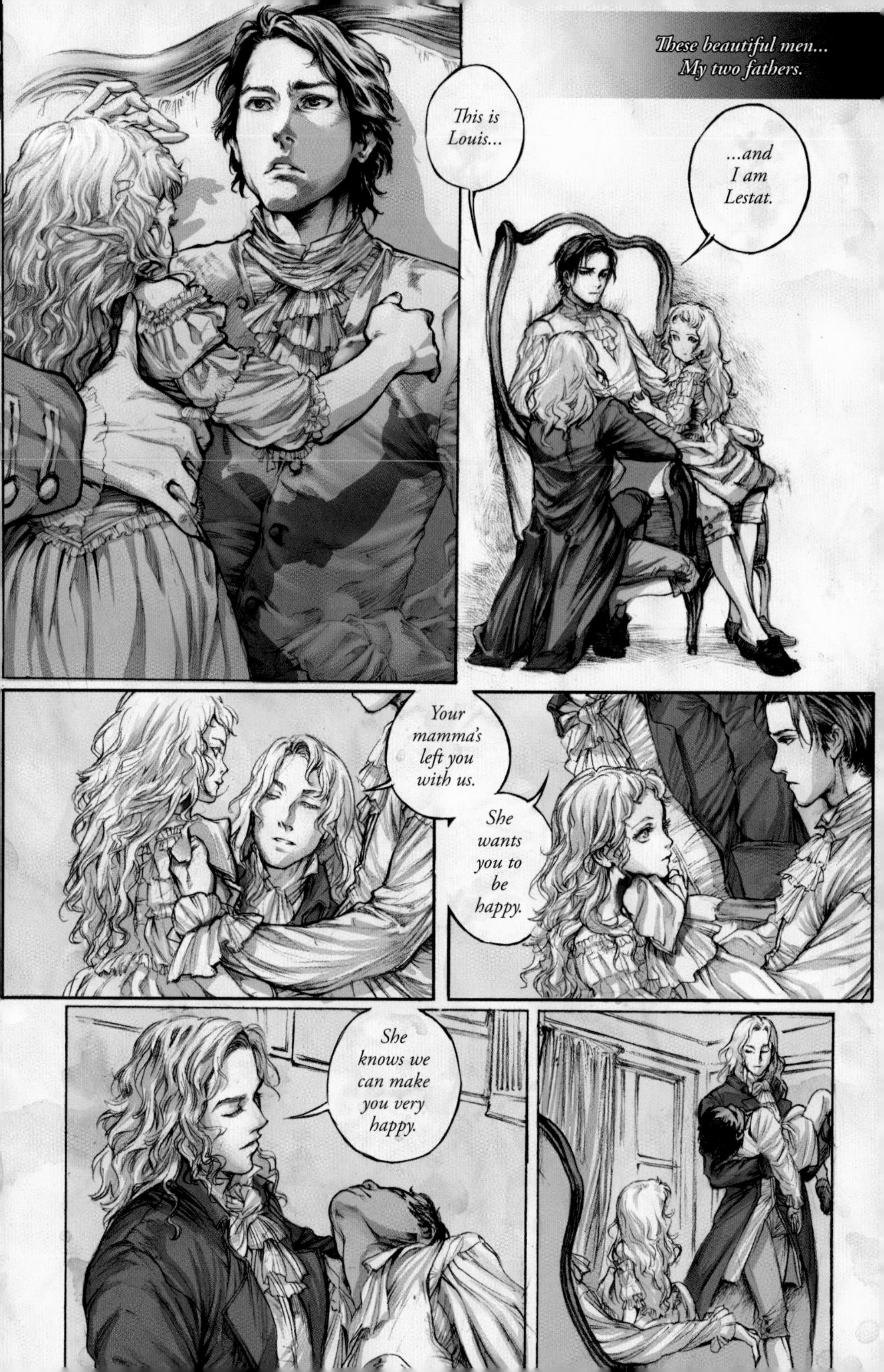
These beautiful men...
My two fathers.
This is Louis...
...and I am Lestat.
Your mamma's left you with us.
She wants you to be happy.
She knows we can make you very happy.

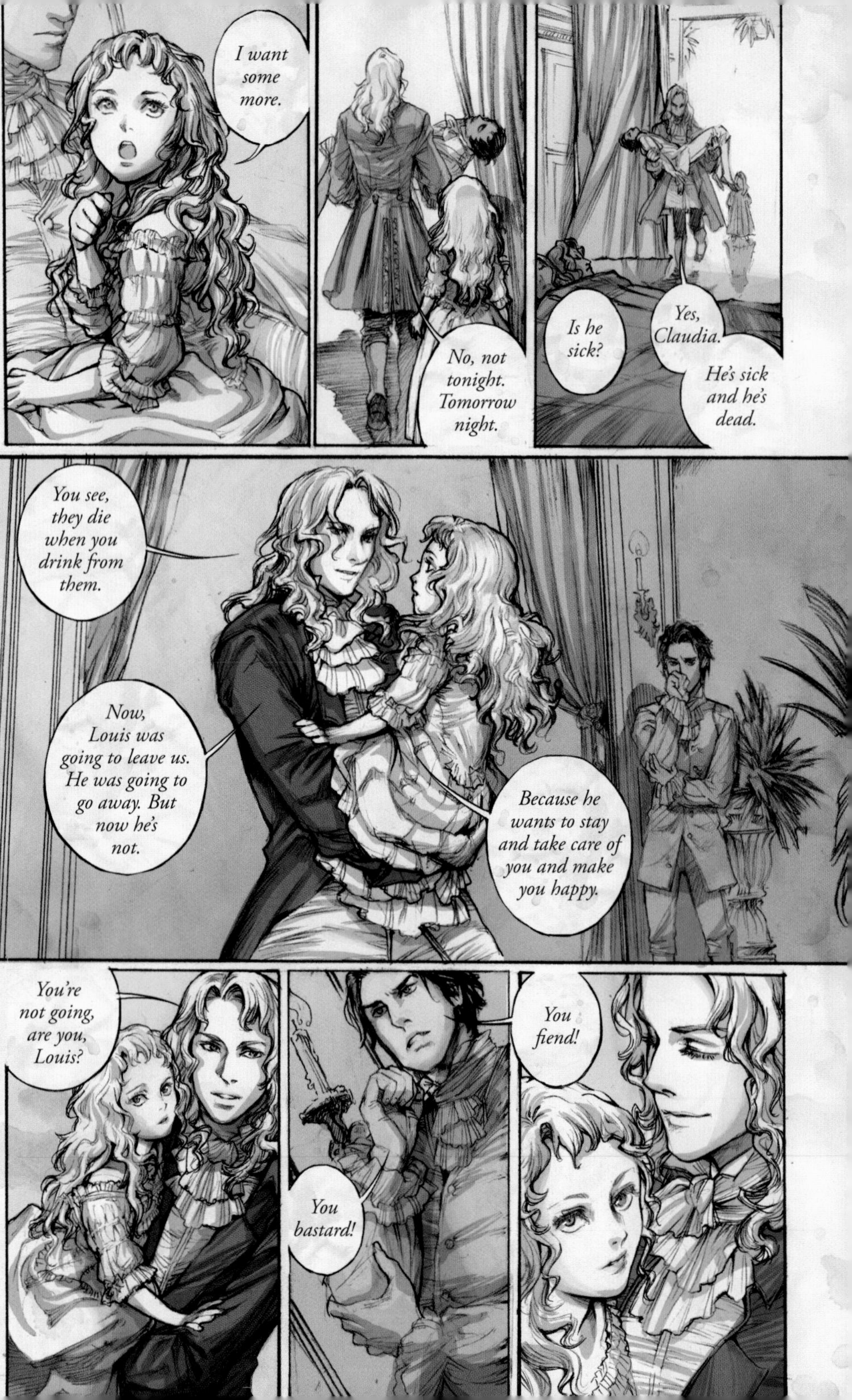
I want some more.
No, not tonight. Tomorrow night.
Is he sick?
Yes, Claudia.
He's sick and he's dead.
You see, they die when you drink from them.
Now, Louis was going to leave us. He was going to go away. But now he's not.
Because he wants to stay and take care of you and make you happy.
You're not going, are you, Louis?
You bastard!
You fiend!

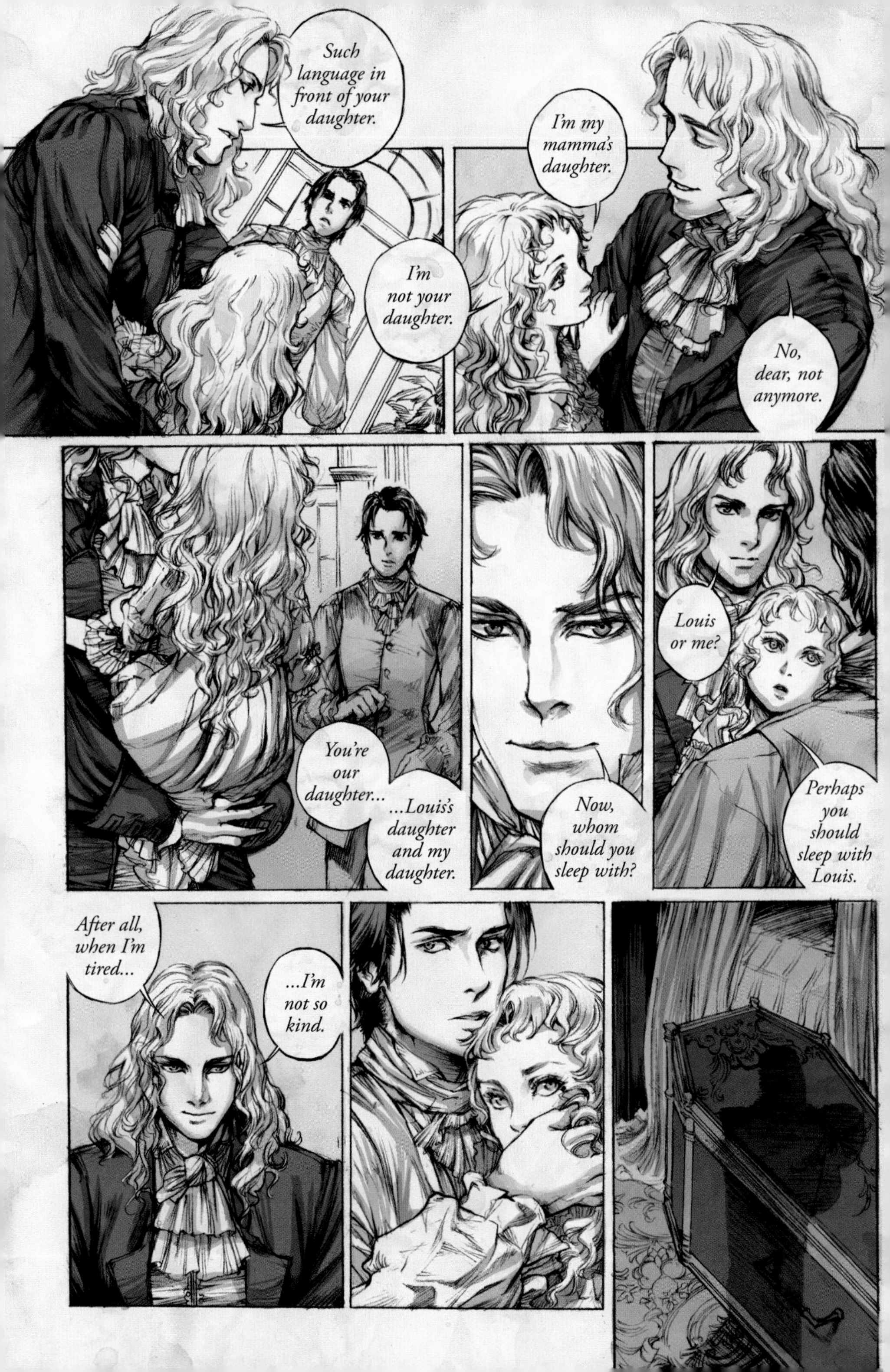
Such language in front of your daughter.
I'm not your daughter.
I'm my mamma's daughter.
No, dear, not anymore.
You're our daughter...
...Louis's daughter and my daughter.
Now, whom should you sleep with?
Louis or me?
Perhaps you should sleep with Louis.
After all, when I'm tired...
...I'm not so kind.

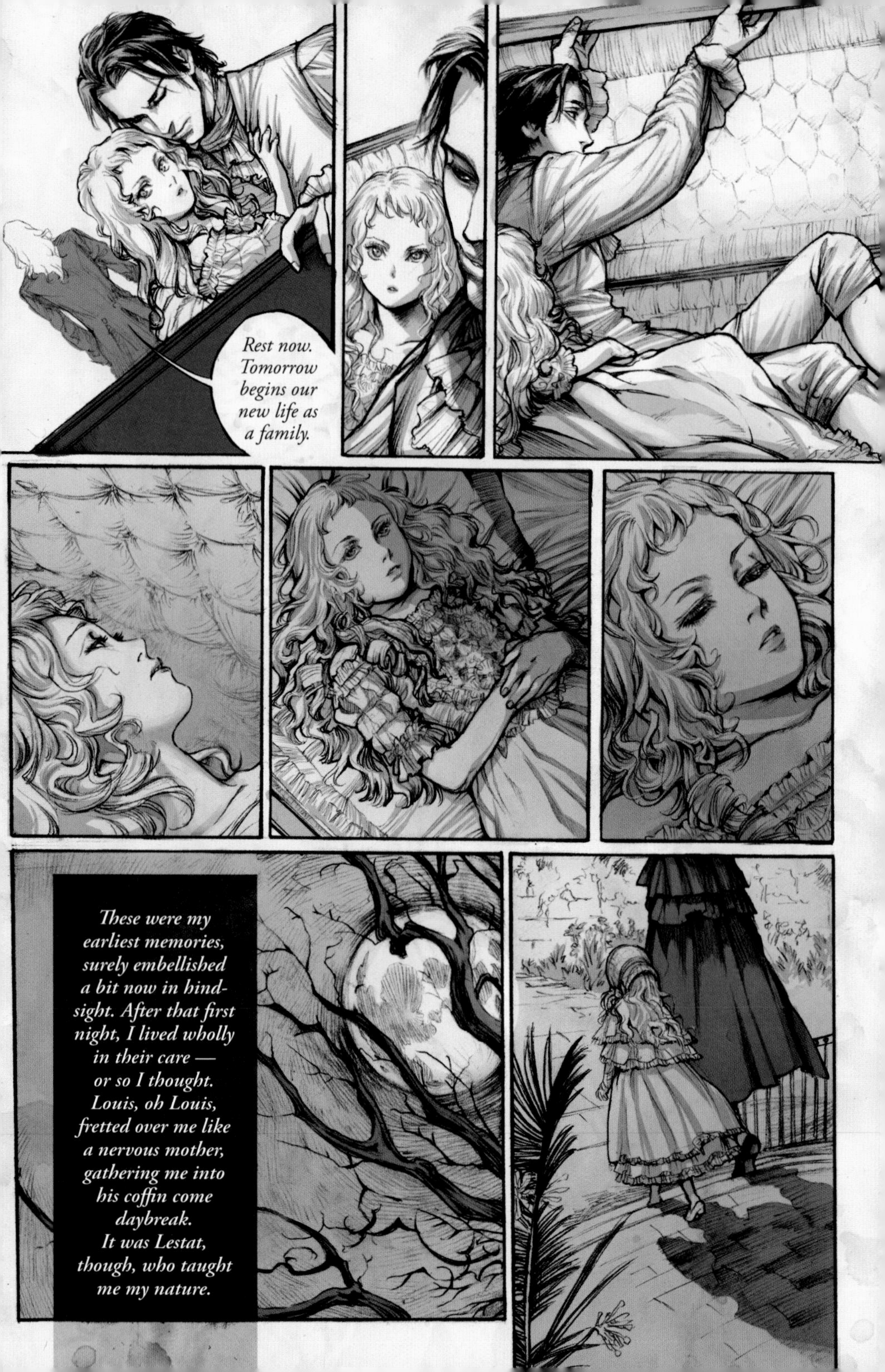
Rest now. Tomorrow begins our new life as a family.
These were my earliest memories, surely embellished a bit now in hindsight. After that first night, I lived wholly in their care — or so I thought. Louis, oh Louis, fretted over me like a nervous mother, gathering me into his coffin come daybreak. It was Lestat, though, who taught me my nature.

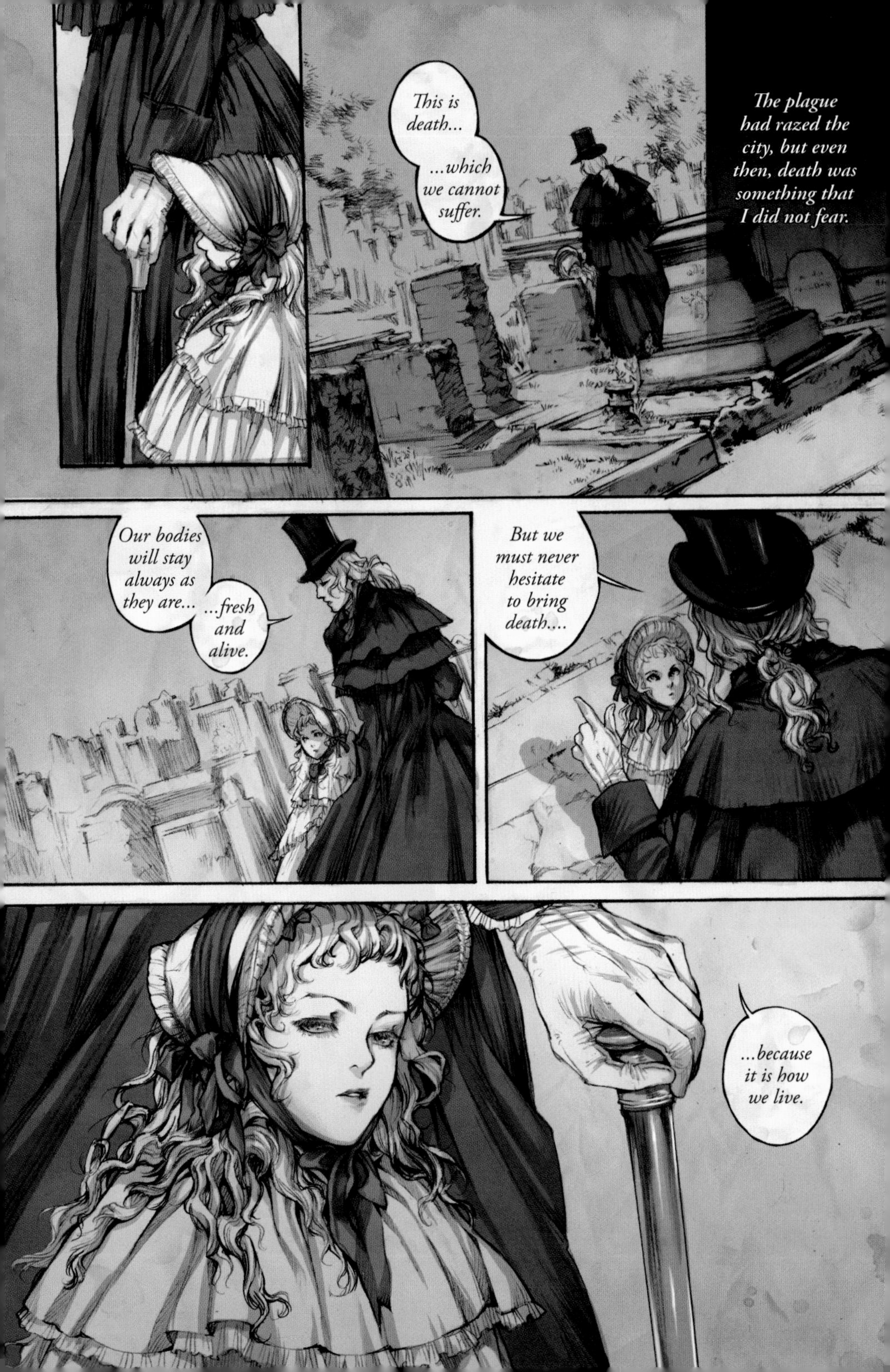
The plague had razed the city, but even then, death was something that I did not fear.
This is death...
...which we cannot suffer.
Our bodies will stay always as they are...
...fresh and alive.
But we must never hesitate to bring death....
...because it is how we live.

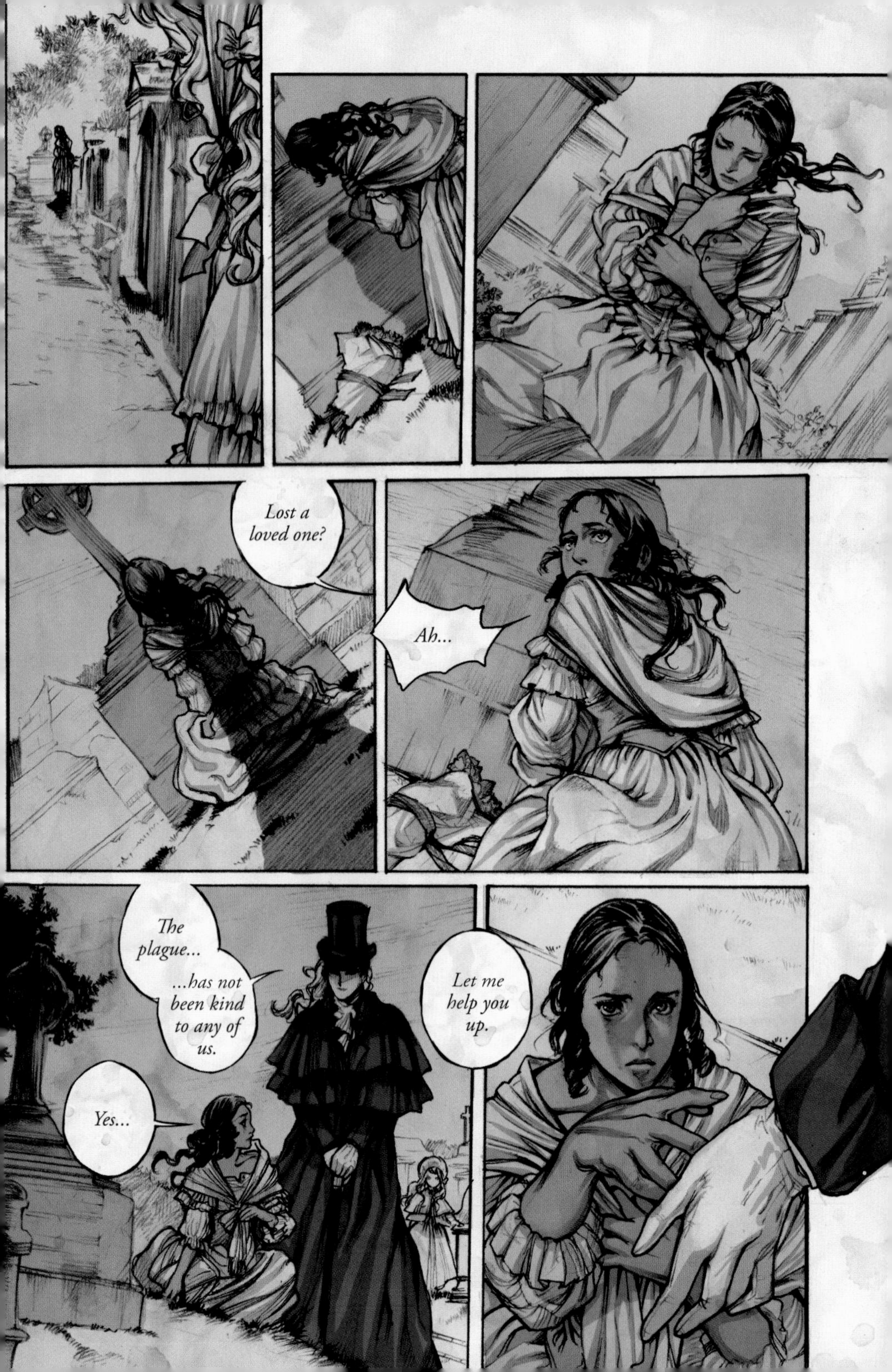
Lost a loved one?
Ah...
The plague...
...has not been kind to any of us.
Yes...
Let me help you up.

I'll...

You shouldn't moan anymore.

...let you join them.

Claudia, come drink.

Hunting and seduction were Lestat's lessons for me, and I came to know and relish death's many moods. Lestat was the perfect tutor, and I absorbed all that he was willing to offer.

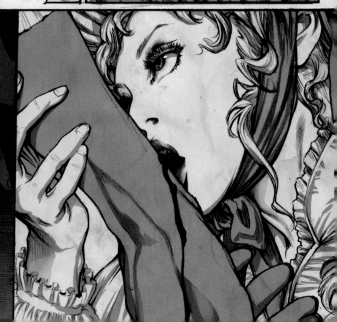

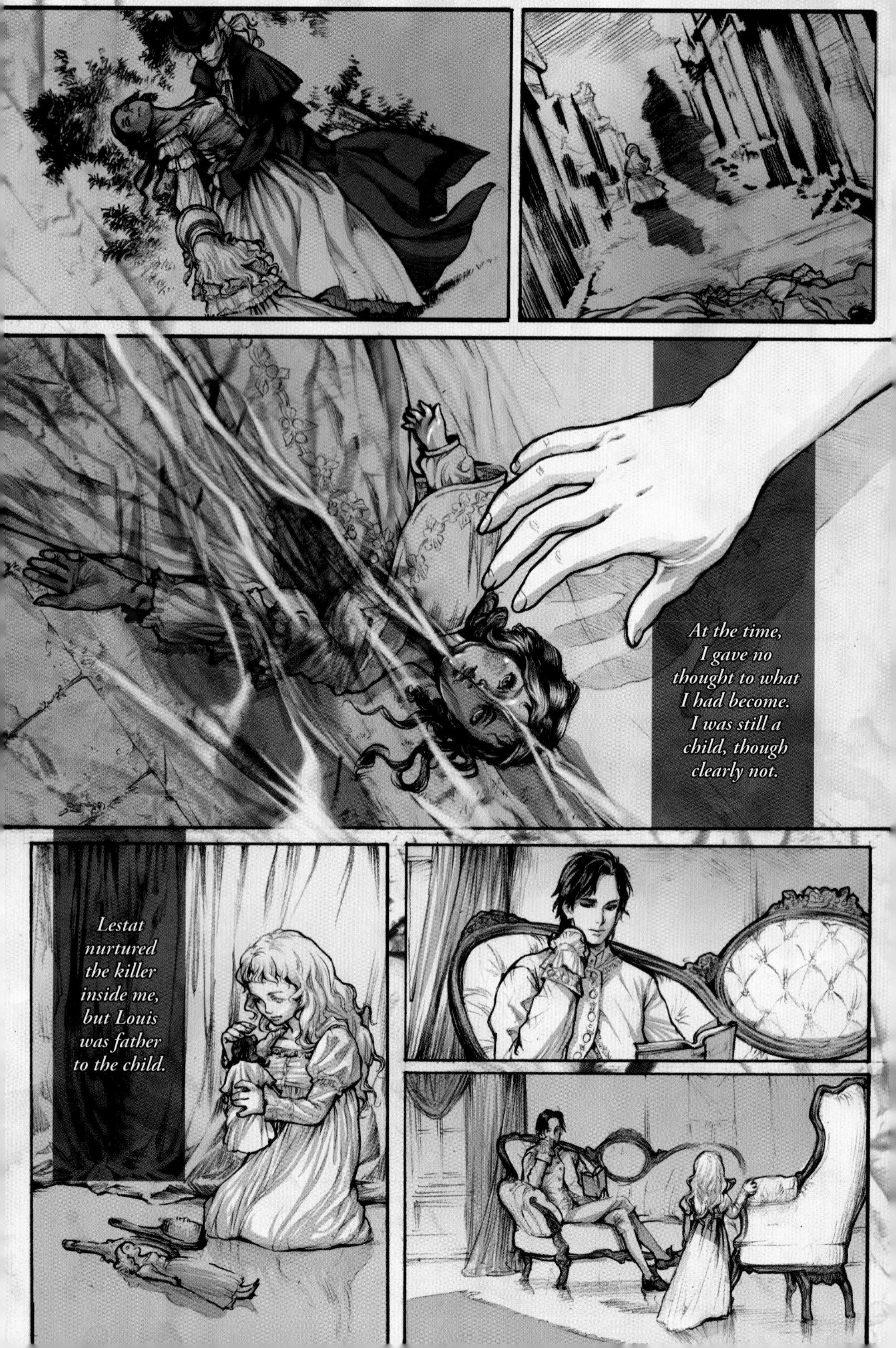
At the time, I gave no thought to what I had become. I was still a child, though clearly not.
Lestat nurtured the killer inside me, but Louis was father to the child.

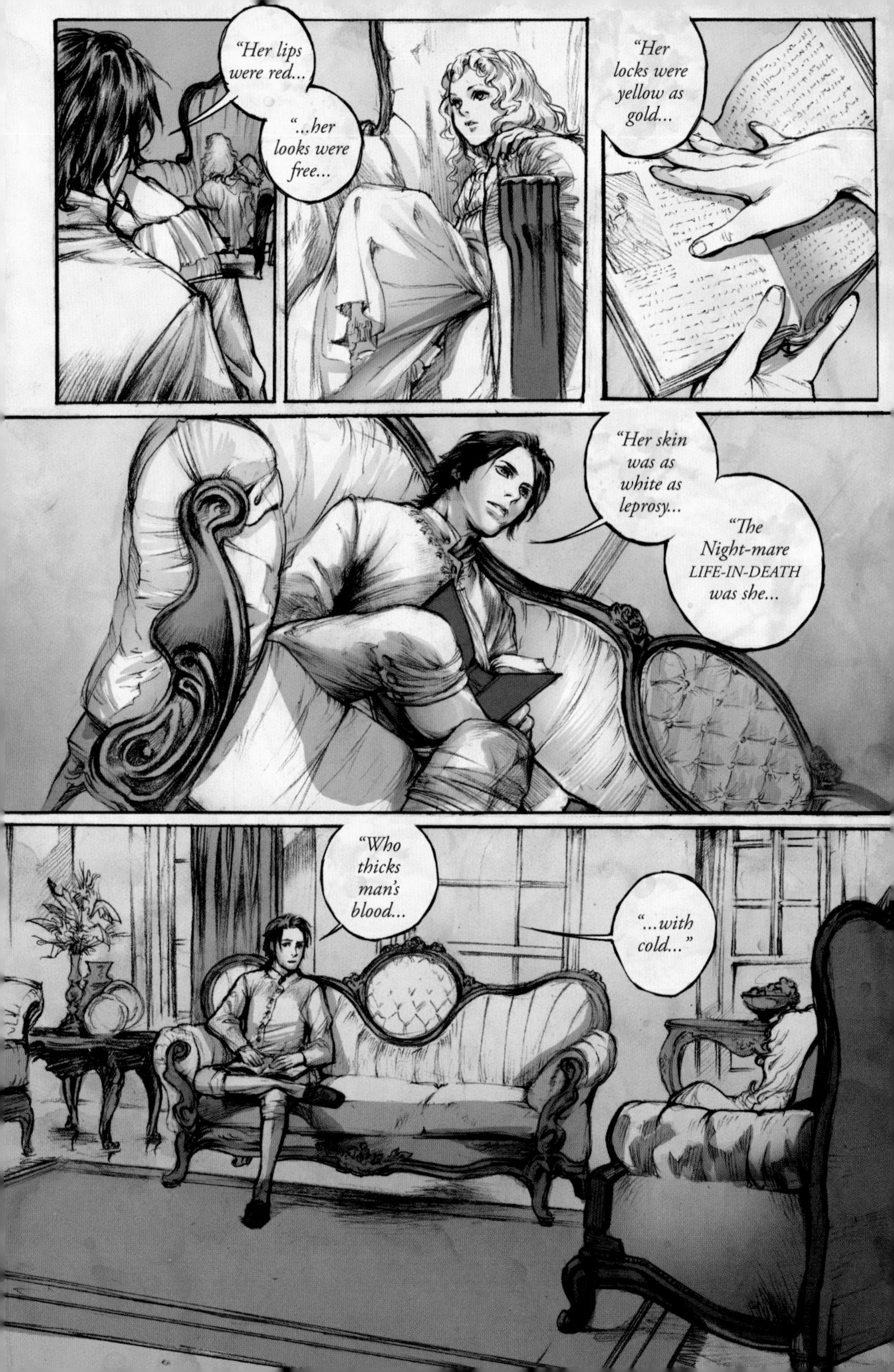
"Her lips were red...
"...her looks were free...
"Her locks were yellow as gold...
"Her skin was as white as leprosy...
"The Night-mare LIFE-IN-DEATH was she...
"Who thicks man's blood...
"...with cold..."

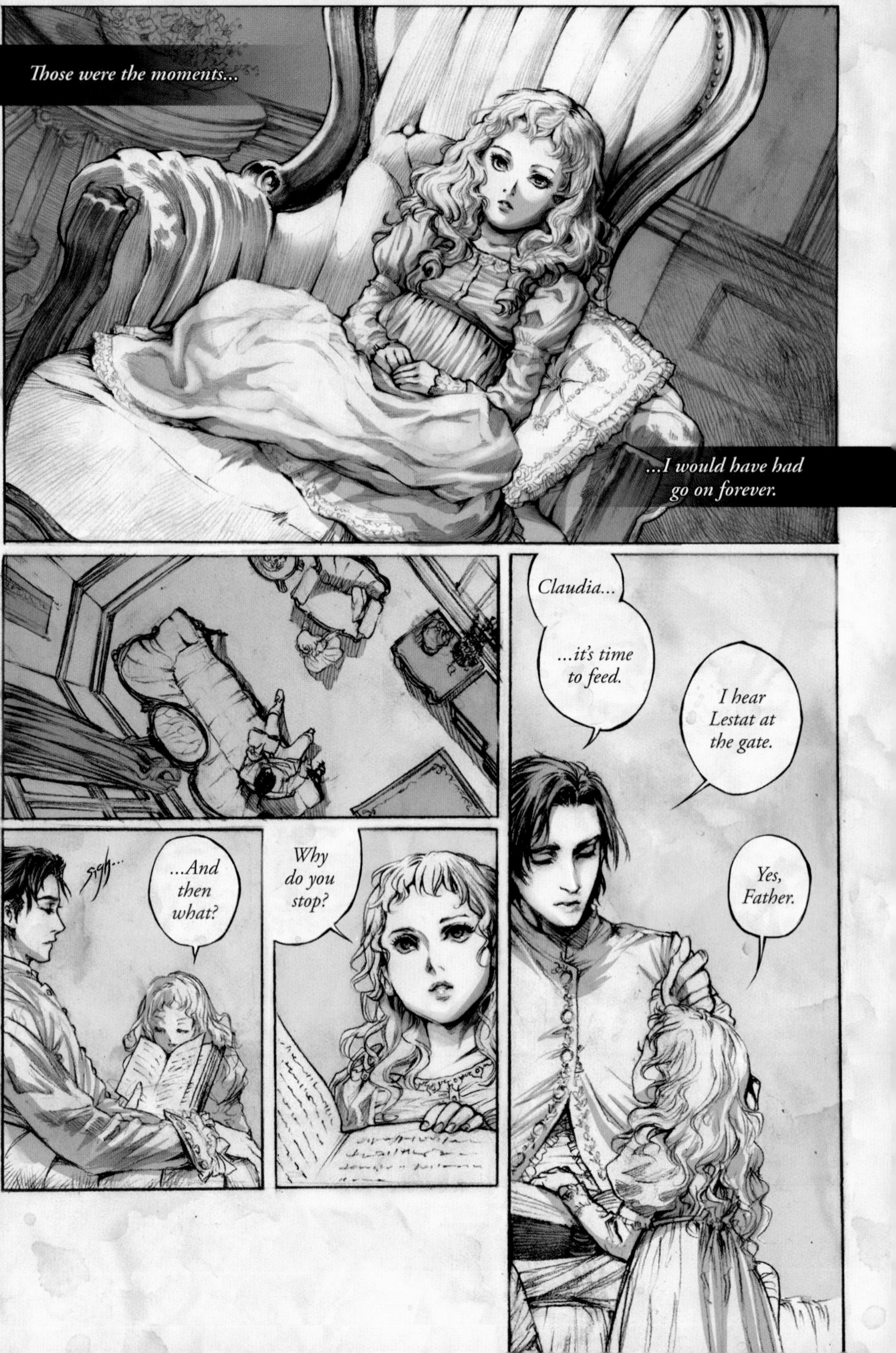

Those were the moments...
...I would have had go on forever.
sigh...
...And then what?
Why do you stop?
Claudia...
...it's time to feed.
I hear Lestat at the gate.
Yes, Father.

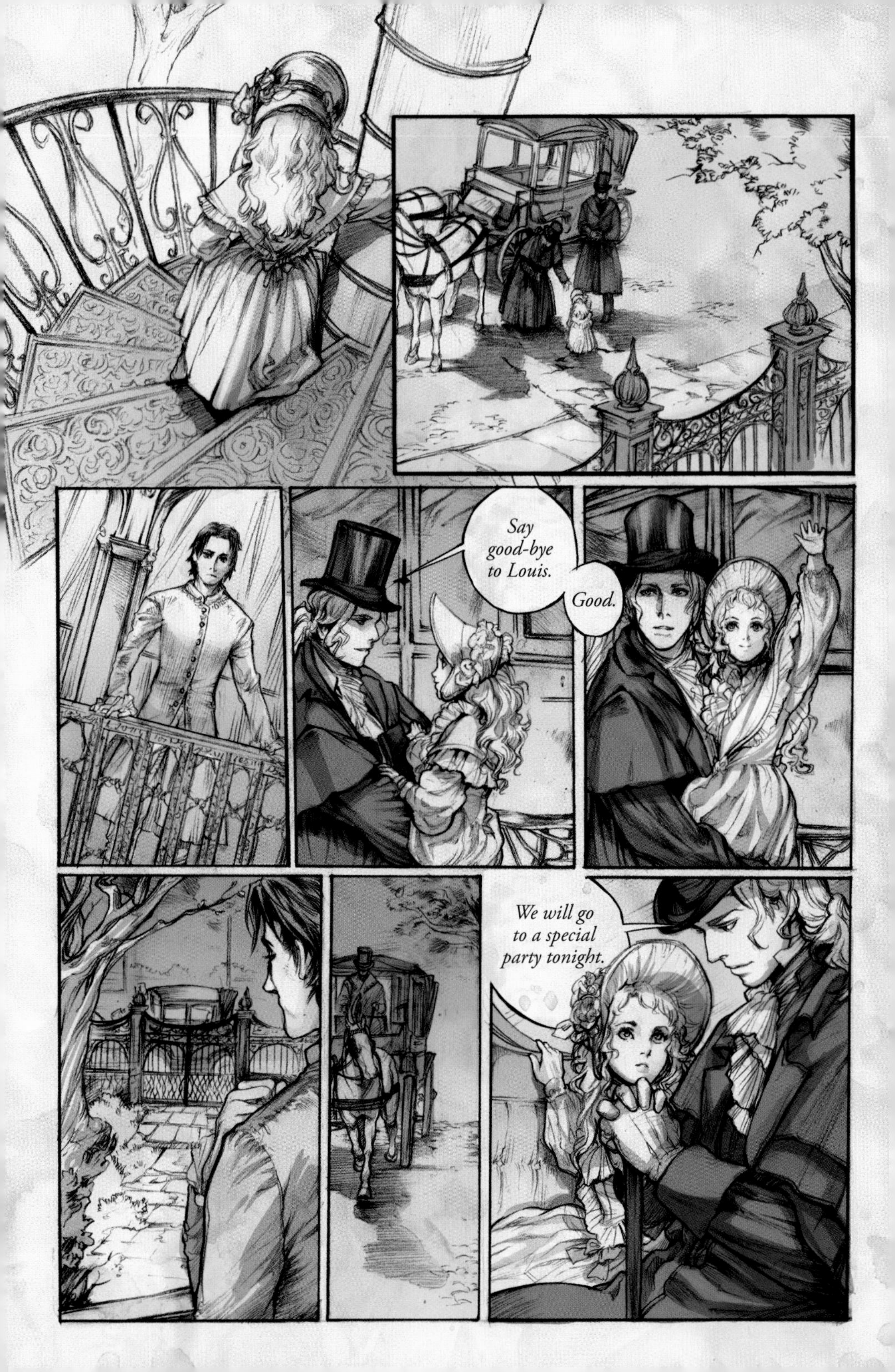
Say good-bye to Louis.
Good.
We will go to a special party tonight.

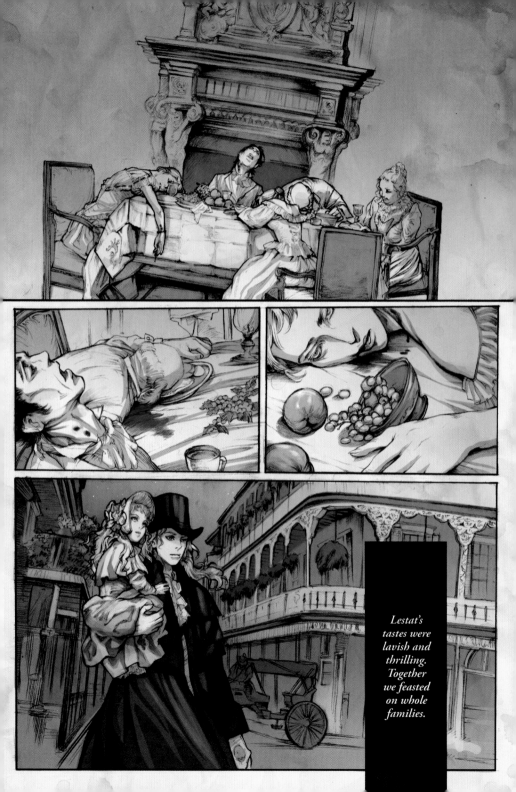

Lestat's tastes were lavish and thrilling. Together we feasted on whole families.

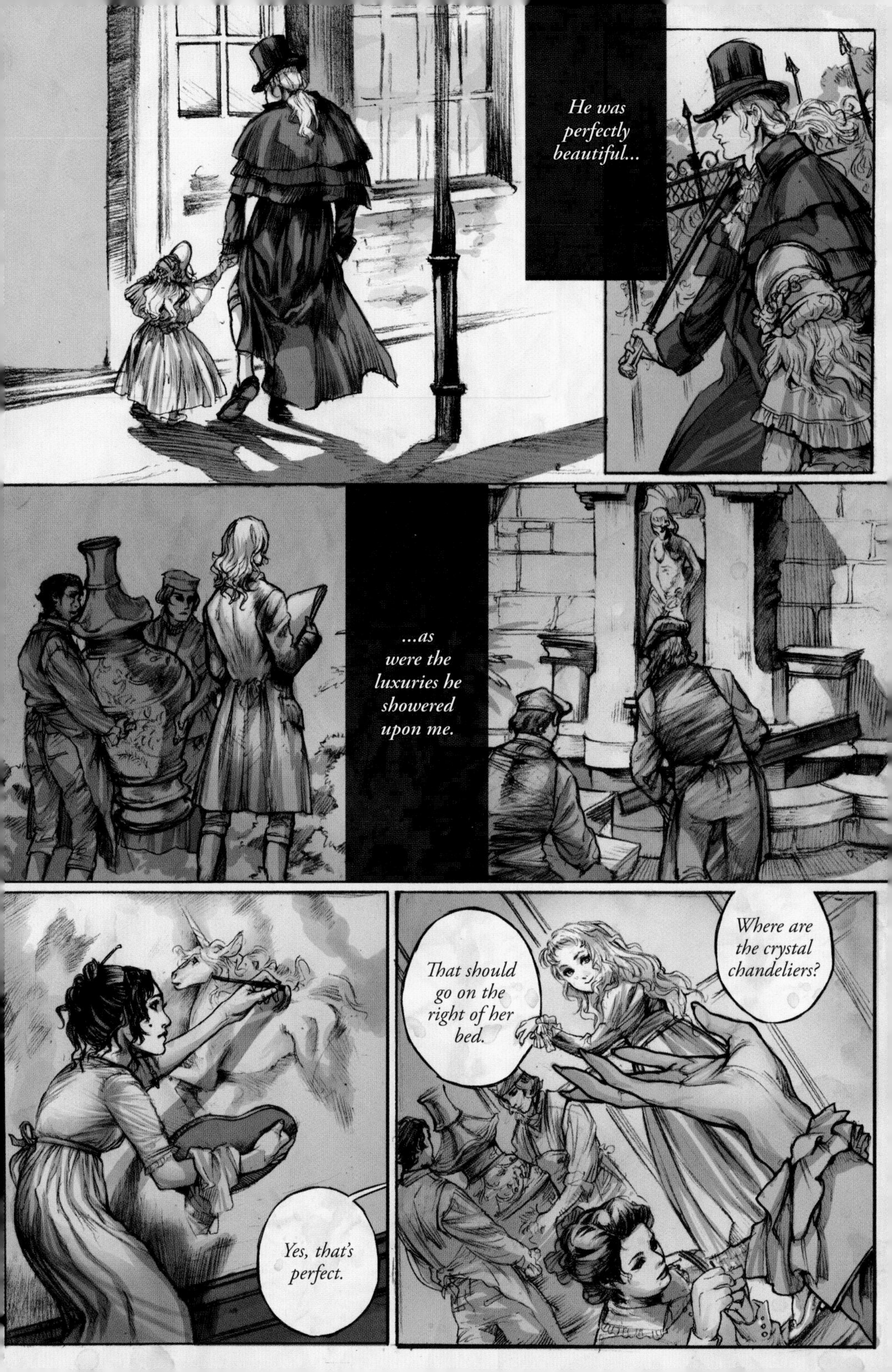
He was perfectly beautiful...
...as were the luxuries he showered upon me.
Yes, that's perfect.
Where are the crystal chandeliers?
That should go on the right of her bed.

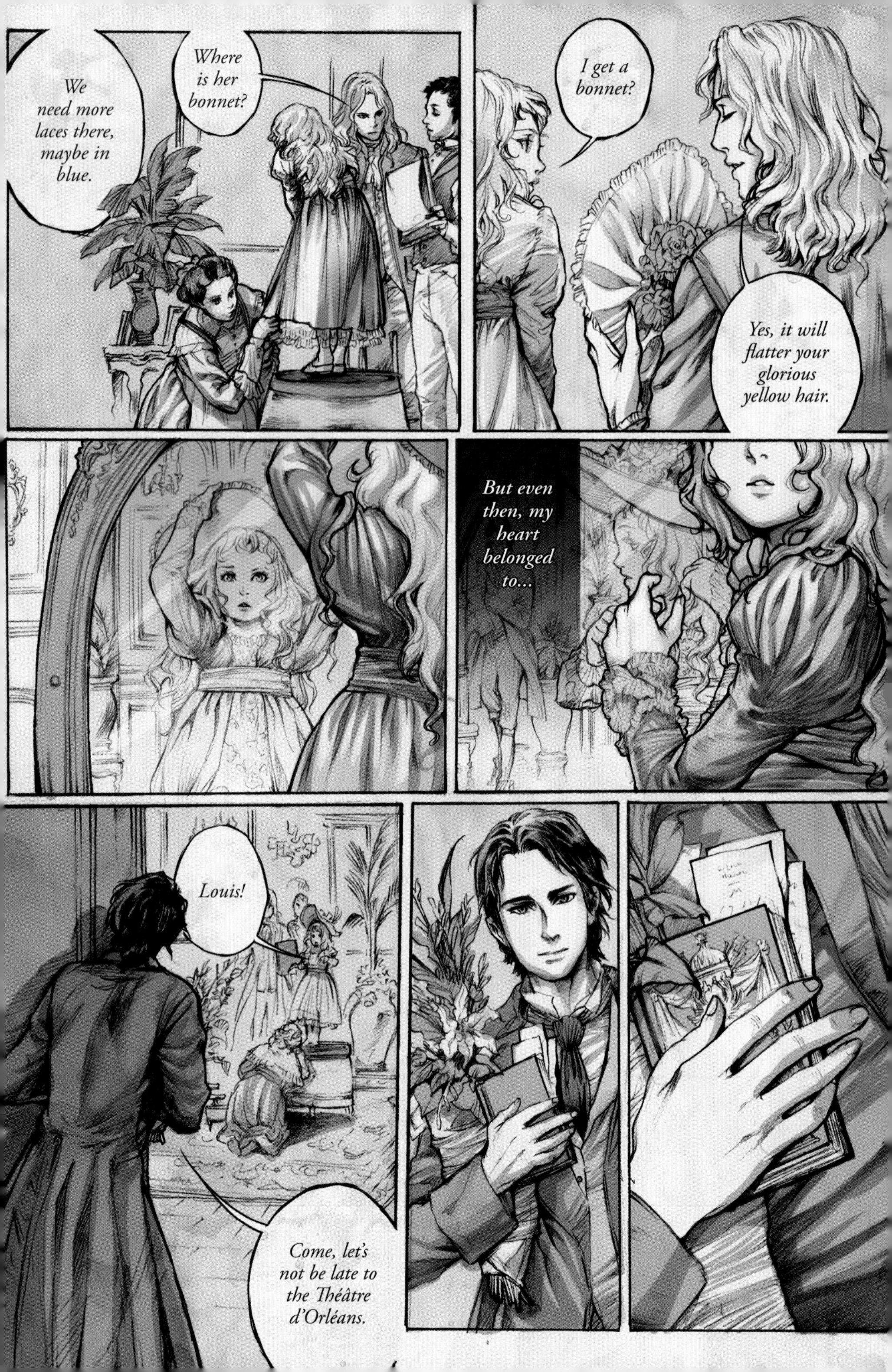
We need more laces there, maybe in blue.
Where is her bonnet?
I get a bonnet?
Yes, it will flatter your glorious yellow hair.
But even then, my heart belonged to...
Louis!
Come, let's not be late to the Théâtre d'Orléans.

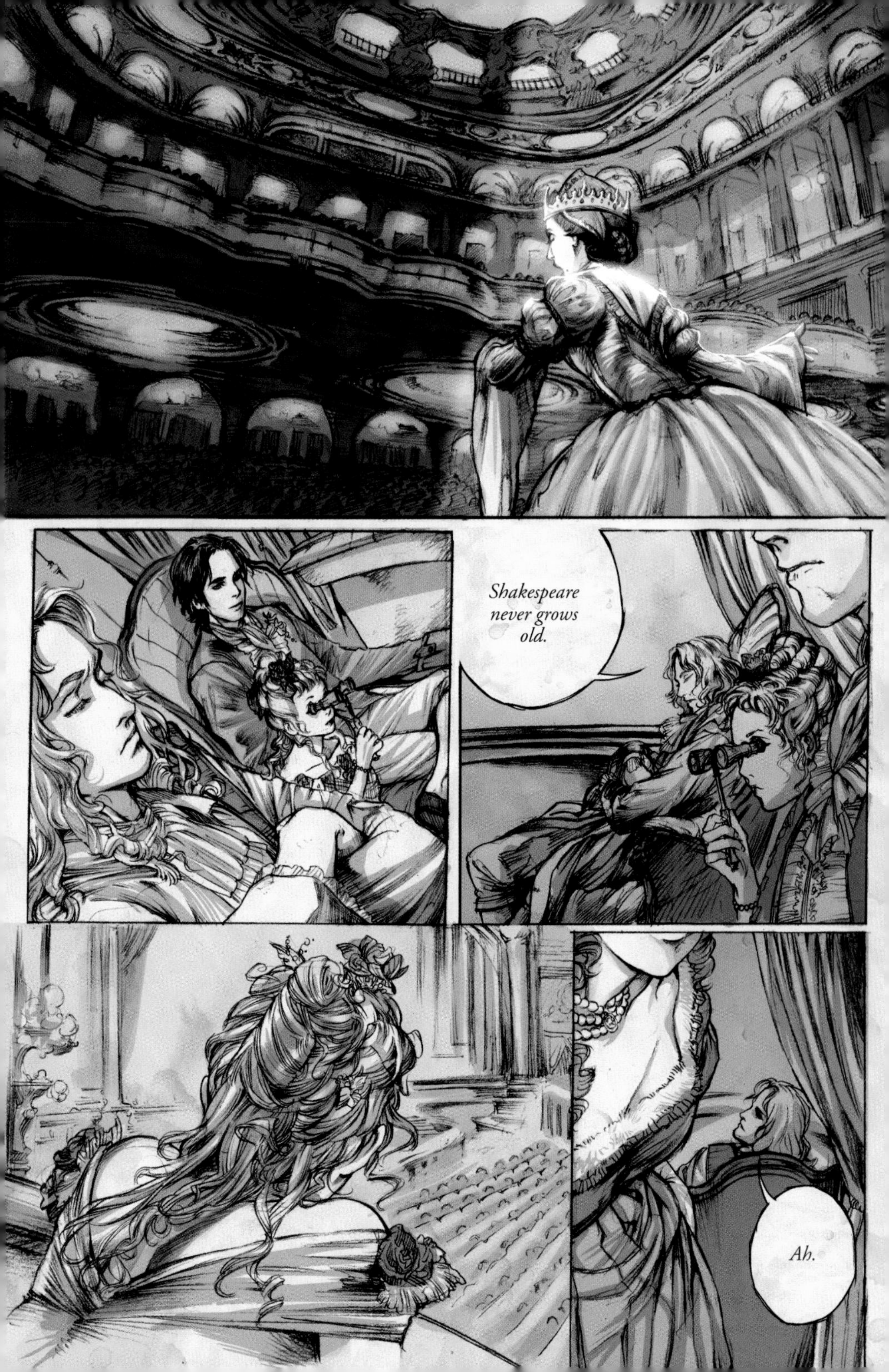
Shakespeare never grows old.
Ah.

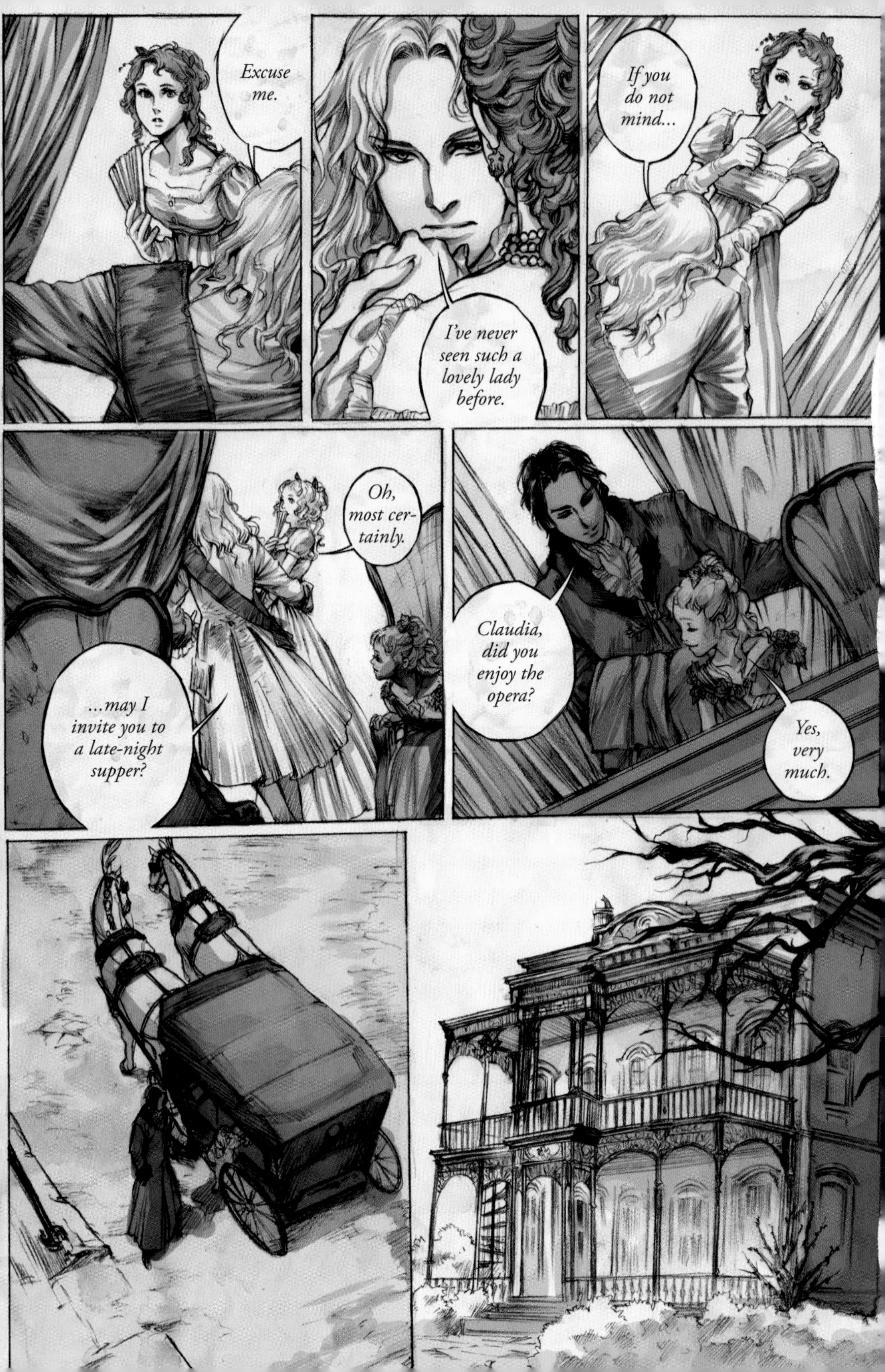
Excuse me.
I've never seen such a lovely lady before.
If you do not mind...
...may I invite you to a late-night supper?
Oh, most cer-tainly.
Claudia, did you enjoy the opera?
Yes, very much.

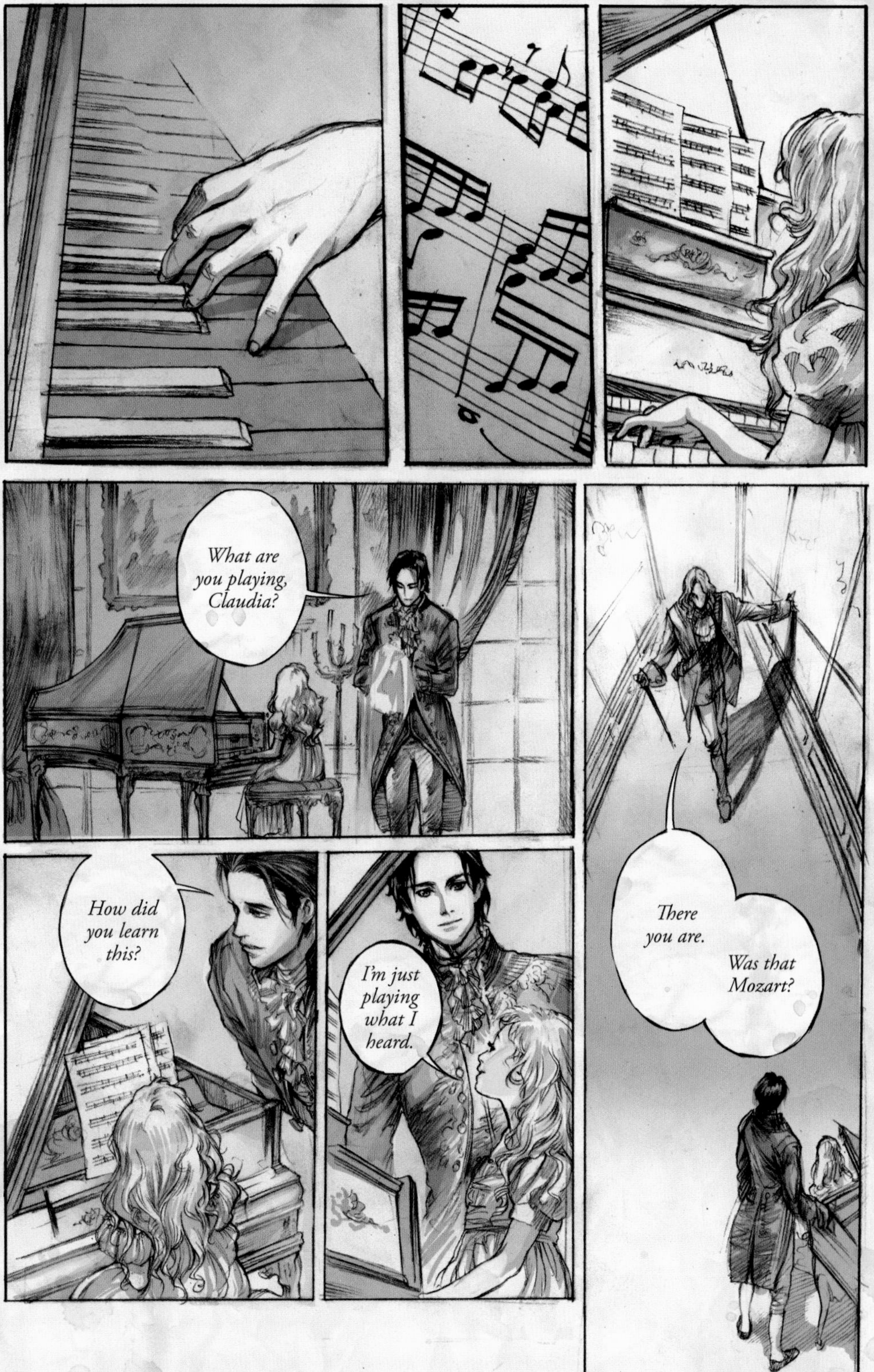
What are you playing, Claudia?
There you are.
Was that Mozart?
How did you learn this?
I'm just playing what I heard.

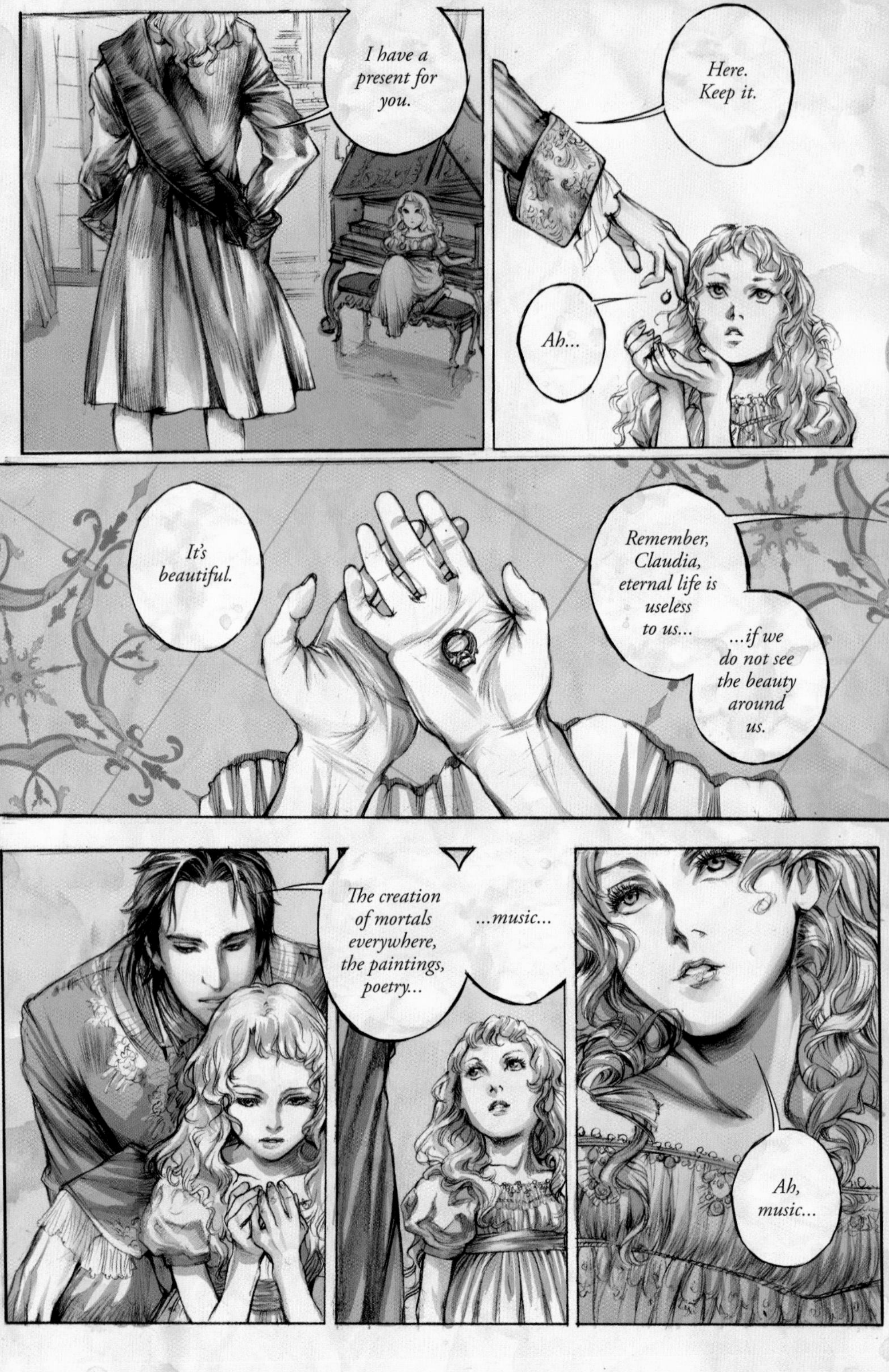
I have a present for you.
Here. Keep it.
Ah...
It's beautiful.
Remember, Claudia, eternal life is useless to us...
...if we do not see the beauty around us.
The creation of mortals everywhere, the paintings, poetry...
...music...
Ah, music...

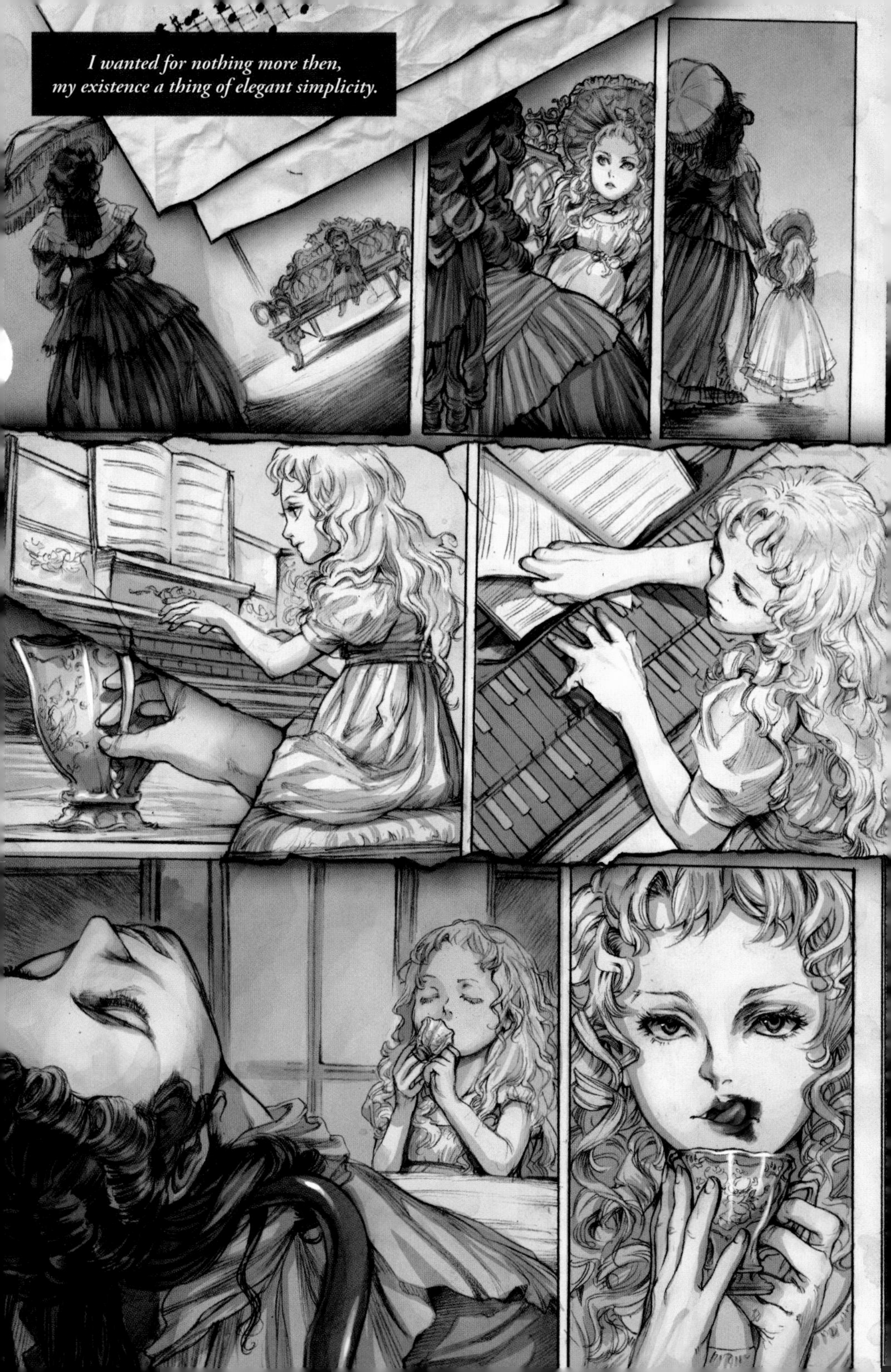
I wanted for nothing more then,
my existence a thing of elegant simplicity.

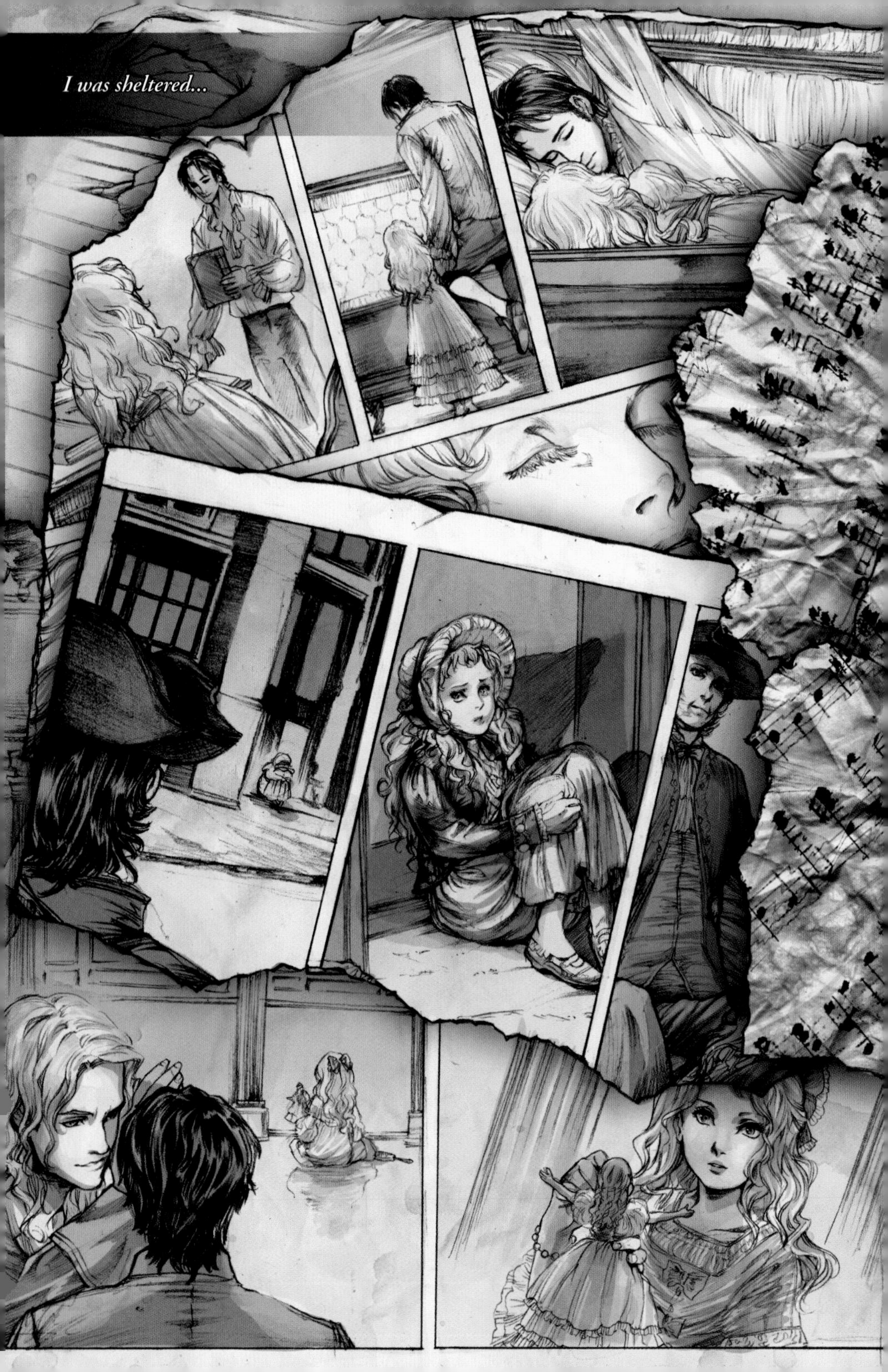
I was sheltered...

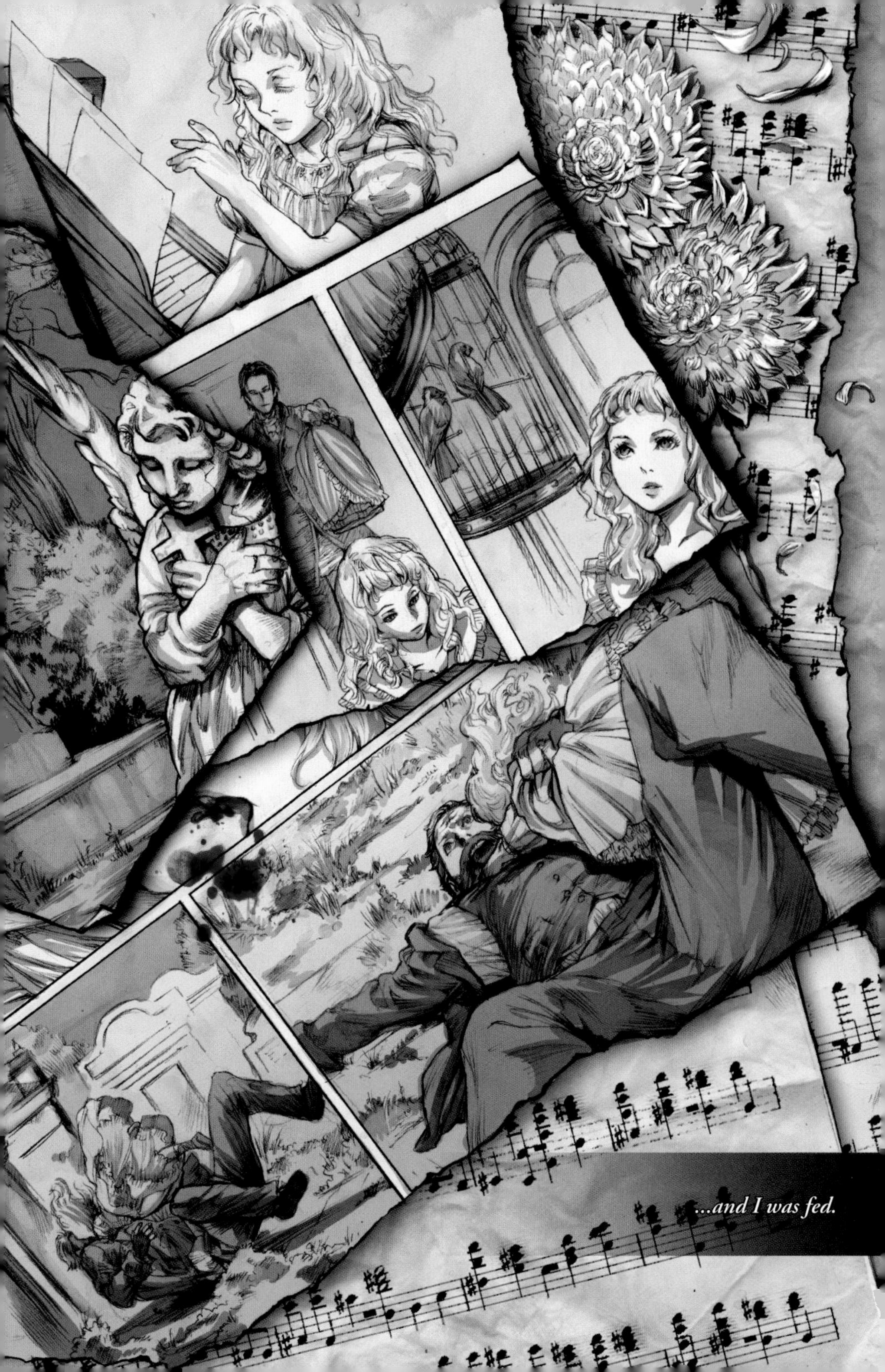
...and I was fed.

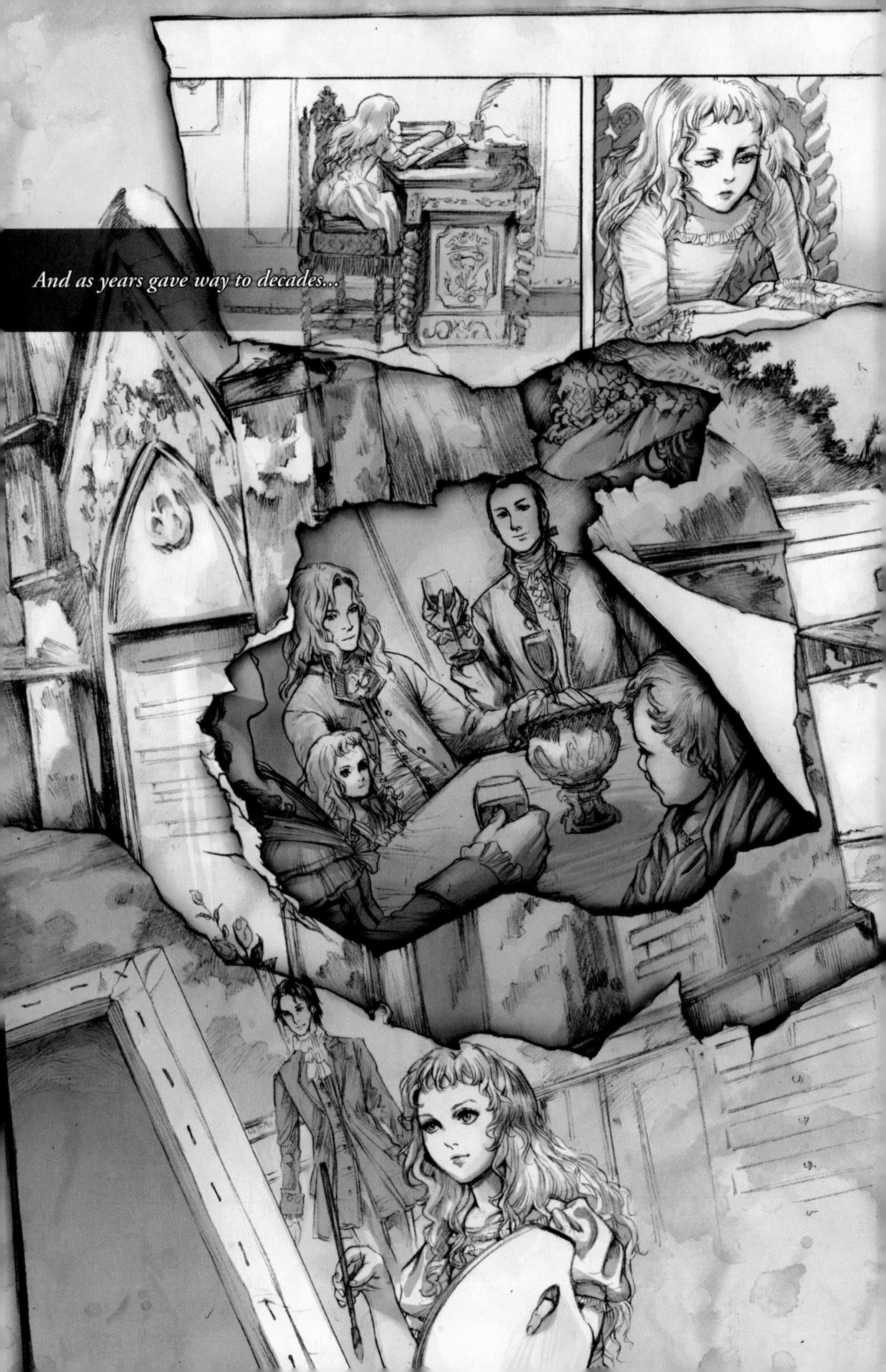
And as years gave way to decades...

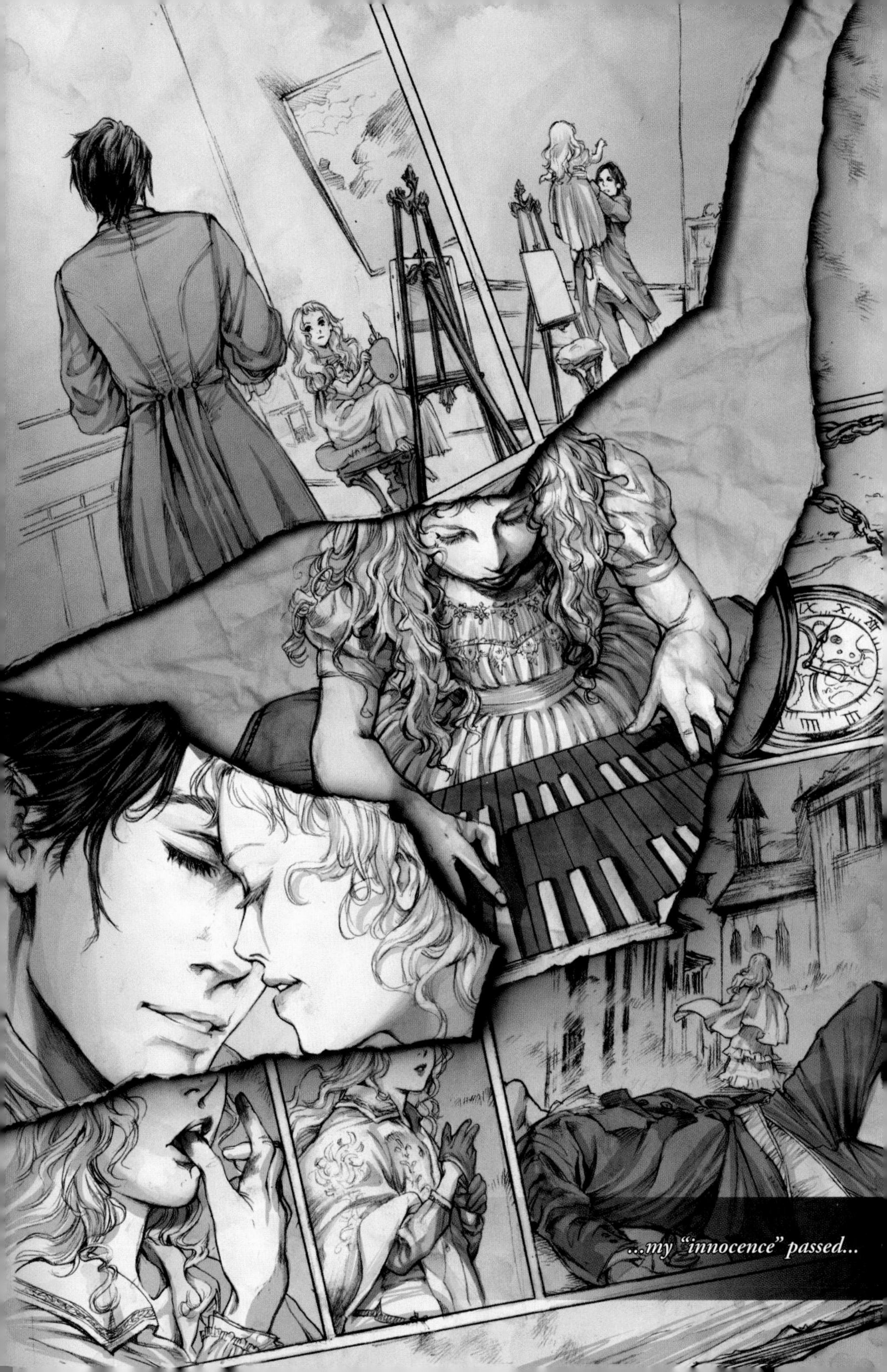
...my "innocence" passed...

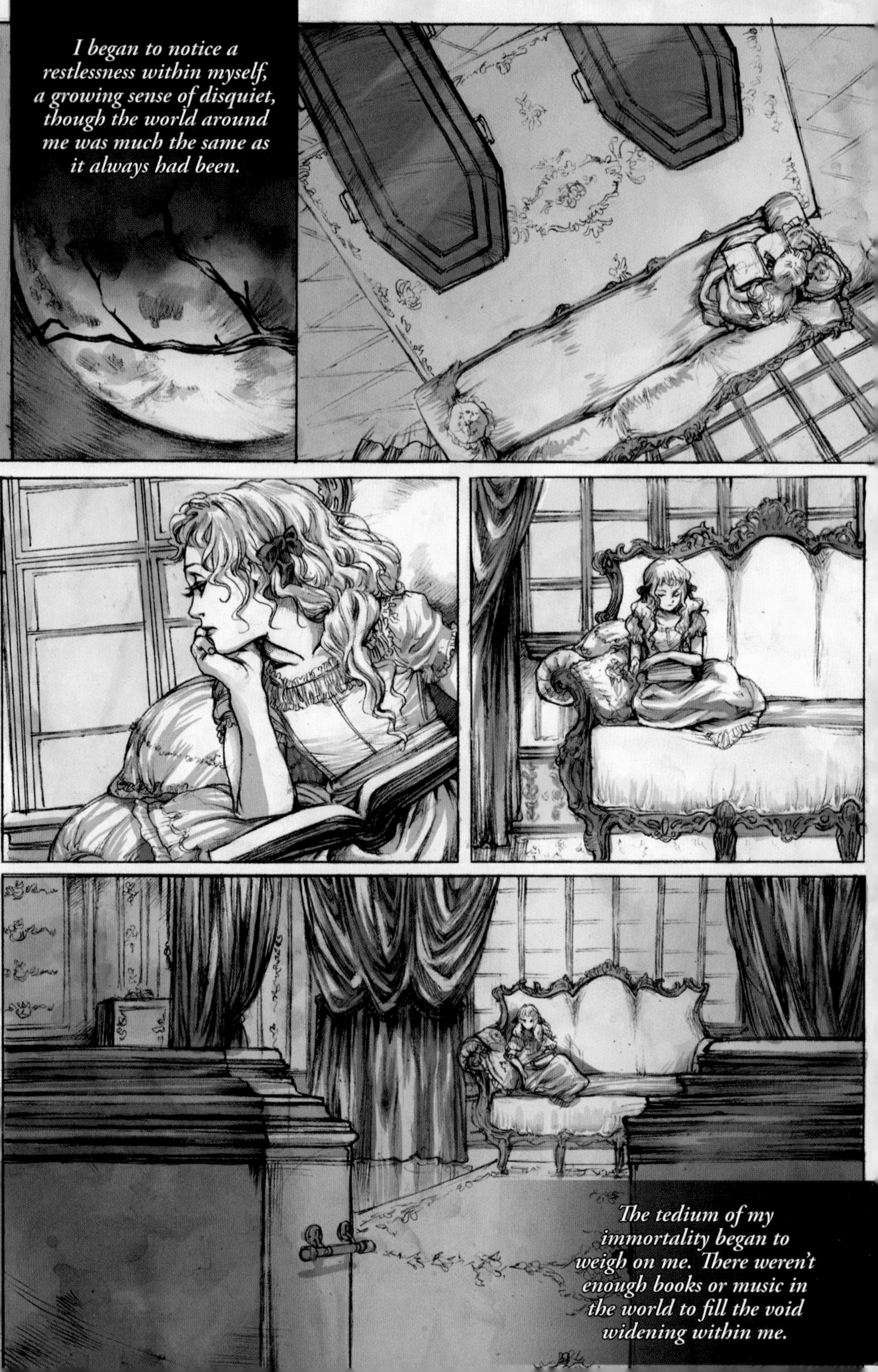
I began to notice a restlessness within myself, a growing sense of disquiet, though the world around me was much the same as it always had been.
The tedium of my immortality began to weigh on me. There weren't enough books or music in the world to fill the void widening within me.

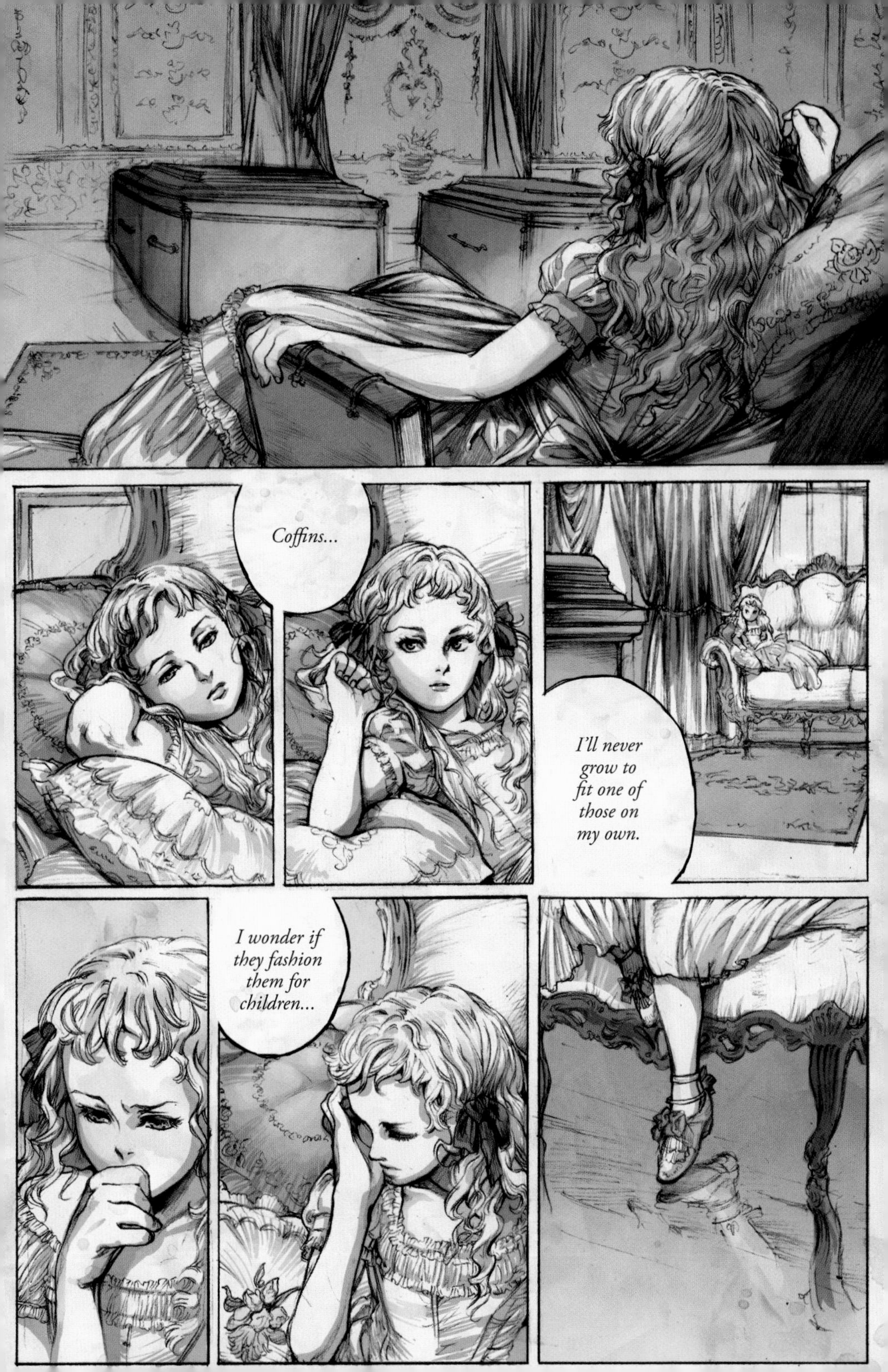
Coffins...
I'll never grow to fit one of those on my own.
I wonder if they fashion them for children...

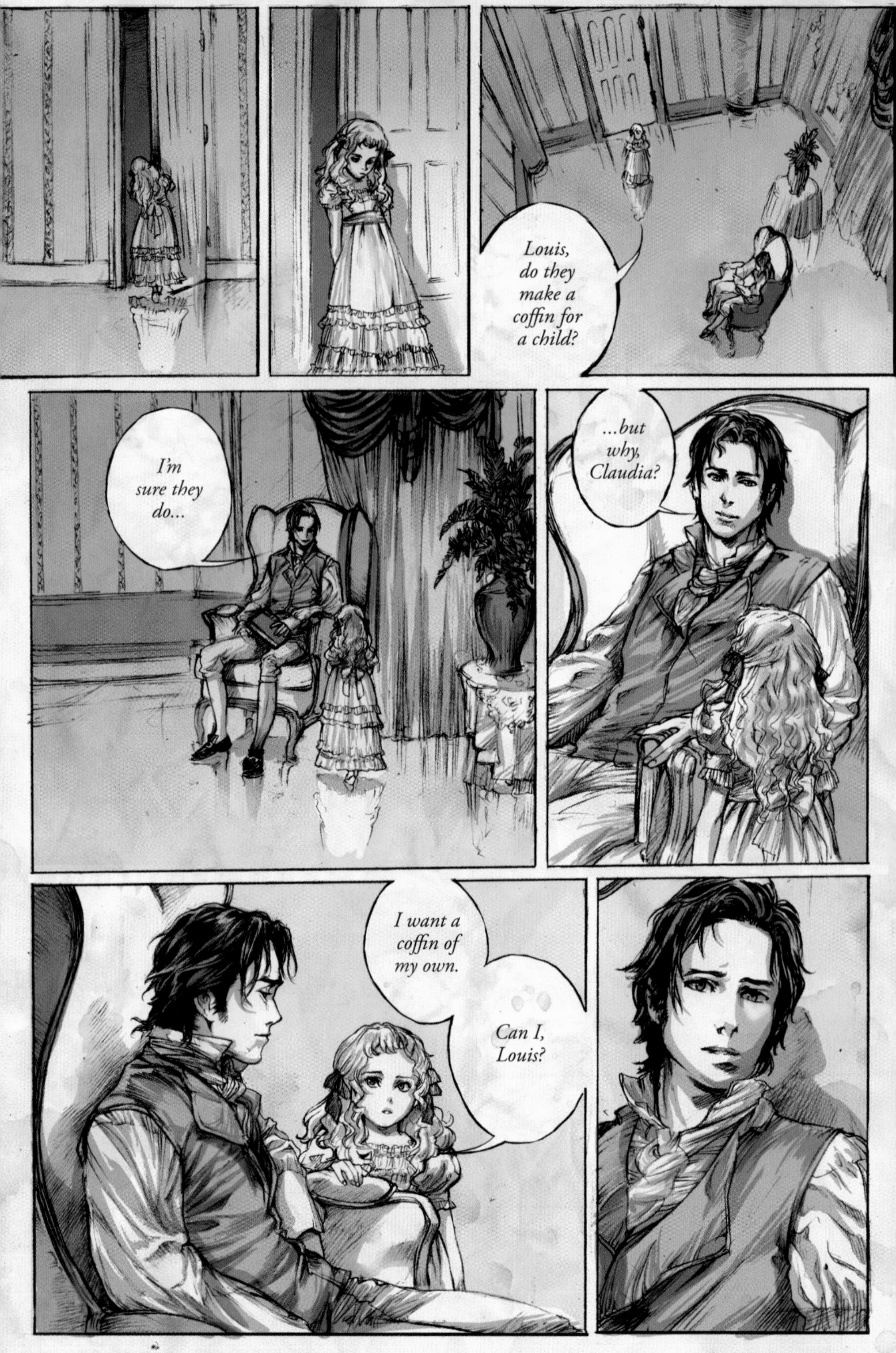
Louis, do they make a coffin for a child?
I'm sure they do...
...but why, Claudia?
I want a coffin of my own.
Can I, Louis?

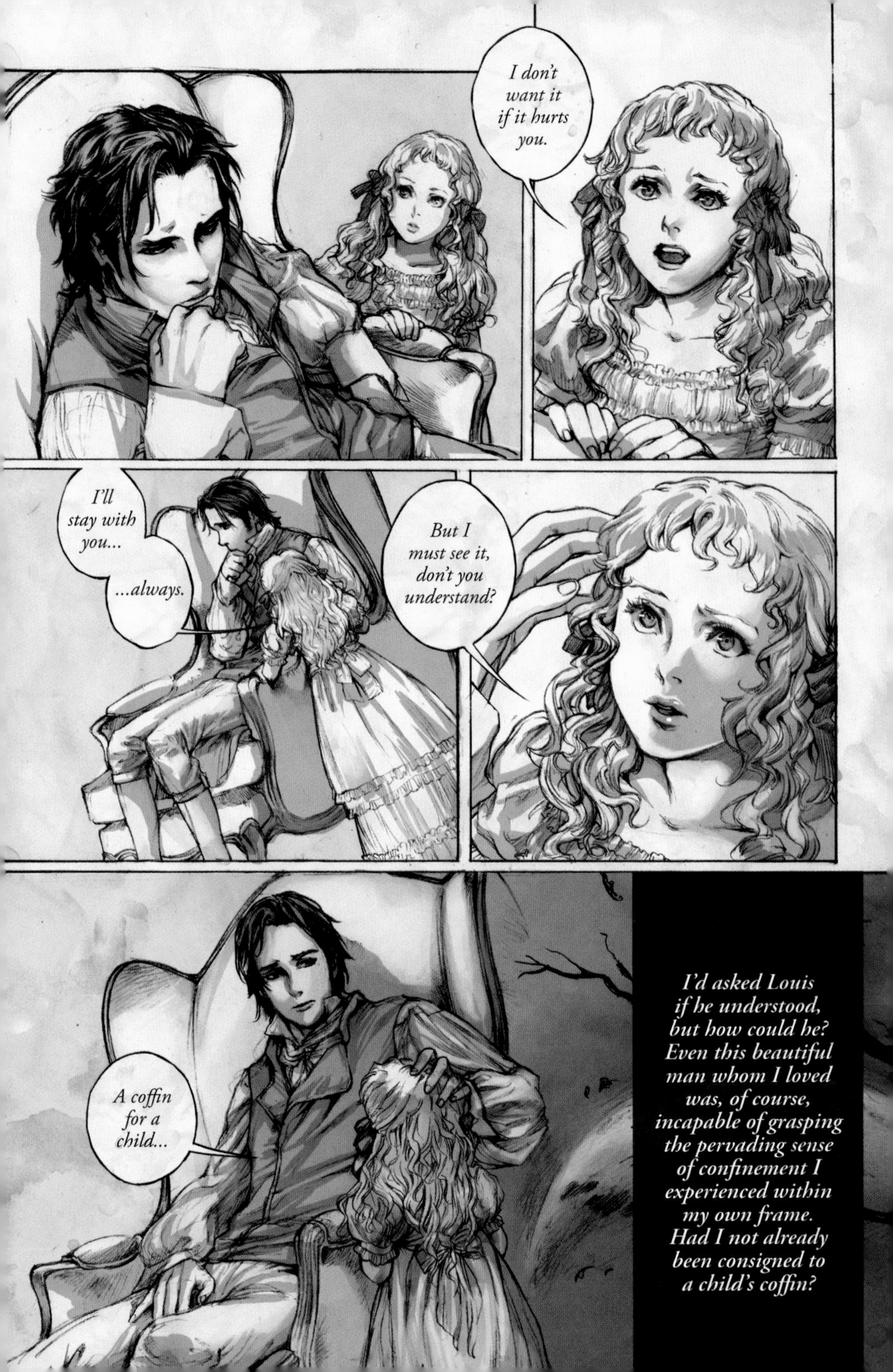
I don't want it if it hurts you.
I'll stay with you...
...always.
But I must see it, don't you understand?
A coffin for a child...
I'd asked Louis if he understood, but how could he? Even this beautiful man whom I loved was, of course, incapable of grasping the pervading sense of confinement I experienced within my own frame. Had I not already been consigned to a child's coffin?

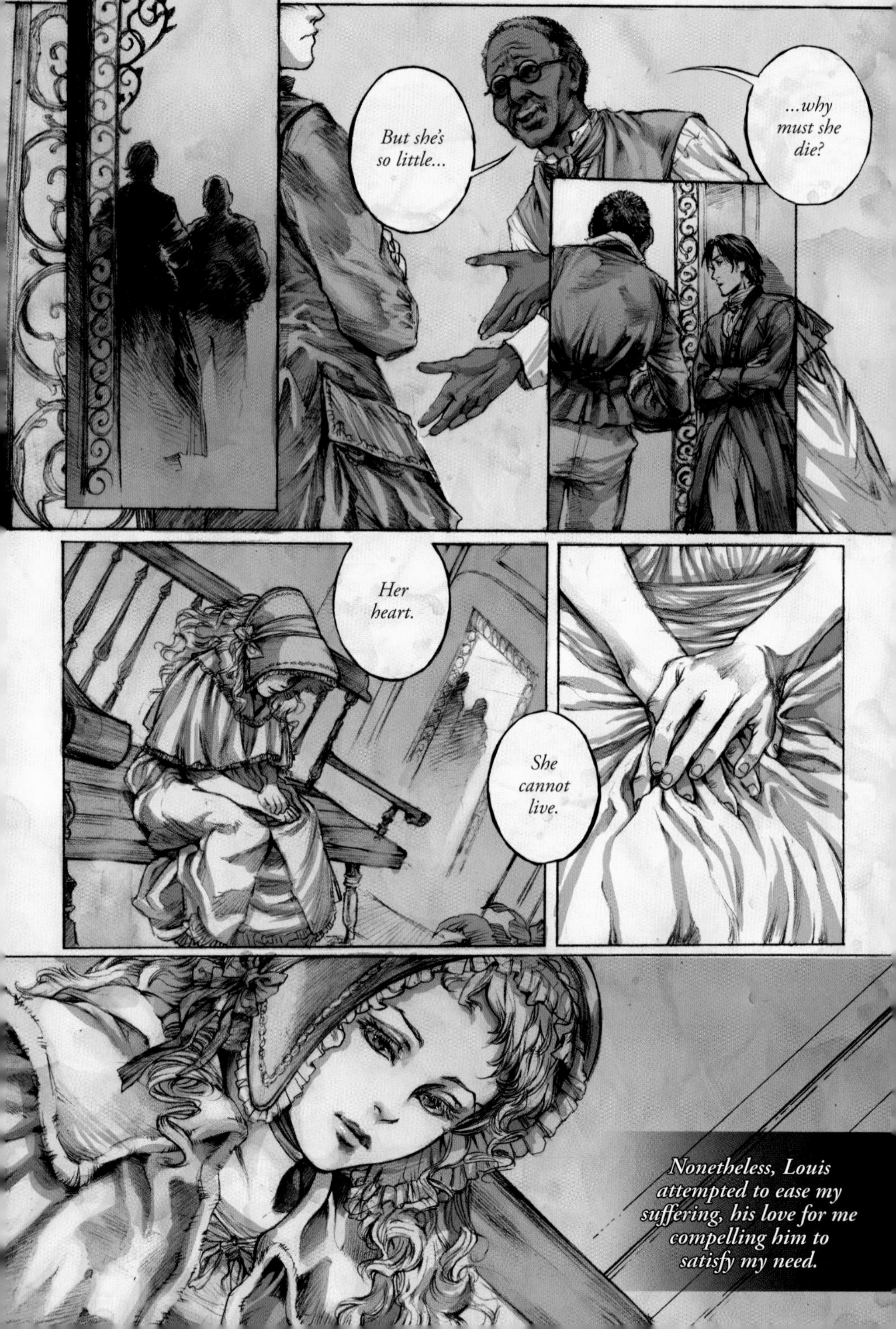
But she's so little...
...why must she die?
Her heart.
She cannot live.
Nonetheless, Louis attempted to ease my suffering, his love for me compelling him to satisfy my need.

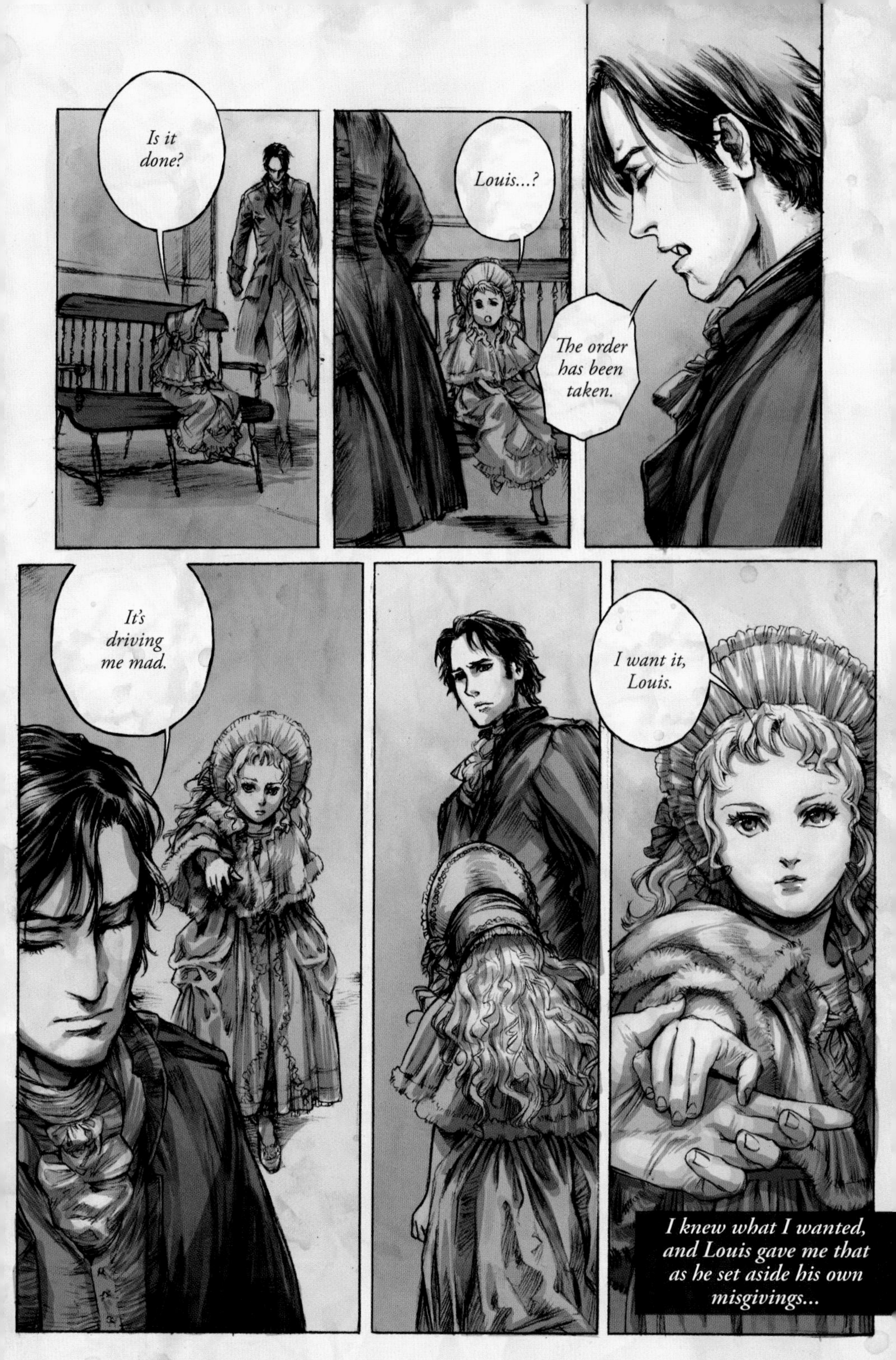
Is it done?
Louis...?
The order has been taken.
It's driving me mad.
I want it, Louis.
I knew what I wanted, and Louis gave me that as he set aside his own misgivings...

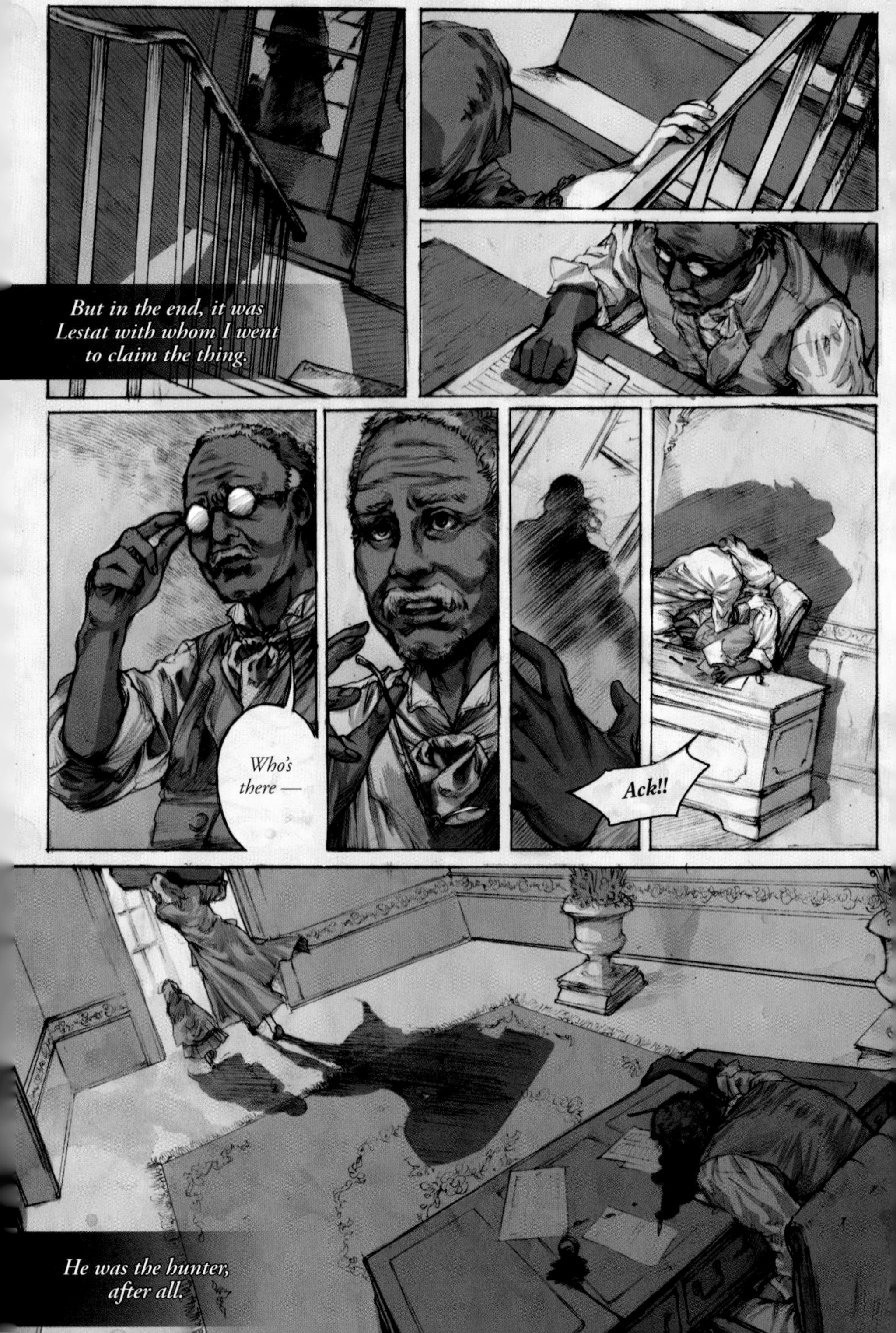
But in the end, it was Lestat with whom I went to claim the thing.
Who's there —
Ack!!
He was the hunter, after all.

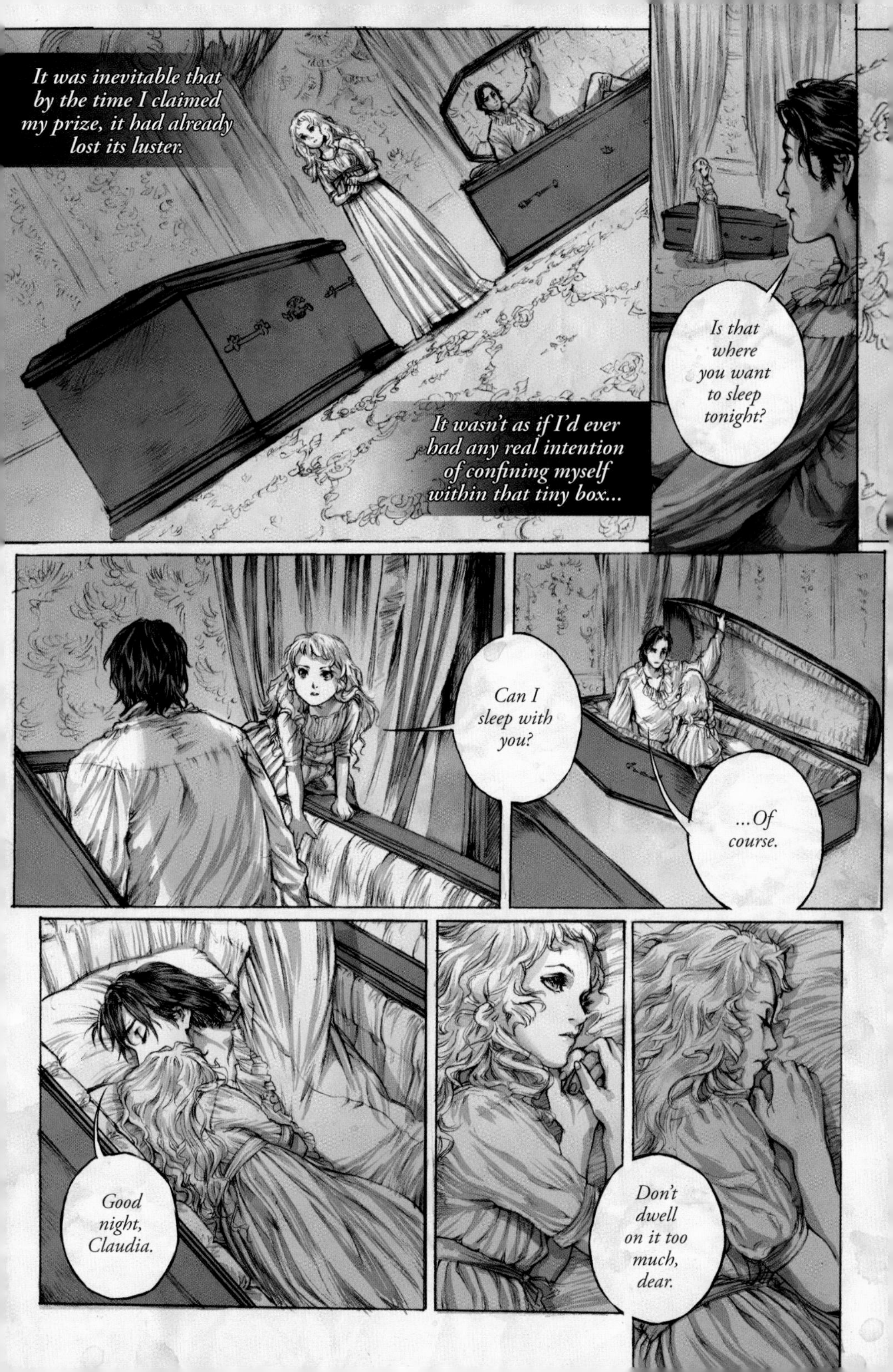
It was inevitable that by the time I claimed my prize, it had already lost its luster.
It wasn't as if I'd ever had any real intention of confining myself within that tiny box...
Is that where you want to sleep tonight?
Can I sleep with you?
...Of course.
Good night, Claudia.
Don't dwell on it too much, dear.

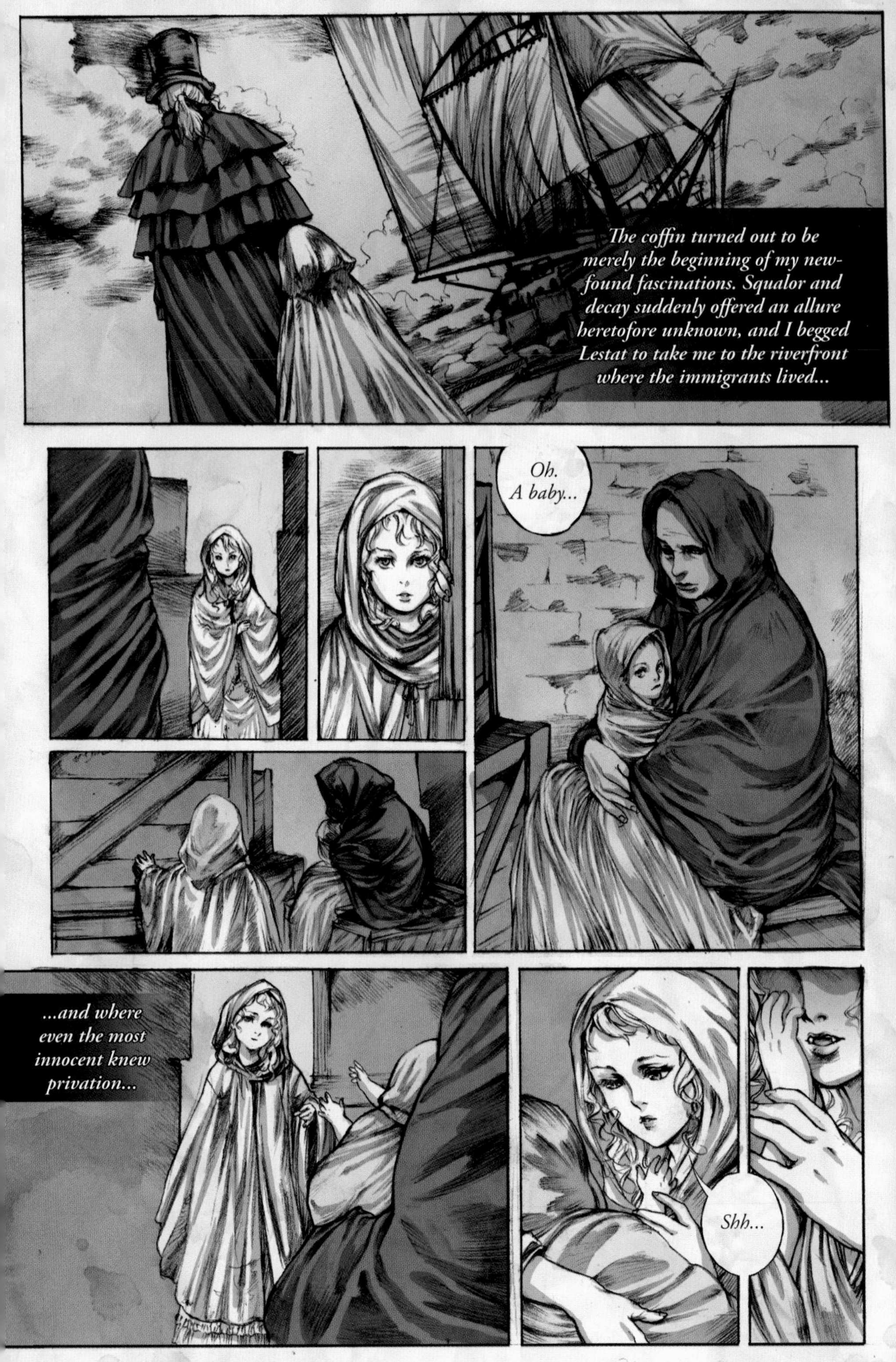
The coffin turned out to be merely the beginning of my new-found fascinations. Squalor and decay suddenly offered an allure heretofore unknown, and I begged Lestat to take me to the riverfront where the immigrants lived...
Oh. A baby...
...and where even the most innocent knew privation...
Shh...

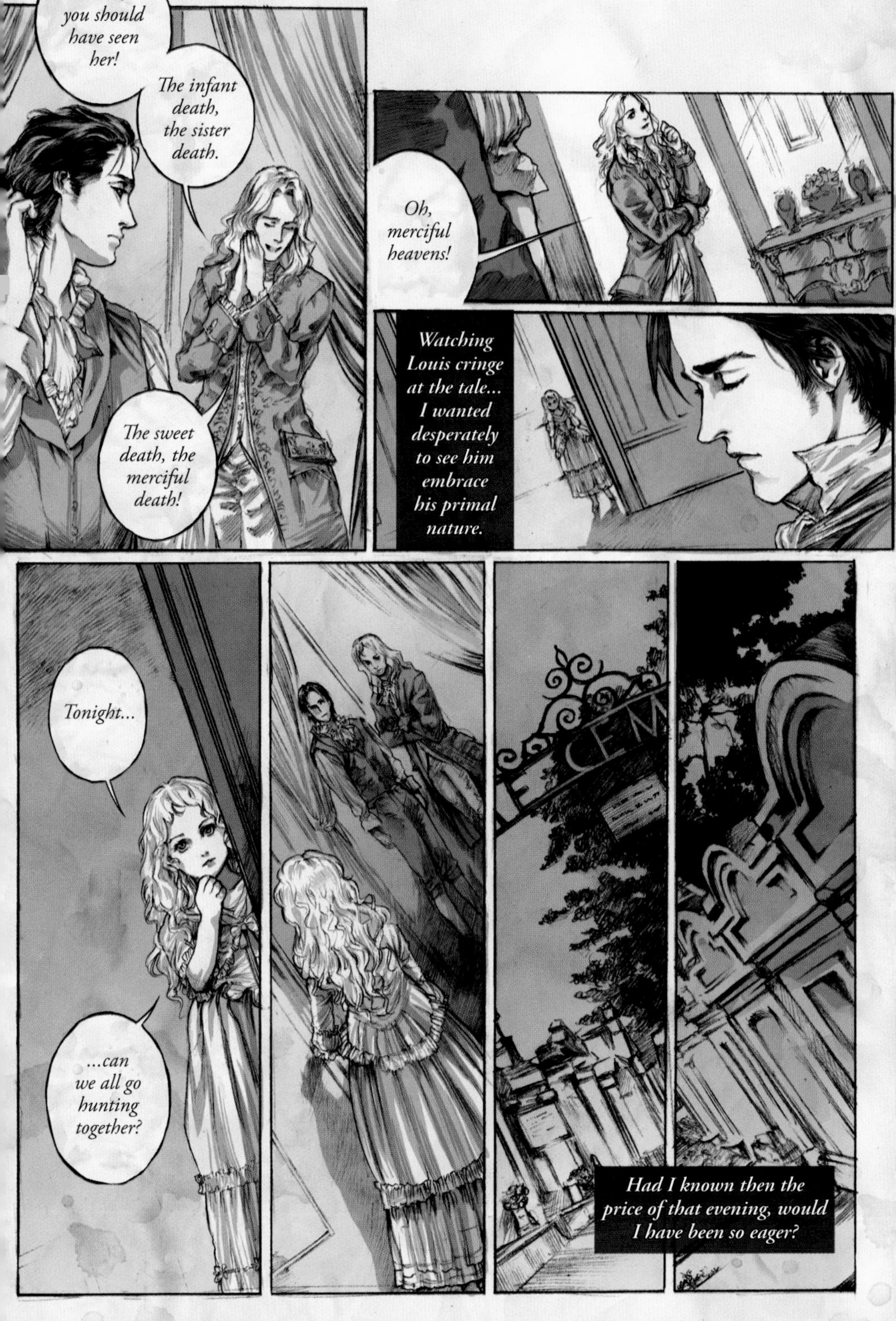
Louis, you should have seen her!
The infant death, the sister death.
The sweet death, the merciful death!
Oh, merciful heavens!
Watching Louis cringe at the tale... I wanted desperately to see him embrace his primal nature.
Tonight...
...can we all go hunting together?
CEM
Had I known then the price of that evening, would I have been so eager?

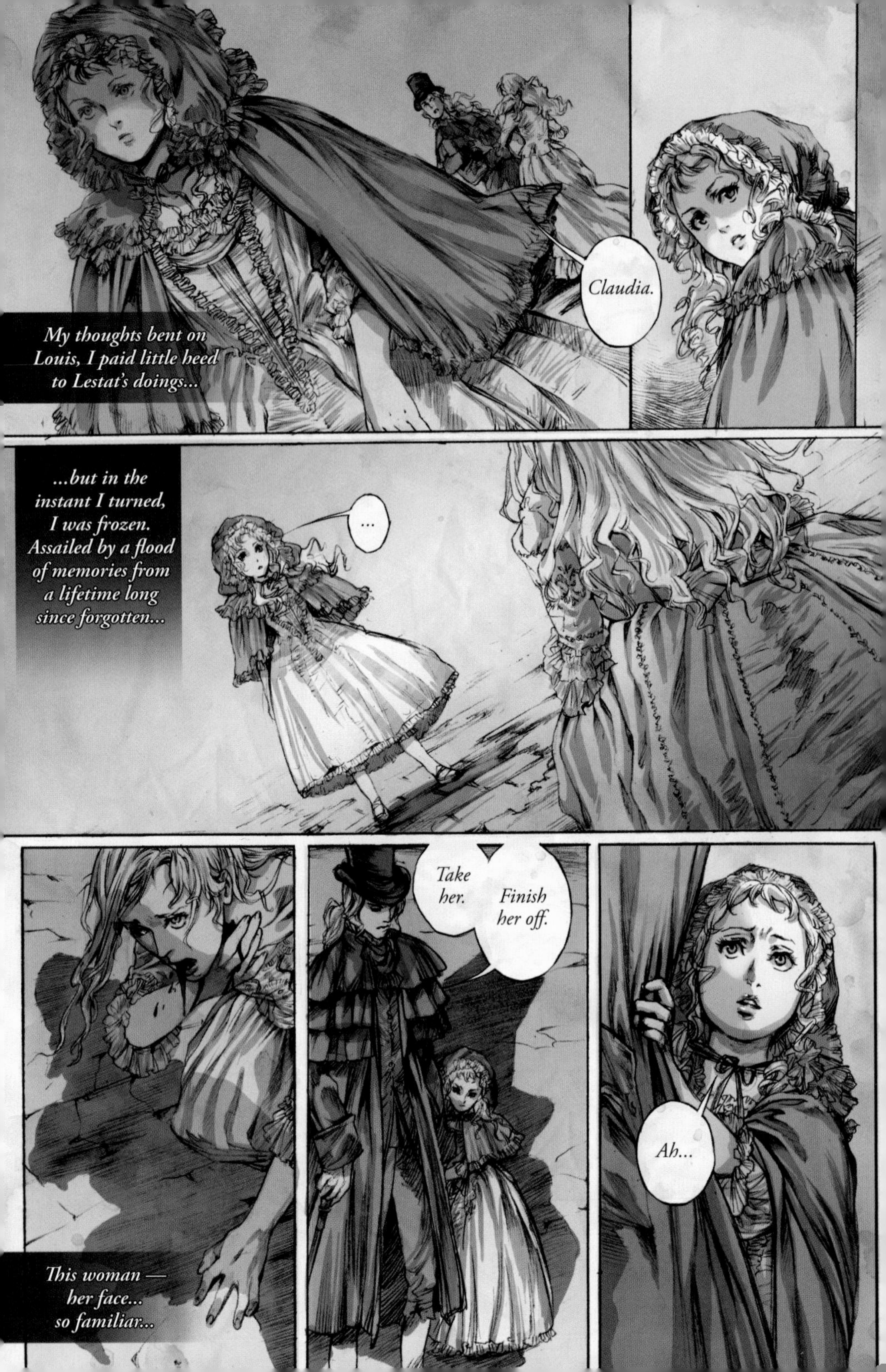

My thoughts bent on Louis, I paid little heed to Lestat's doings...
Claudia.
...but in the instant I turned, I was frozen. Assailed by a flood of memories from a lifetime long since forgotten...
...
This woman — her face... so familiar...
Take her.
Finish her off.
Ah...

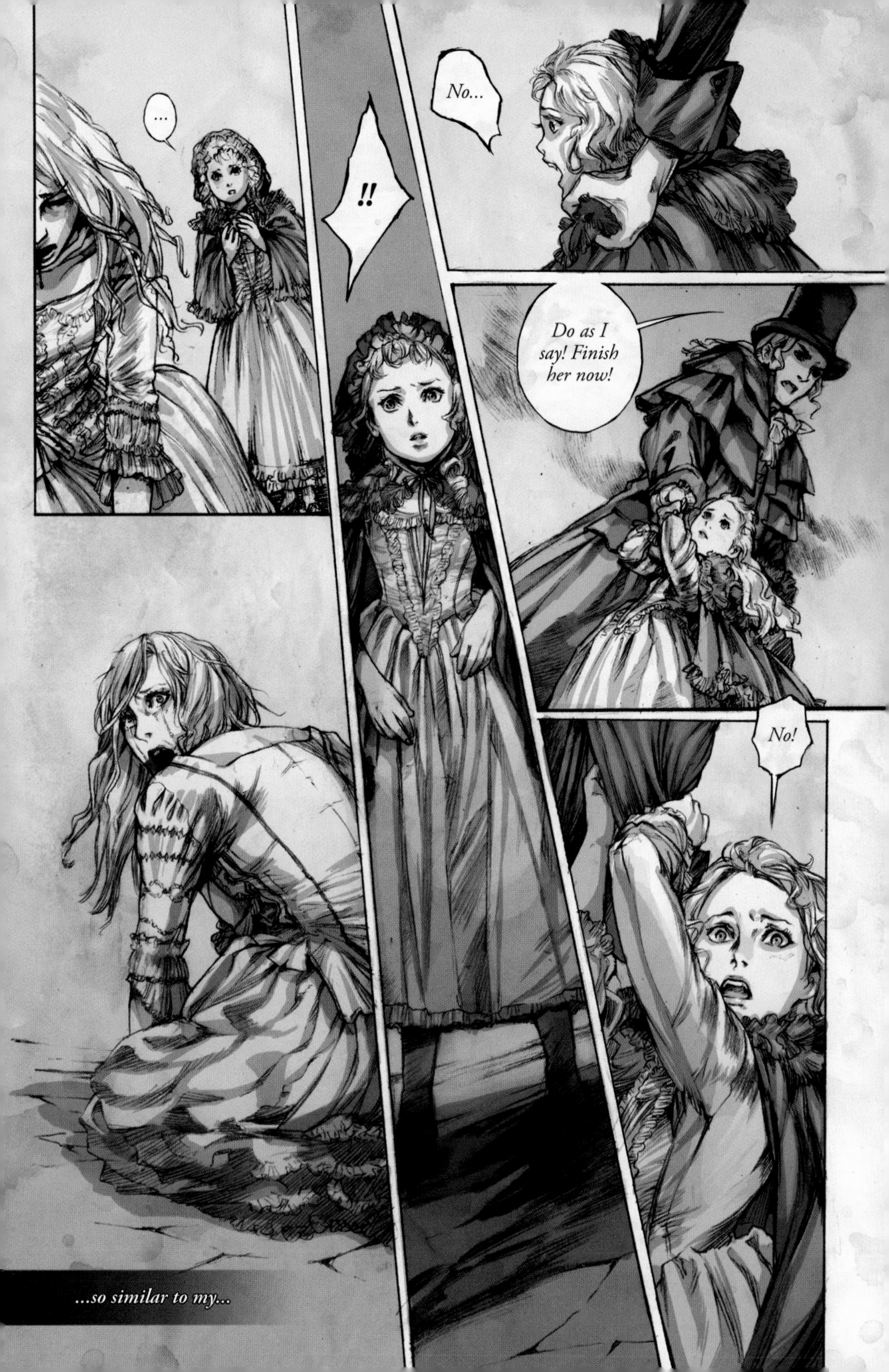
...
!!
No...
Do as I say! Finish her now!
No!
...so similar to my...

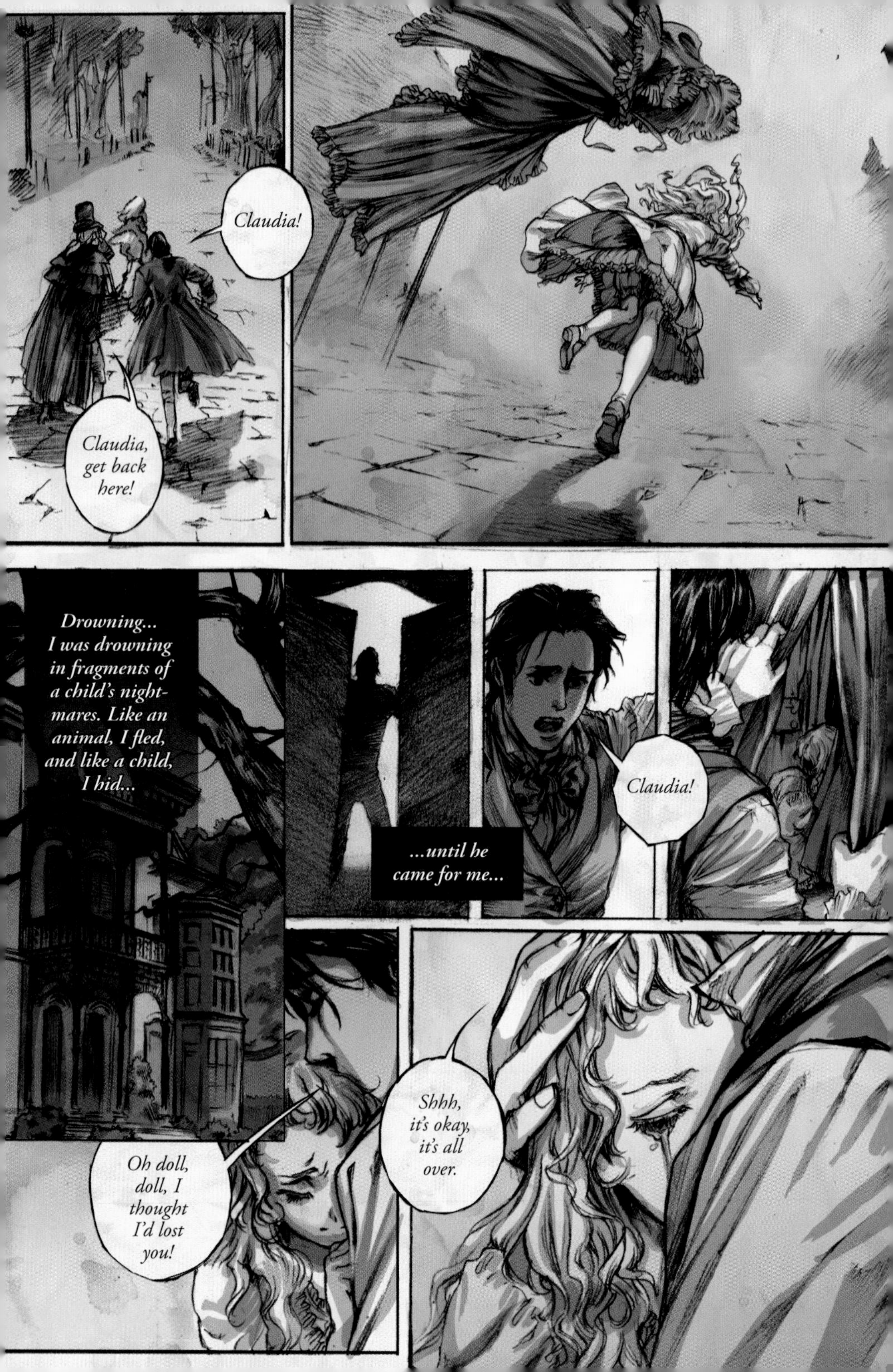
Claudia!
Claudia, get back here!
Drowning... I was drowning in fragments of a child's night-mares. Like an animal, I fled, and like a child, I hid...
...until he came for me...
Claudia!
Oh doll, doll, I thought I'd lost you!
Shhh, it's okay, it's all over.

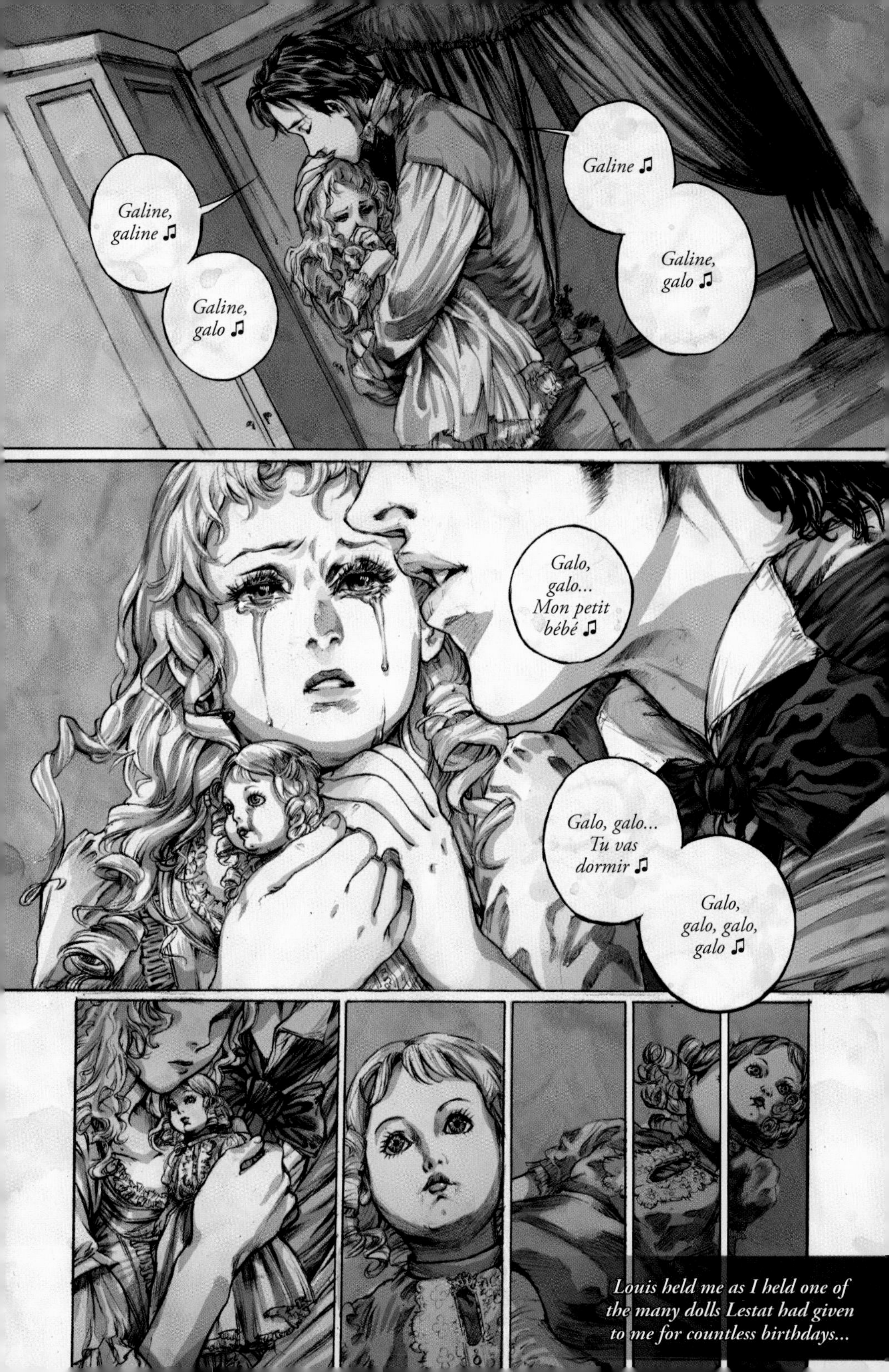

Galine, galine ♫
Galine, galo ♫
Galine ♫
Galine, galo ♫
Galo, galo... Mon petit bébé ♫
Galo, galo... Tu vas dormir ♫
Galo, galo, galo, galo ♫
Louis held me as I held one of the many dolls Lestat had given to me for countless birthdays...

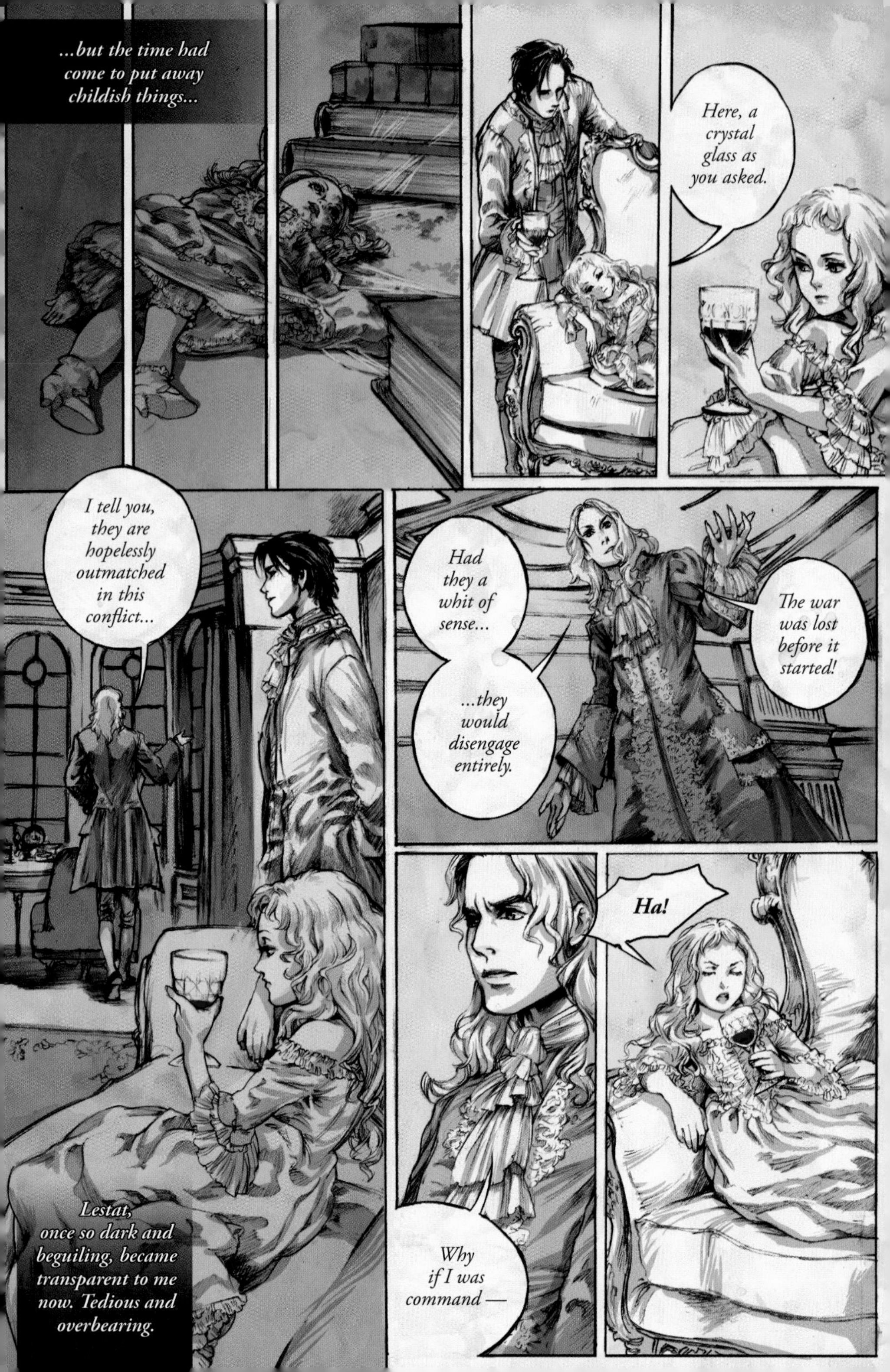
...but the time had come to put away childish things...
Here, a crystal glass as you asked.
I tell you, they are hopelessly outmatched in this conflict...
Had they a whit of sense...
...they would disengage entirely.
The war was lost before it started!
Lestat, once so dark and beguiling, became transparent to me now. Tedious and overbearing.
Ha!
Why if I was command —

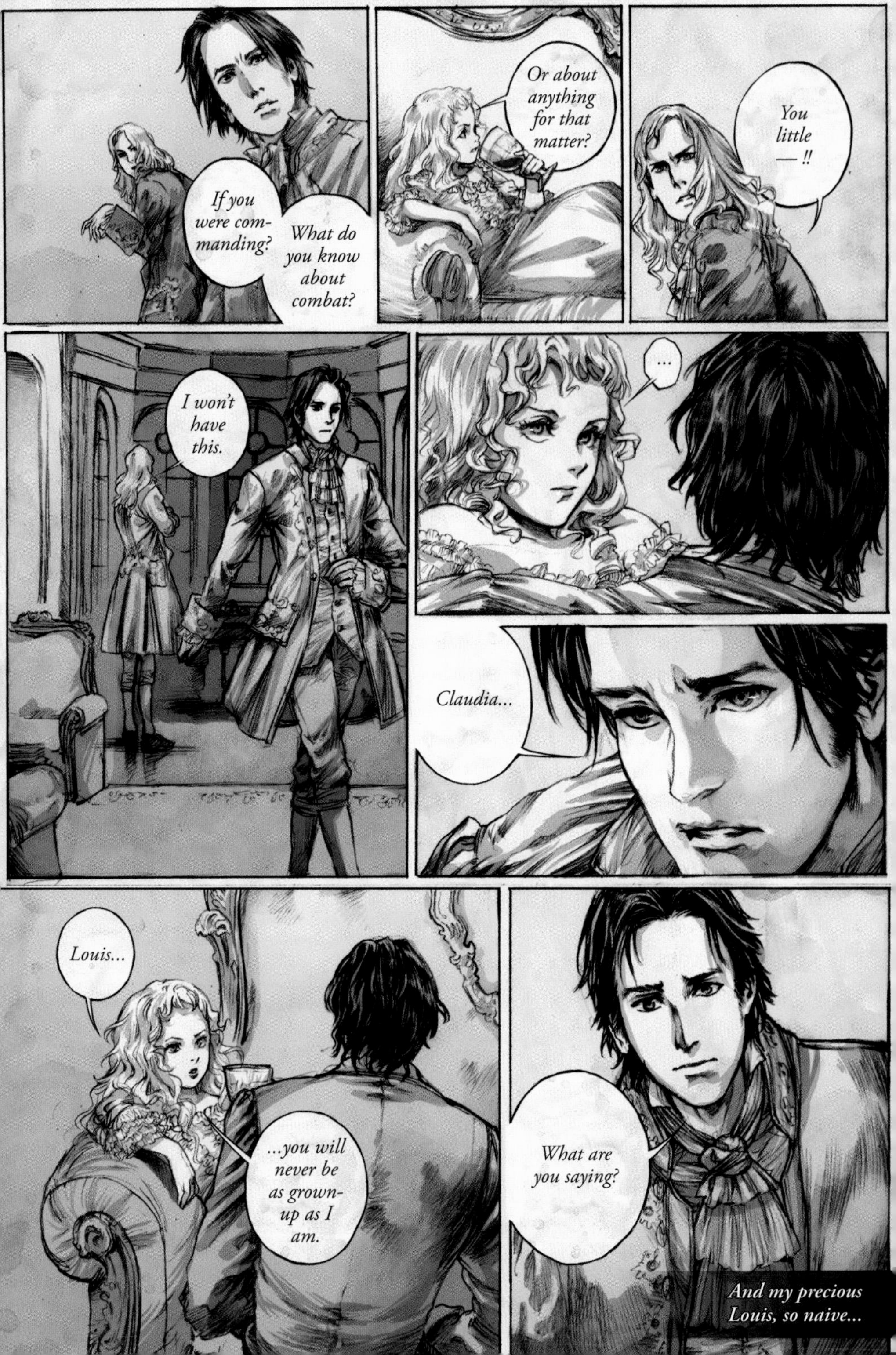
If you were com-manding?
What do you know about combat?
Or about anything for that matter?
You little — !!
I won't have this.
...
Claudia...
Louis...
...you will never be as grown-up as I am.
What are you saying?
And my precious Louis, so naive...

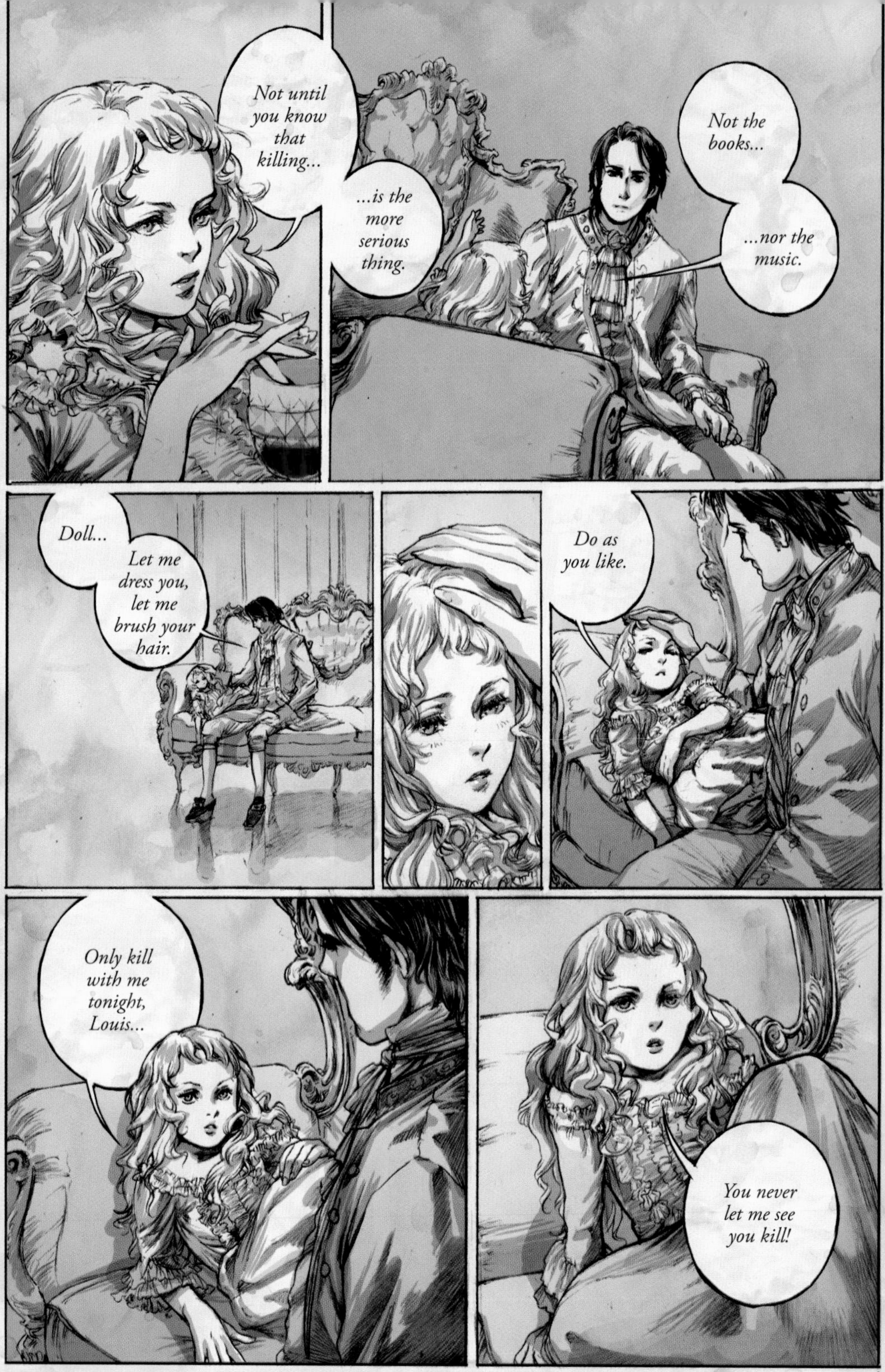
Not until you know that killing...
...is the more serious thing.
Not the books...
...nor the music.
Doll...
Let me dress you, let me brush your hair.
Do as you like.
Only kill with me tonight, Louis...
You never let me see you kill!

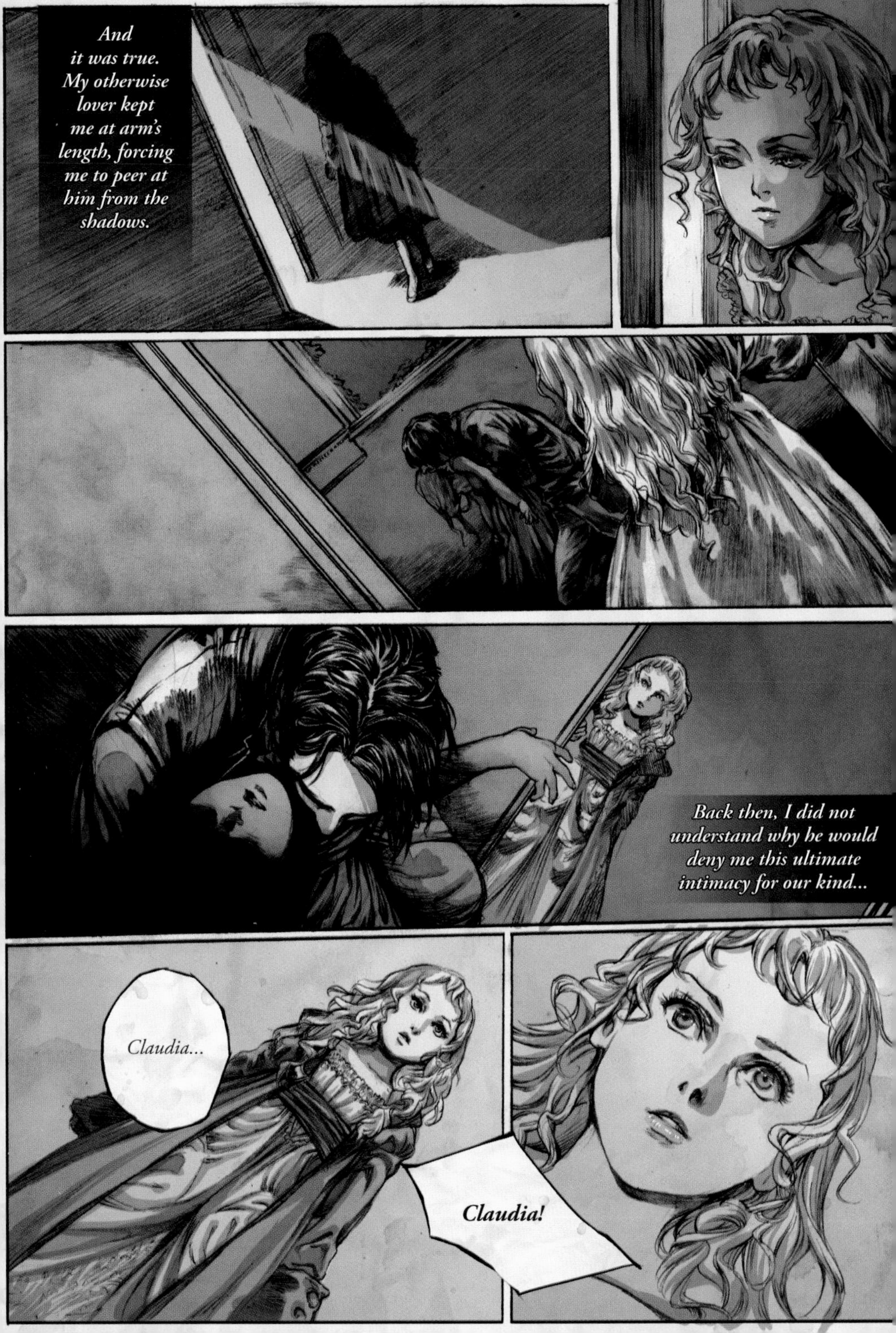
And it was true. My otherwise lover kept me at arm's length, forcing me to peer at him from the shadows.
Back then, I did not understand why he would deny me this ultimate intimacy for our kind...
Claudia...
Claudia!

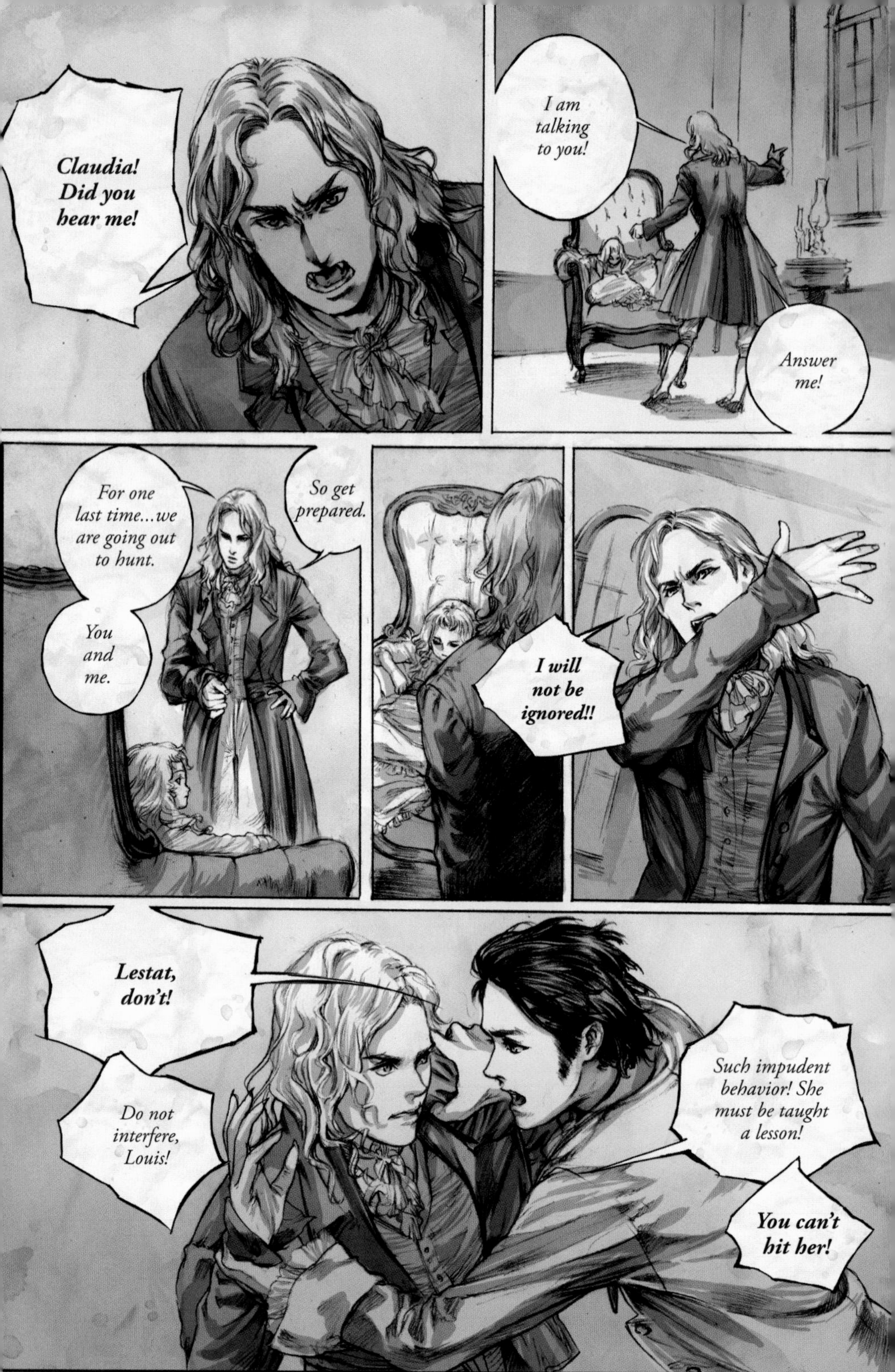
Claudia! Did you hear me!
I am talking to you!
Answer me!
For one last time...we are going out to hunt.
You and me.
So get prepared.
I will not be ignored!!
Lestat, don't!
Do not interfere, Louis!
Such impudent behavior! She must be taught a lesson!
You can't hit her!

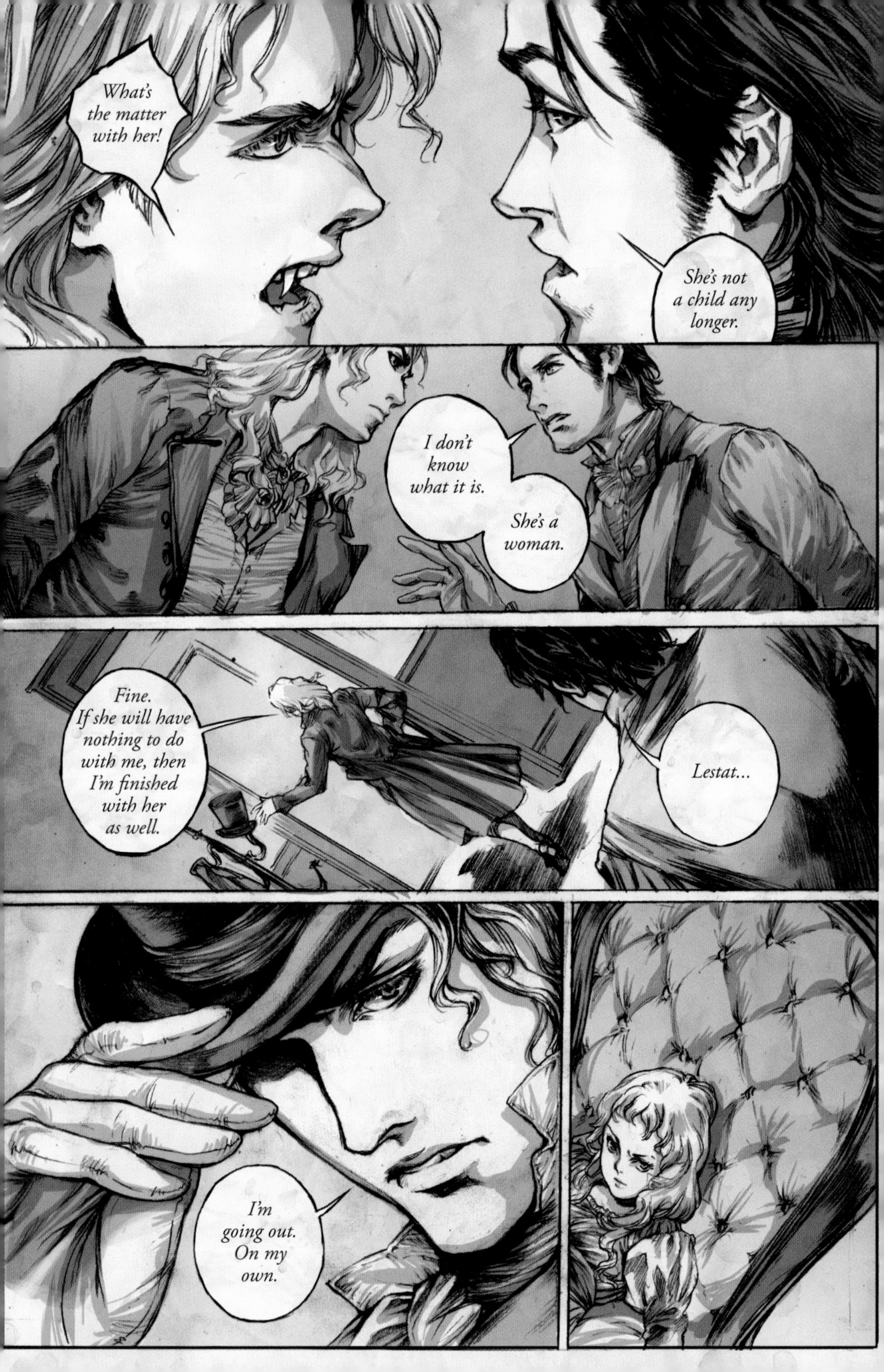

What's the matter with her!
She's not a child any longer.
I don't know what it is.
She's a woman.
Fine. If she will have nothing to do with me, then I'm finished with her as well.
Lestat...
I'm going out. On my own.

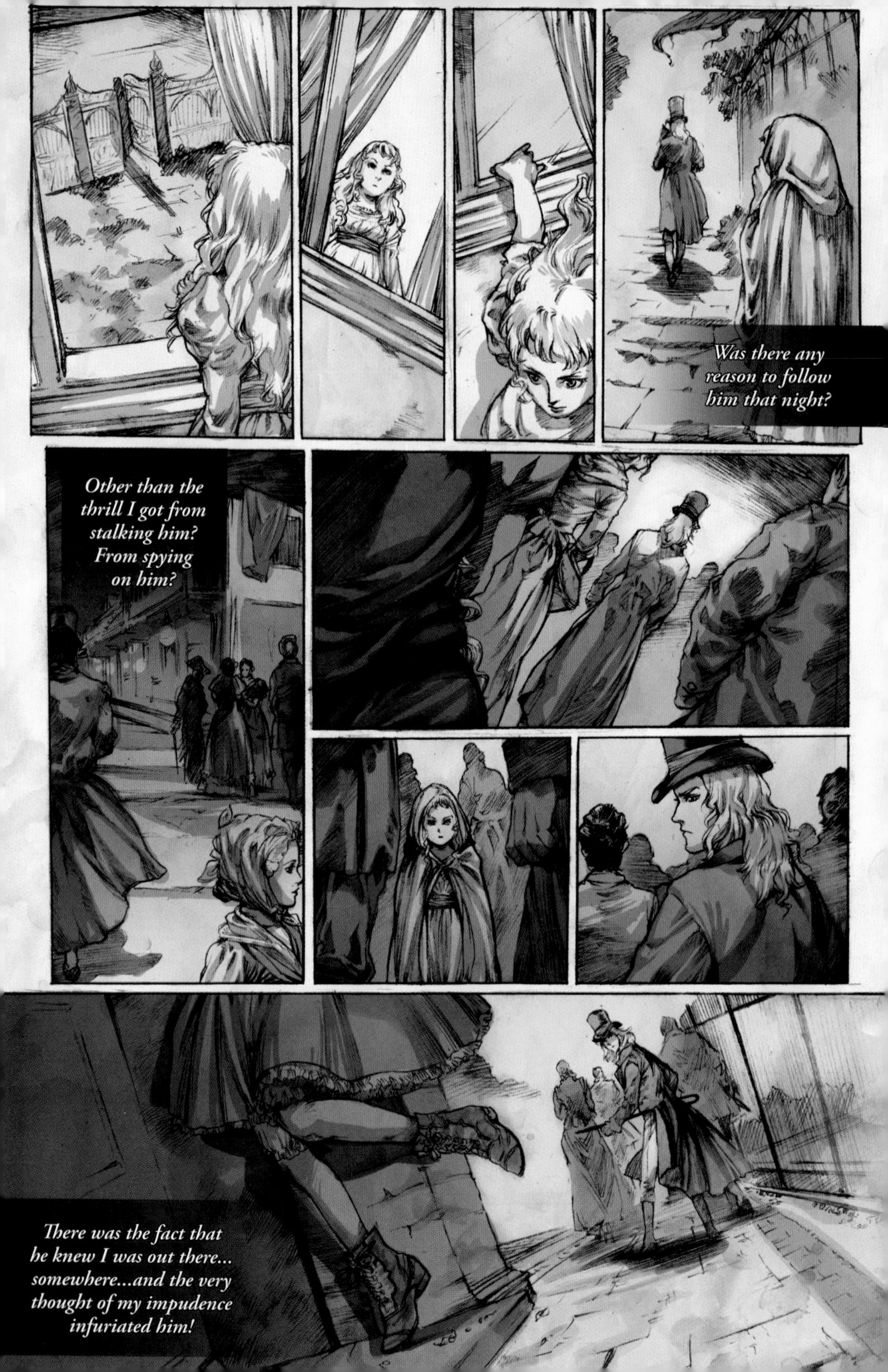
Was there any reason to follow him that night?
Other than the thrill I got from stalking him? From spying on him?
There was the fact that he knew I was out there... somewhere...and the very thought of my impudence infuriated him!

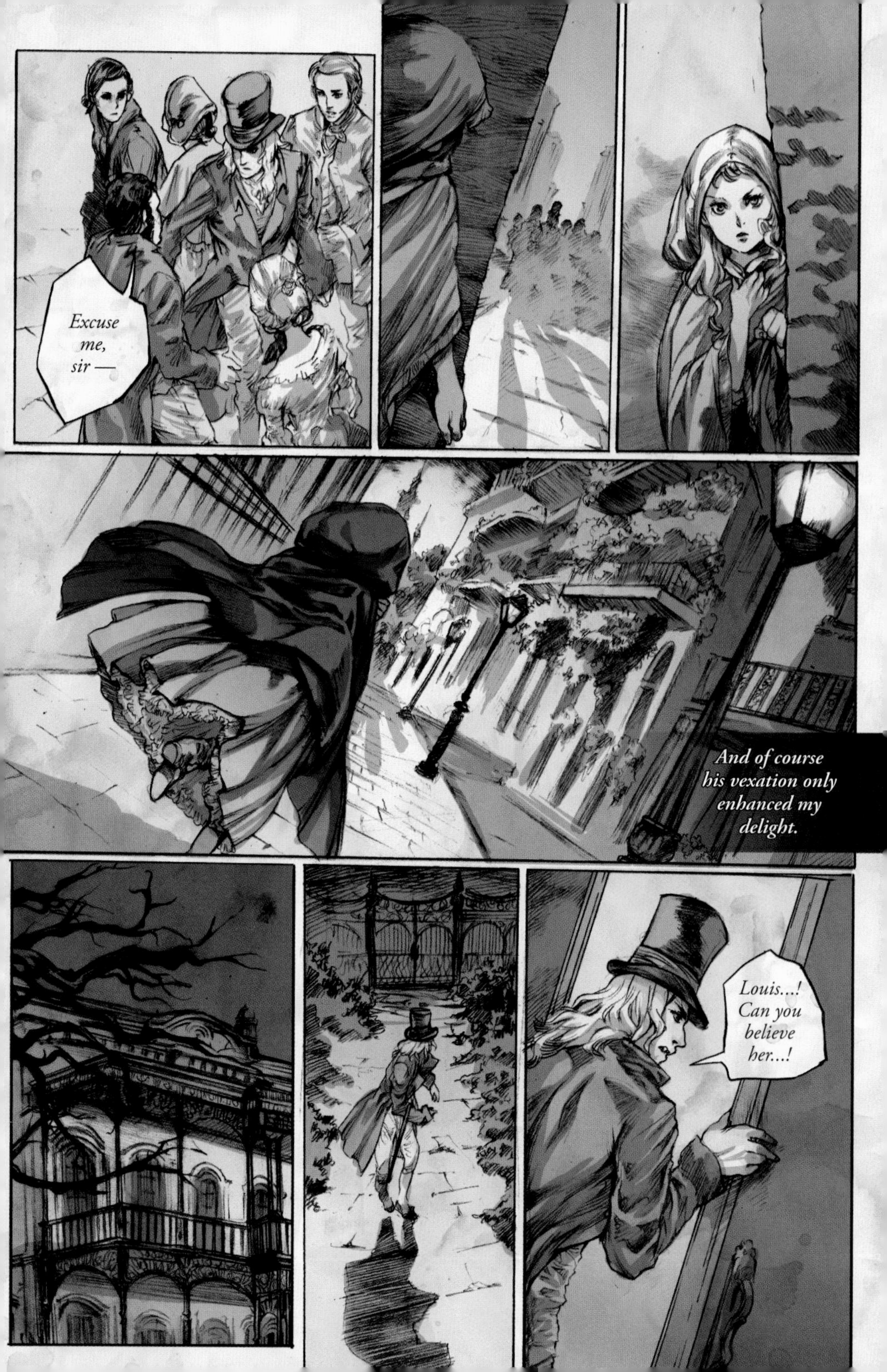
Excuse me, sir —
And of course his vexation only enhanced my delight.
Louis...! Can you believe her...!

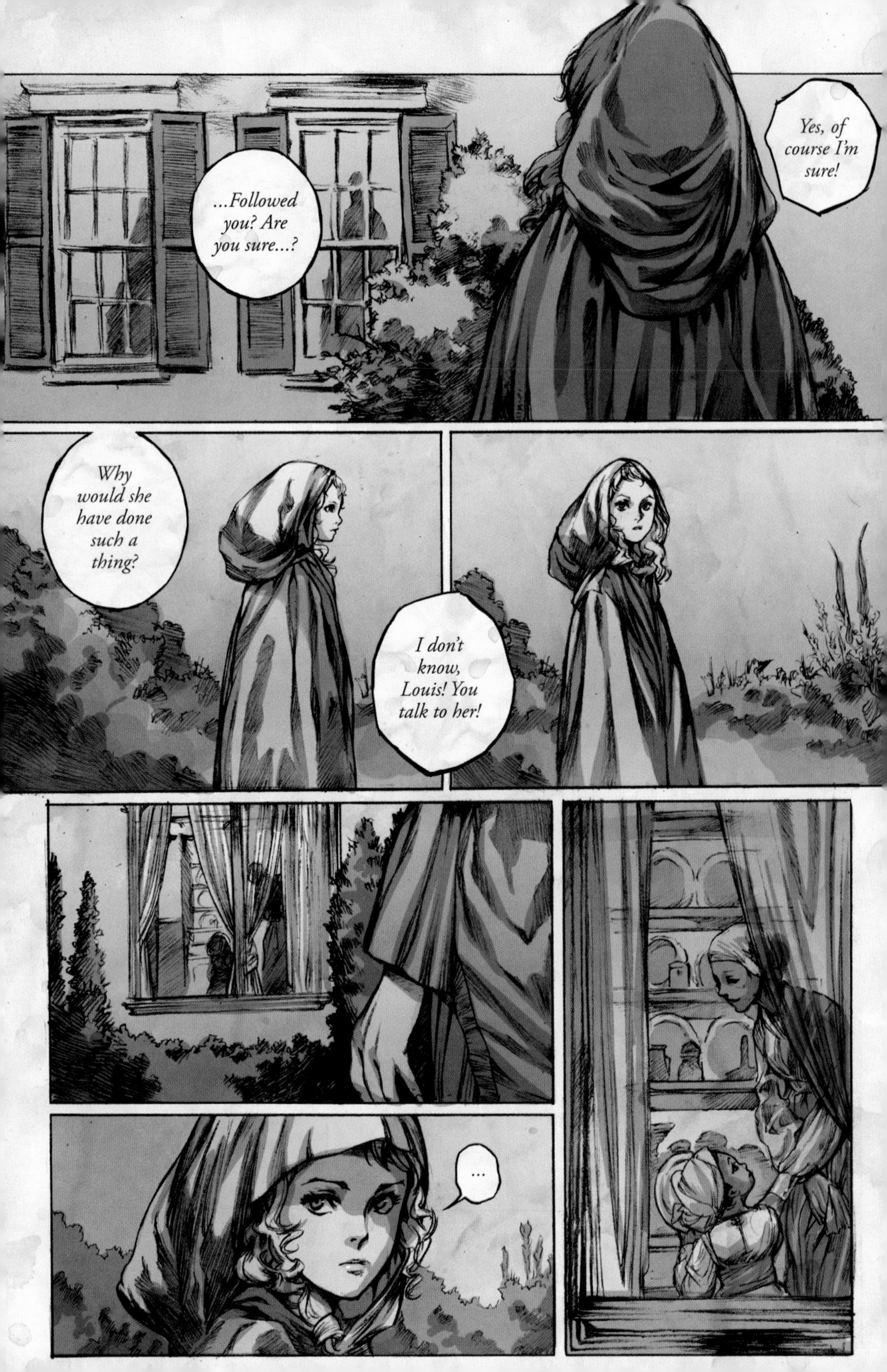
...Followed you? Are you sure...?
Yes, of course I'm sure!
Why would she have done such a thing?
I don't know, Louis! You talk to her!
...

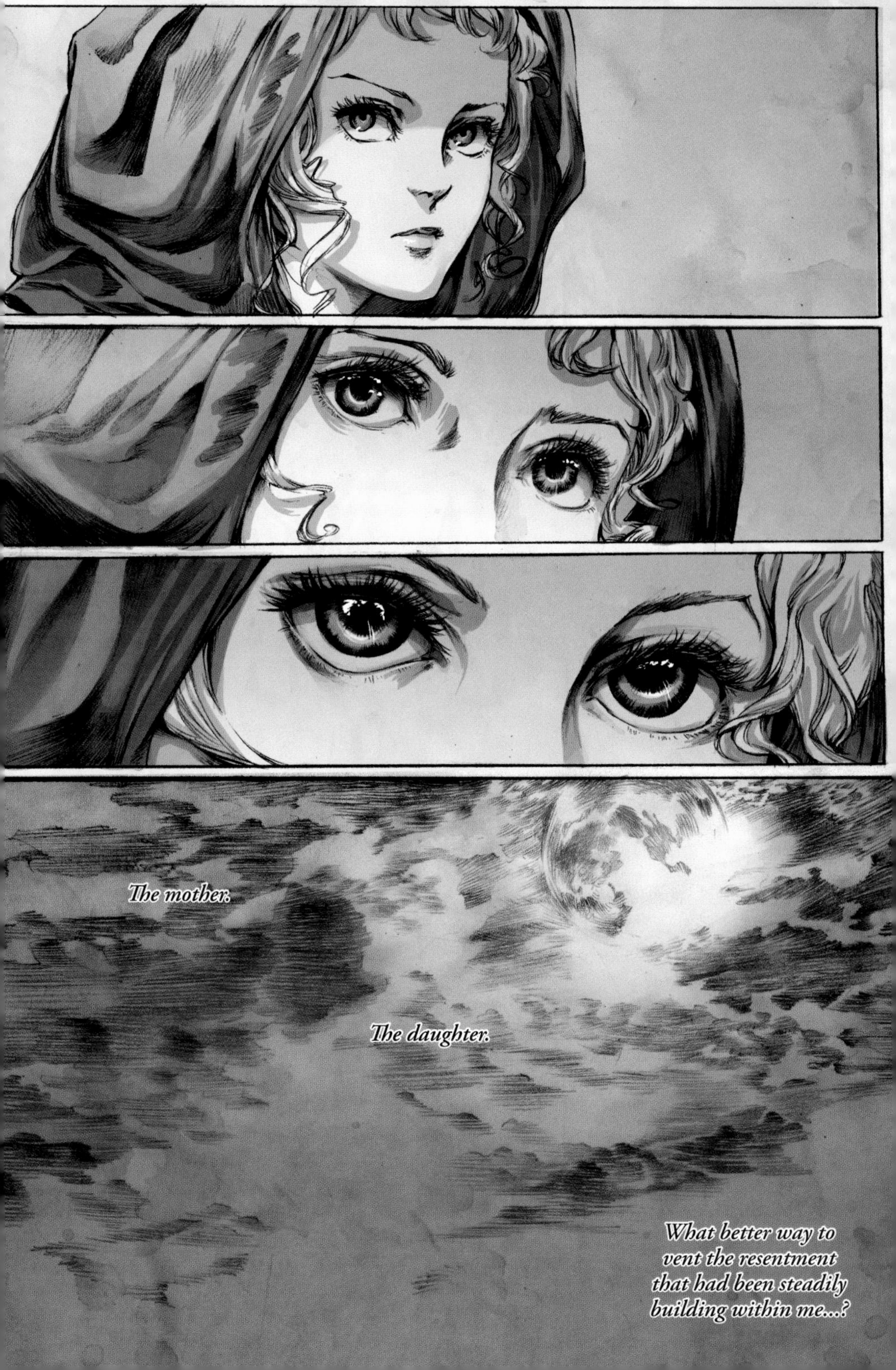
The mother.
The daughter.
What better way to vent the resentment that had been steadily building within me...?

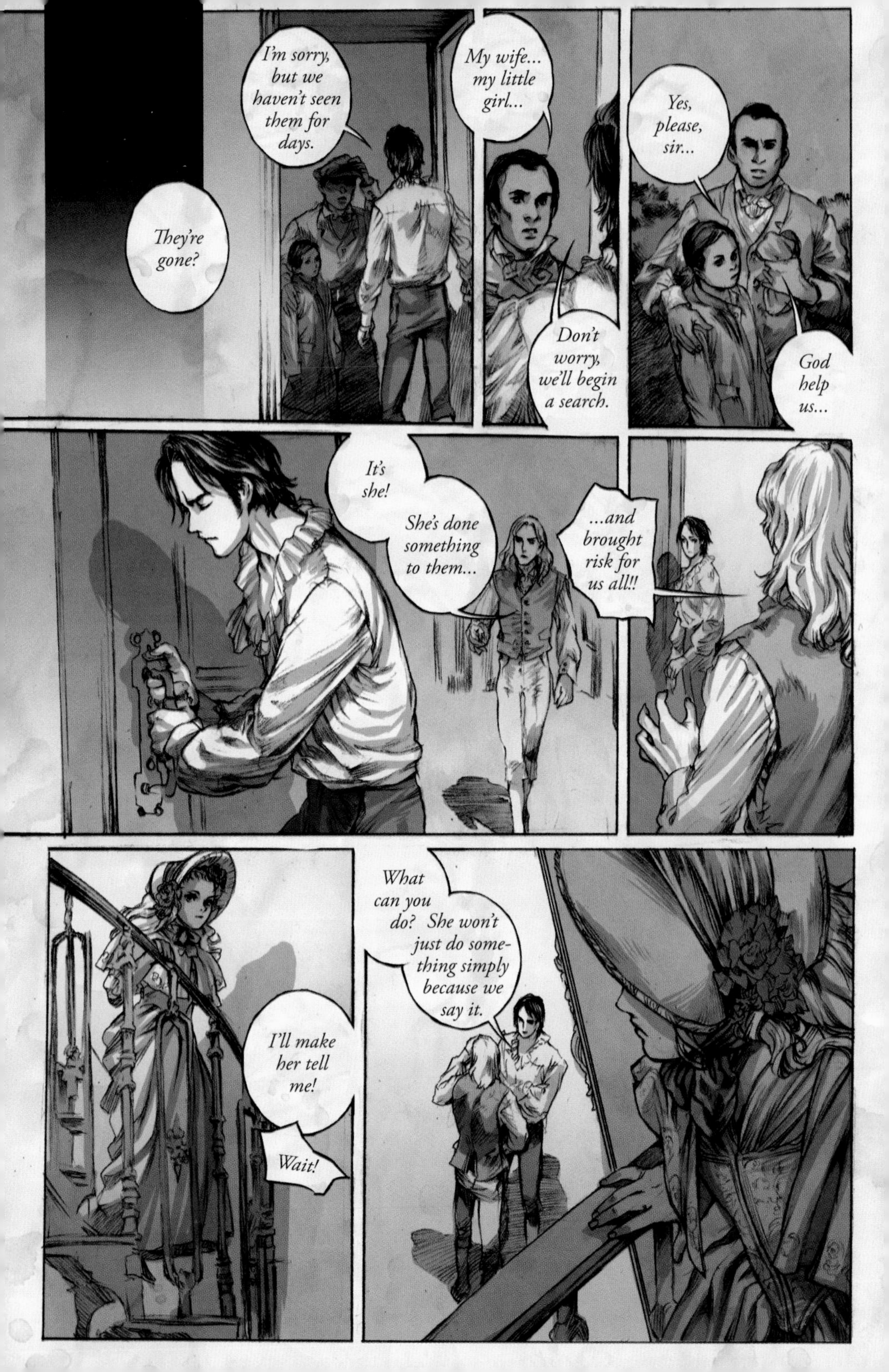
They're gone?
I'm sorry, but we haven't seen them for days.
My wife... my little girl...
Don't worry, we'll begin a search.
Yes, please, sir...
God help us...
It's she!
She's done something to them...
...and brought risk for us all!!
I'll make her tell me!
Wait!
What can you do? She won't just do some-thing simply because we say it.

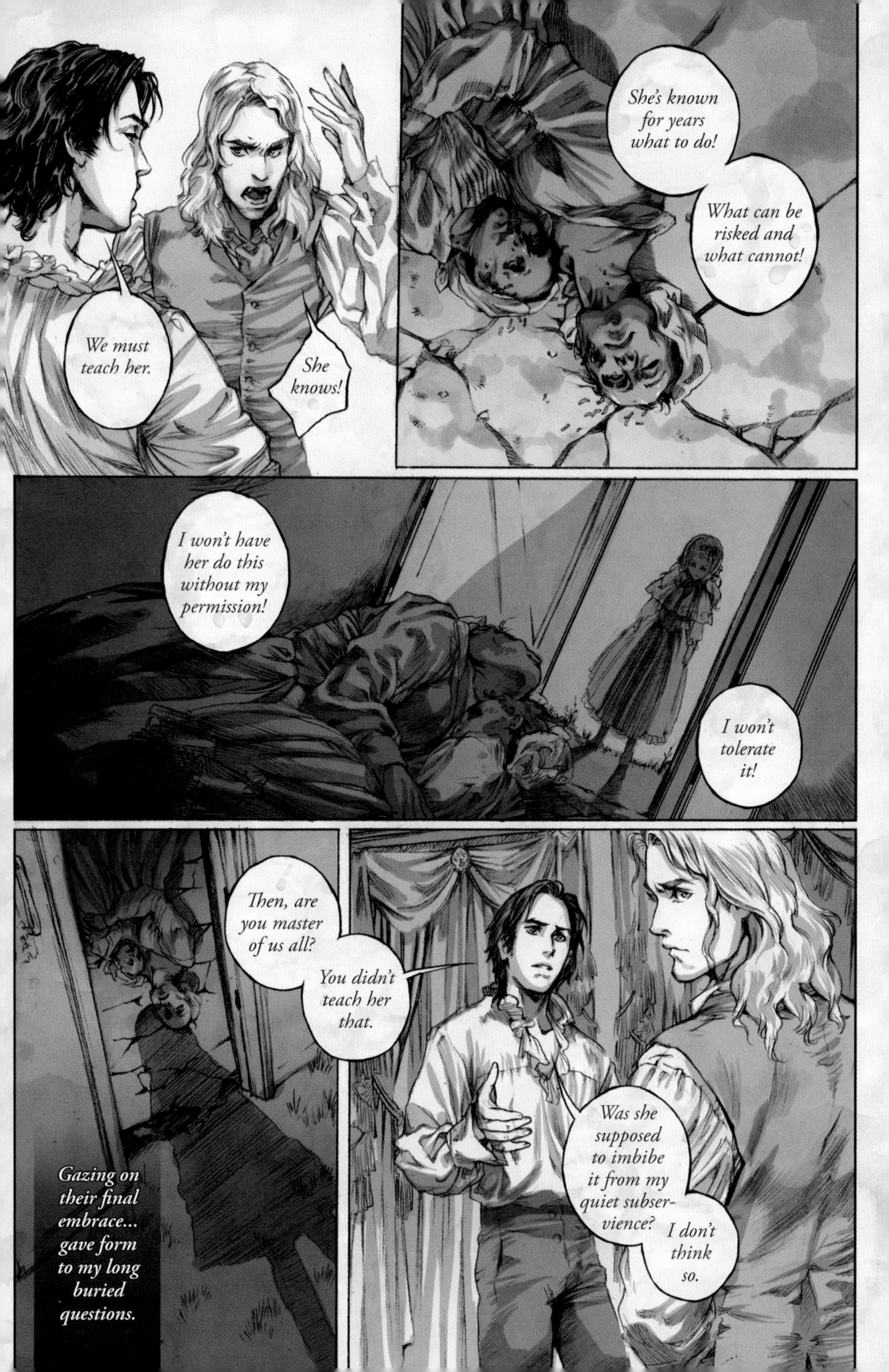
We must teach her.
She knows!
She's known for years what to do!
What can be risked and what cannot!
I won't have her do this without my permission!
I won't tolerate it!
Gazing on their final embrace... gave form to my long buried questions.
Then, are you master of us all?
You didn't teach her that.
Was she supposed to imbibe it from my quiet subser-vience?
I don't think so.

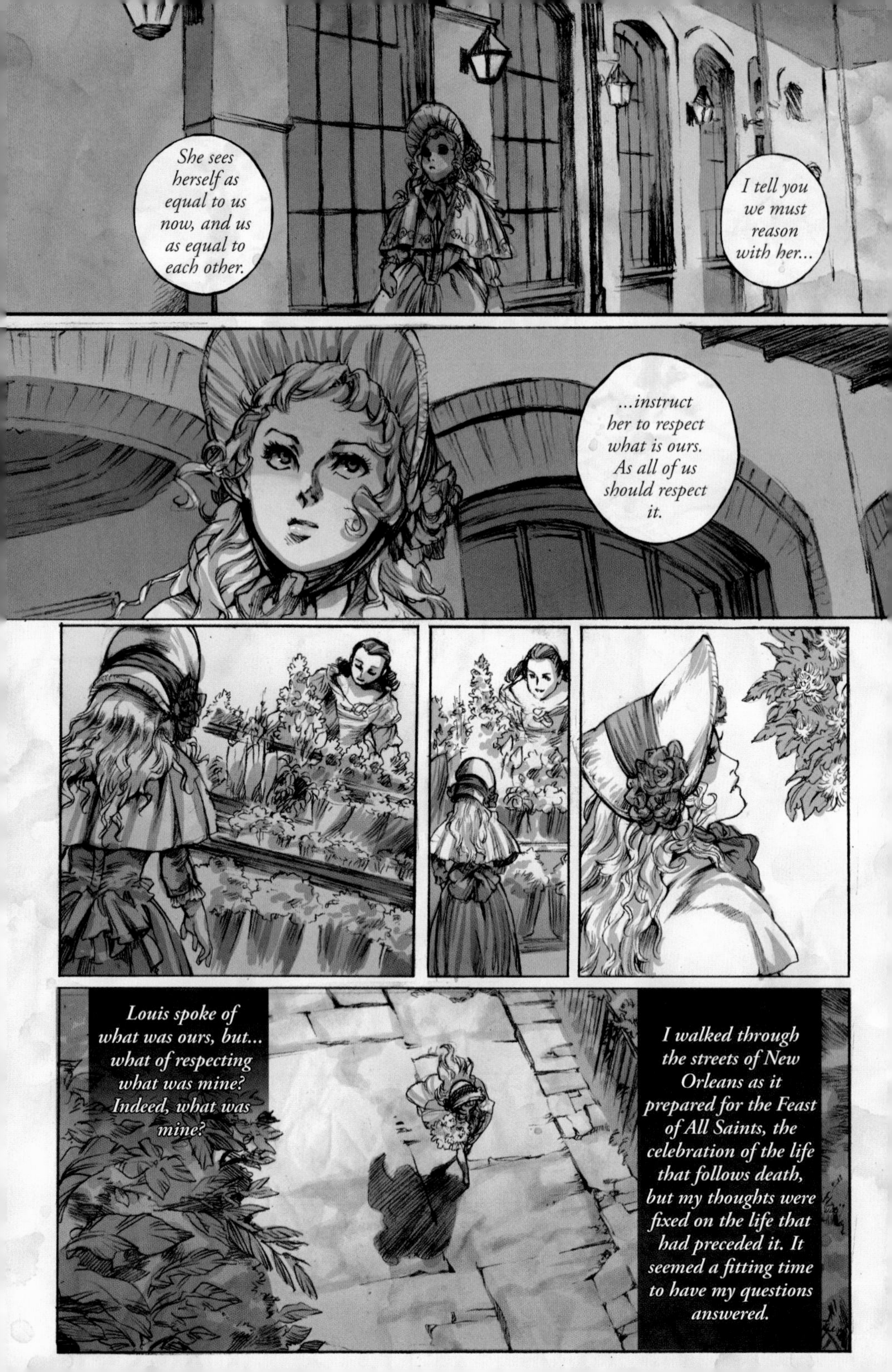
She sees herself as equal to us now, and us as equal to each other.
I tell you we must reason with her...
...instruct her to respect what is ours. As all of us should respect it.
Louis spoke of what was ours, but... what of respecting what was mine? Indeed, what was mine?
I walked through the streets of New Orleans as it prepared for the Feast of All Saints, the celebration of the life that follows death, but my thoughts were fixed on the life that had preceded it. It seemed a fitting time to have my questions answered.

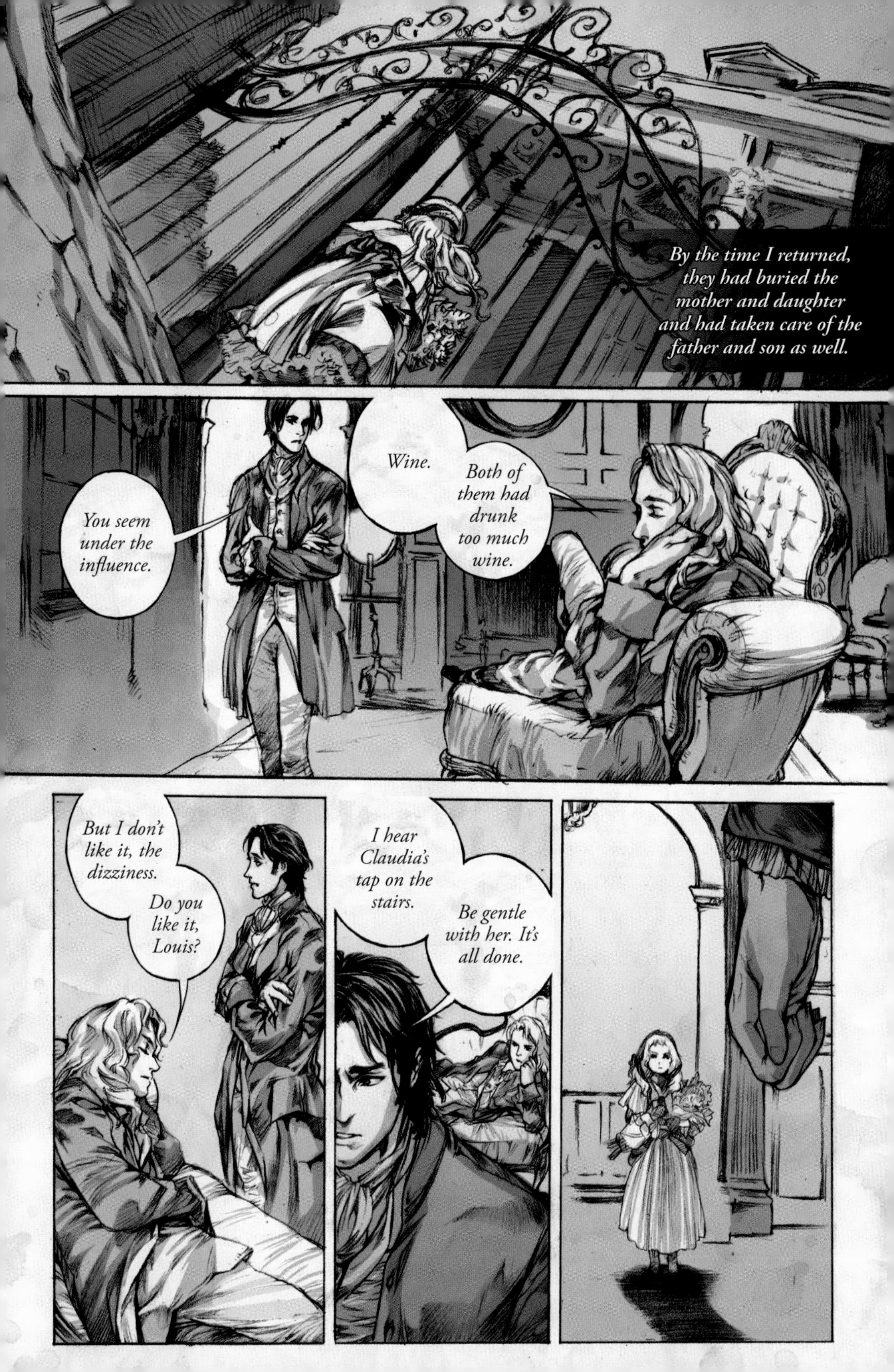
By the time I returned, they had buried the mother and daughter and had taken care of the father and son as well.
You seem under the influence.
Wine.
Both of them had drunk too much wine.
But I don't like it, the dizziness.
Do you like it, Louis?
I hear Claudia's tap on the stairs.
Be gentle with her. It's all done.

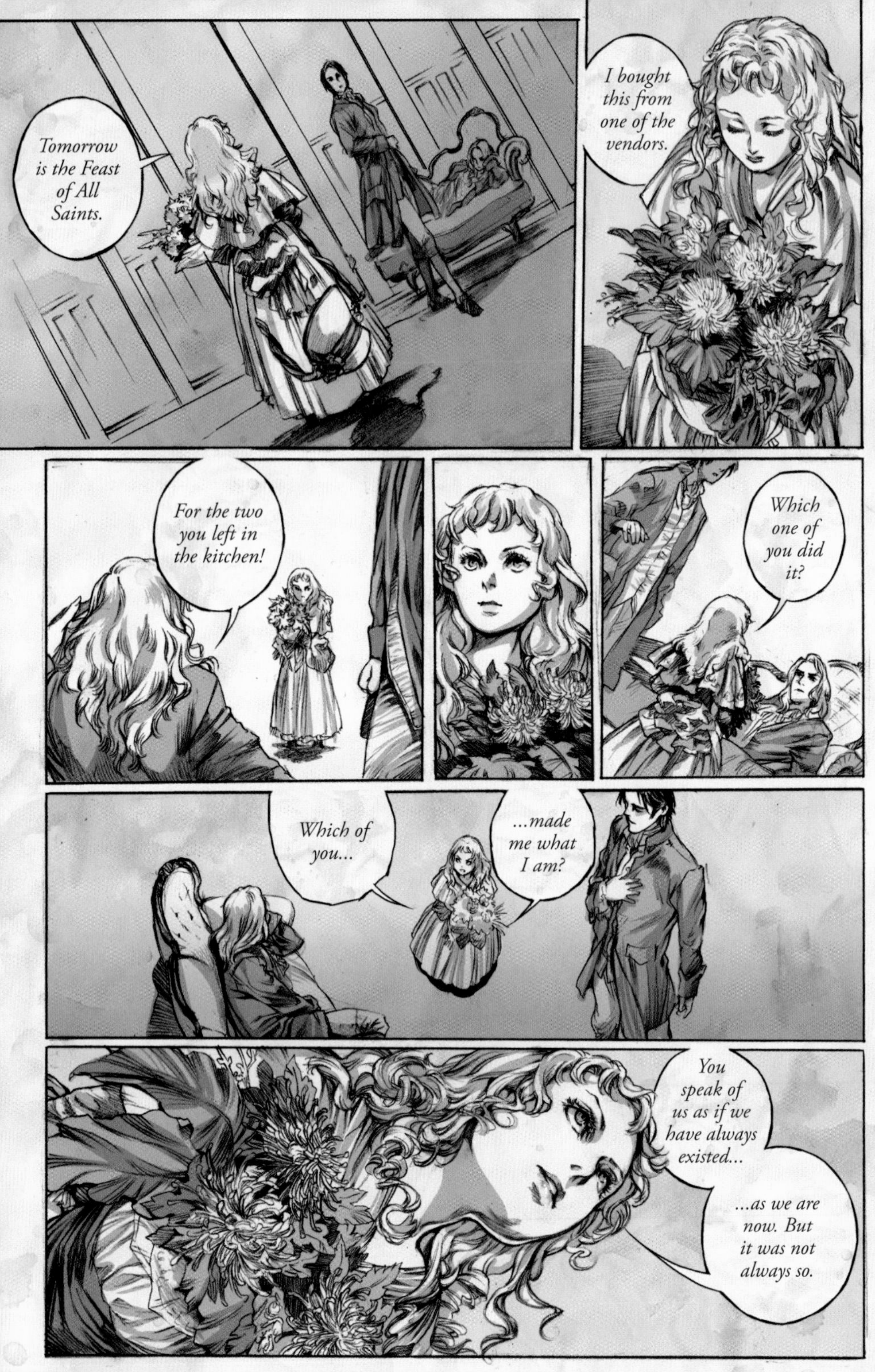
Tomorrow is the Feast of All Saints.
I bought this from one of the vendors.
For the two you left in the kitchen!
Which one of you did it?
Which of you...
...made me what I am?
You speak of us as if we have always existed...
...as we are now. But it was not always so.

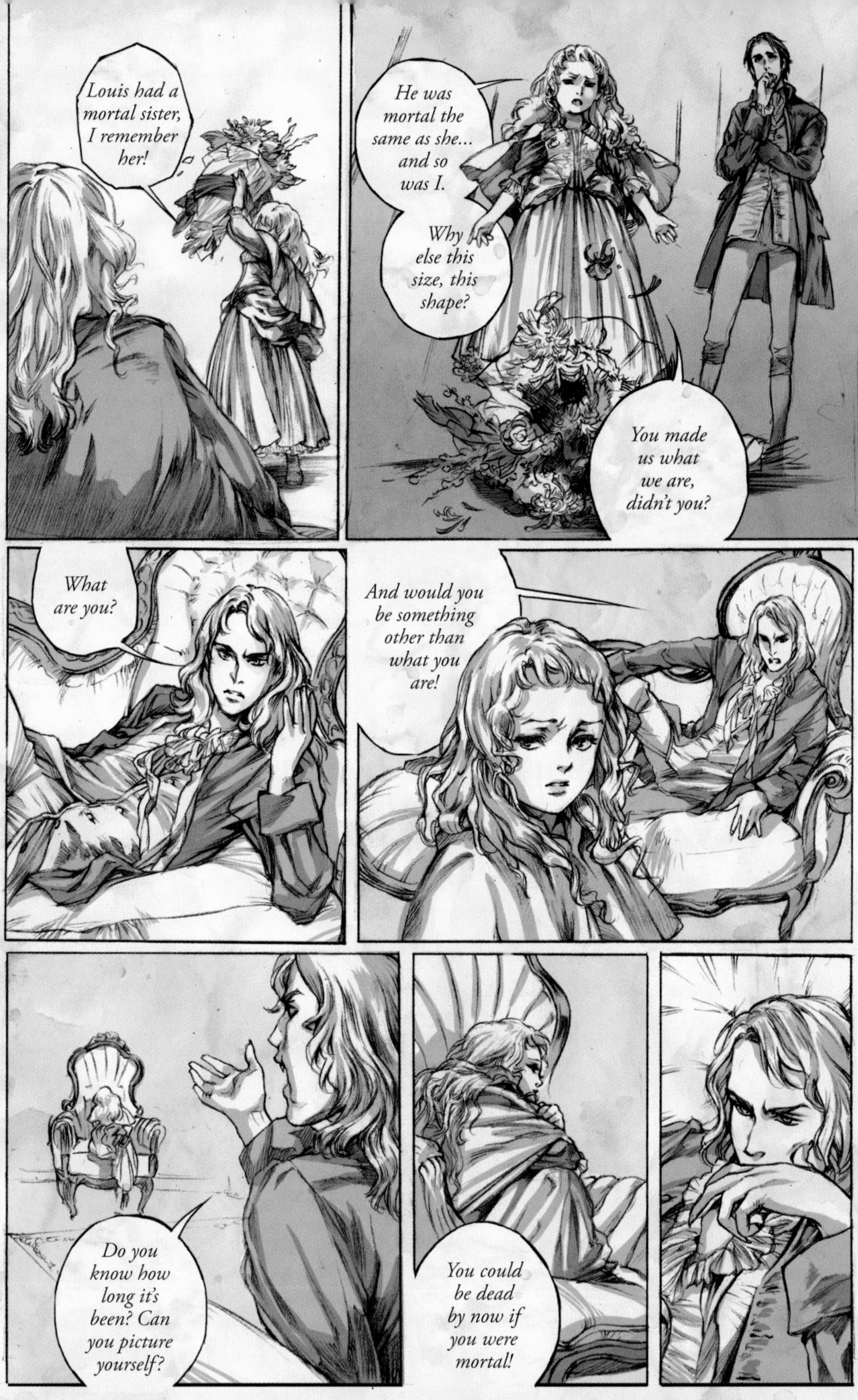
Louis had a mortal sister, I remember her!
He was mortal the same as she... and so was I.
Why else this size, this shape?
You made us what we are, didn't you?
What are you?
And would you be something other than what you are!
Do you know how long it's been? Can you picture yourself?
You could be dead by now if you were mortal!

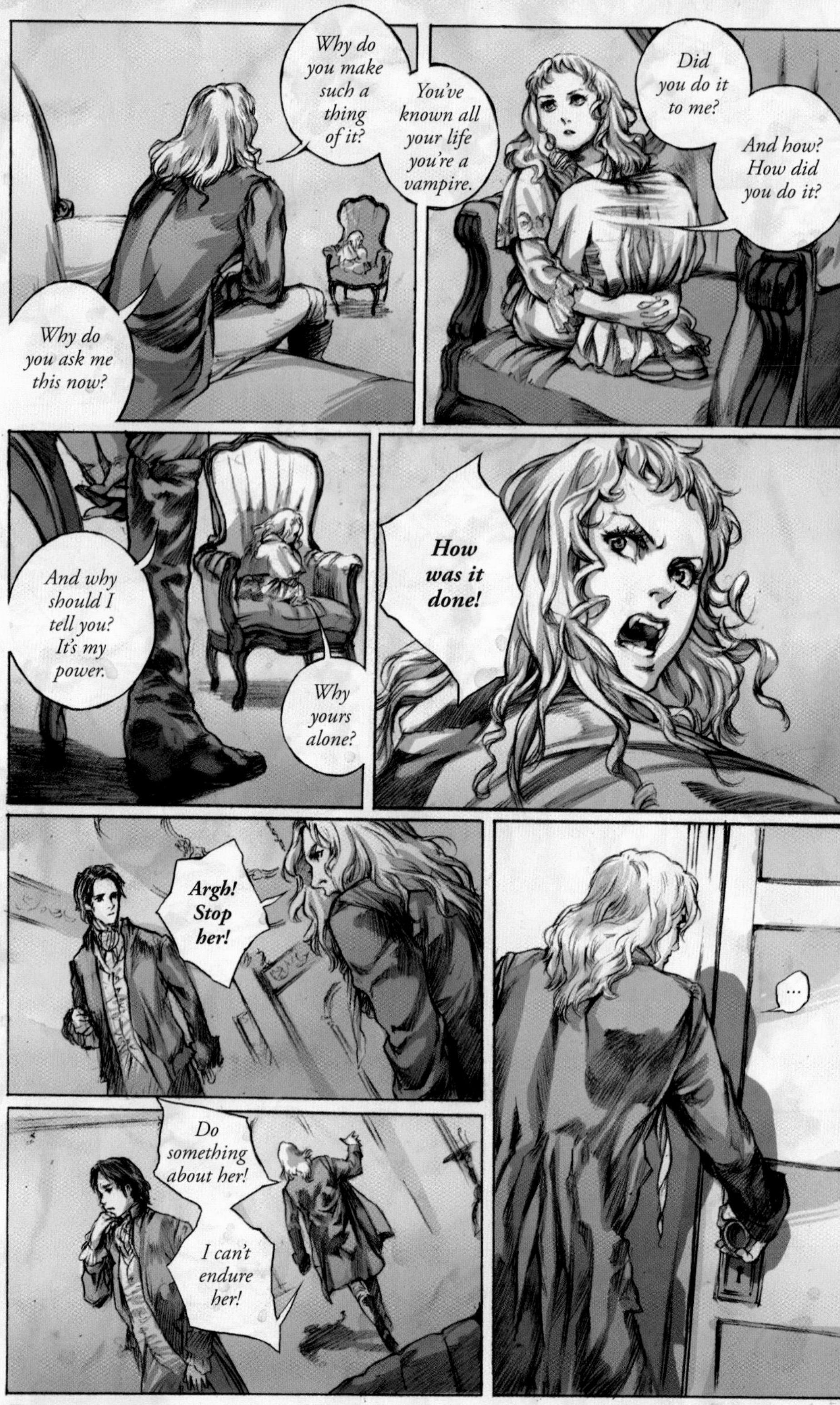
Why do you make such a thing of it?
You've known all your life you're a vampire.
Why do you ask me this now?
Did you do it to me?
And how? How did you do it?
And why should I tell you? It's my power.
Why yours alone?
How was it done!
Argh! Stop her!
Do something about her!
I can't endure her!
...

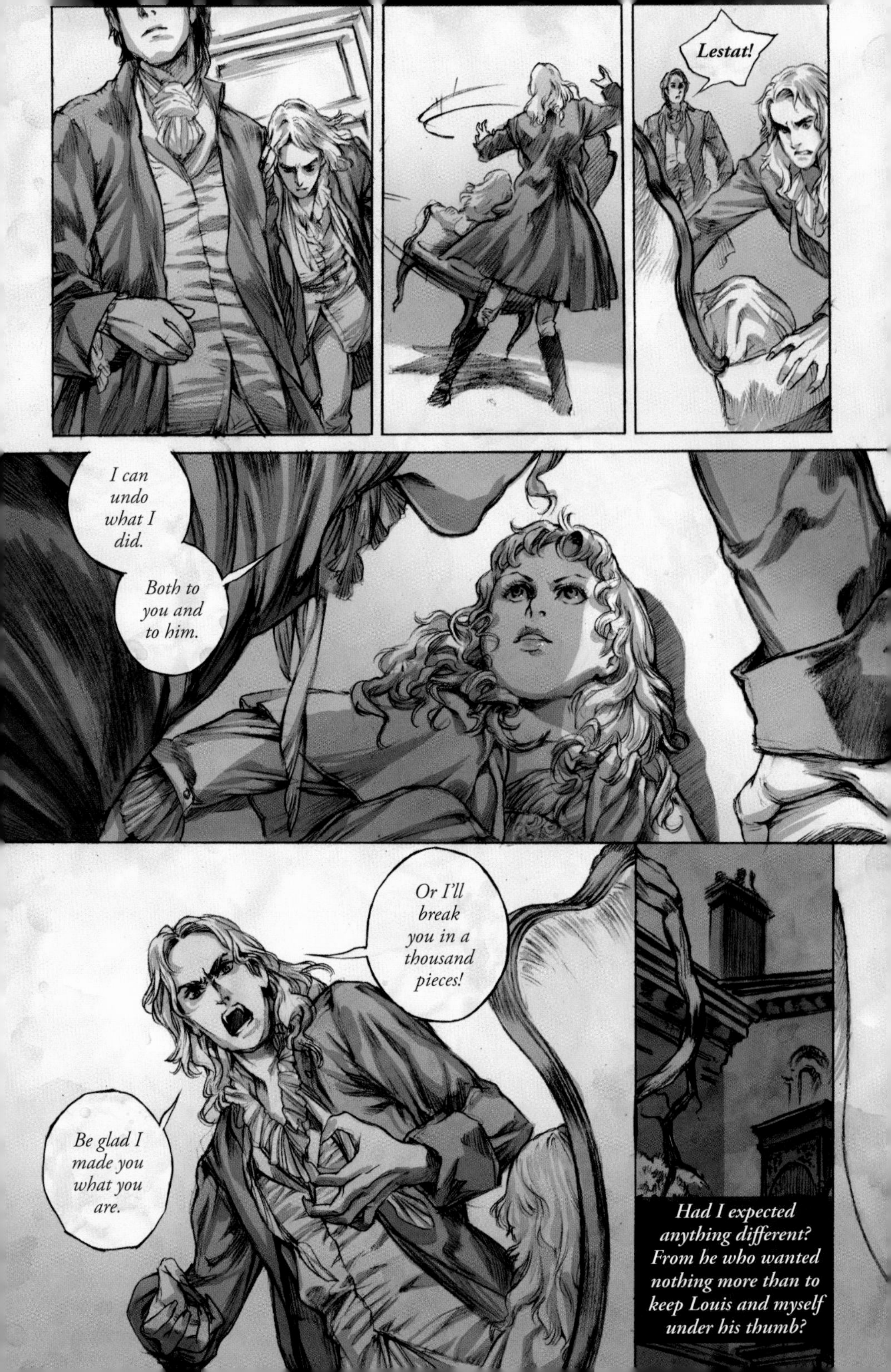
Lestat!
I can undo what I did.
Both to you and to him.
Or I'll break you in a thousand pieces!
Be glad I made you what you are.
Had I expected anything different? From he who wanted nothing more than to keep Louis and myself under his thumb?

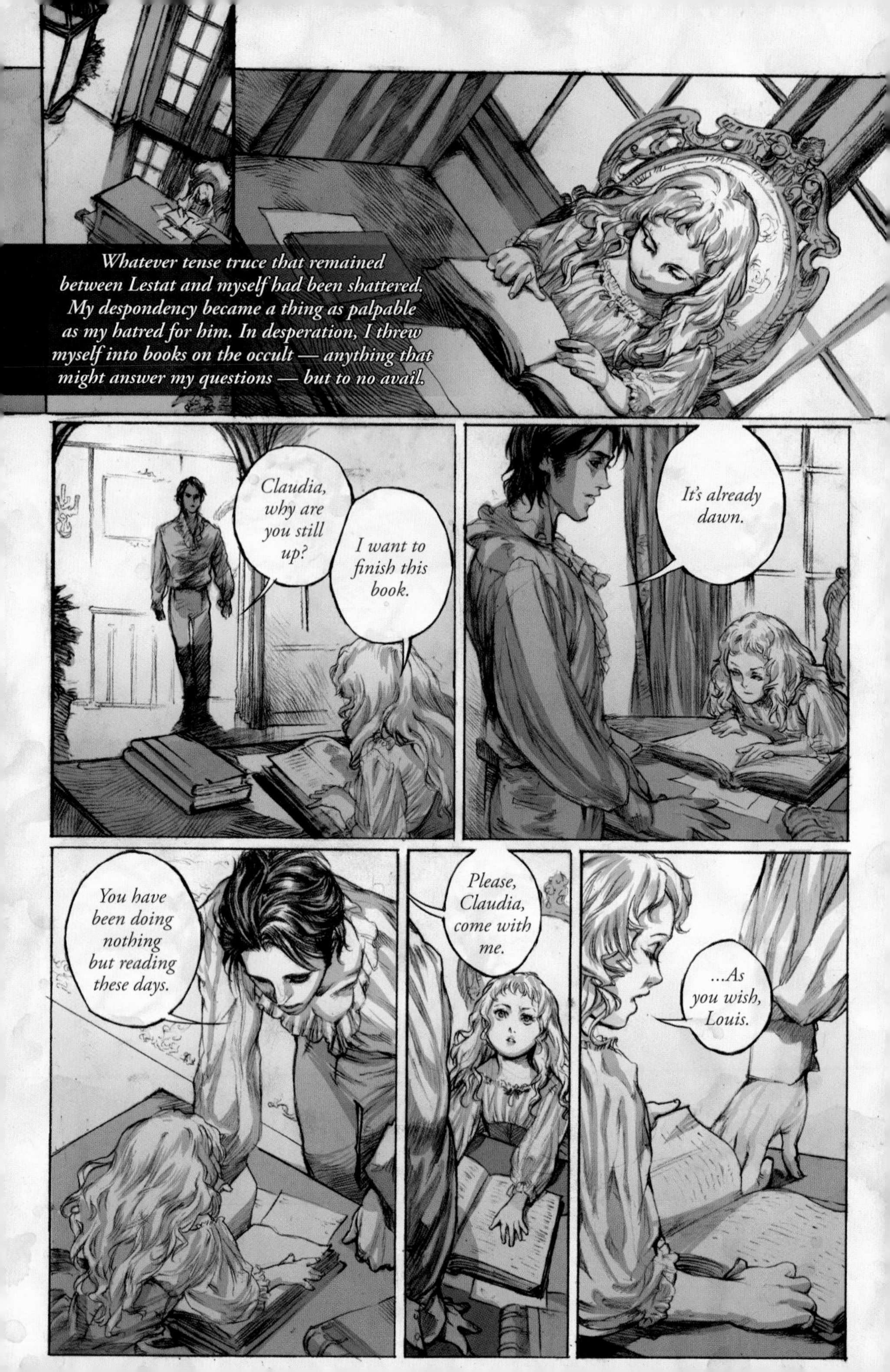
Whatever tense truce that remained between Lestat and myself had been shattered. My despondency became a thing as palpable as my hatred for him. In desperation, I threw myself into books on the occult — anything that might answer my questions — but to no avail.
Claudia, why are you still up?
I want to finish this book.
It's already dawn.
You have been doing nothing but reading these days.
Please, Claudia, come with me.
...As you wish, Louis.

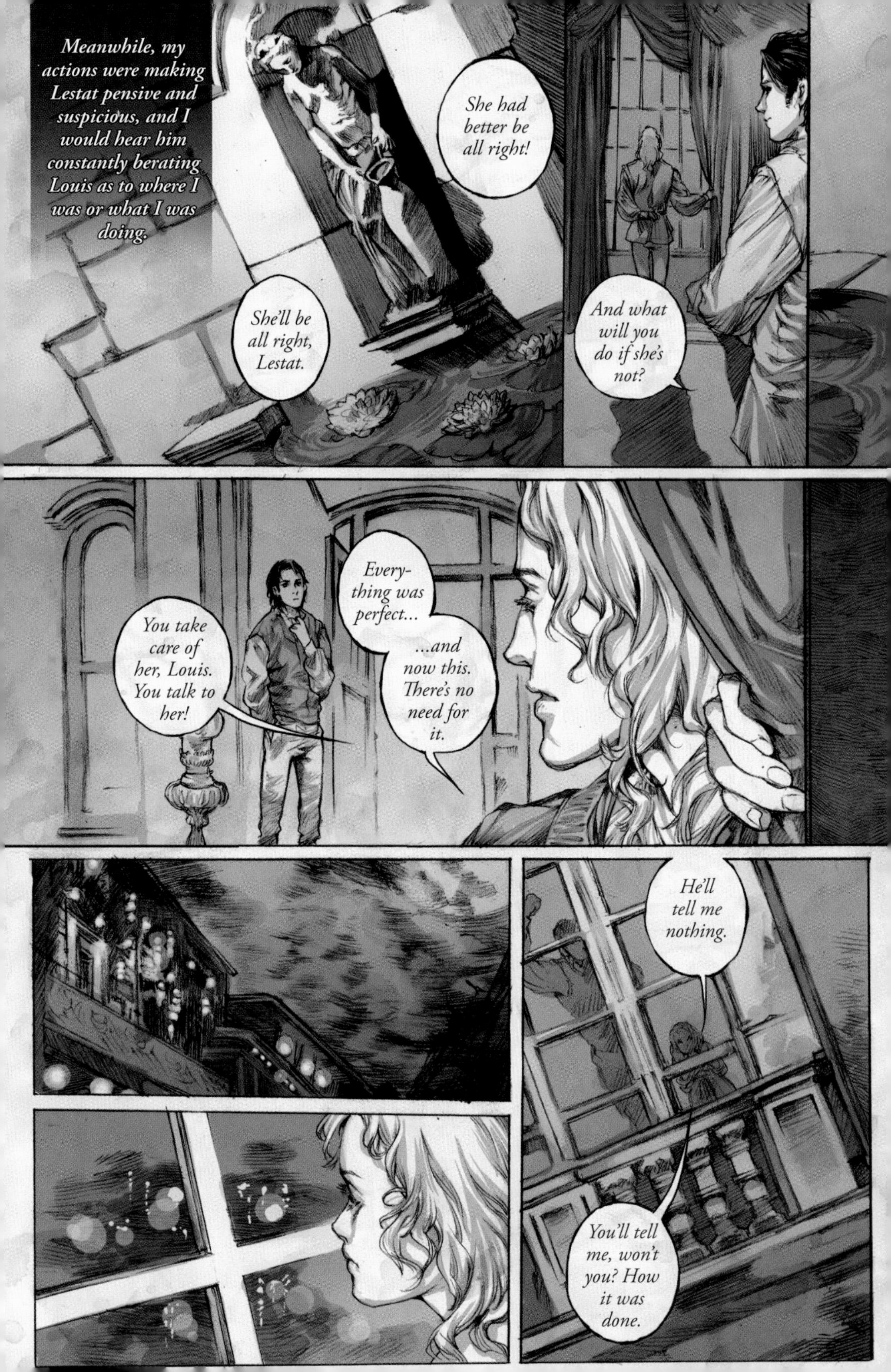
Meanwhile, my actions were making Lestat pensive and suspicious, and I would hear him constantly berating Louis as to where I was or what I was doing.
She had better be all right!
She'll be all right, Lestat.
And what will you do if she's not?
Every-thing was perfect...
...and now this. There's no need for it.
You take care of her, Louis. You talk to her!
He'll tell me nothing.
You'll tell me, won't you? How it was done.

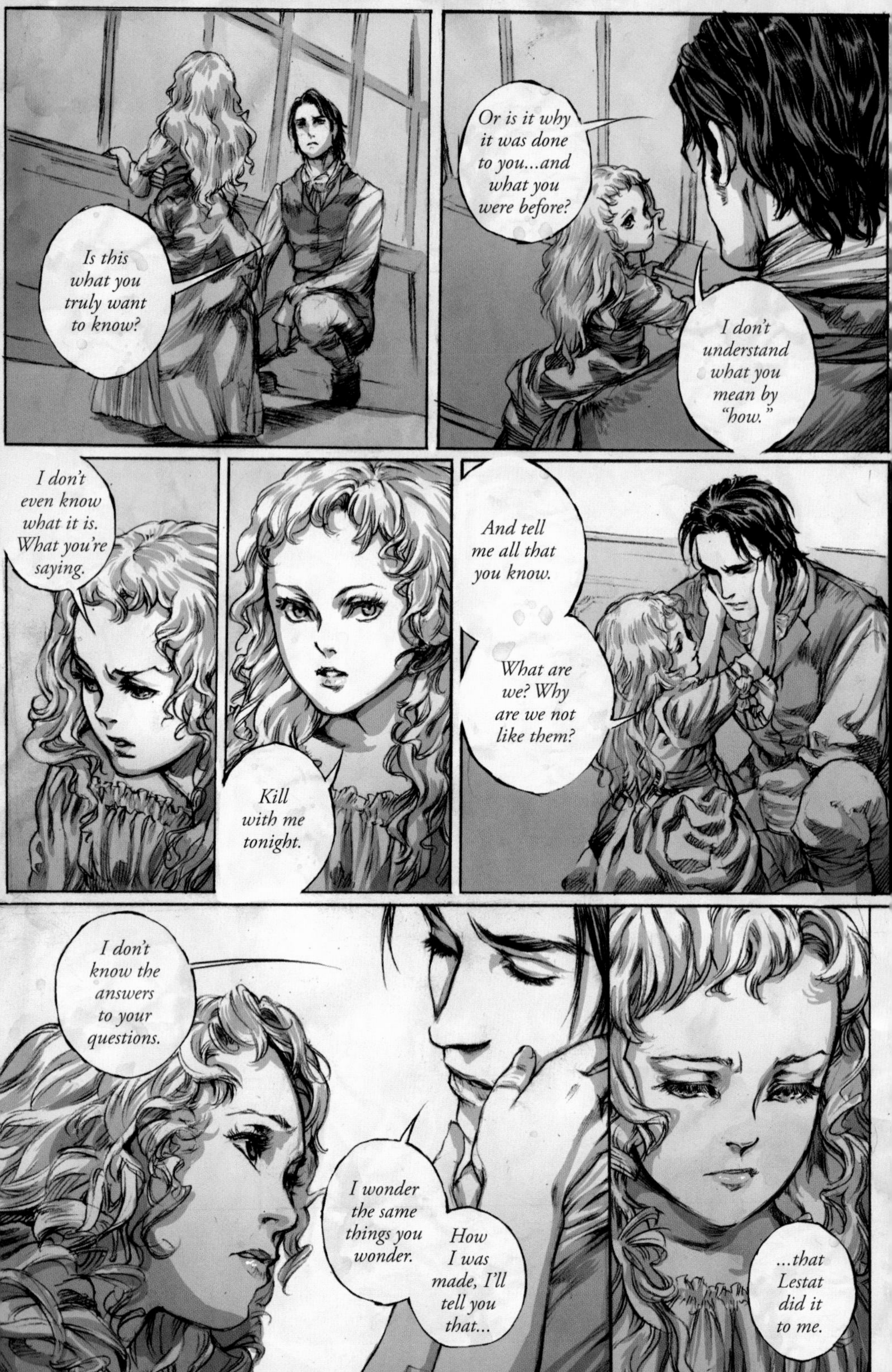
Is this what you truly want to know?
Or is it why it was done to you...and what you were before?
I don't understand what you mean by "how."
I don't even know what it is. What you're saying.
Kill with me tonight.
And tell me all that you know.
What are we? Why are we not like them?
I don't know the answers to your questions.
I wonder the same things you wonder.
How I was made, I'll tell you that...
...that Lestat did it to me.

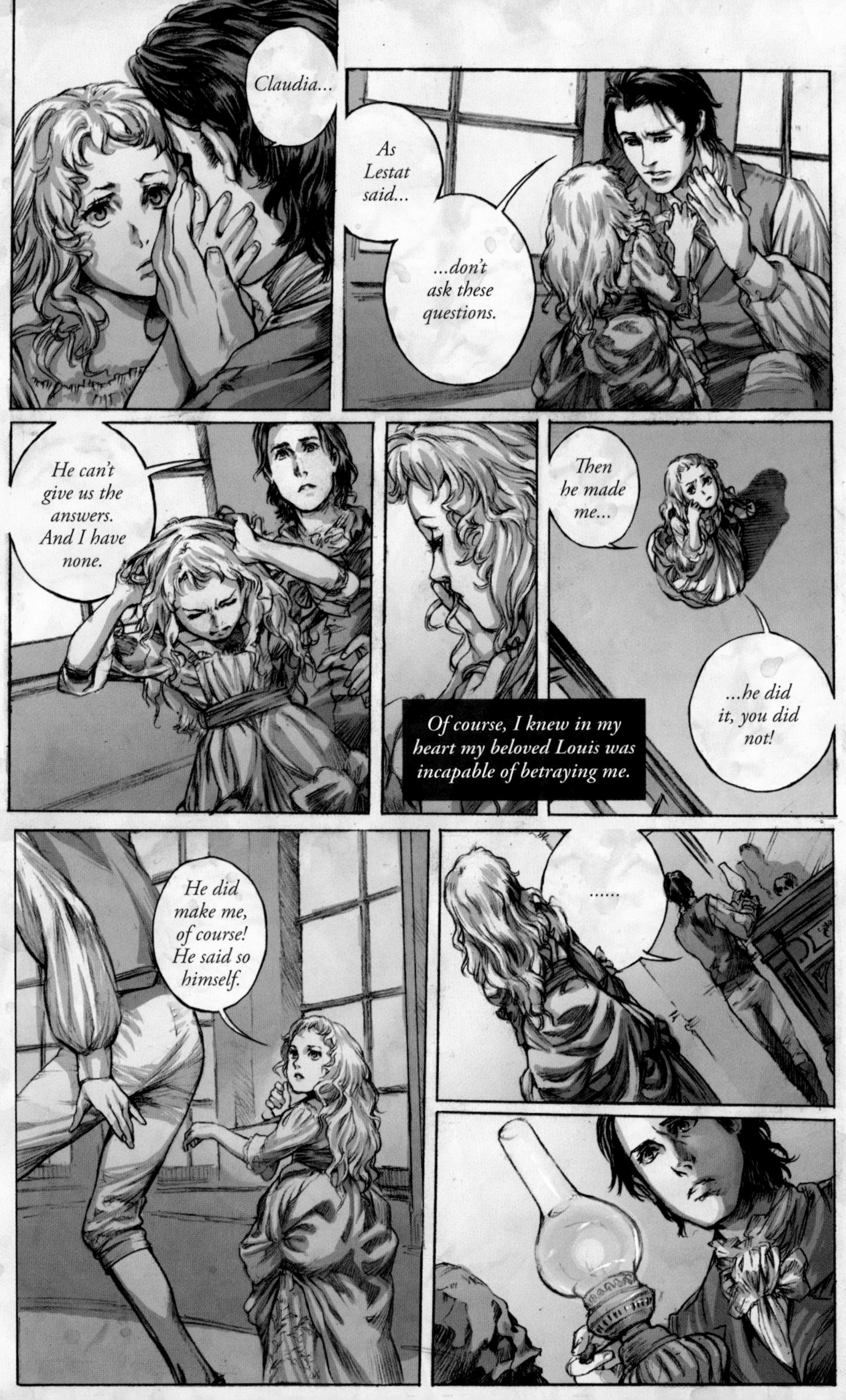
Claudia...
As Lestat said...
...don't ask these questions.
He can't give us the answers. And I have none.
Then he made me...
...he did it, you did not!
Of course, I knew in my heart my beloved Louis was incapable of betraying me.
He did make me, of course! He said so himself.
......

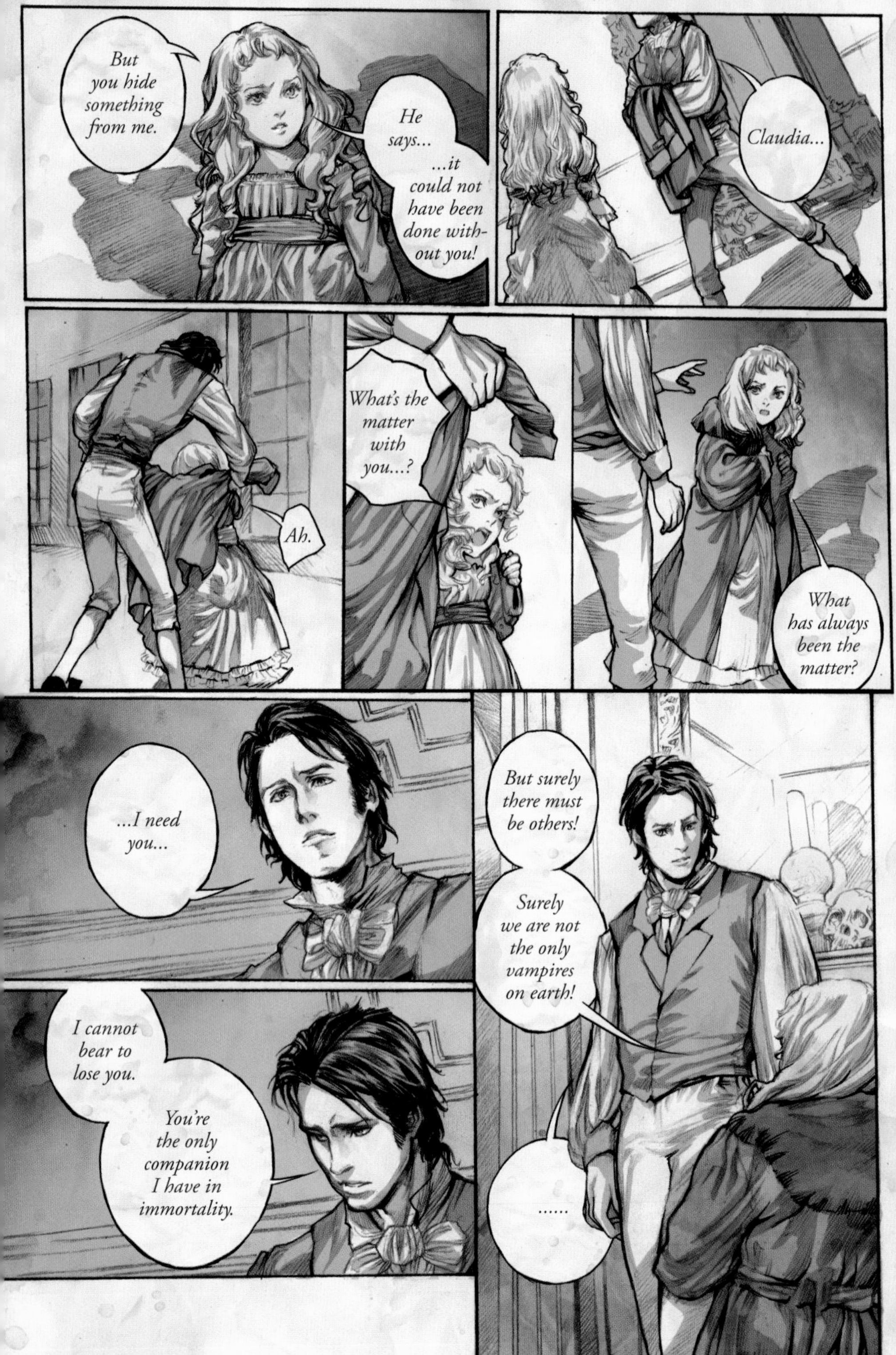
But you hide something from me.
He says... ...it could not have been done without you!
Claudia...
Ah.
What's the matter with you...?
What has always been the matter?
...I need you...
I cannot bear to lose you.
You're the only companion I have in immortality.
But surely there must be others!
Surely we are not the only vampires on earth!
......

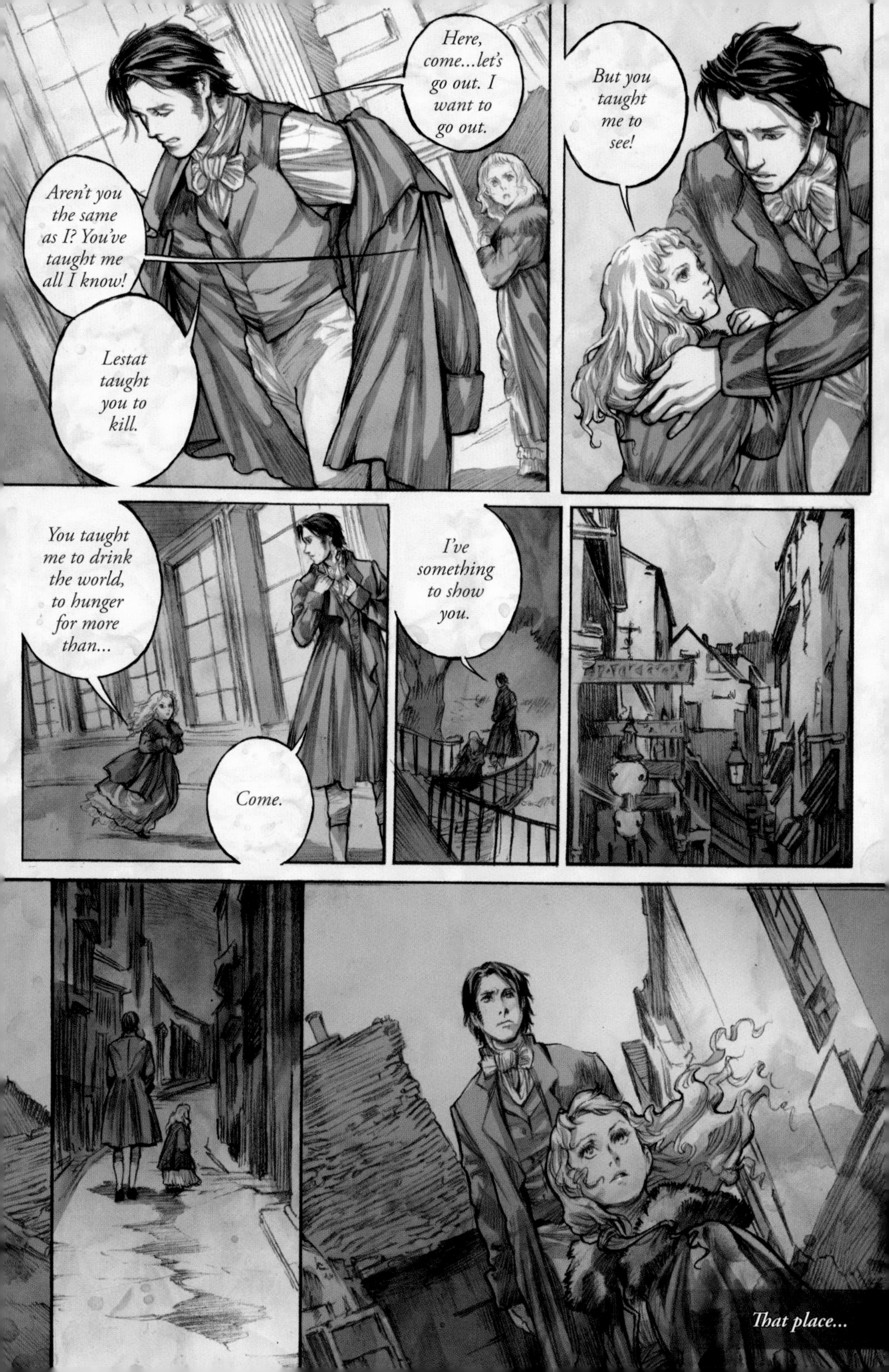
Here, come...let's go out. I want to go out.
Aren't you the same as I? You've taught me all I know!
Lestat taught you to kill.
But you taught me to see!
You taught me to drink the world, to hunger for more than...
Come.
I've something to show you.
That place...

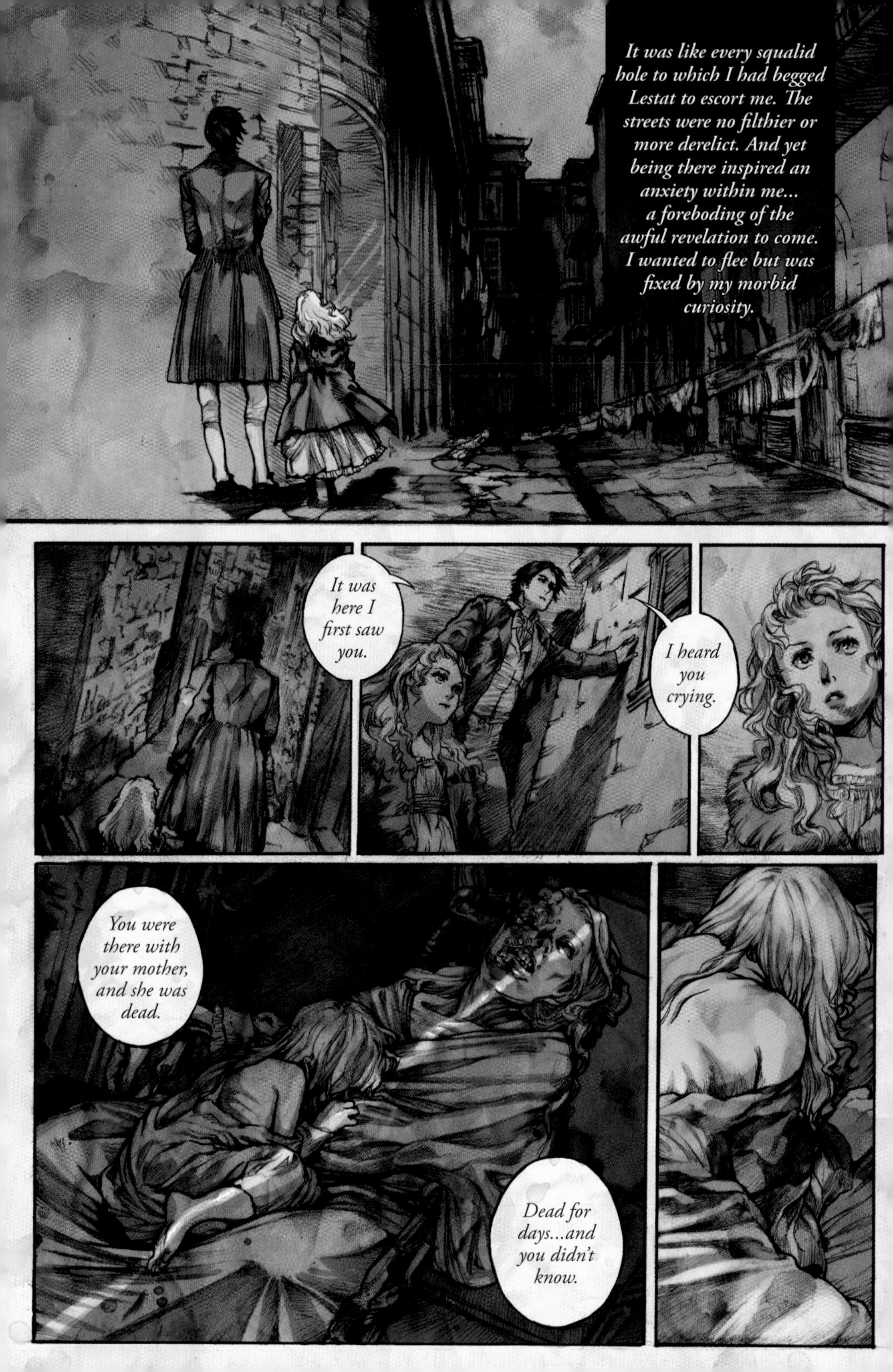
It was like every squalid hole to which I had begged Lestat to escort me. The streets were no filthier or more derelict. And yet being there inspired an anxiety within me... a foreboding of the awful revelation to come. I wanted to flee but was fixed by my morbid curiosity.
It was here I first saw you.
I heard you crying.
You were there with your mother, and she was dead.
Dead for days...and you didn't know.

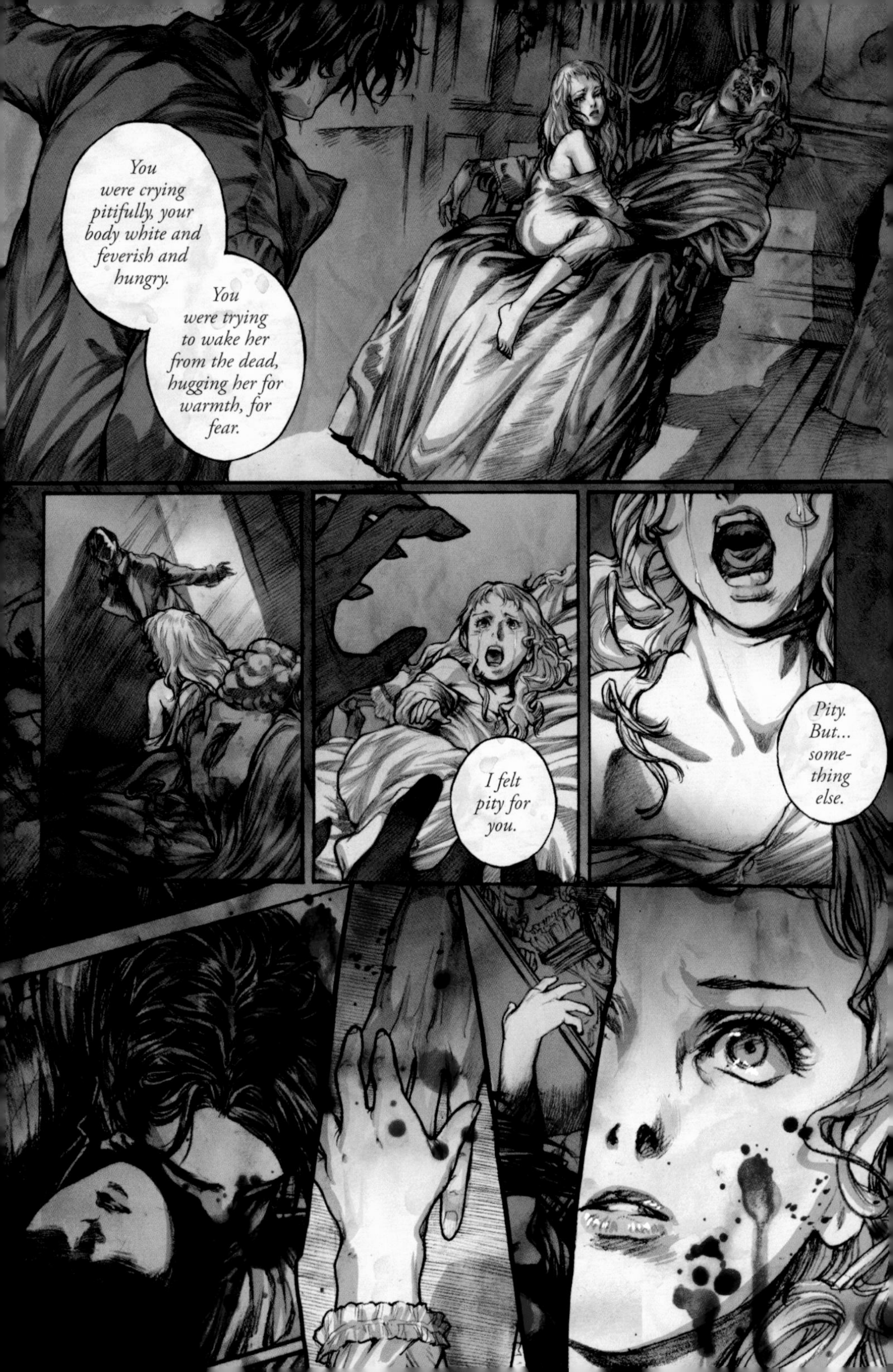
You were crying pitifully, your body white and feverish and hungry.
You were trying to wake her from the dead, hugging her for warmth, for fear.
I felt pity for you.
Pity. But... some-thing else.

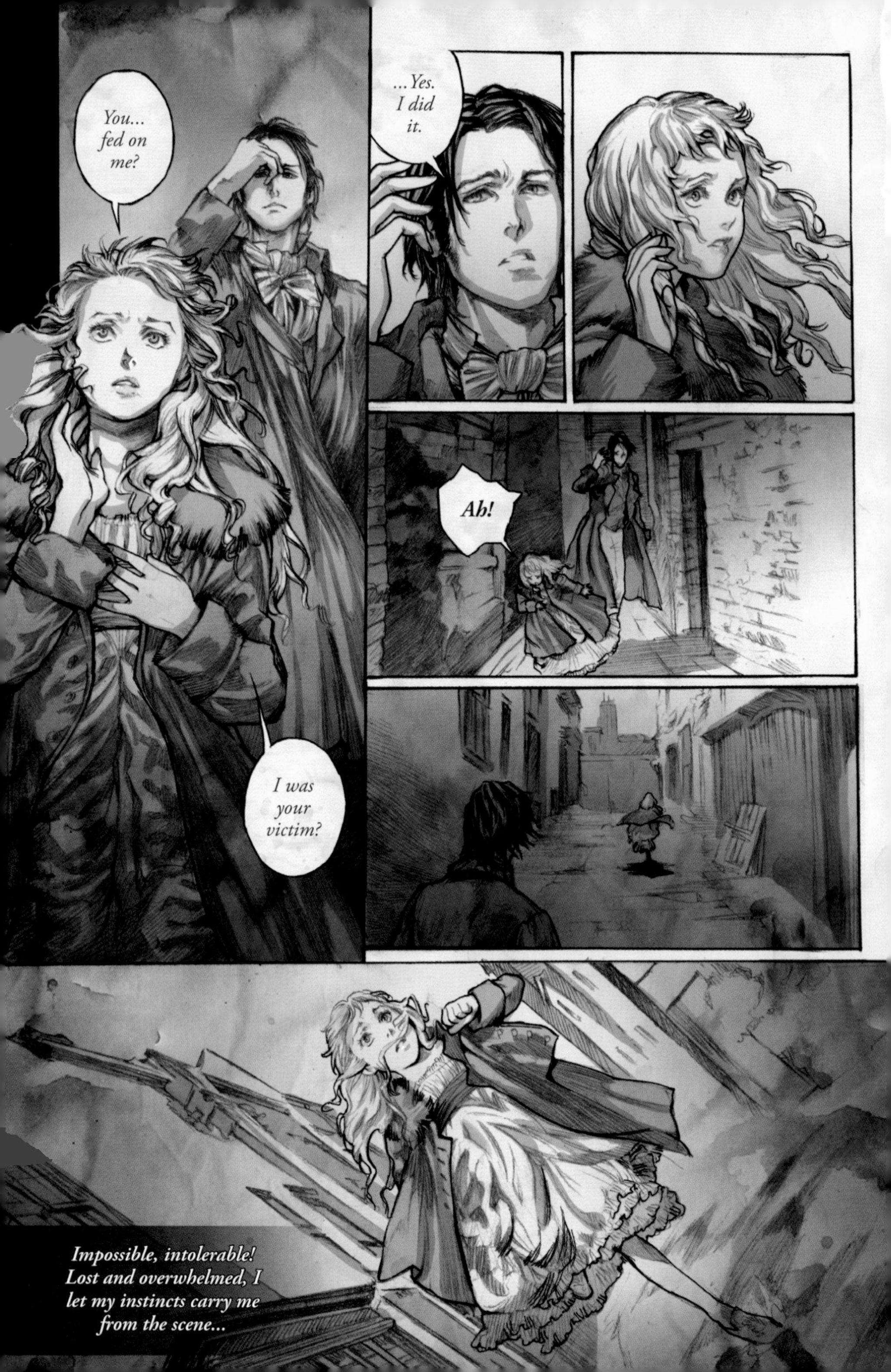
You... fed on me?
...Yes. I did it.
I was your victim?
Ah!
Impossible, intolerable! Lost and overwhelmed, I let my instincts carry me from the scene...

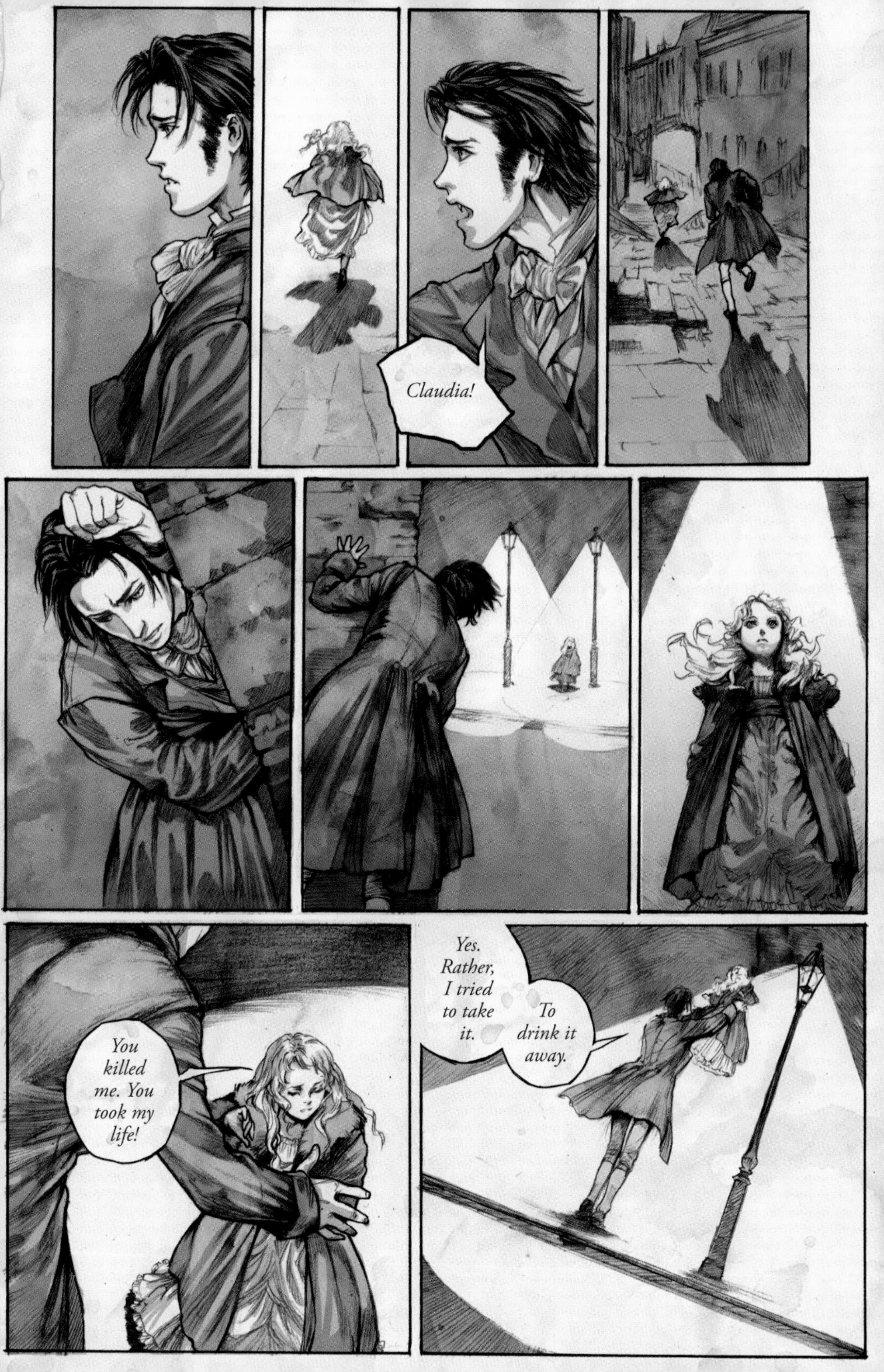
Claudia!
You killed me. You took my life!
Yes. Rather, I tried to take it.
To drink it away.

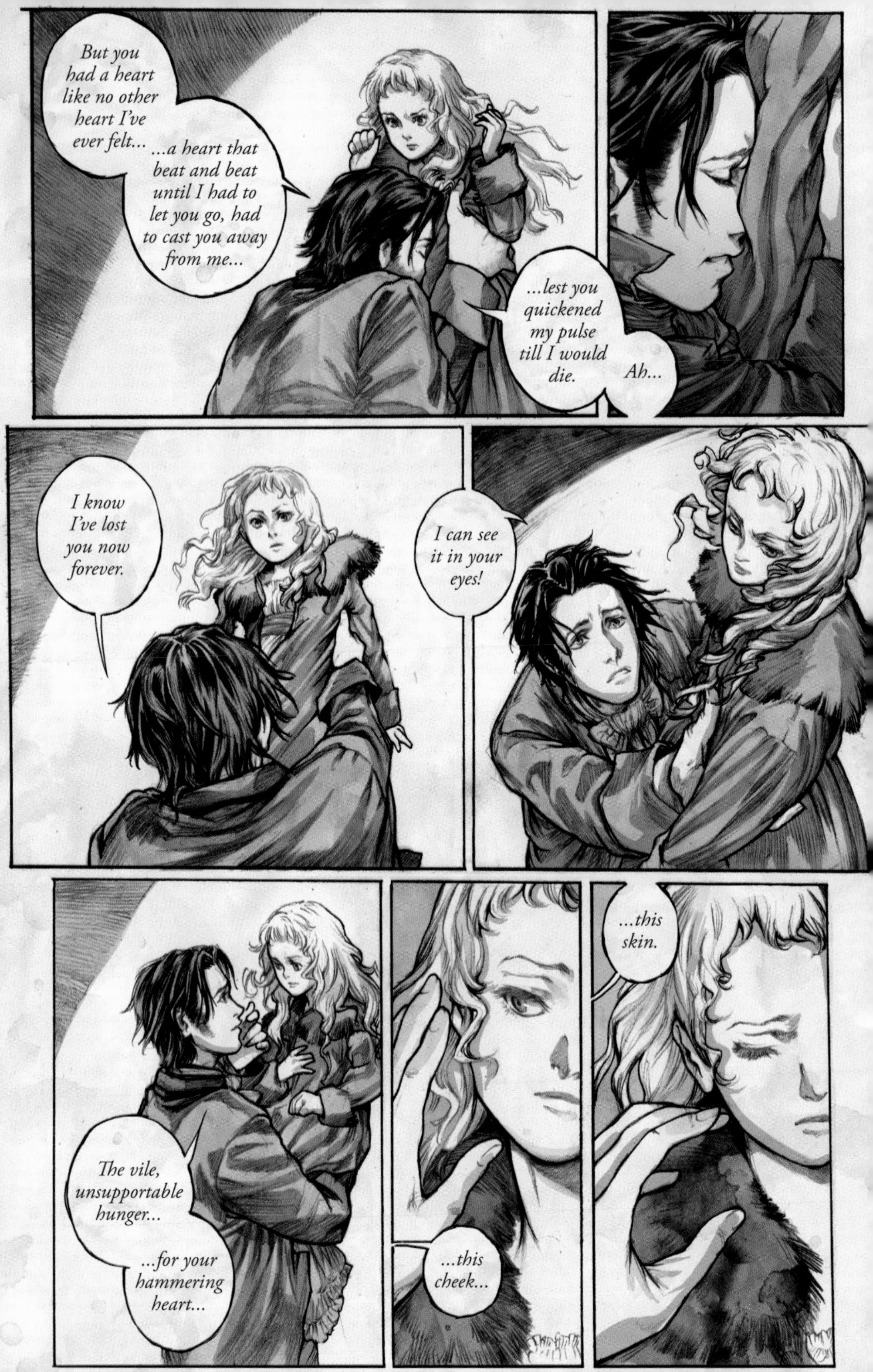
But you had a heart like no other heart I've ever felt...
...a heart that beat and beat until I had to let you go, had to cast you away from me...
...lest you quickened my pulse till I would die.
Ah...
I know I've lost you now forever.
I can see it in your eyes!
The vile, unsupportable hunger...
...for your hammering heart...
...this cheek...
...this skin.

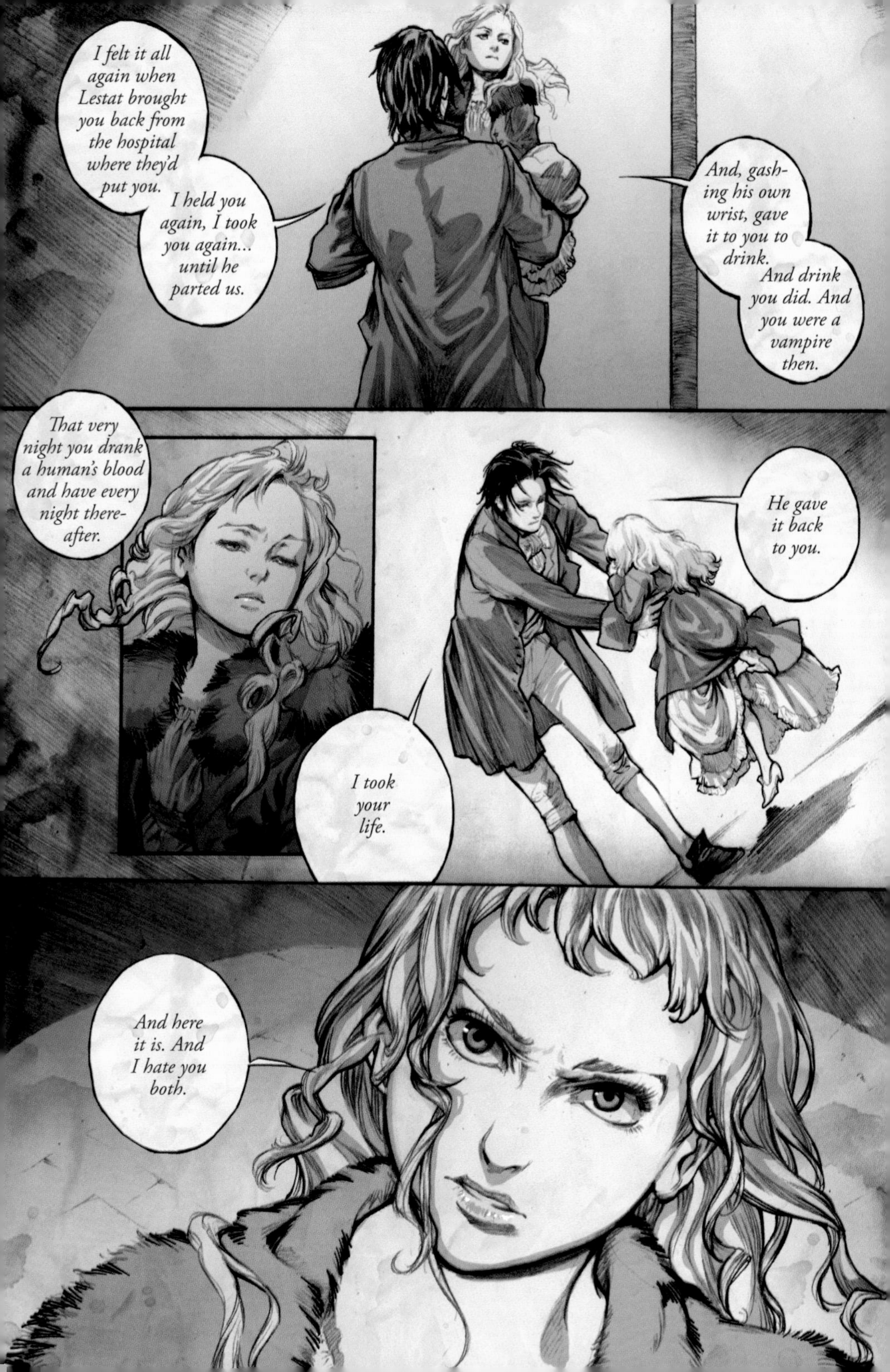
I felt it all again when Lestat brought you back from the hospital where they'd put you.
I held you again, I took you again... until he parted us.
And, gashing his own wrist, gave it to you to drink.
And drink you did. And you were a vampire then.
That very night you drank a human's blood and have every night thereafter.
He gave it back to you.
I took your life.
And here it is. And I hate you both.

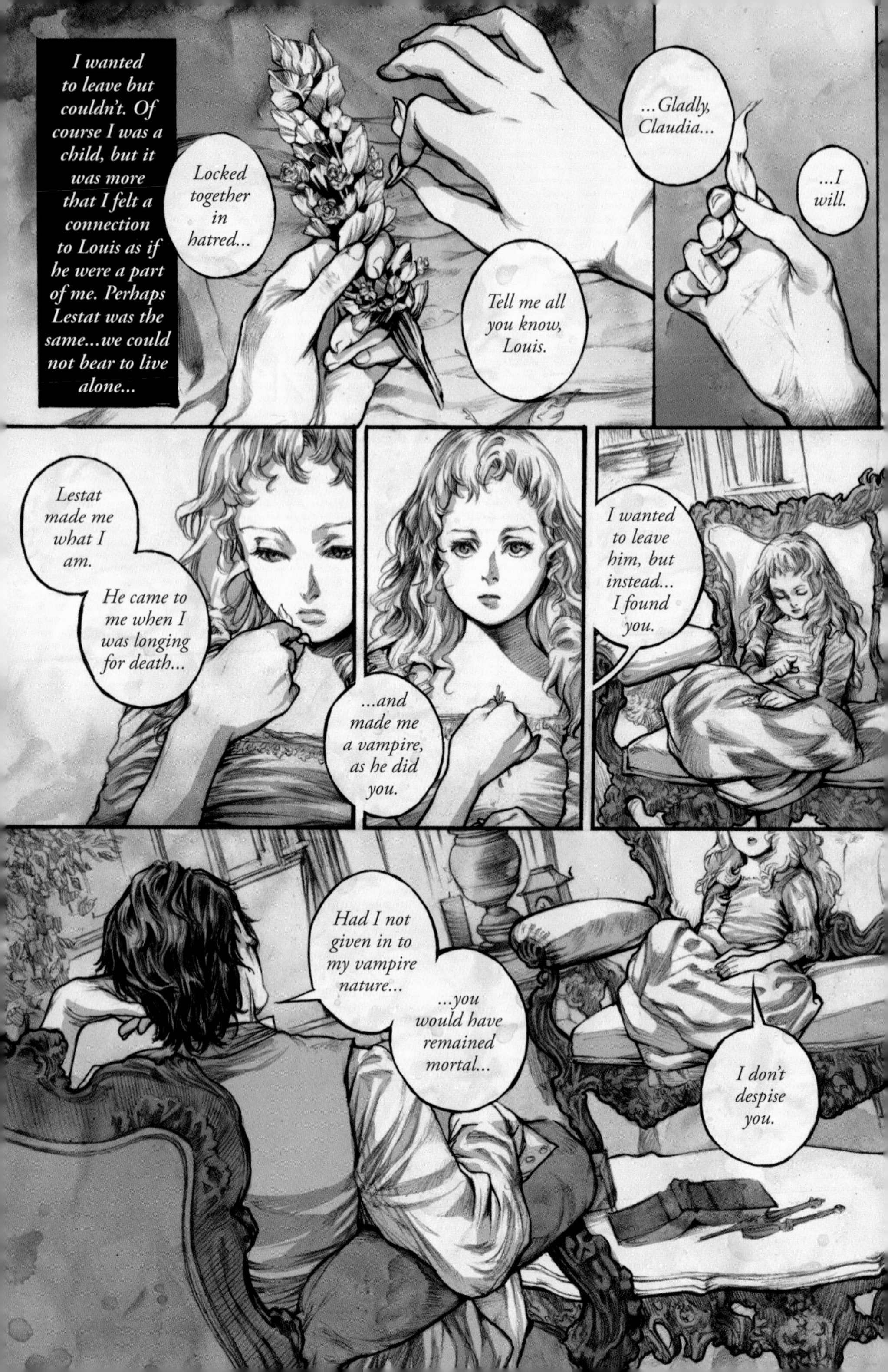
I wanted to leave but couldn't. Of course I was a child, but it was more that I felt a connection to Louis as if he were a part of me. Perhaps Lestat was the same...we could not bear to live alone...
Locked together in hatred...
Tell me all you know, Louis.
...Gladly, Claudia...
...I will.
Lestat made me what I am.
He came to me when I was longing for death...
...and made me a vampire, as he did you.
I wanted to leave him, but instead... I found you.
Had I not given in to my vampire nature...
...you would have remained mortal...
I don't despise you.

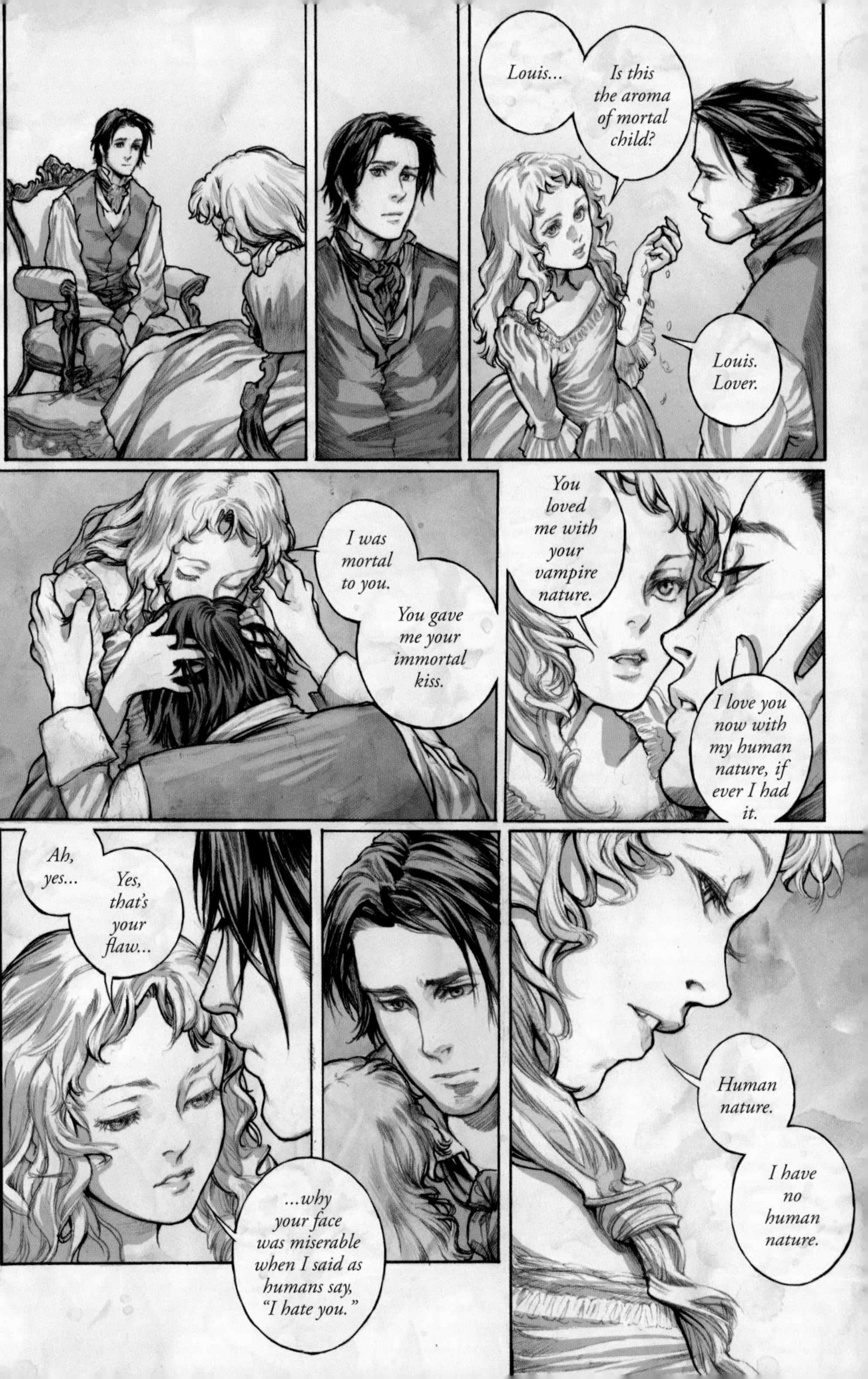
Louis...
Is this the aroma of mortal child?
Louis. Lover.
I was mortal to you.
You gave me your immortal kiss.
You loved me with your vampire nature.
I love you now with my human nature, if ever I had it.
Ah, yes...
Yes, that's your flaw...
...why your face was miserable when I said as humans say, "I hate you."
Human nature.
I have no human nature.

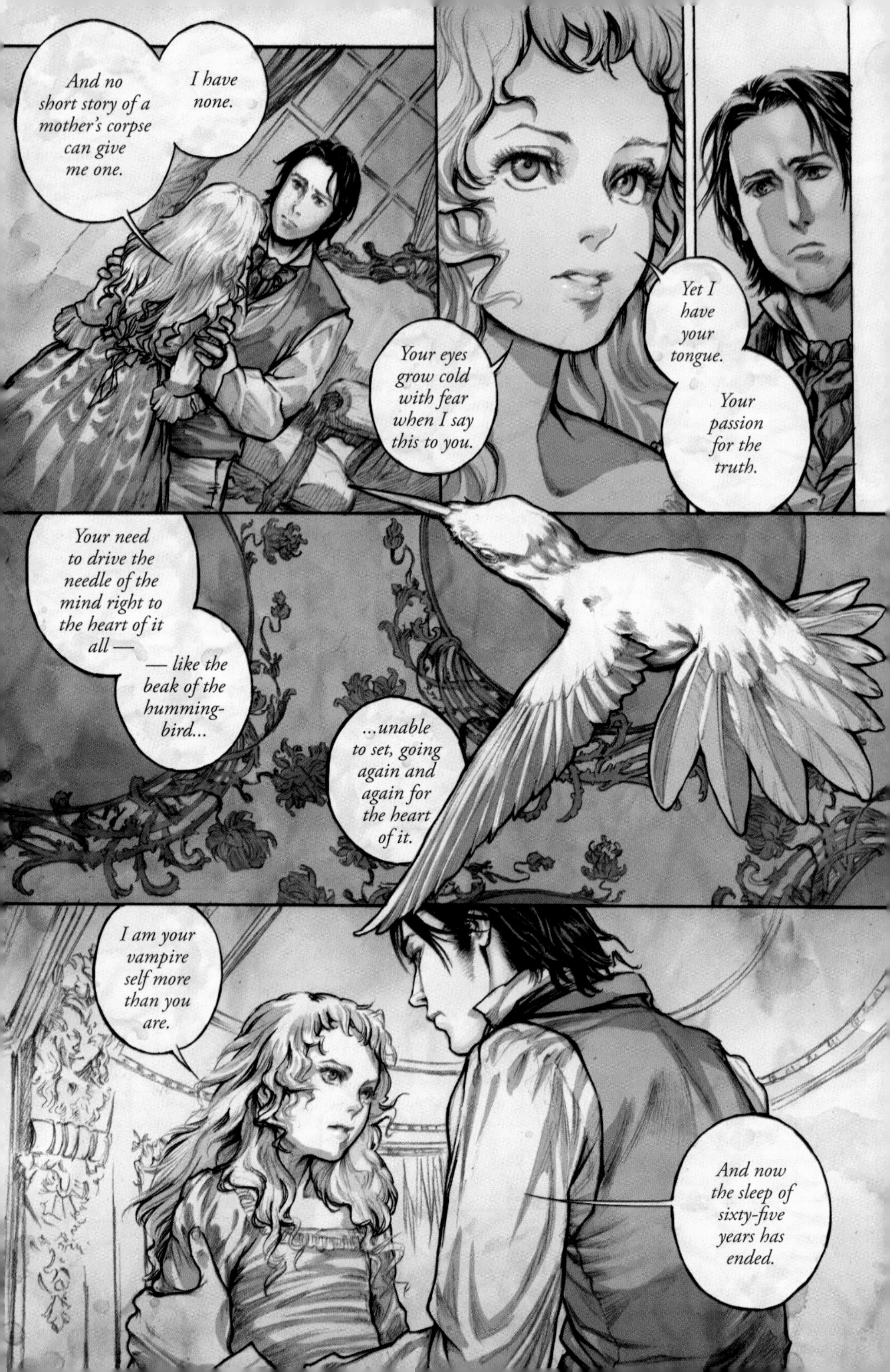
I have none.
And no short story of a mother's corpse can give me one.
Yet I have your tongue.
Your eyes grow cold with fear when I say this to you.
Your passion for the truth.
Your need to drive the needle of the mind right to the heart of it all —
— like the beak of the humming-bird...
...unable to set, going again and again for the heart of it.
I am your vampire self more than you are.
And now the sleep of sixty-five years has ended.

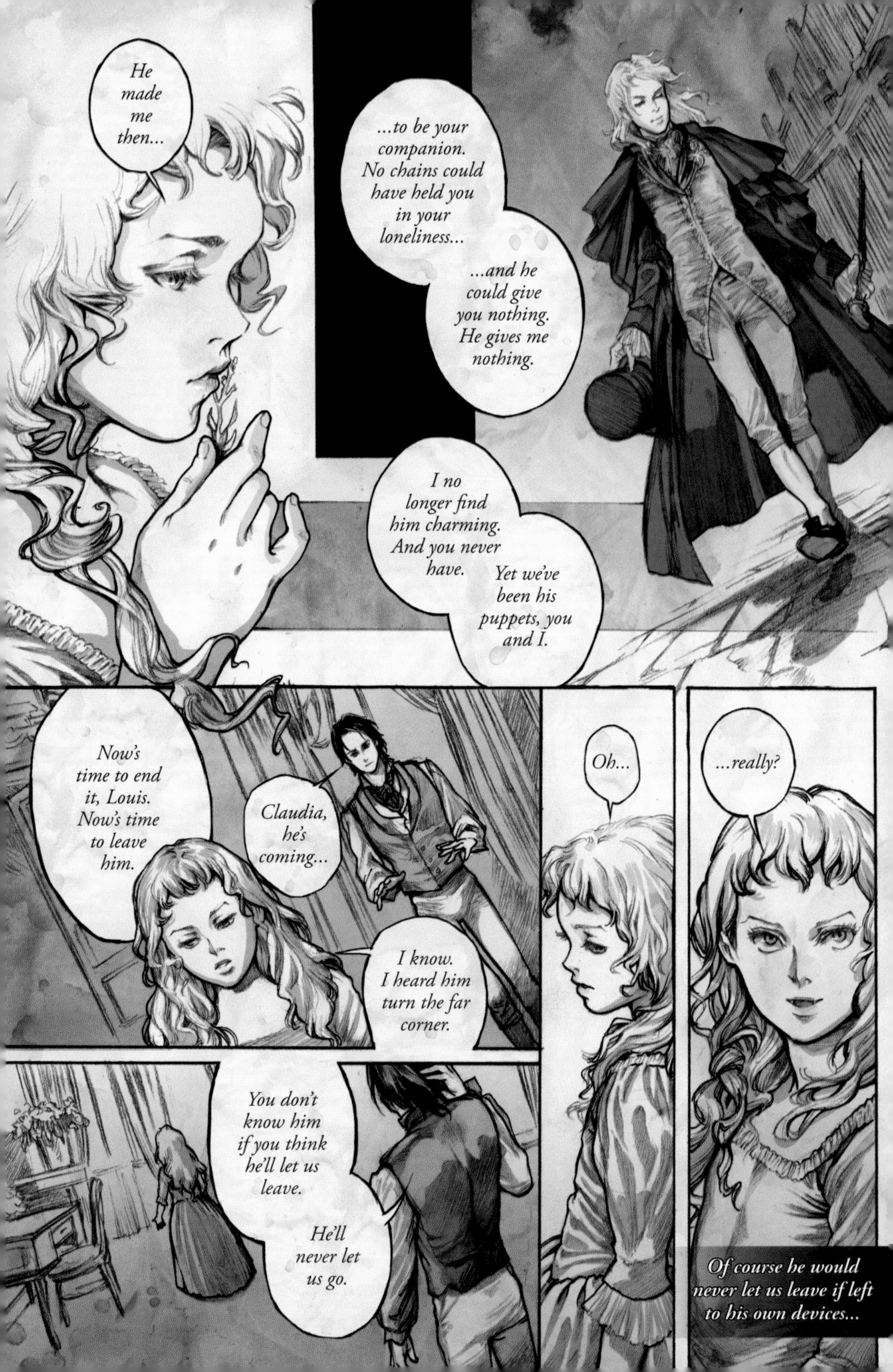
He made me then...
...to be your companion. No chains could have held you in your loneliness...
...and he could give you nothing. He gives me nothing.
I no longer find him charming. And you never have.
Yet we've been his puppets, you and I.
Now's time to end it, Louis. Now's time to leave him.
Claudia, he's coming...
I know. I heard him turn the far corner.
Oh...
...really?
You don't know him if you think he'll let us leave.
He'll never let us go.
Of course he would never let us leave if left to his own devices...

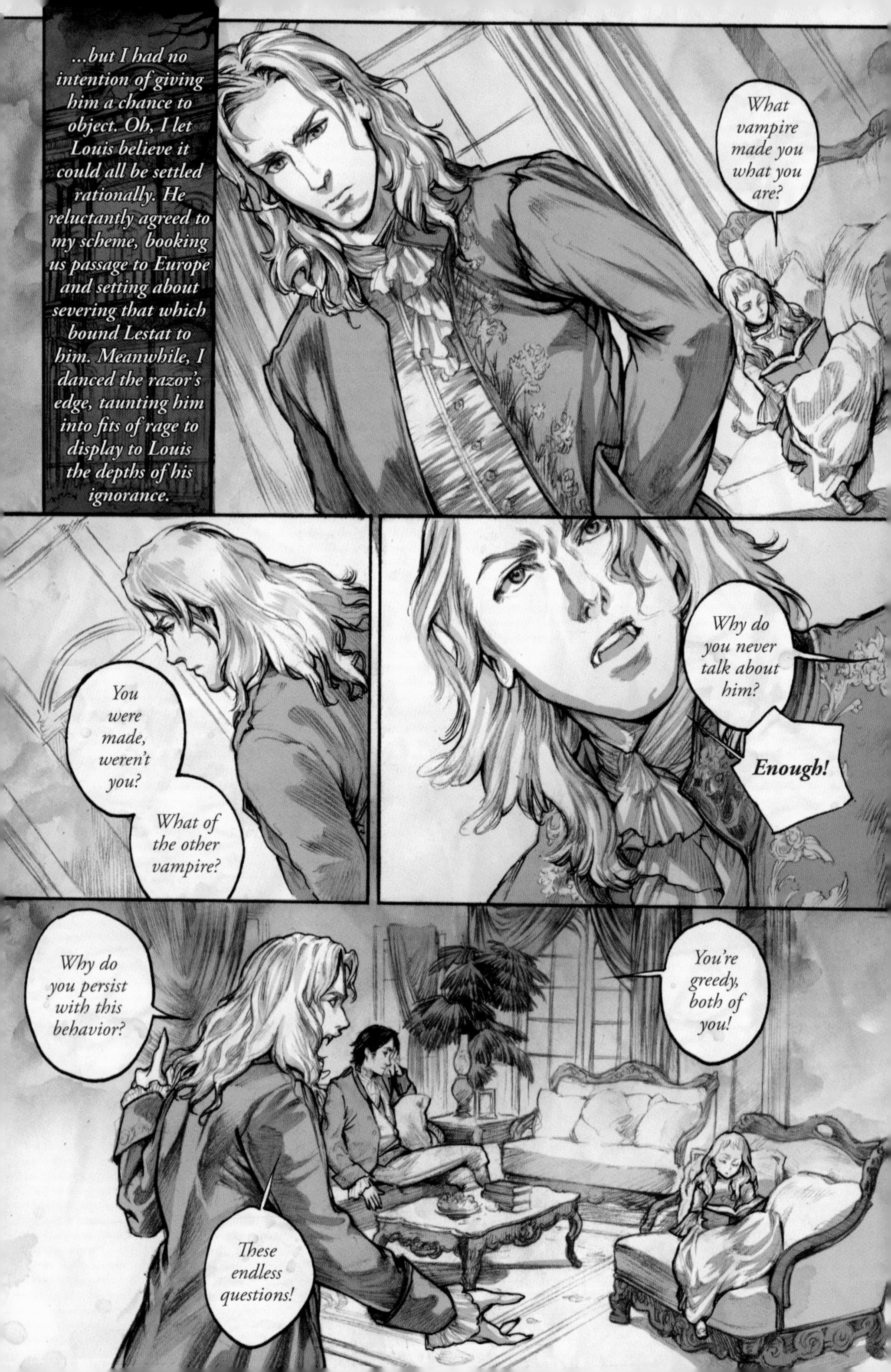
...but I had no intention of giving him a chance to object. Oh, I let Louis believe it could all be settled rationally. He reluctantly agreed to my scheme, booking us passage to Europe and setting about severing that which bound Lestat to him. Meanwhile, I danced the razor's edge, taunting him into fits of rage to display to Louis the depths of his ignorance.
What vampire made you what you are?
You were made, weren't you?
What of the other vampire?
Why do you never talk about him?
Enough!
Why do you persist with this behavior?
You're greedy, both of you!
These endless questions!

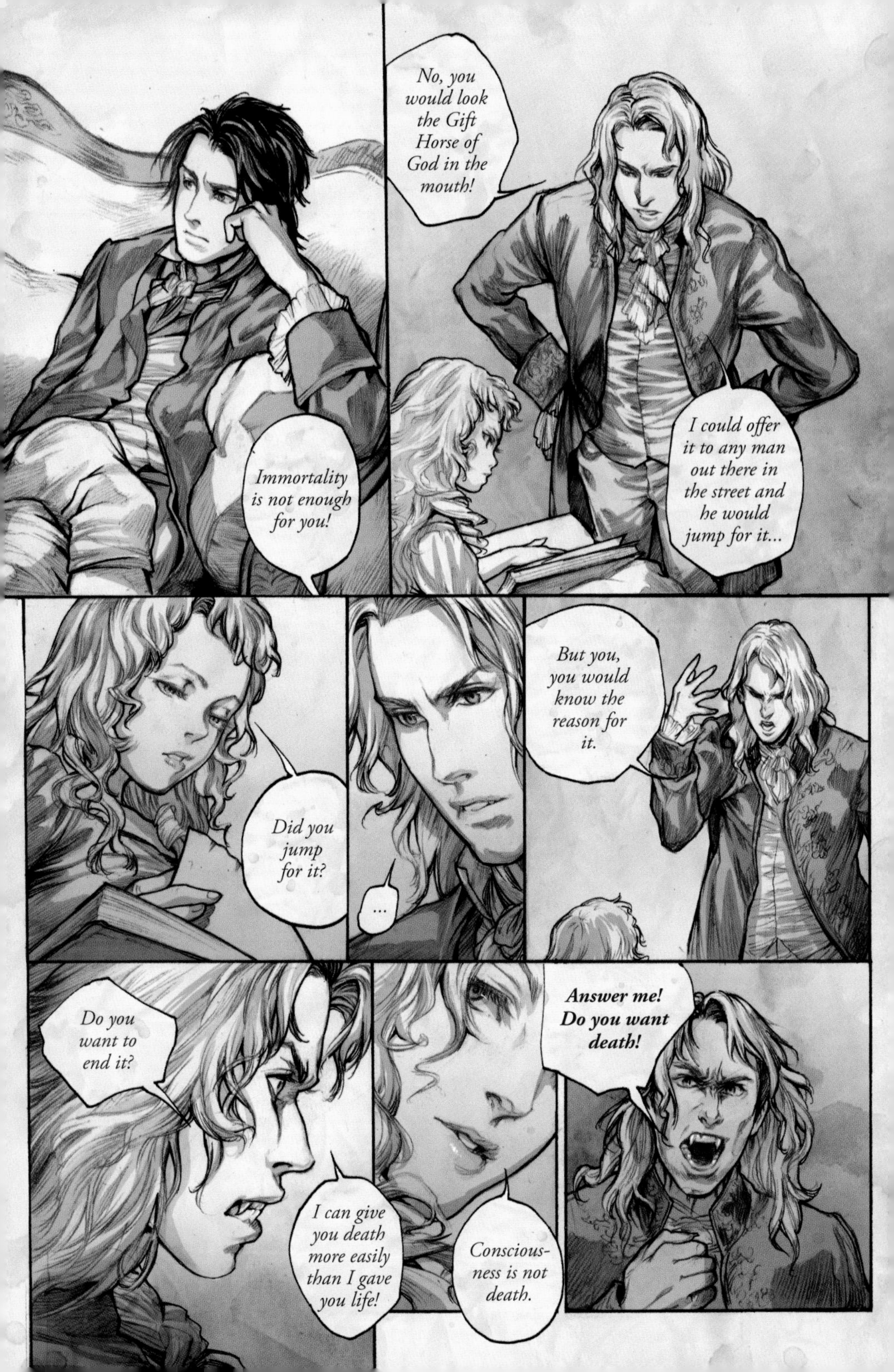
Immortality is not enough for you!
No, you would look the Gift Horse of God in the mouth!
I could offer it to any man out there in the street and he would jump for it...
Did you jump for it?
...
But you, you would know the reason for it.
Do you want to end it?
I can give you death more easily than I gave you life!
Conscious-ness is not death.
Answer me! Do you want death!

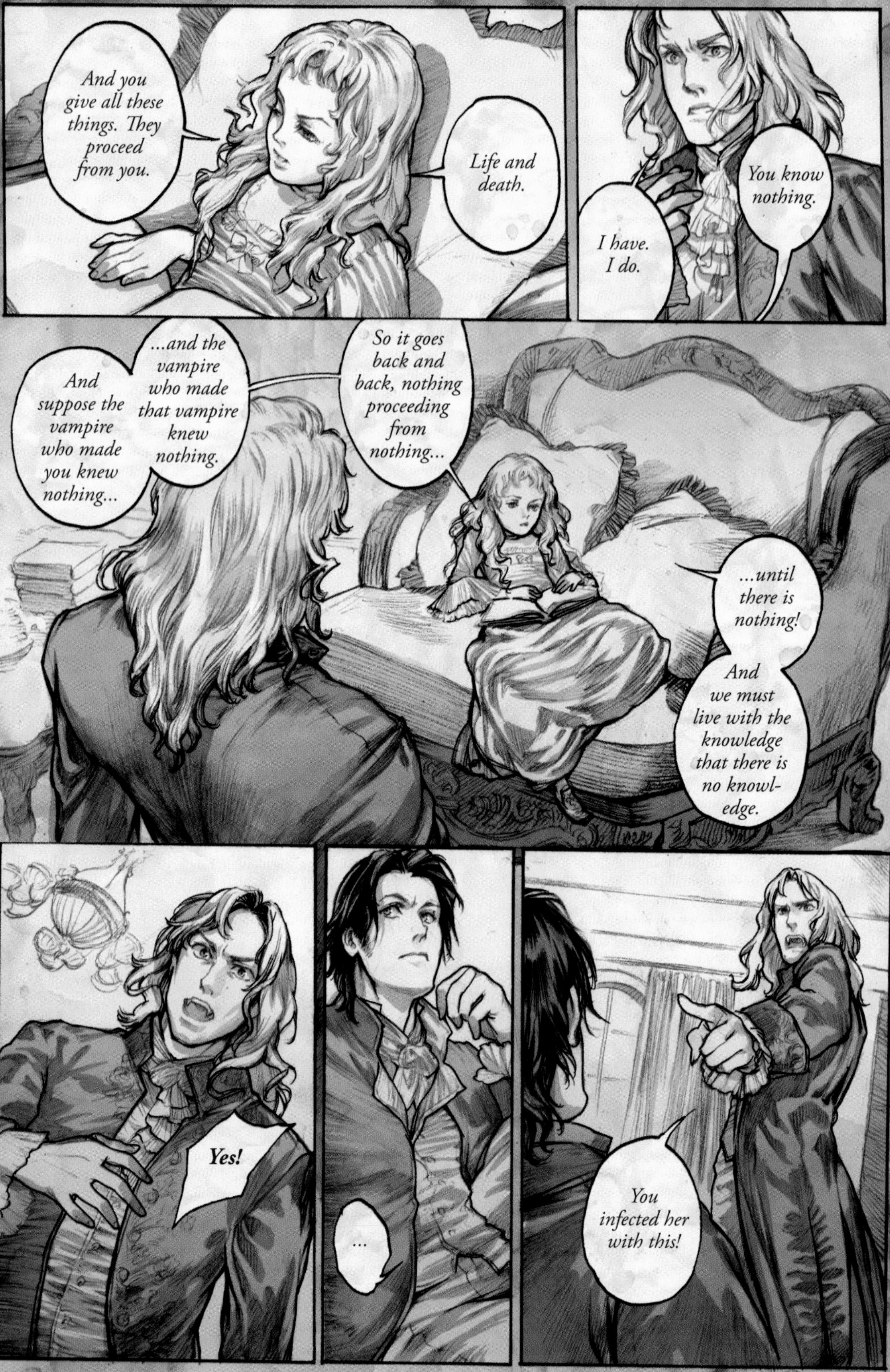
And you give all these things. They proceed from you.
Life and death.
You know nothing.
I have. I do.
And suppose the vampire who made you knew nothing...
...and the vampire who made that vampire knew nothing.
So it goes back and back, nothing proceeding from nothing...
...until there is nothing!
And we must live with the knowledge that there is no knowl-edge.
Yes!
...
You infected her with this!

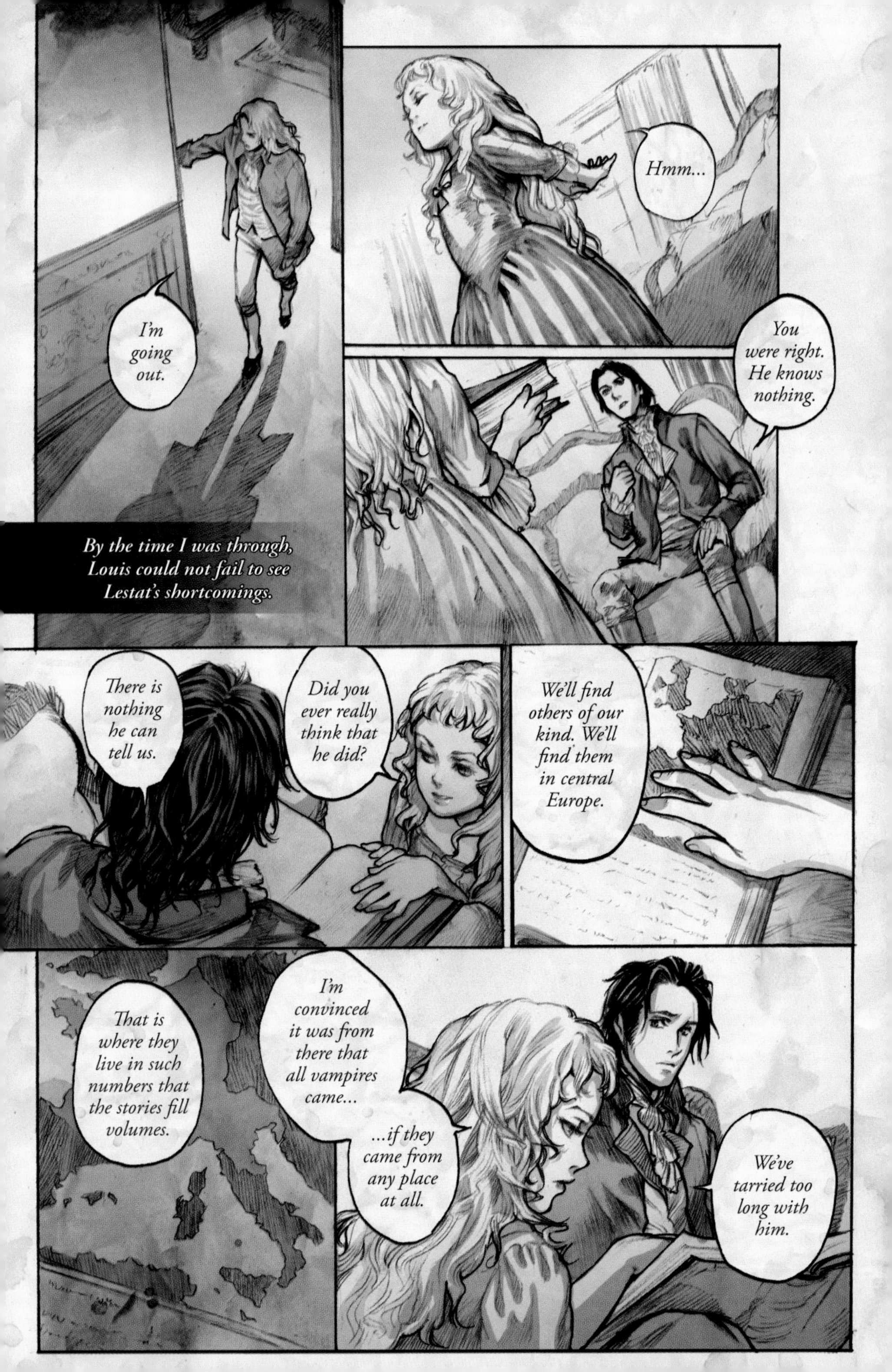
I'm going out.
Hmm...
By the time I was through, Louis could not fail to see Lestat's shortcomings.
You were right. He knows nothing.
There is nothing he can tell us.
Did you ever really think that he did?
We'll find others of our kind. We'll find them in central Europe.
That is where they live in such numbers that the stories fill volumes.
I'm convinced it was from there that all vampires came...
...if they came from any place at all.
We've tarried too long with him.

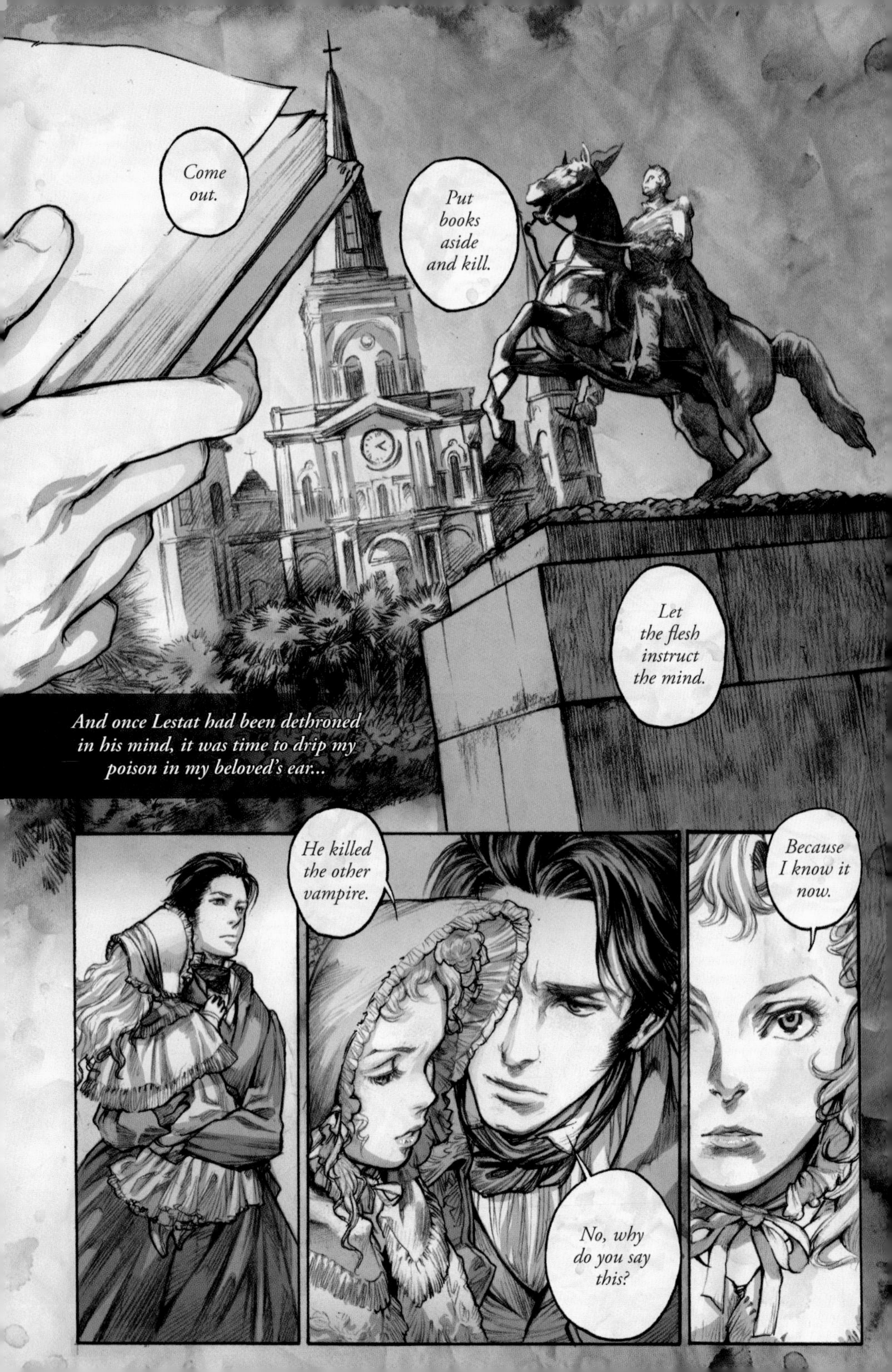
Come out.
Put books aside and kill.
Let the flesh instruct the mind.
And once Lestat had been dethroned in his mind, it was time to drip my poison in my beloved's ear...
He killed the other vampire.
No, why do you say this?
Because I know it now.

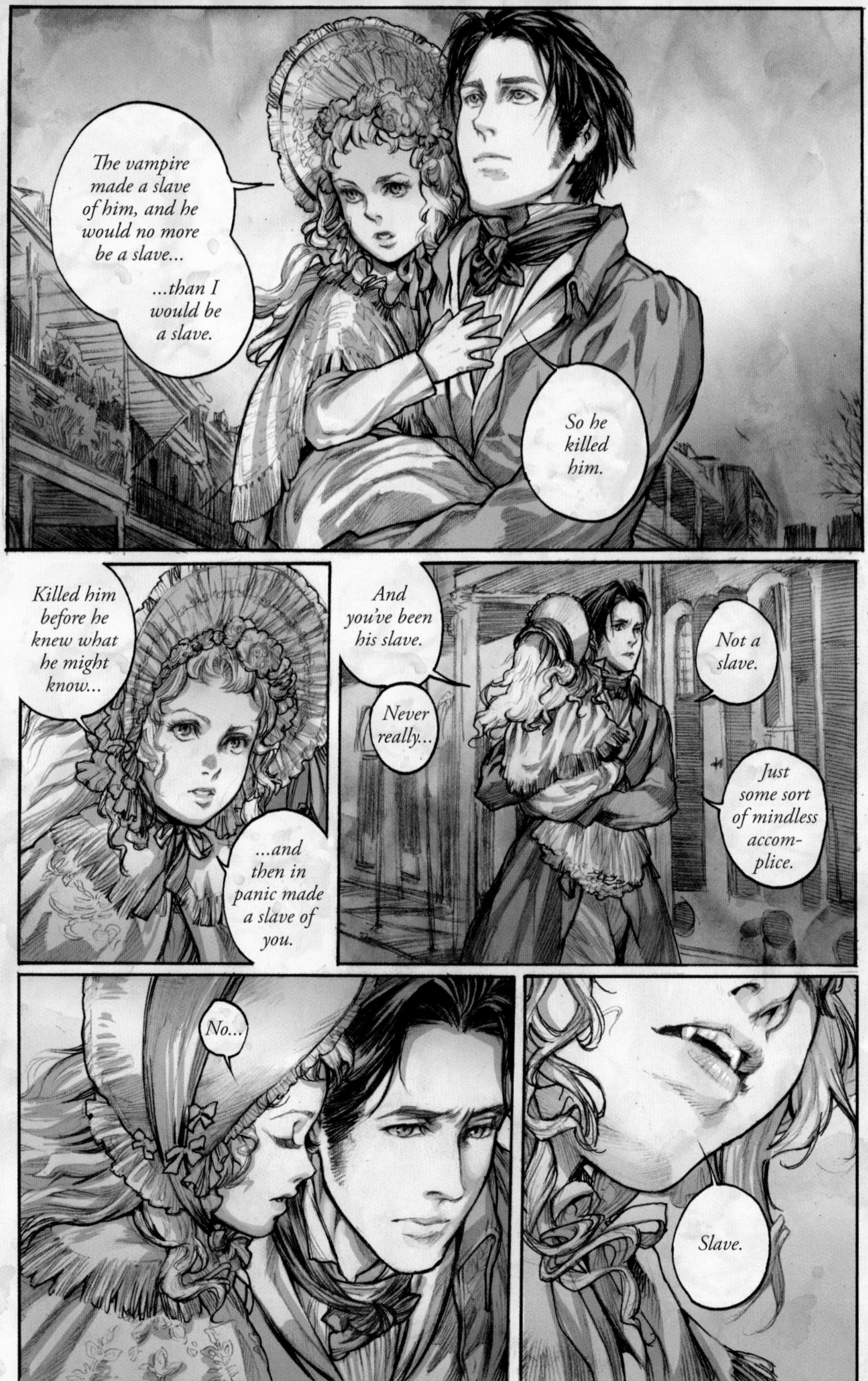
The vampire made a slave of him, and he would no more be a slave...
...than I would be a slave.
So he killed him.
Killed him before he knew what he might know...
...and then in panic made a slave of you.
And you've been his slave.
Never really...
Not a slave.
Just some sort of mindless accomplice.
No...
Slave.

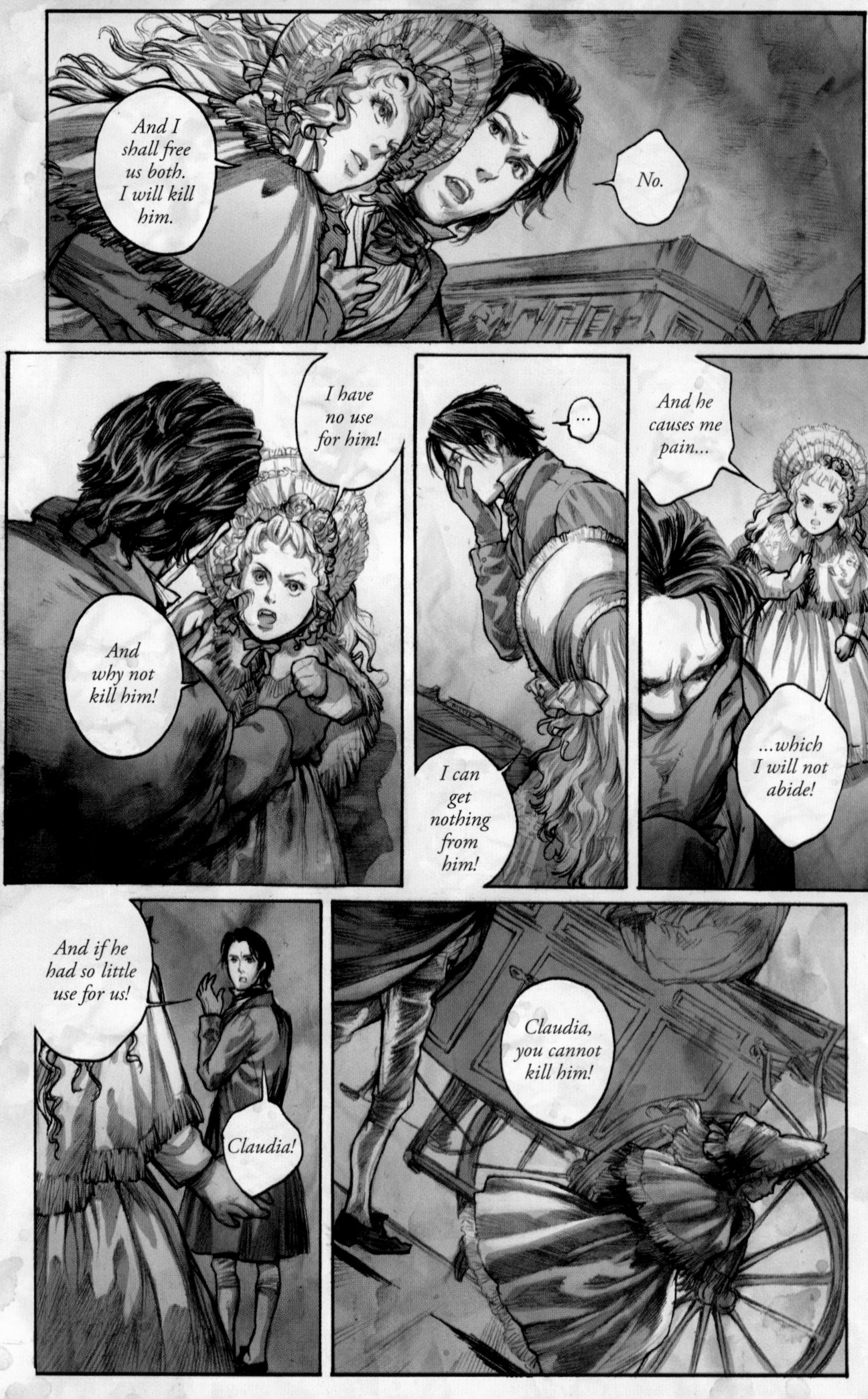
And I shall free us both. I will kill him.
No.
I have no use for him!
And why not kill him!
...
I can get nothing from him!
And he causes me pain...
...which I will not abide!
And if he had so little use for us!
Claudia!
Claudia, you cannot kill him!

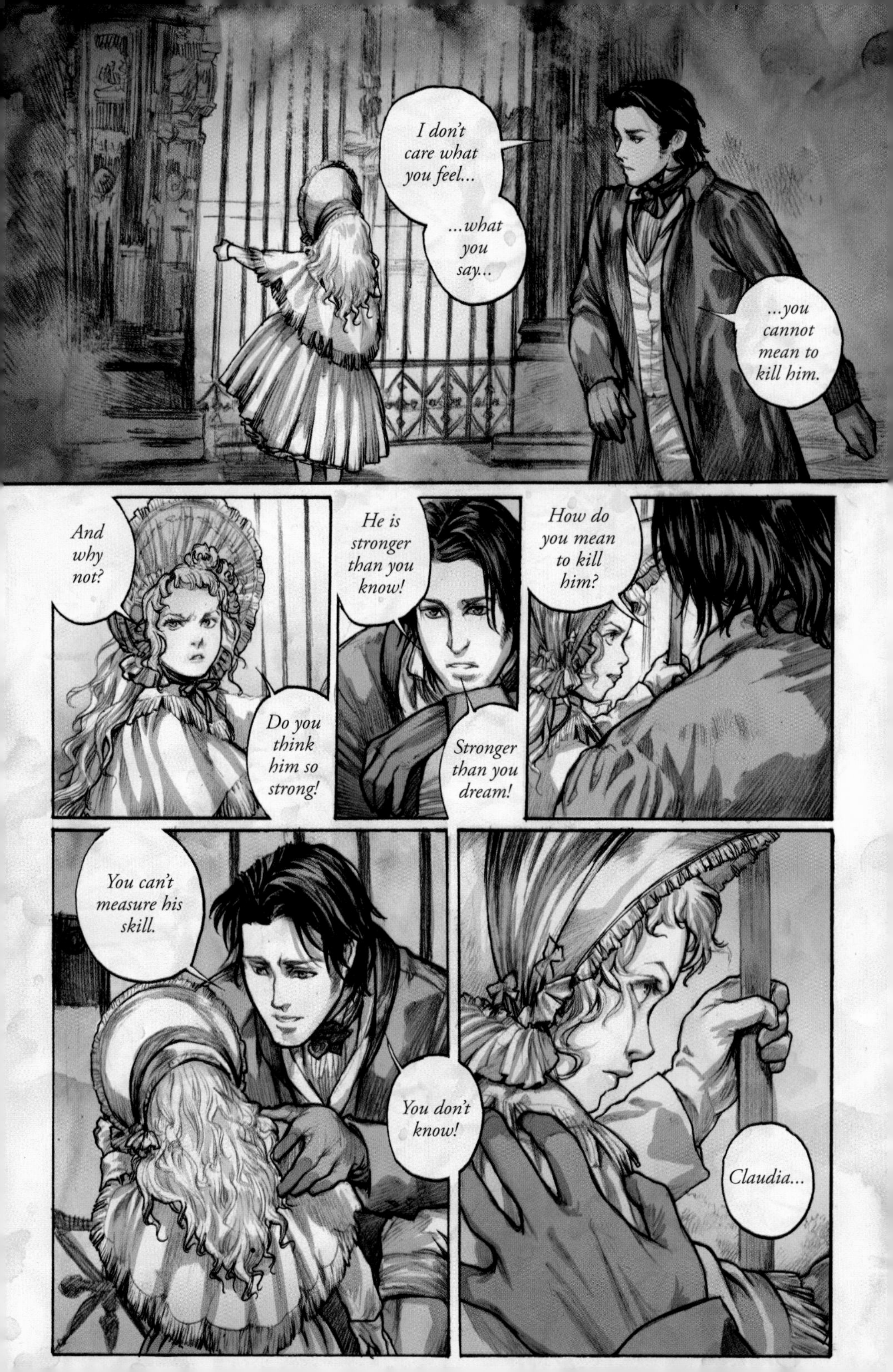
I don't care what you feel...
...what you say...
...you cannot mean to kill him.
And why not?
Do you think him so strong!
He is stronger than you know!
Stronger than you dream!
How do you mean to kill him?
You can't measure his skill.
You don't know!
Claudia...

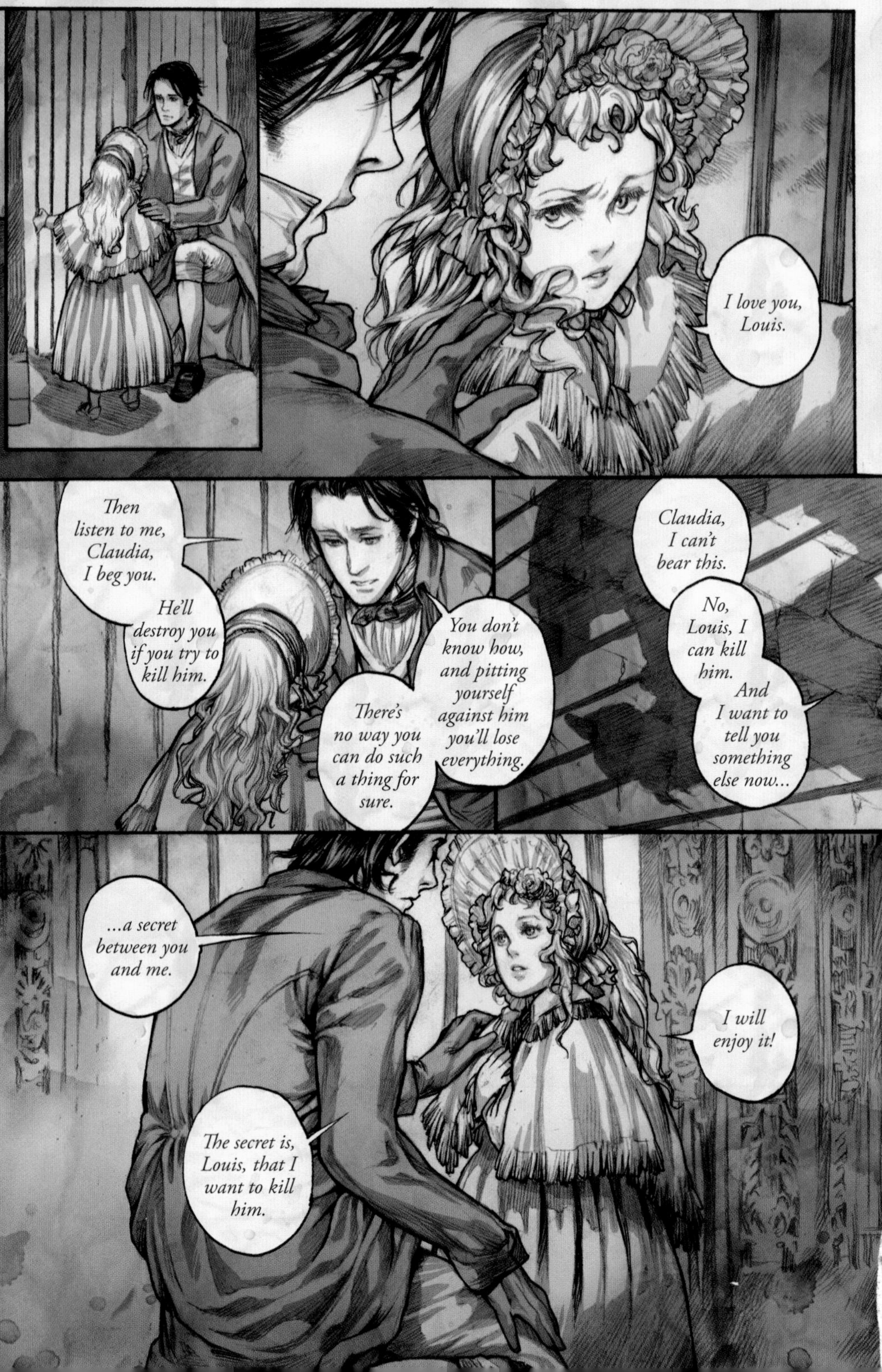
I love you, Louis.
Then listen to me, Claudia, I beg you.
He'll destroy you if you try to kill him.
There's no way you can do such a thing for sure.
You don't know how, and pitting yourself against him you'll lose everything.
Claudia, I can't bear this.
No, Louis, I can kill him.
And I want to tell you something else now...
...a secret between you and me.
The secret is, Louis, that I want to kill him.
I will enjoy it!

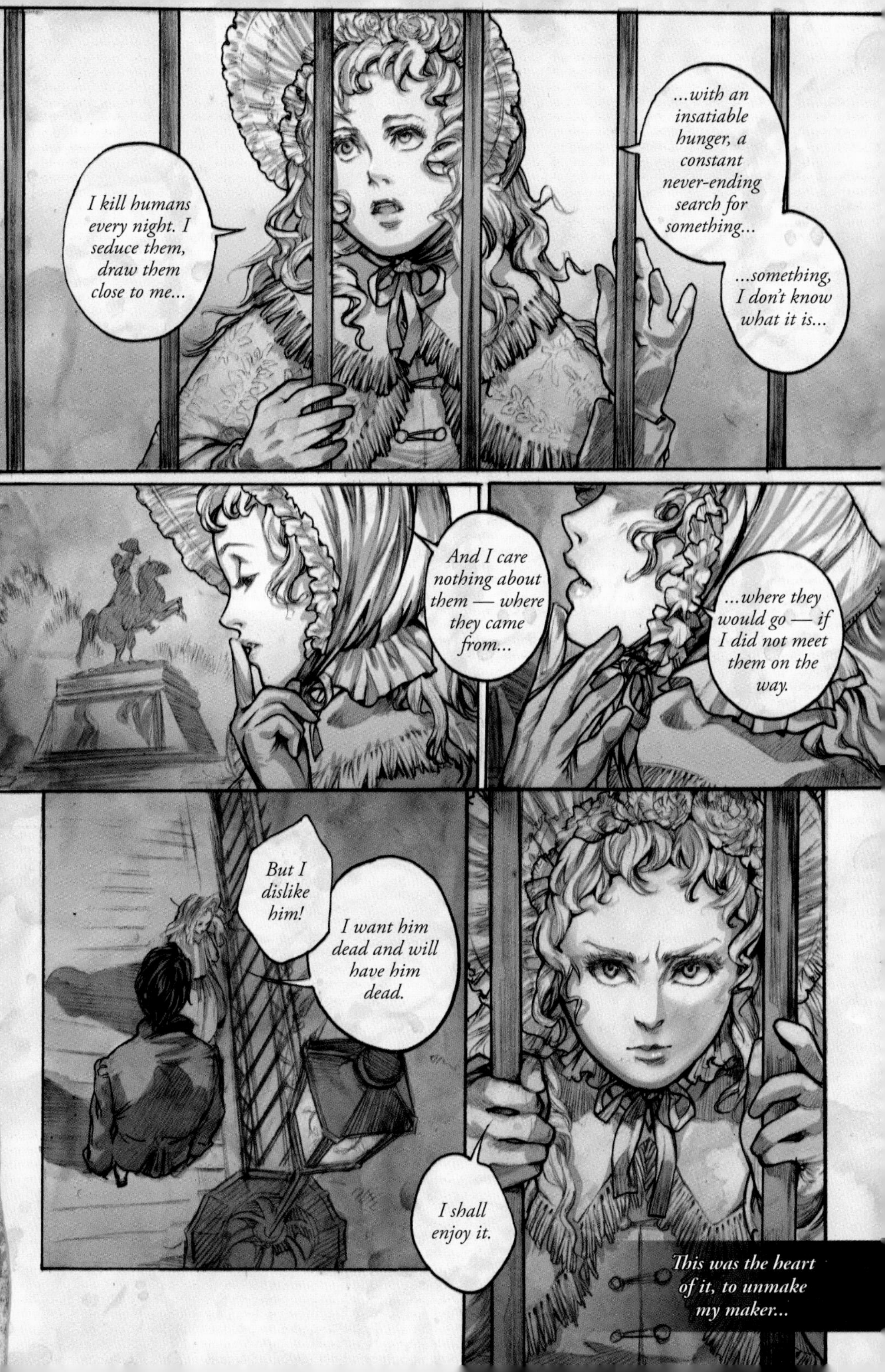
I kill humans every night. I seduce them, draw them close to me...
...with an insatiable hunger, a constant never-ending search for something...
...something, I don't know what it is...
And I care nothing about them — where they came from...
...where they would go — if I did not meet them on the way.
But I dislike him!
I want him dead and will have him dead.
I shall enjoy it.
This was the heart of it, to unmake my maker...

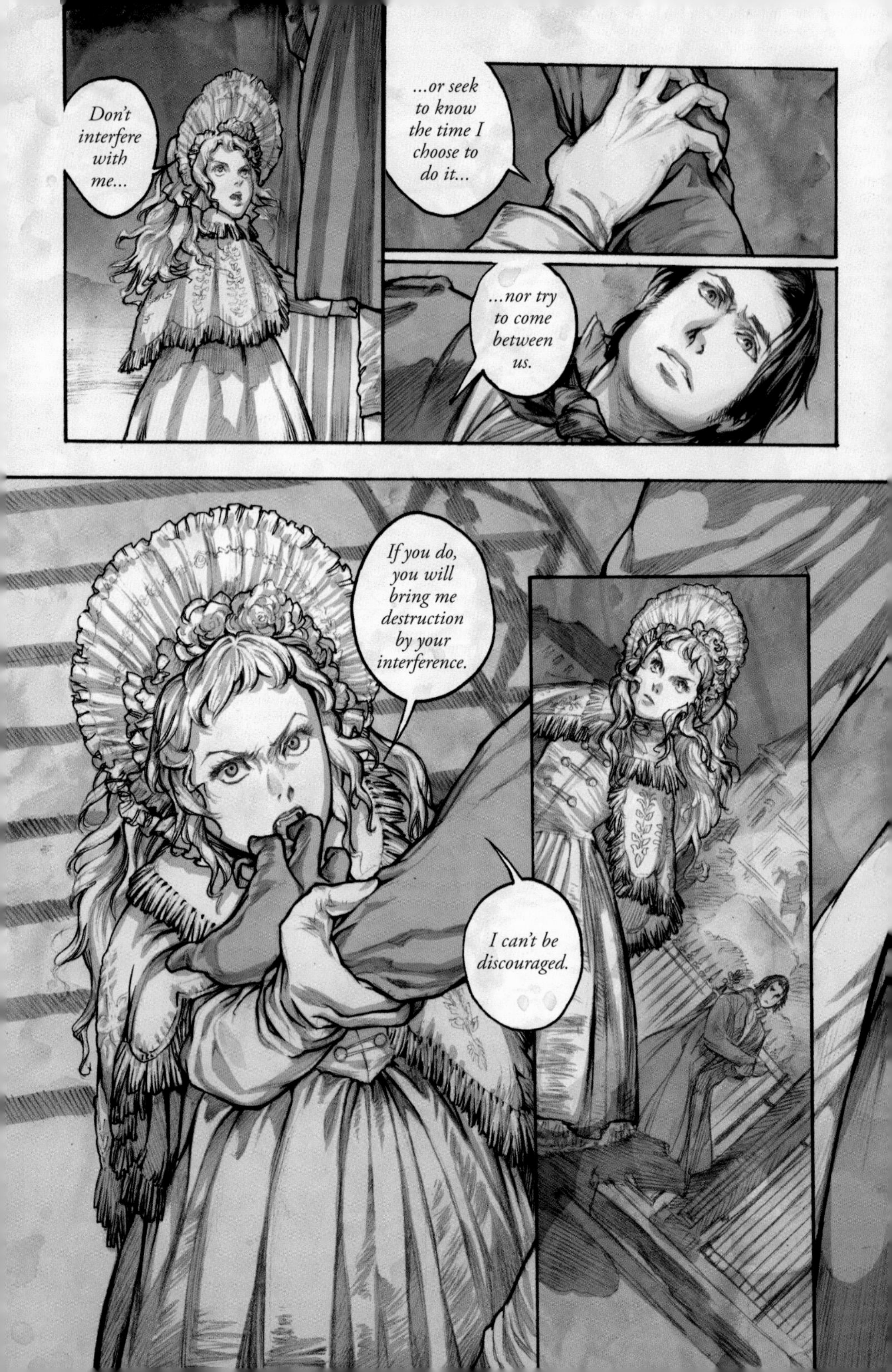

Don't interfere with me...
...or seek to know the time I choose to do it...
...nor try to come between us.
If you do, you will bring me destruction by your interference.
I can't be discouraged.

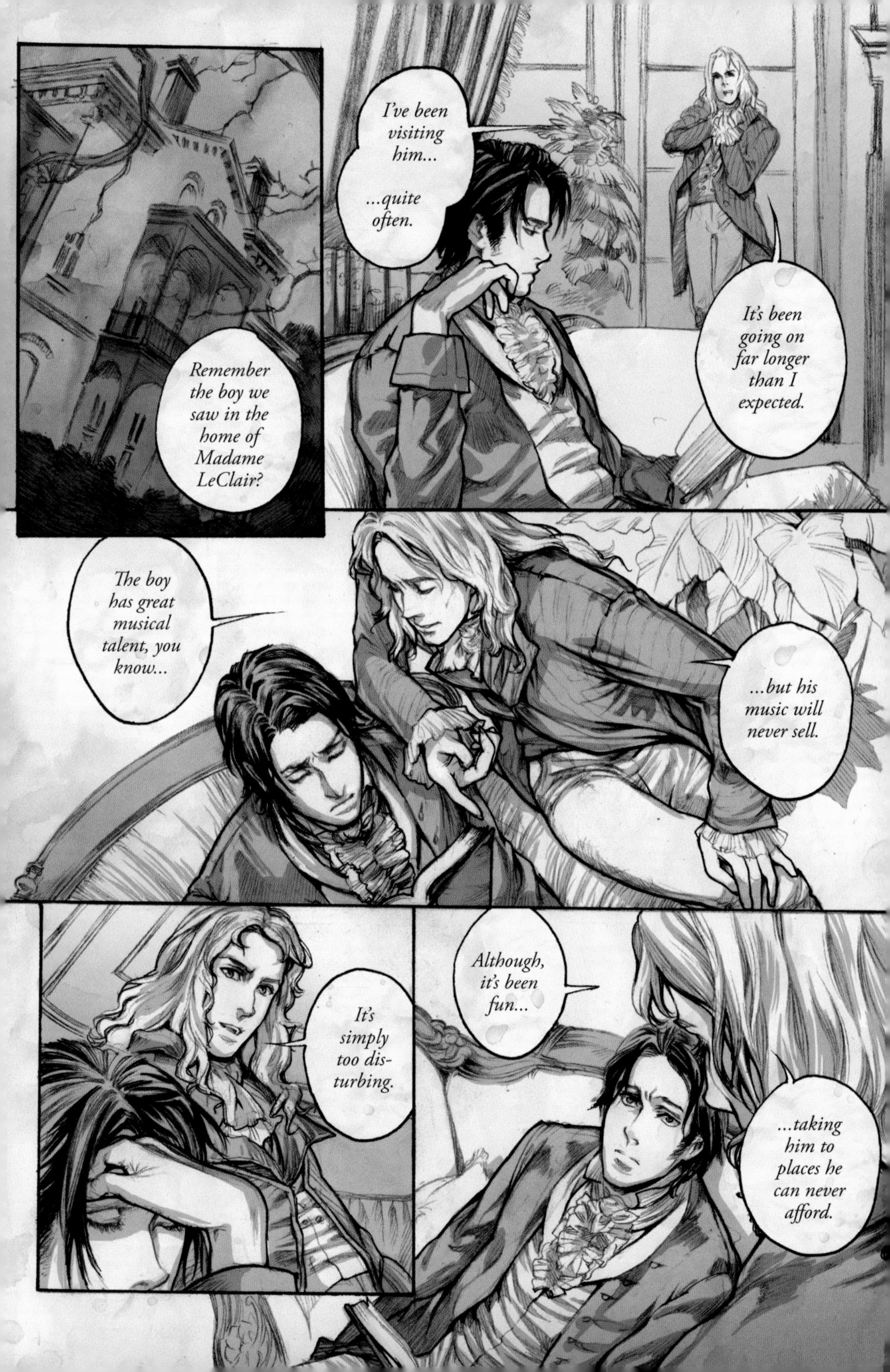
I've been visiting him...
...quite often.
Remember the boy we saw in the home of Madame LeClair?
It's been going on far longer than I expected.
The boy has great musical talent, you know...
...but his music will never sell.
It's simply too dis-turbing.
Although, it's been fun...
...taking him to places he can never afford.

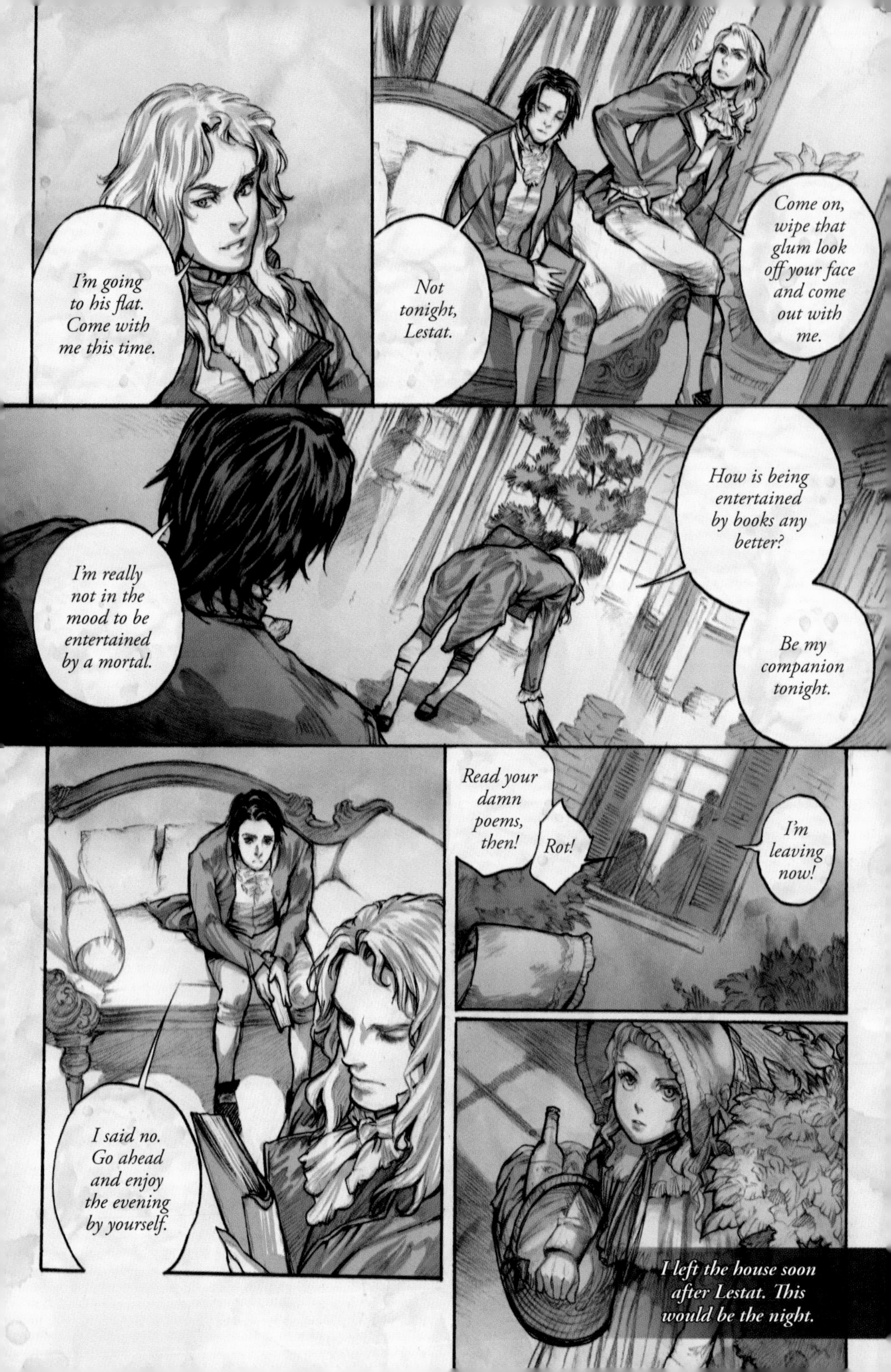
I'm going to his flat. Come with me this time.
Not tonight, Lestat.
Come on, wipe that glum look off your face and come out with me.
I'm really not in the mood to be entertained by a mortal.
How is being entertained by books any better?
Be my companion tonight.
I said no. Go ahead and enjoy the evening by yourself.
Read your damn poems, then!
Rot!
I'm leaving now!
I left the house soon after Lestat. This would be the night.

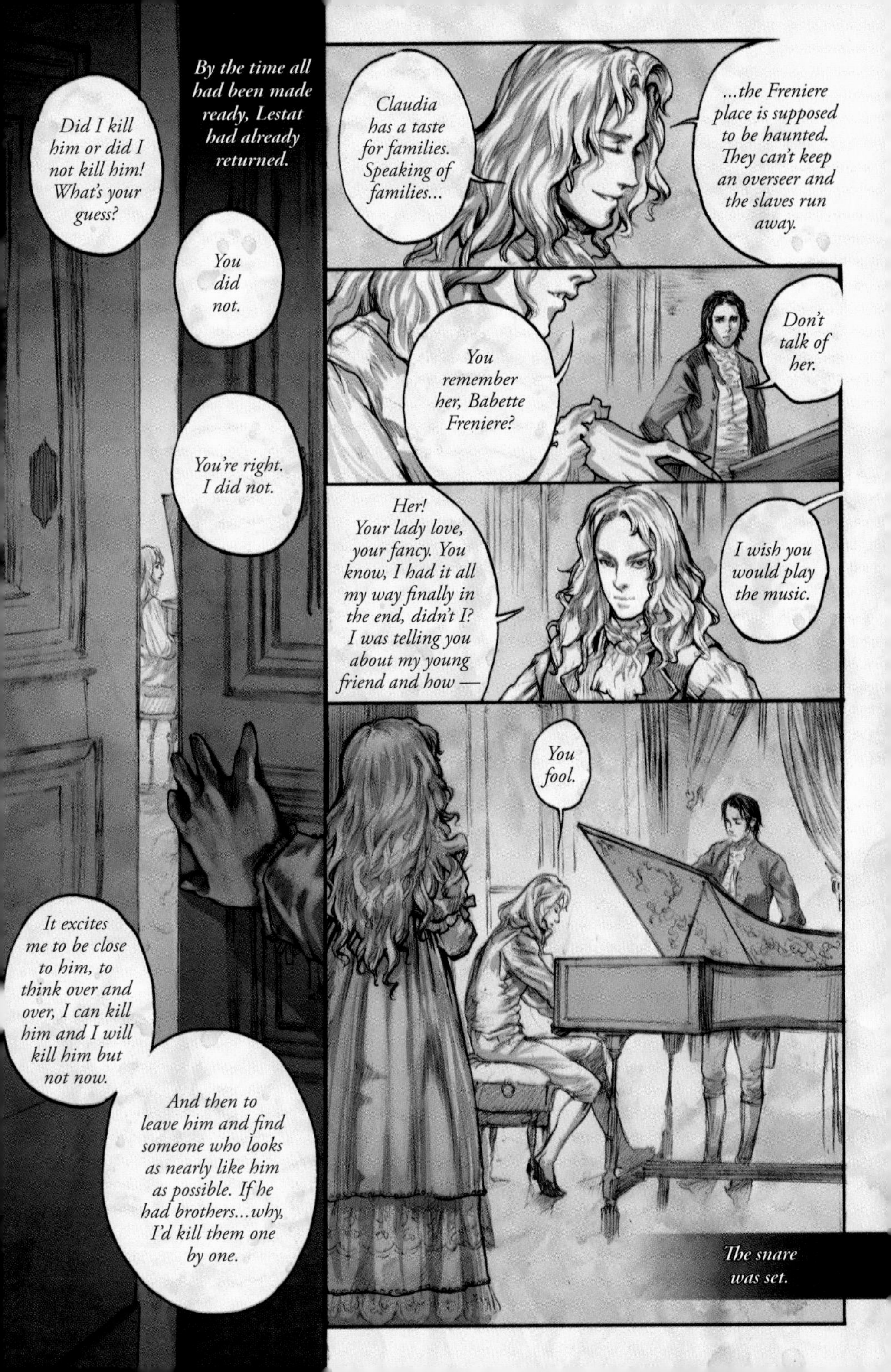
By the time all had been made ready, Lestat had already returned.
Did I kill him or did I not kill him! What's your guess?
You did not.
You're right. I did not.
Claudia has a taste for families. Speaking of families...
...the Freniere place is supposed to be haunted. They can't keep an overseer and the slaves run away.
You remember her, Babette Freniere?
Don't talk of her.
Her! Your lady love, your fancy. You know, I had it all my way finally in the end, didn't I? I was telling you about my young friend and how —
I wish you would play the music.
You fool.
It excites me to be close to him, to think over and over, I can kill him and I will kill him but not now.
And then to leave him and find someone who looks as nearly like him as possible. If he had brothers...why, I'd kill them one by one.
The snare was set.

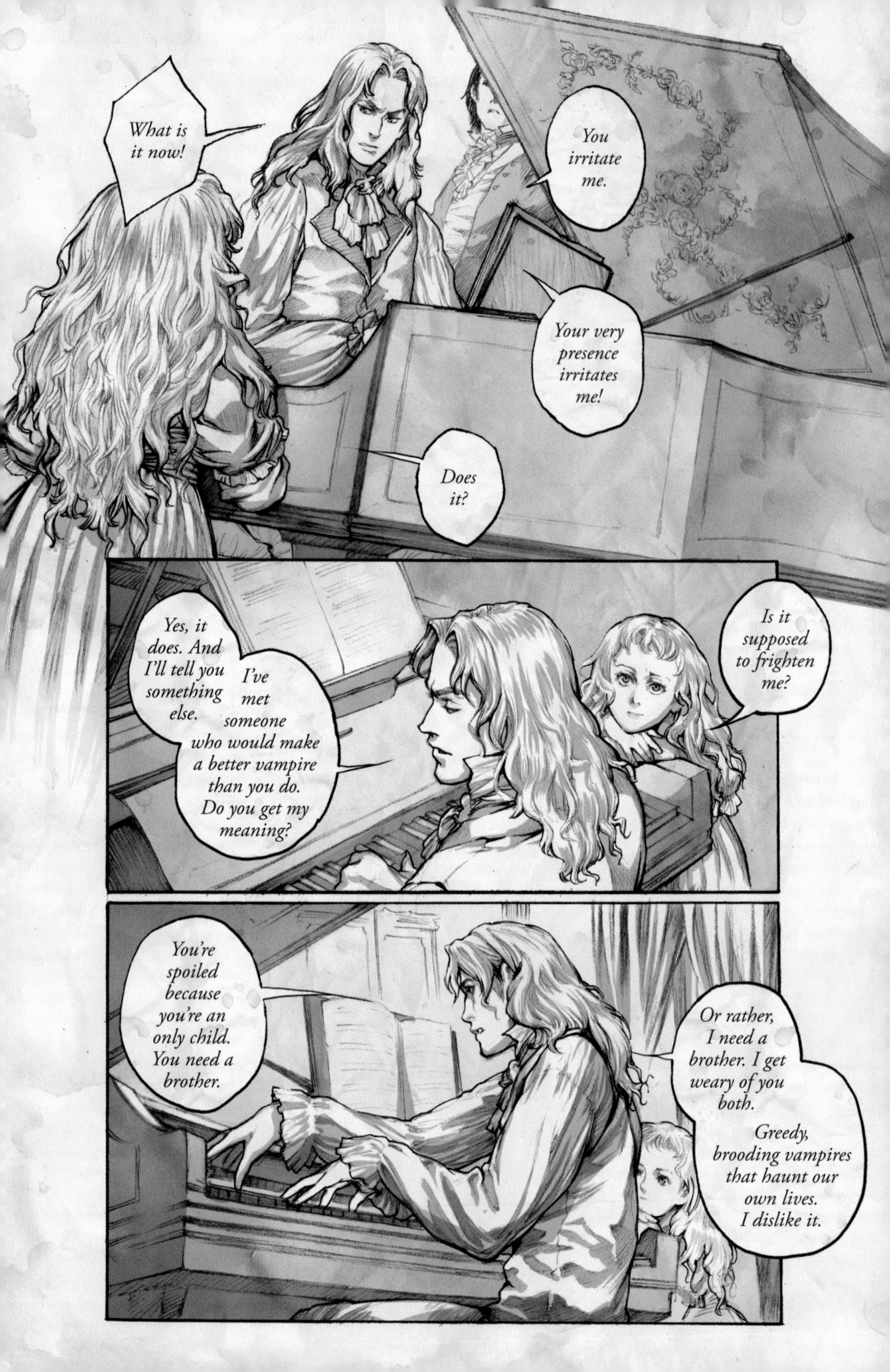
What is it now!
You irritate me.
Your very presence irritates me!
Does it?
Yes, it does. And I'll tell you something else.
I've met someone who would make a better vampire than you do. Do you get my meaning?
Is it supposed to frighten me?
You're spoiled because you're an only child. You need a brother.
Or rather, I need a brother. I get weary of you both.
Greedy, brooding vampires that haunt our own lives. I dislike it.

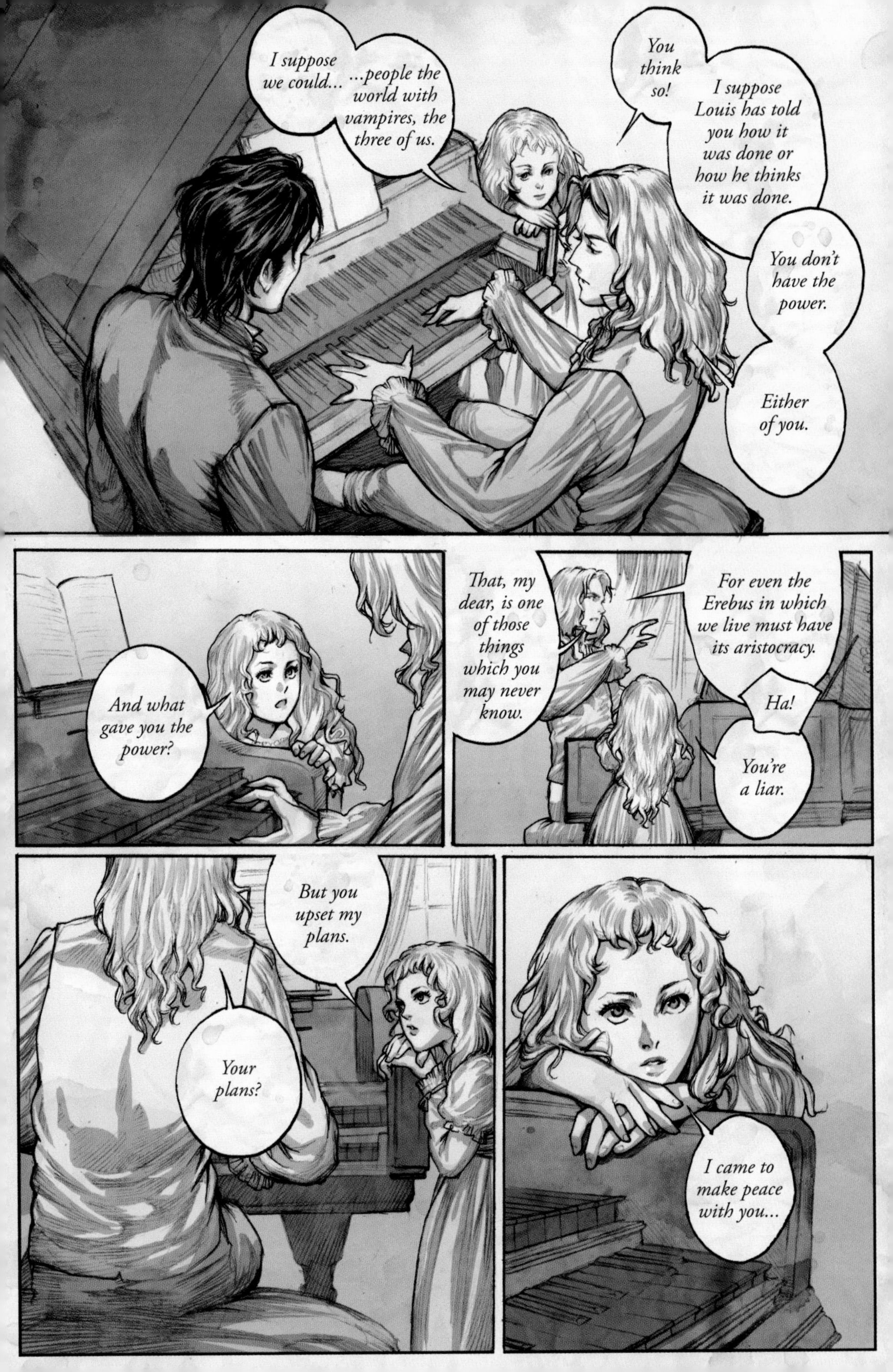
I suppose we could...
...people the world with vampires, the three of us.
You think so!
I suppose Louis has told you how it was done or how he thinks it was done.
You don't have the power.
Either of you.
And what gave you the power?
That, my dear, is one of those things which you may never know.
For even the Erebus in which we live must have its aristocracy.
Ha!
You're a liar.
But you upset my plans.
Your plans?
I came to make peace with you...

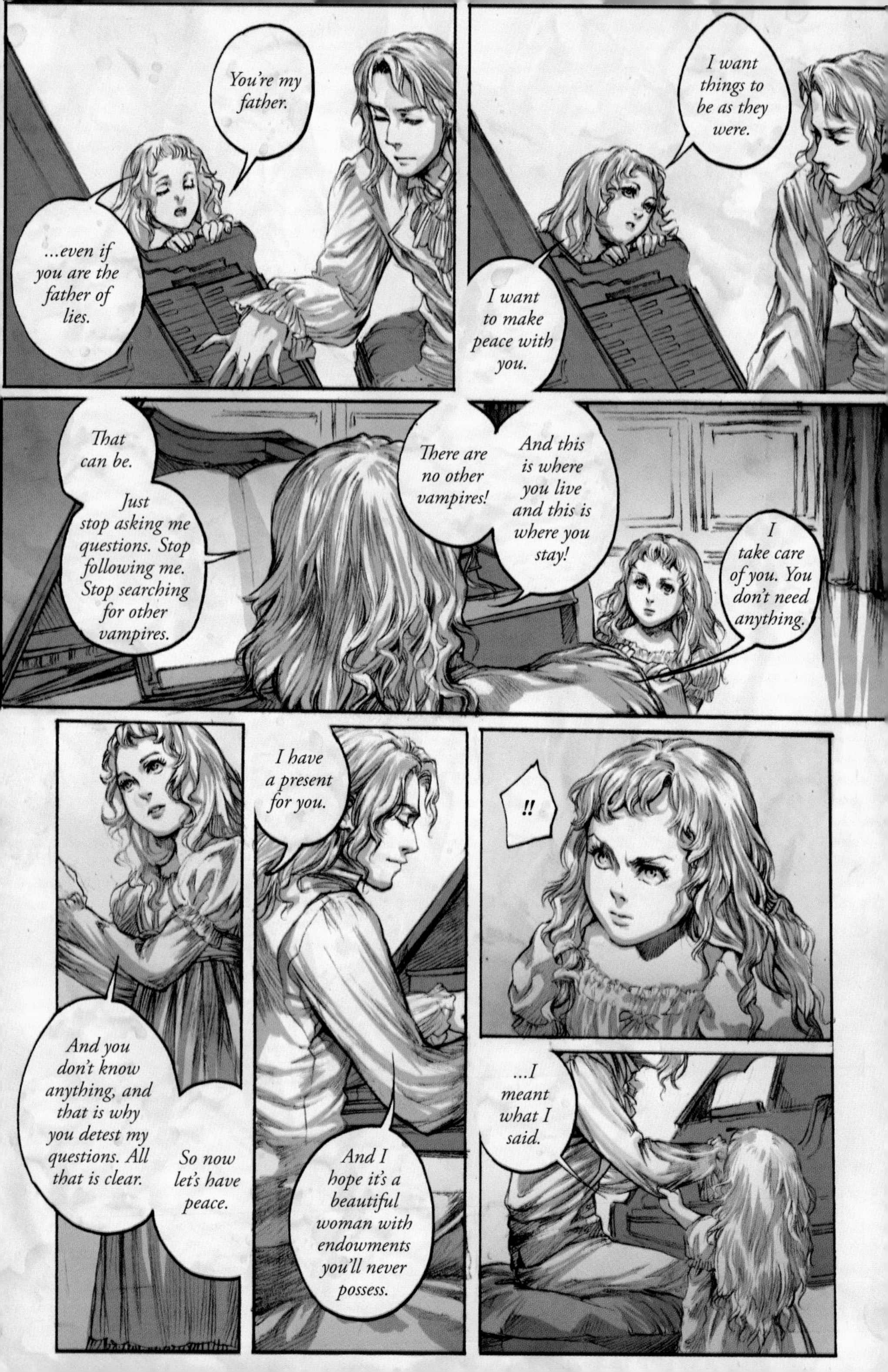
You're my father.
...even if you are the father of lies.
I want things to be as they were.
I want to make peace with you.
That can be.
Just stop asking me questions. Stop following me. Stop searching for other vampires.
There are no other vampires!
And this is where you live and this is where you stay!
I take care of you. You don't need anything.
And you don't know anything, and that is why you detest my questions. All that is clear.
So now let's have peace.
I have a present for you.
And I hope it's a beautiful woman with endowments you'll never possess.
!!
...I meant what I said.

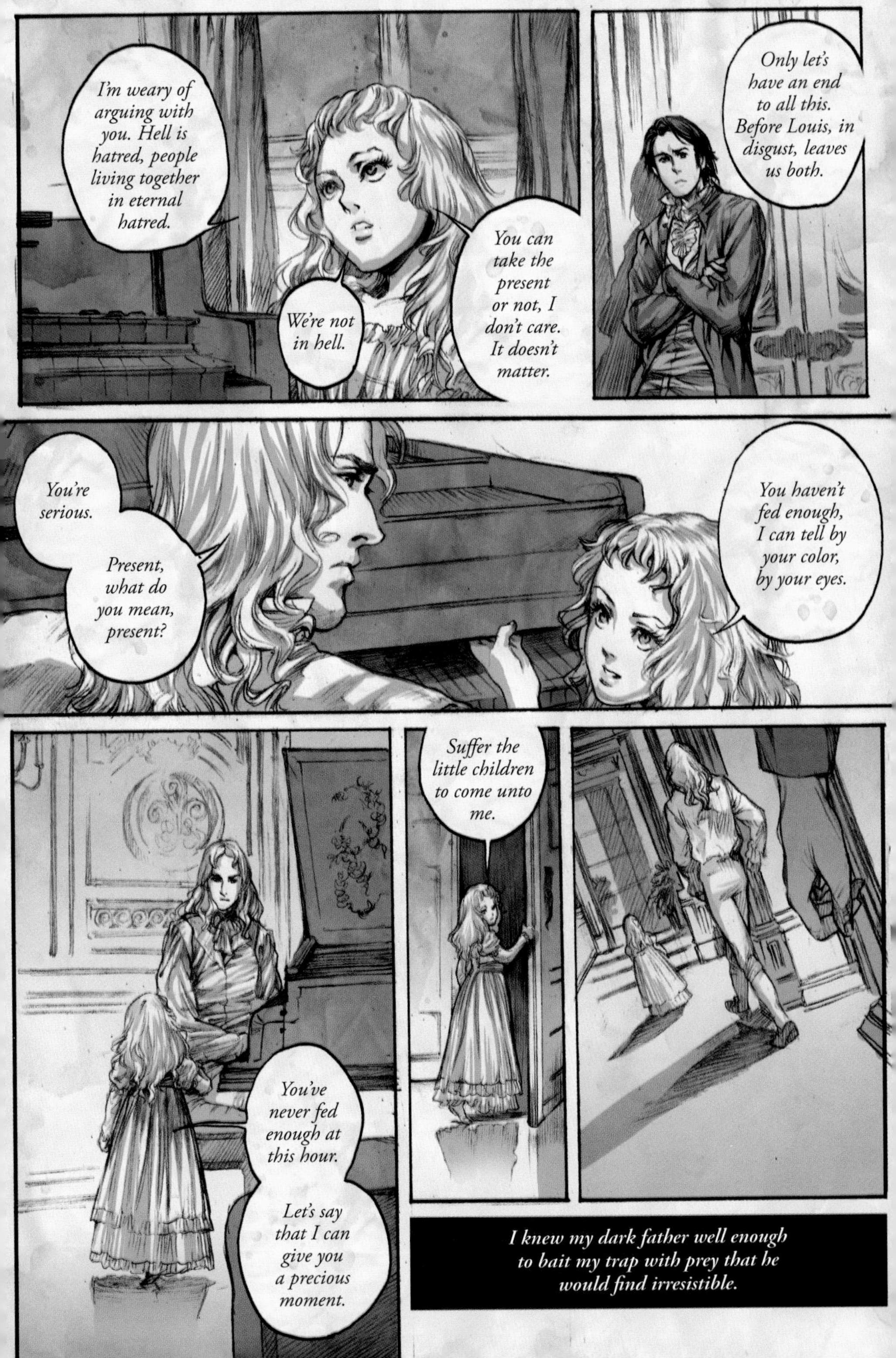
I'm weary of arguing with you. Hell is hatred, people living together in eternal hatred.
We're not in hell.
You can take the present or not, I don't care. It doesn't matter.
Only let's have an end to all this. Before Louis, in disgust, leaves us both.
You're serious.
Present, what do you mean, present?
You haven't fed enough, I can tell by your color, by your eyes.
You've never fed enough at this hour.
Let's say that I can give you a precious moment.
Suffer the little children to come unto me.
I knew my dark father well enough to bait my trap with prey that he would find irresistible.

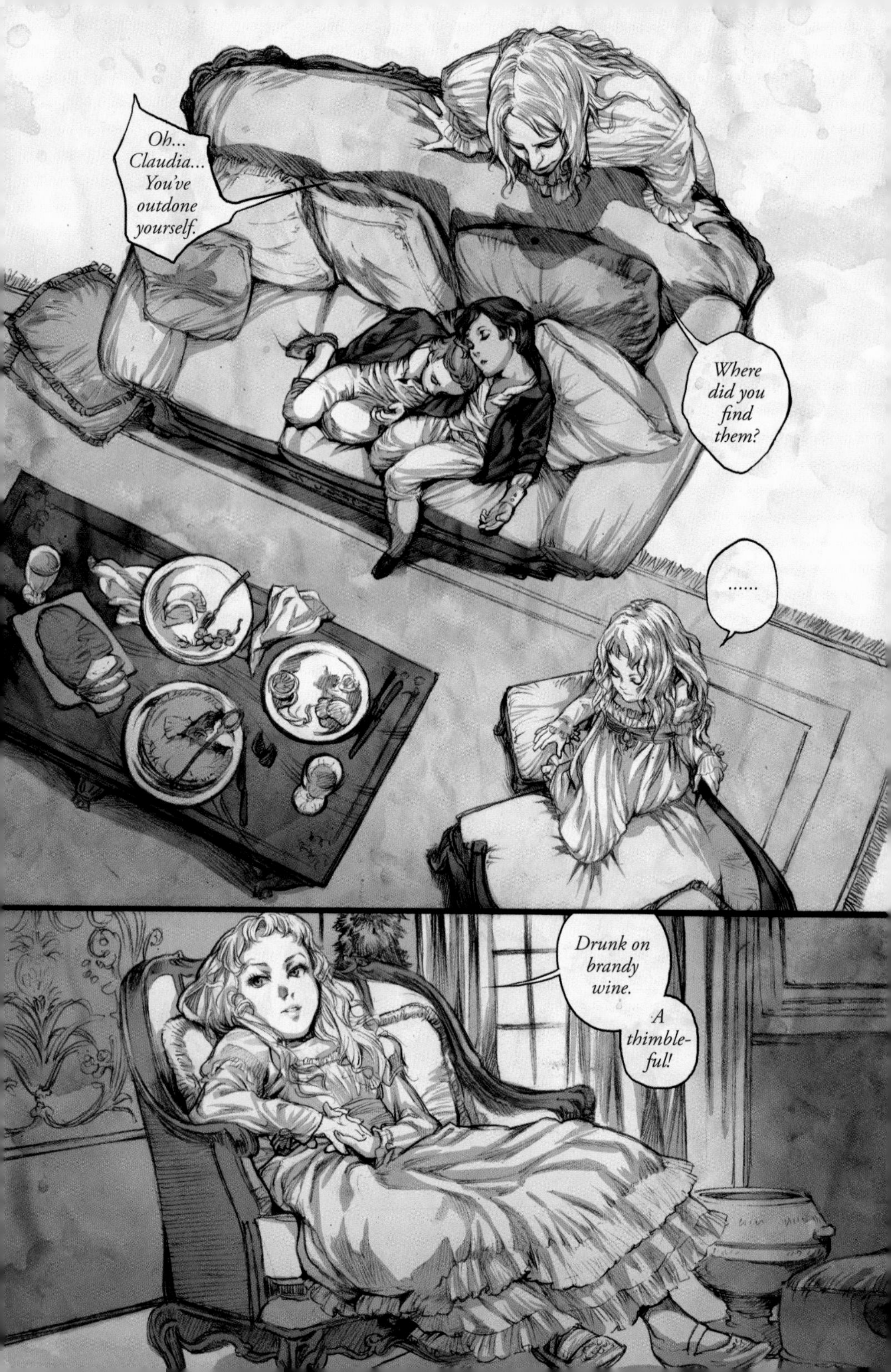
Oh... Claudia... You've outdone yourself.
Where did you find them?
......
Drunk on brandy wine.
A thimble-ful!

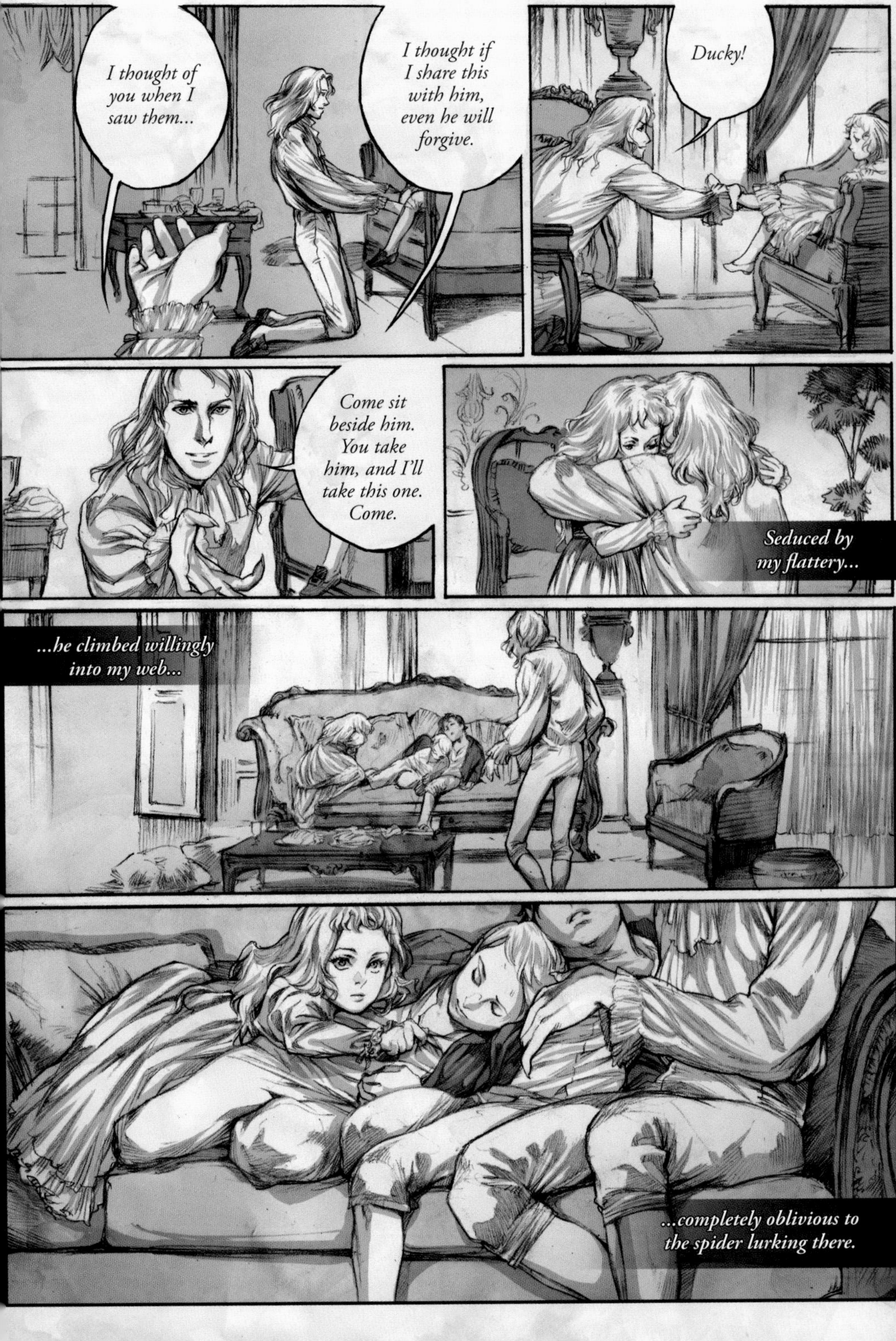
I thought of you when I saw them...
I thought if I share this with him, even he will forgive.
Ducky!
Come sit beside him. You take him, and I'll take this one. Come.
Seduced by my flattery...
...he climbed willingly into my web...
...completely oblivious to the spider lurking there.

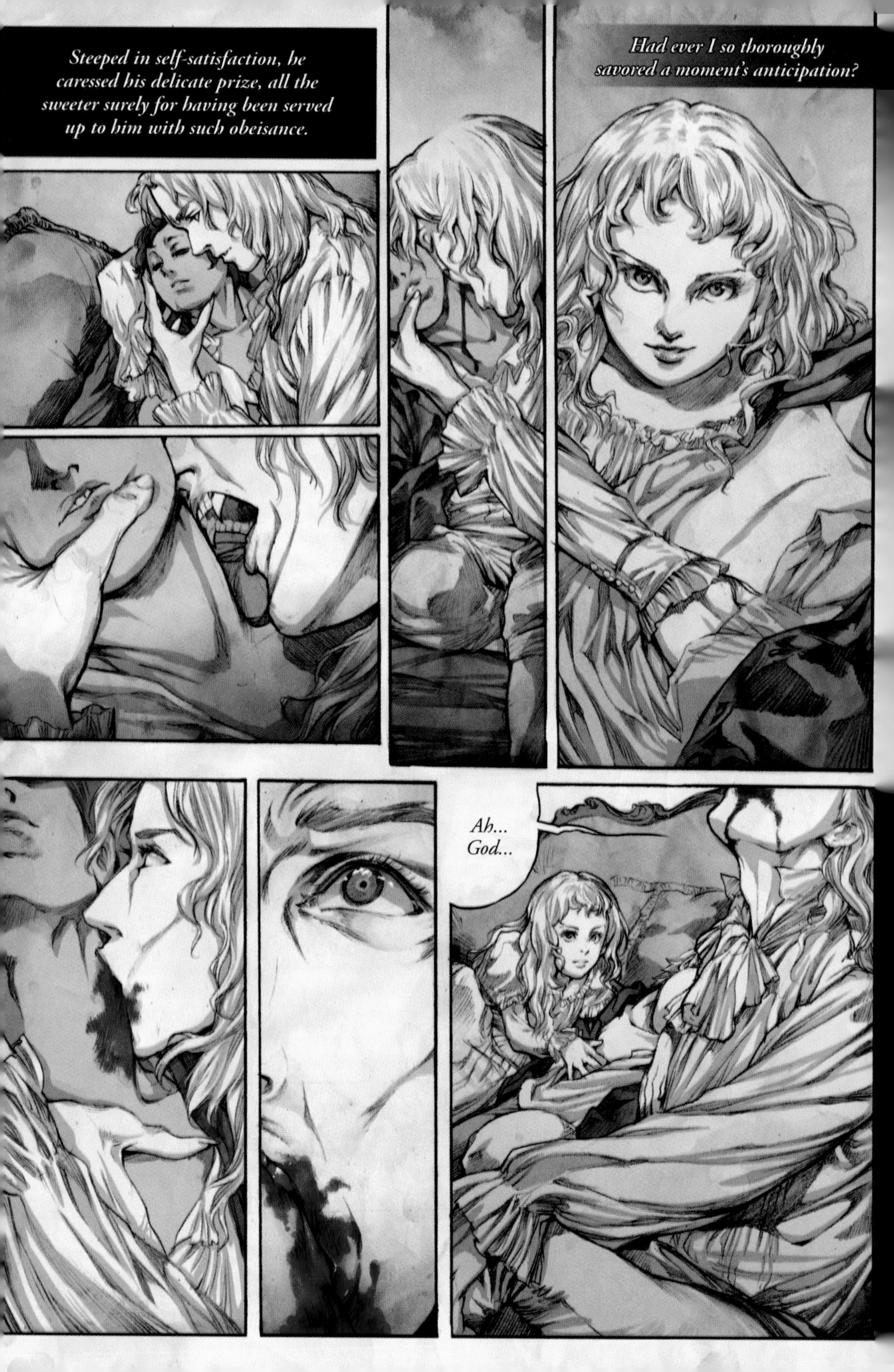
Steeped in self-satisfaction, he caressed his delicate prize, all the sweeter surely for having been served up to him with such obeisance.
Had ever I so thoroughly savored a moment's anticipation?
Ah... God...

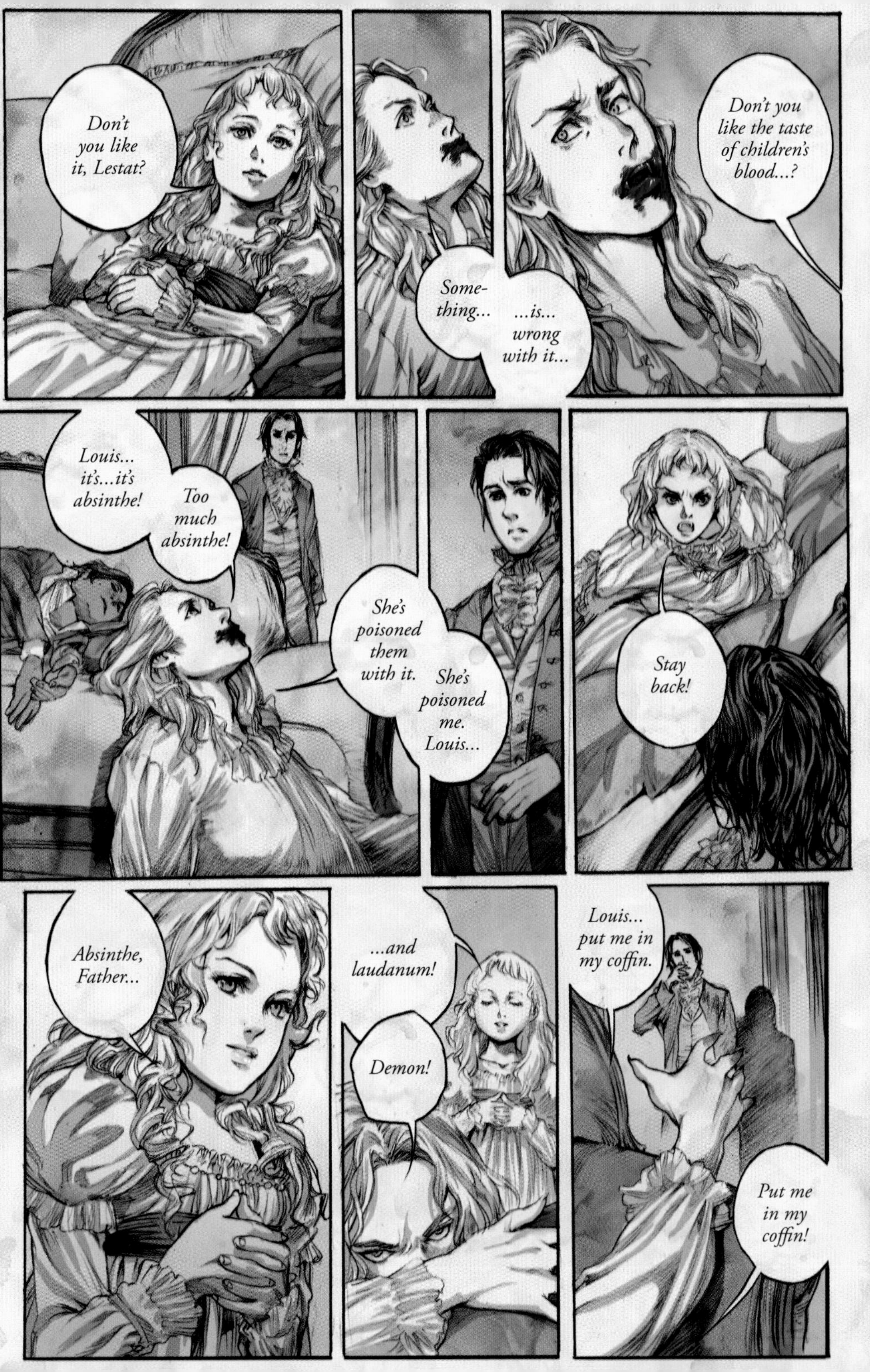
Don't you like it, Lestat?
Something...
...is... wrong with it...
Don't you like the taste of children's blood...?
Louis... it's...it's absinthe!
Too much absinthe!
She's poisoned them with it.
She's poisoned me. Louis...
Stay back!
Absinthe, Father...
...and laudanum!
Demon!
Louis... put me in my coffin.
Put me in my coffin!

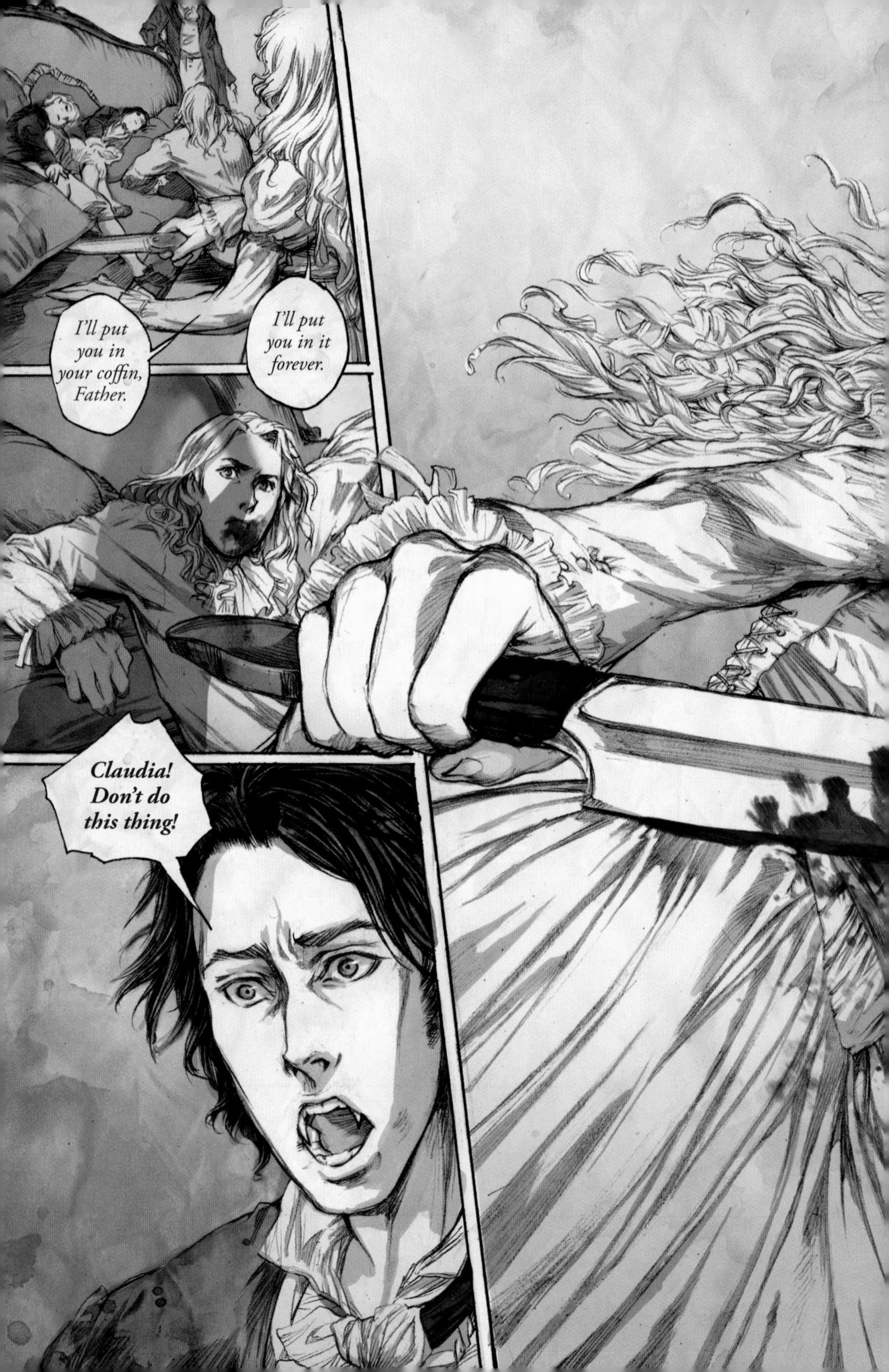
I'll put you in your coffin, Father.
I'll put you in it forever.
Claudia! Don't do this thing!

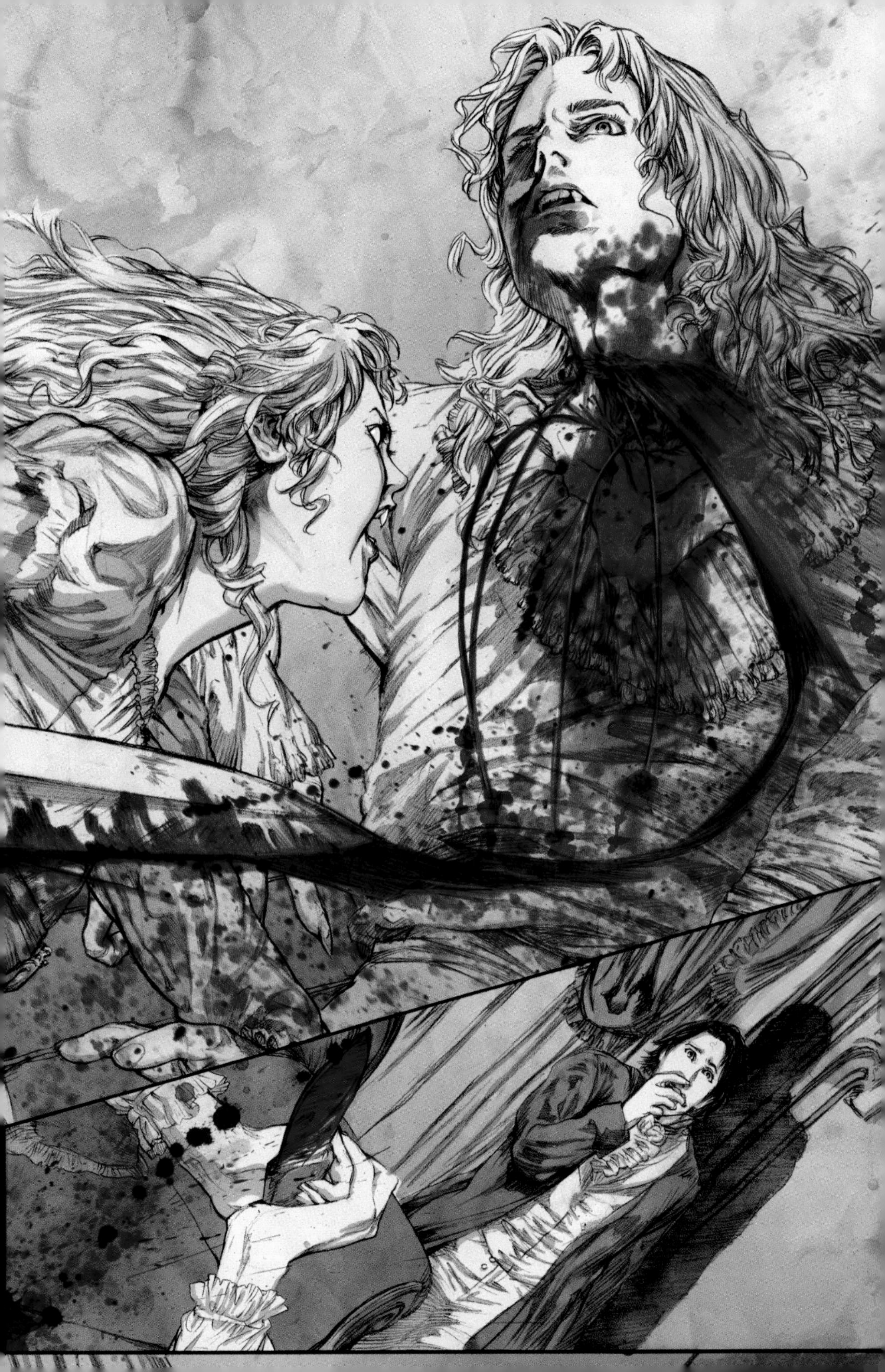

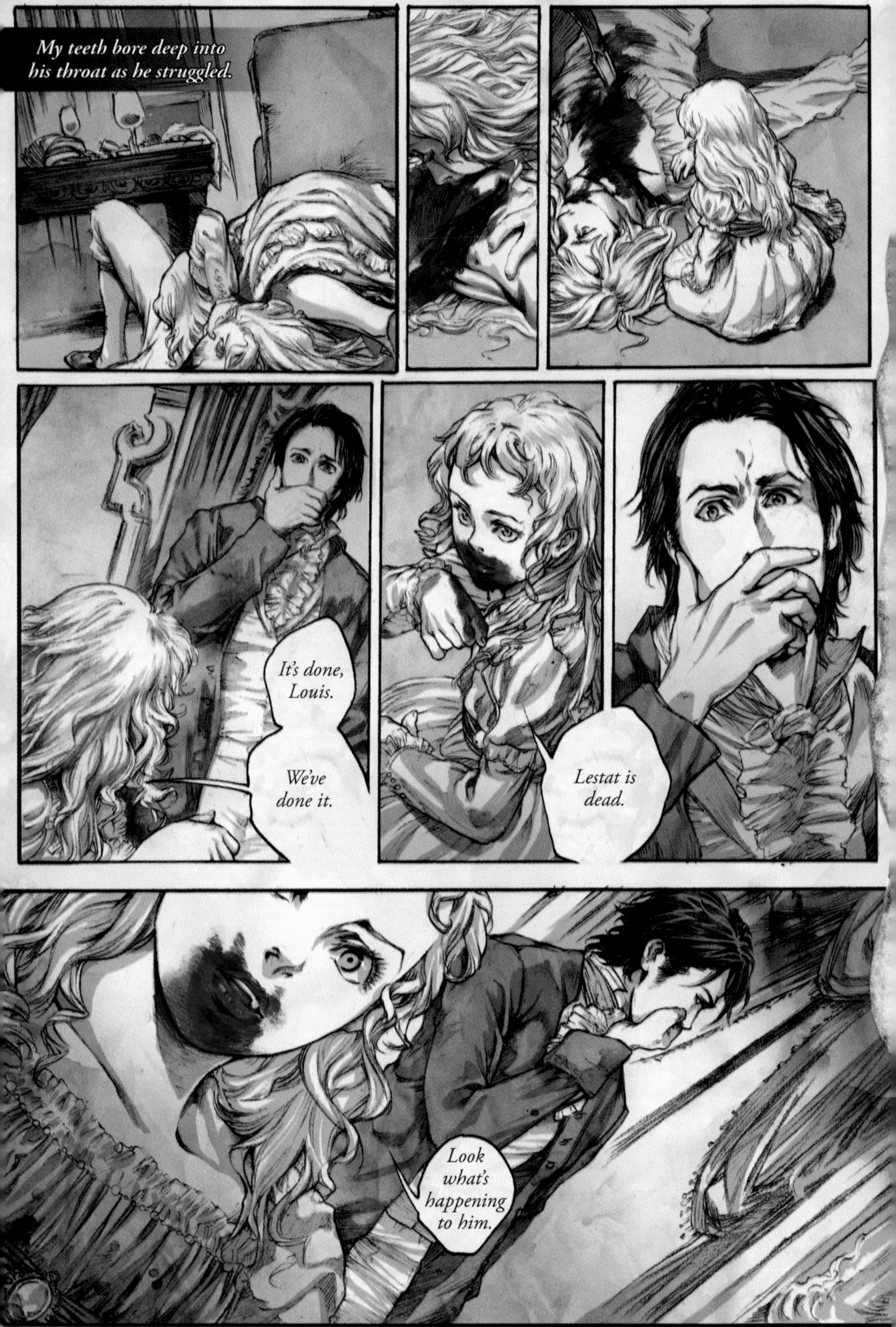
My teeth bore deep into his throat as he struggled.
It's done, Louis.
We've done it.
Lestat is dead.
Look what's happening to him.

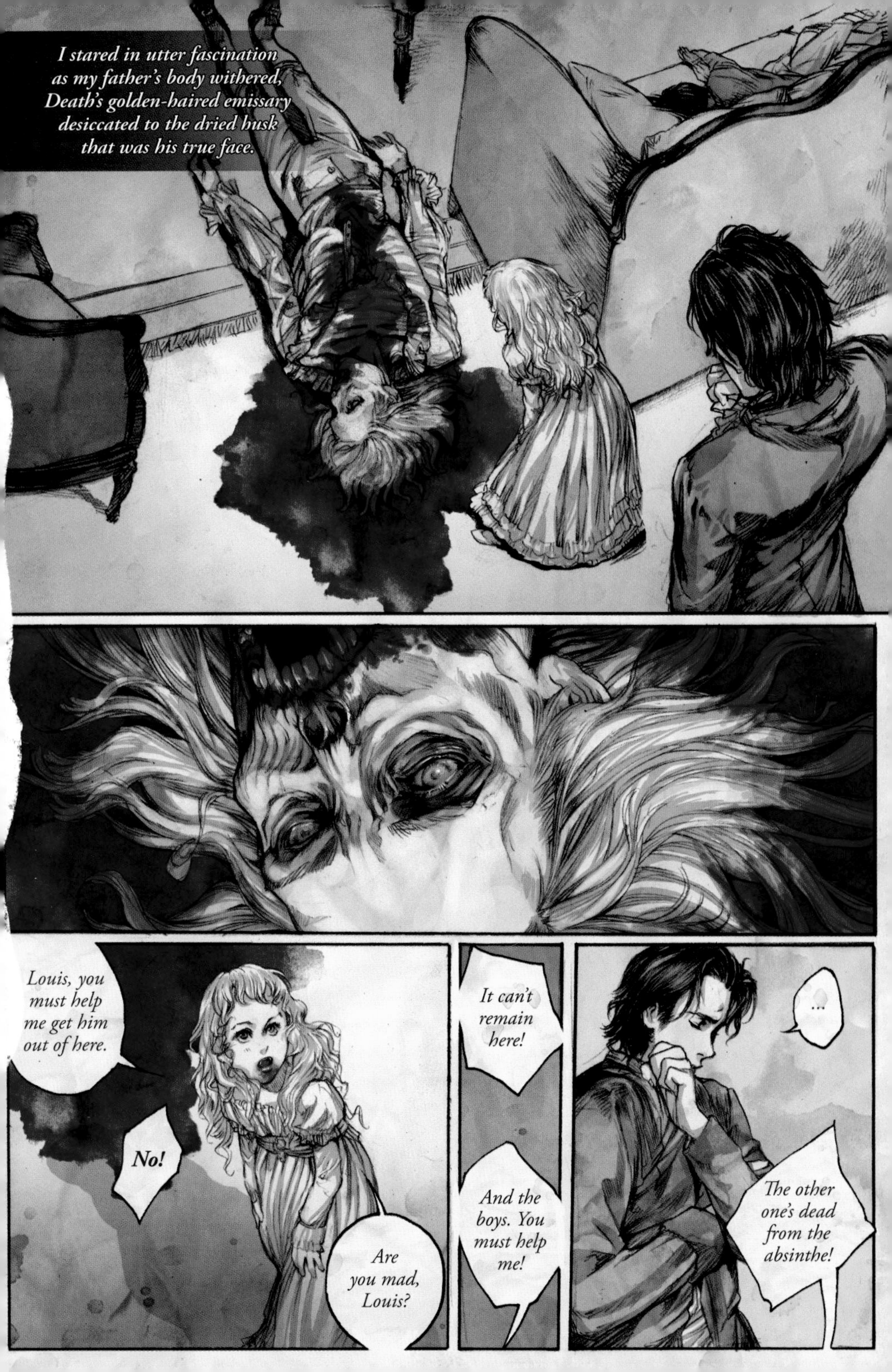

I stared in utter fascination as my father's body withered, Death's golden-haired emissary desiccated to the dried husk that was his true face.
Louis, you must help me get him out of here.
No!
Are you mad, Louis?
It can't remain here!
And the boys. You must help me!
...
The other one's dead from the absinthe!

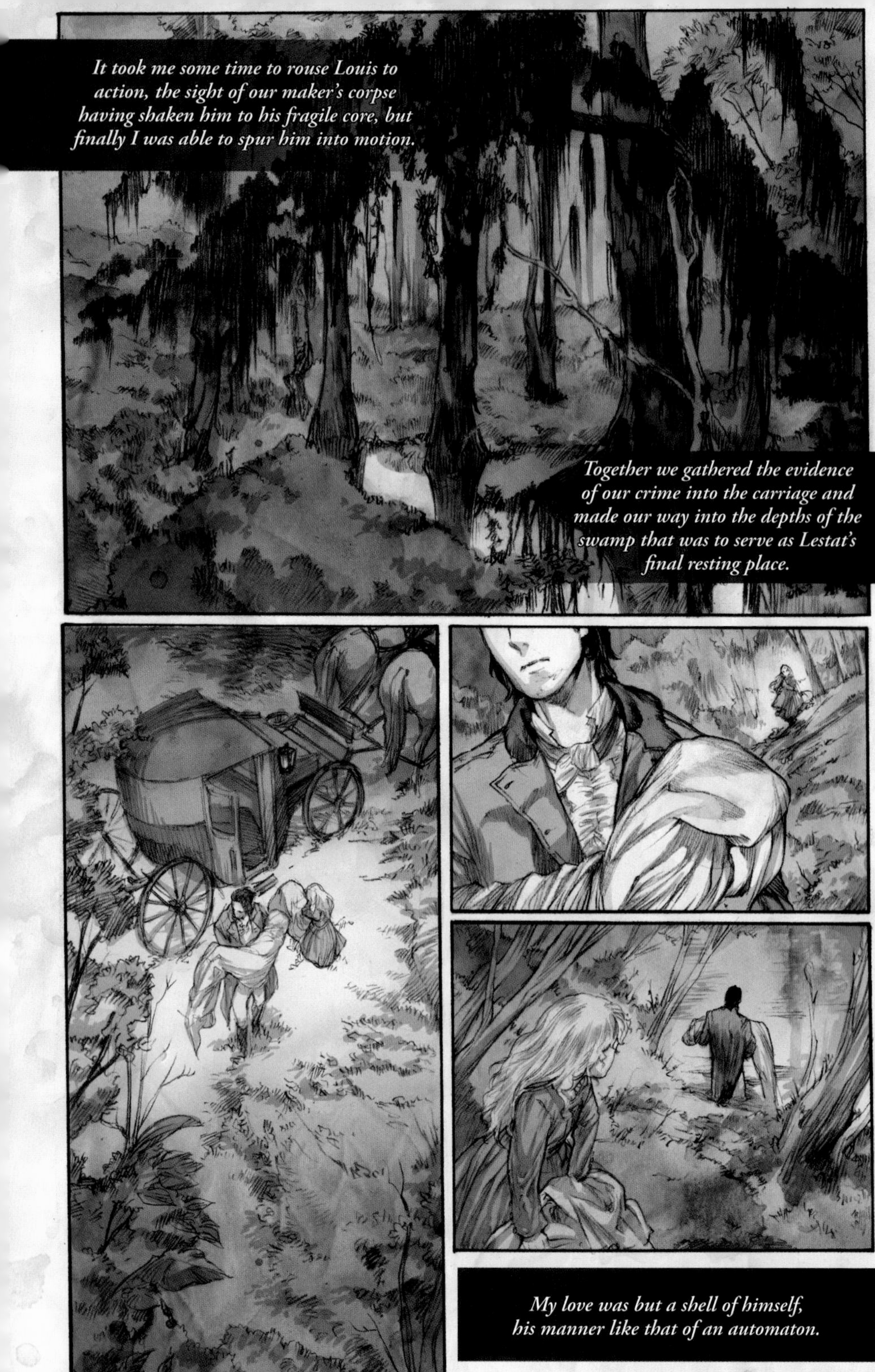
It took me some time to rouse Louis to action, the sight of our maker's corpse having shaken him to his fragile core, but finally I was able to spur him into motion.
Together we gathered the evidence of our crime into the carriage and made our way into the depths of the swamp that was to serve as Lestat's final resting place.
My love was but a shell of himself, his manner like that of an automaton.

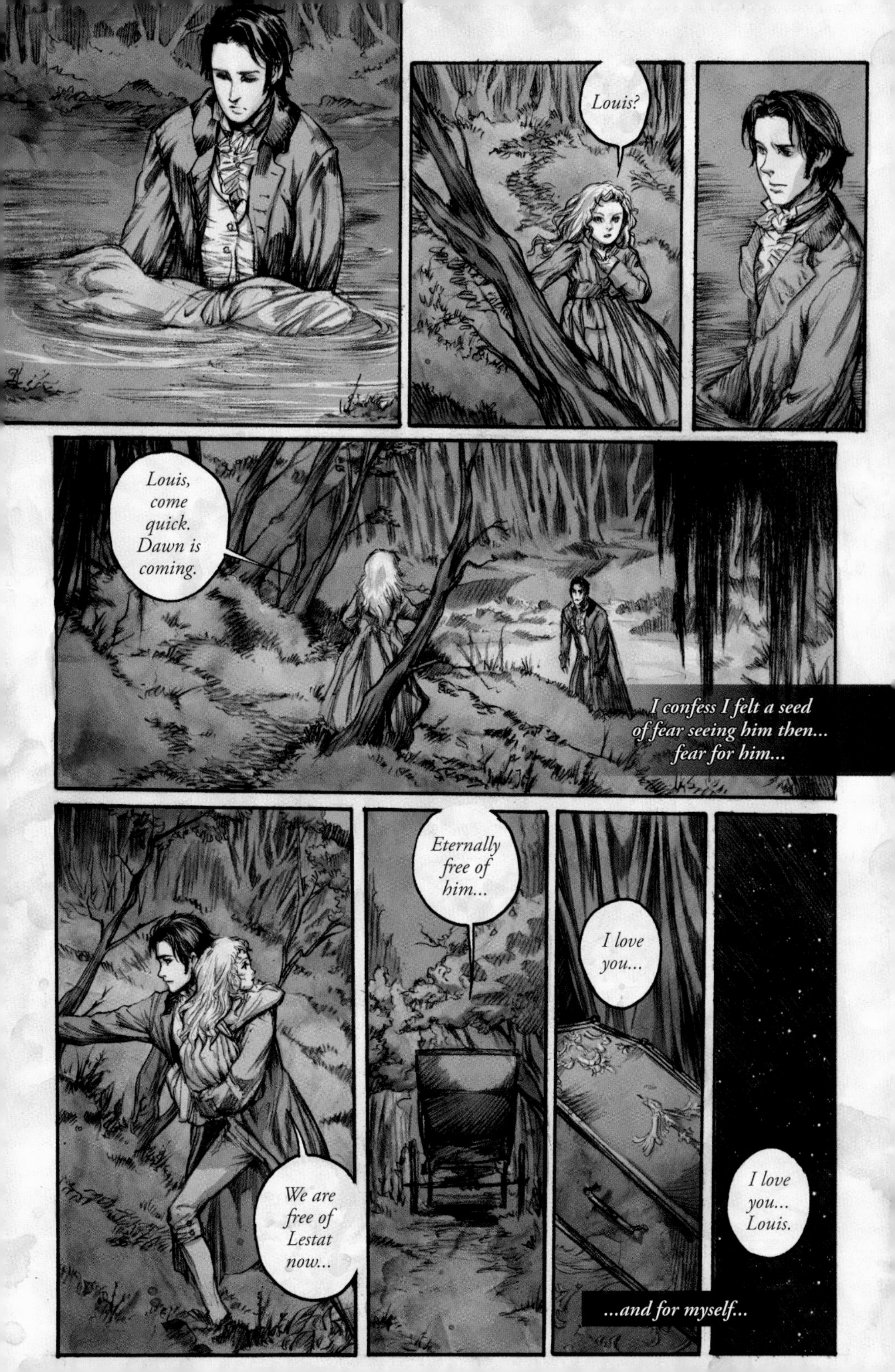
Louis?
Louis, come quick. Dawn is coming.
I confess I felt a seed of fear seeing him then... fear for him...
We are free of Lestat now...
Eternally free of him...
I love you...
I love you... Louis.
...and for myself...

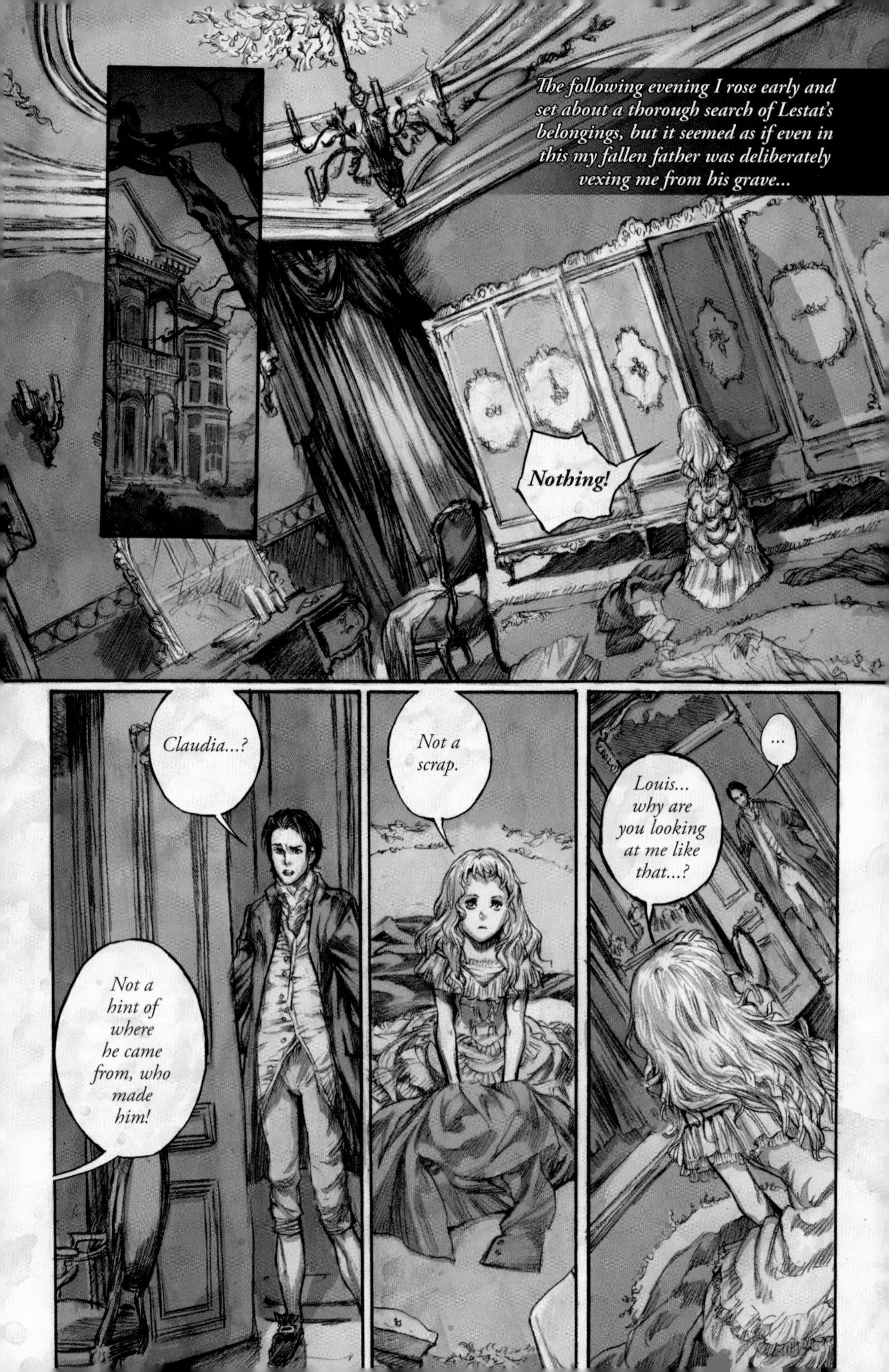
The following evening I rose early and set about a thorough search of Lestat's belongings, but it seemed as if even in this my fallen father was deliberately vexing me from his grave...
Nothing!
Claudia...?
Not a hint of where he came from, who made him!
Not a scrap.
...
Louis... why are you looking at me like that...?

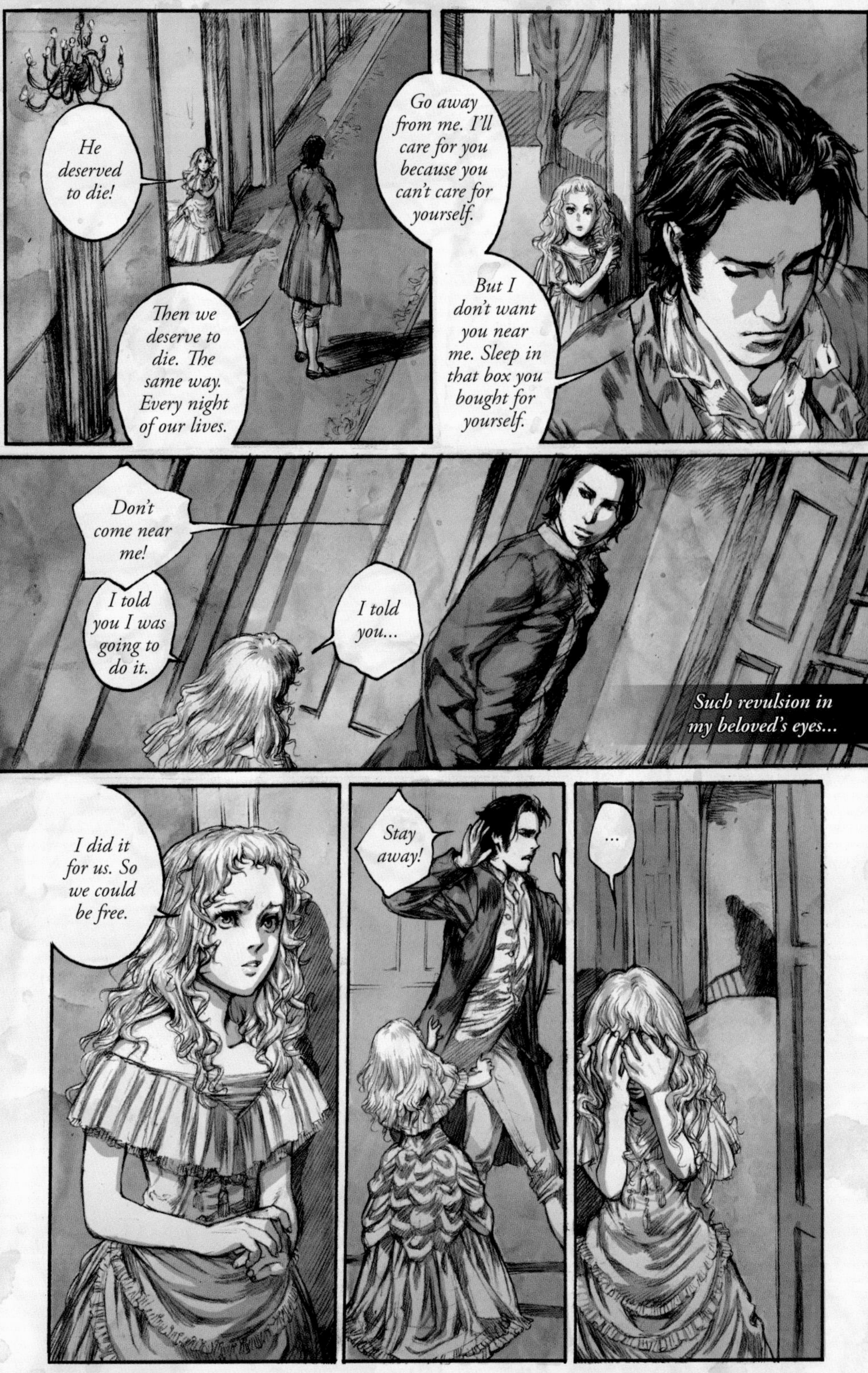
He deserved to die!
Then we deserve to die. The same way. Every night of our lives.
Go away from me. I'll care for you because you can't care for yourself.
But I don't want you near me. Sleep in that box you bought for yourself.
Don't come near me!
I told you I was going to do it.
I told you...
Such revulsion in my beloved's eyes...
I did it for us. So we could be free.
Stay away!
...

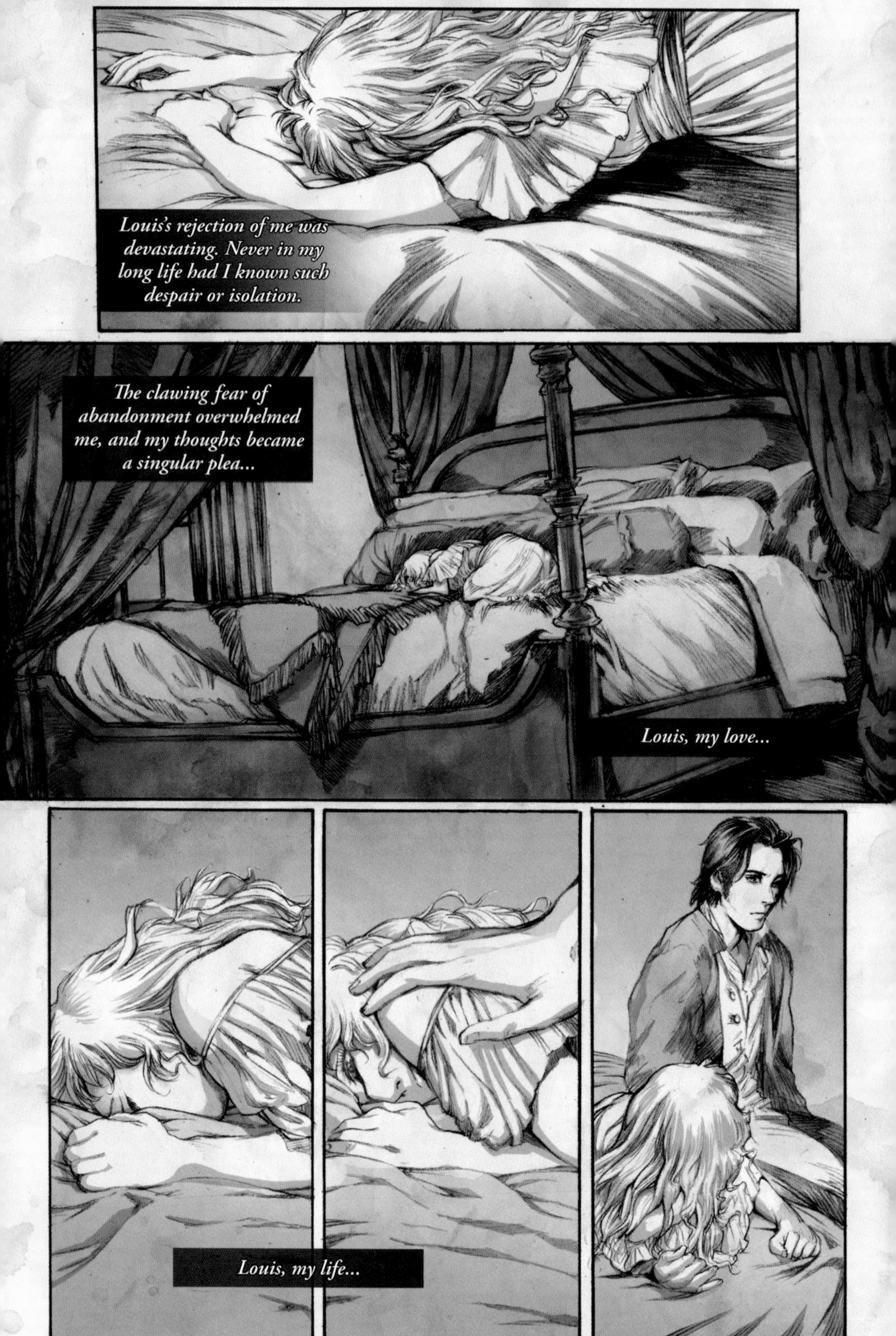
Louis's rejection of me was devastating. Never in my long life had I known such despair or isolation.
The clawing fear of abandonment overwhelmed me, and my thoughts became a singular plea...
Louis, my love...
Louis, my life...

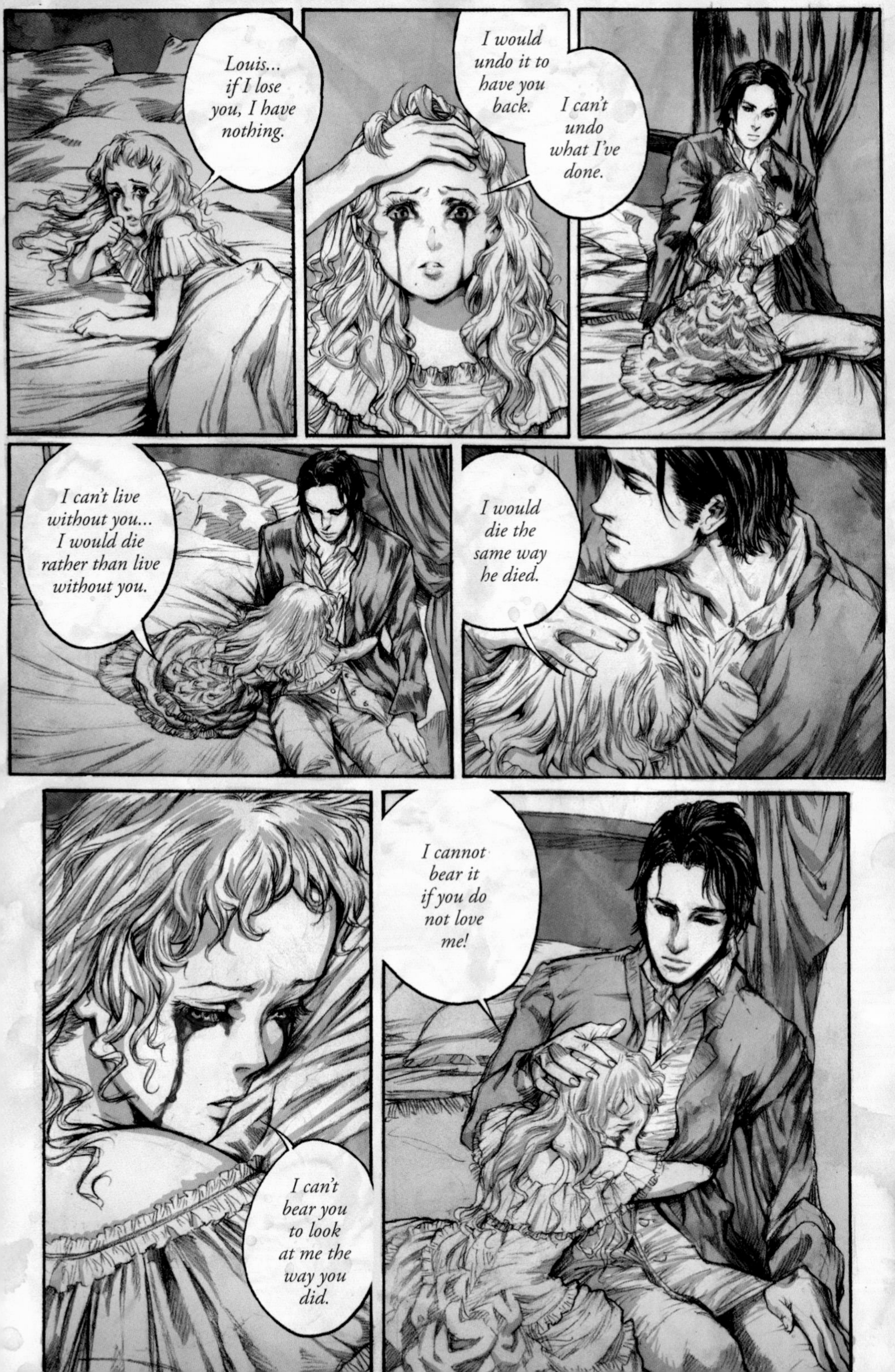
Louis... if I lose you, I have nothing.
I would undo it to have you back.
I can't undo what I've done.
I can't live without you... I would die rather than live without you.
I would die the same way he died.
I can't bear you to look at me the way you did.
I cannot bear it if you do not love me!

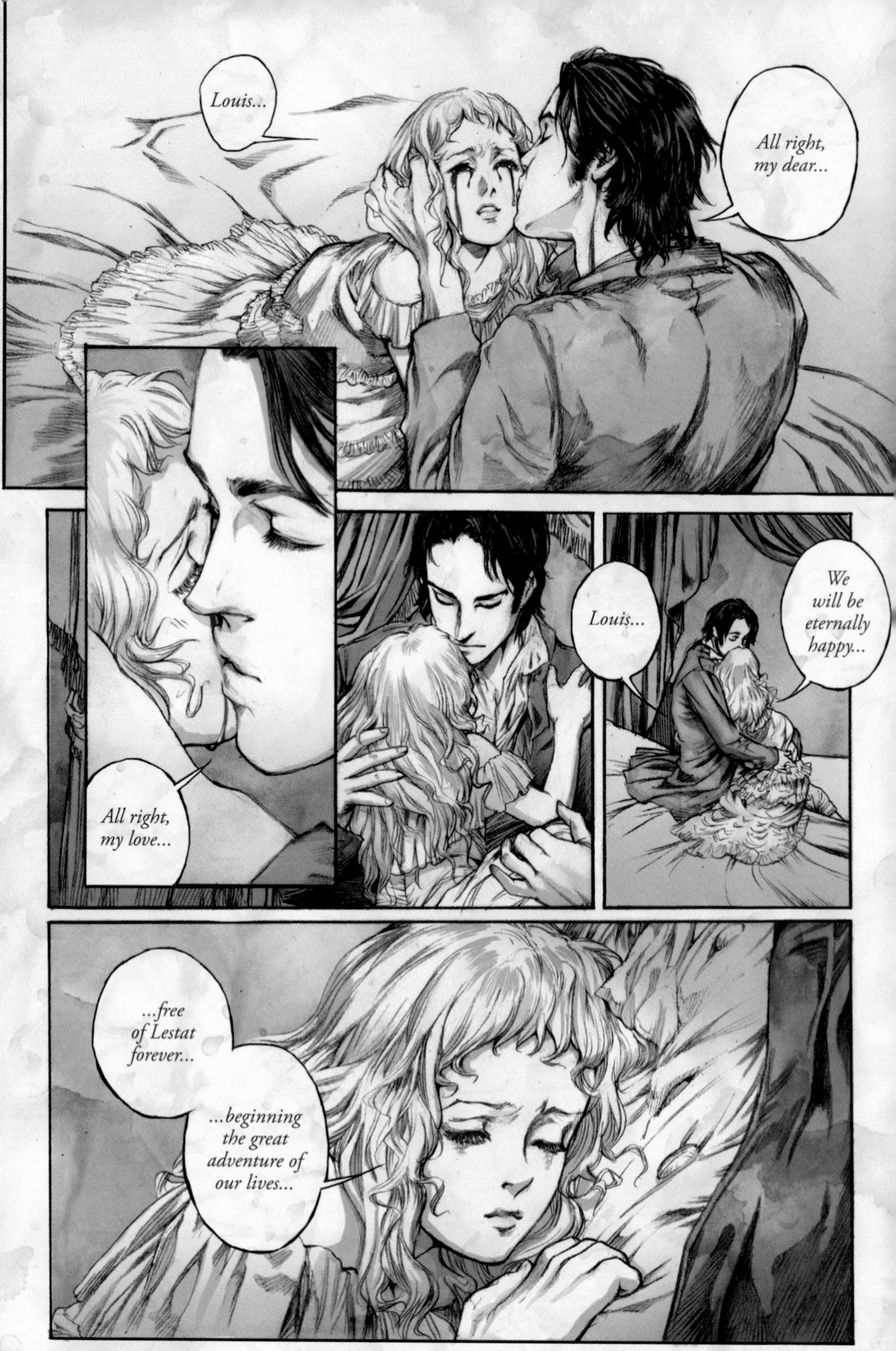
Louis...
All right, my dear...
All right, my love...
Louis...
We will be eternally happy...
...free of Lestat forever...
...beginning the great adventure of our lives...

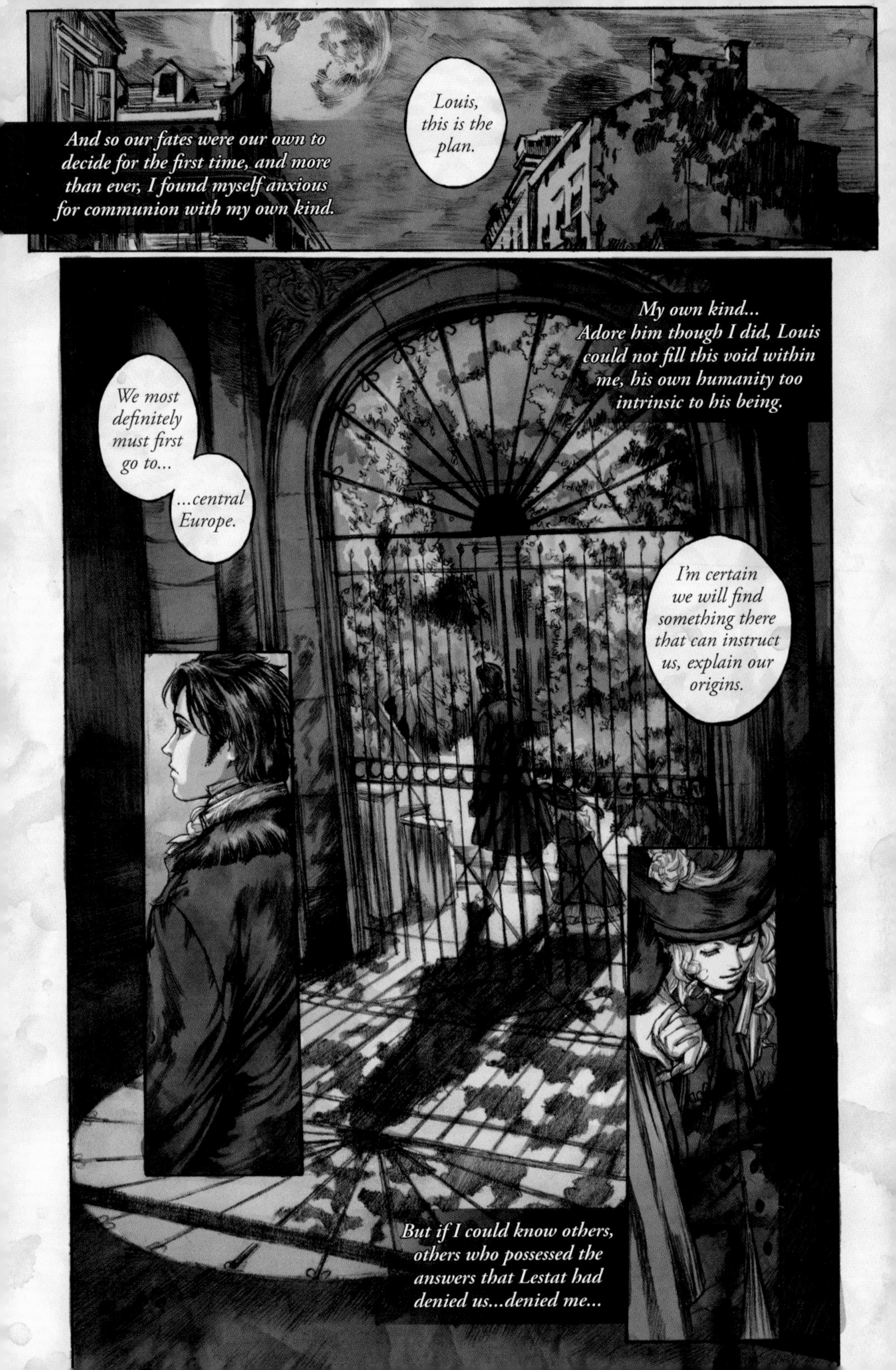

And so our fates were our own to decide for the first time, and more than ever, I found myself anxious for communion with my own kind.
Louis, this is the plan.
My own kind... Adore him though I did, Louis could not fill this void within me, his own humanity too intrinsic to his being.
We most definitely must first go to...
...central Europe.
I'm certain we will find something there that can instruct us, explain our origins.
But if I could know others, others who possessed the answers that Lestat had denied us...denied me...

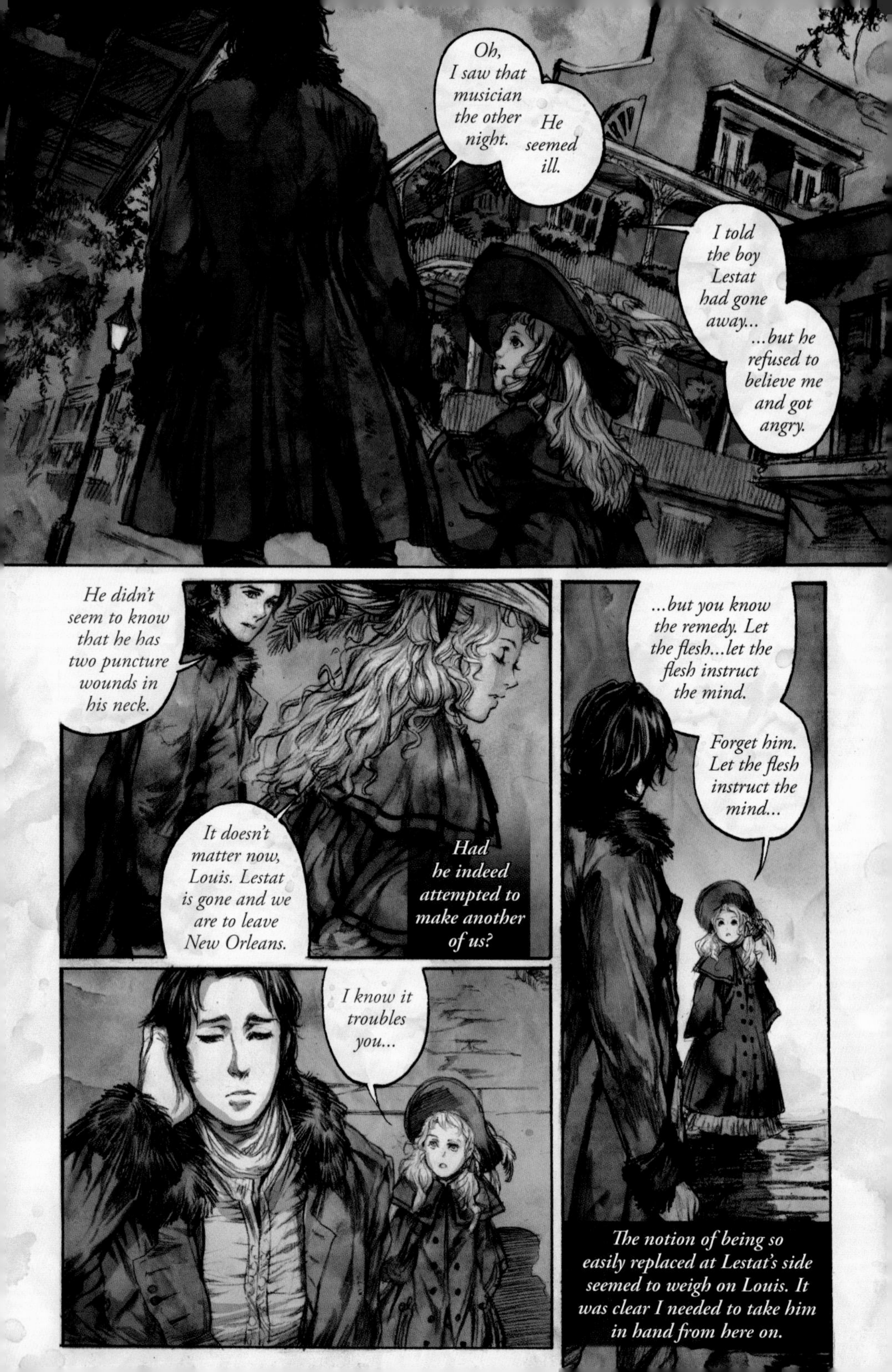
Oh, I saw that musician the other night.
He seemed ill.
I told the boy Lestat had gone away...
...but he refused to believe me and got angry.
He didn't seem to know that he has two puncture wounds in his neck.
It doesn't matter now, Louis. Lestat is gone and we are to leave New Orleans.
Had he indeed attempted to make another of us?
I know it troubles you...
...but you know the remedy. Let the flesh...let the flesh instruct the mind.
Forget him. Let the flesh instruct the mind...
The notion of being so easily replaced at Lestat's side seemed to weigh on Louis. It was clear I needed to take him in hand from here on.

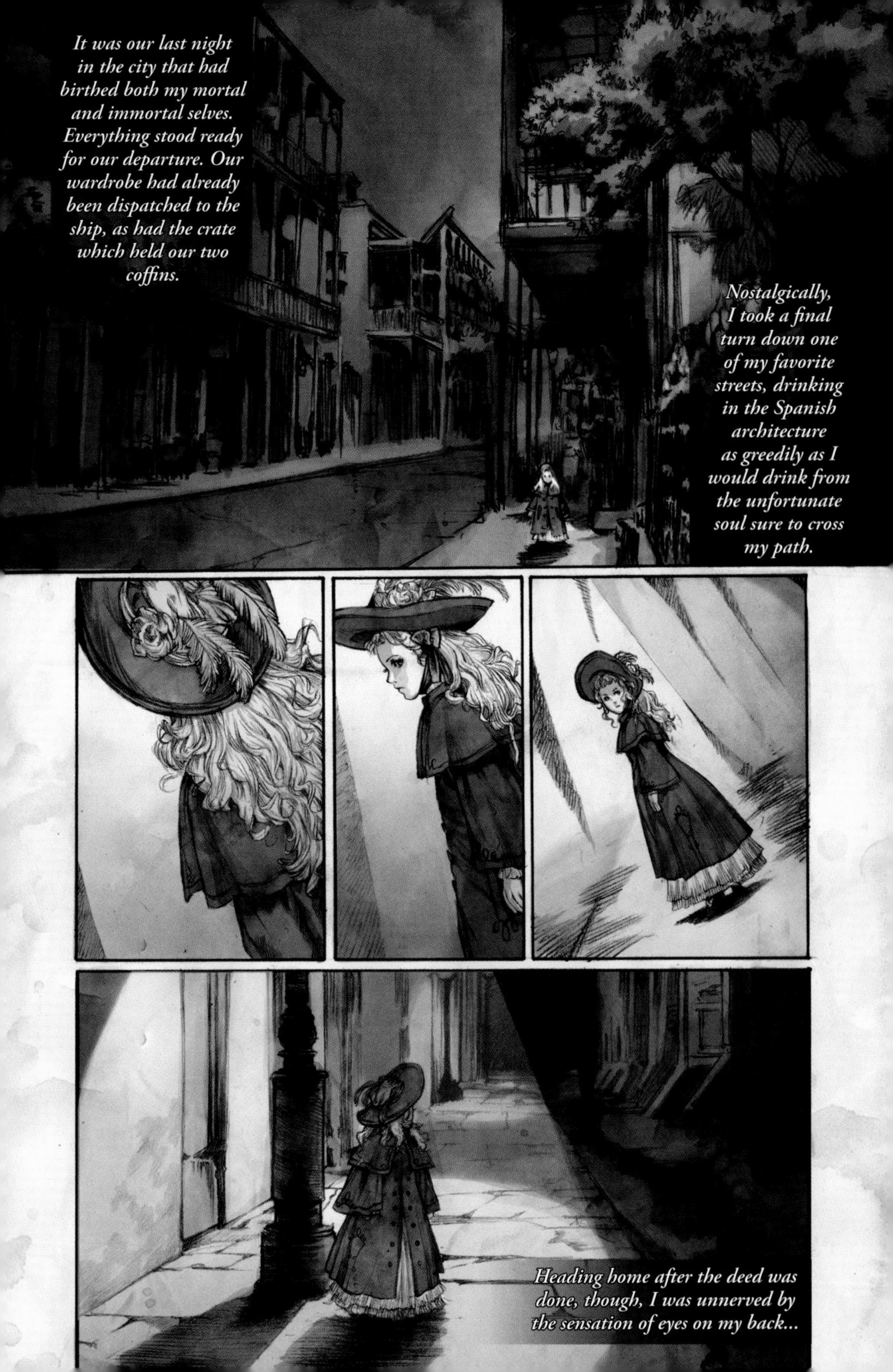
It was our last night in the city that had birthed both my mortal and immortal selves. Everything stood ready for our departure. Our wardrobe had already been dispatched to the ship, as had the crate which held our two coffins.
Nostalgically, I took a final turn down one of my favorite streets, drinking in the Spanish architecture as greedily as I would drink from the unfortunate soul sure to cross my path.
Heading home after the deed was done, though, I was unnerved by the sensation of eyes on my back...

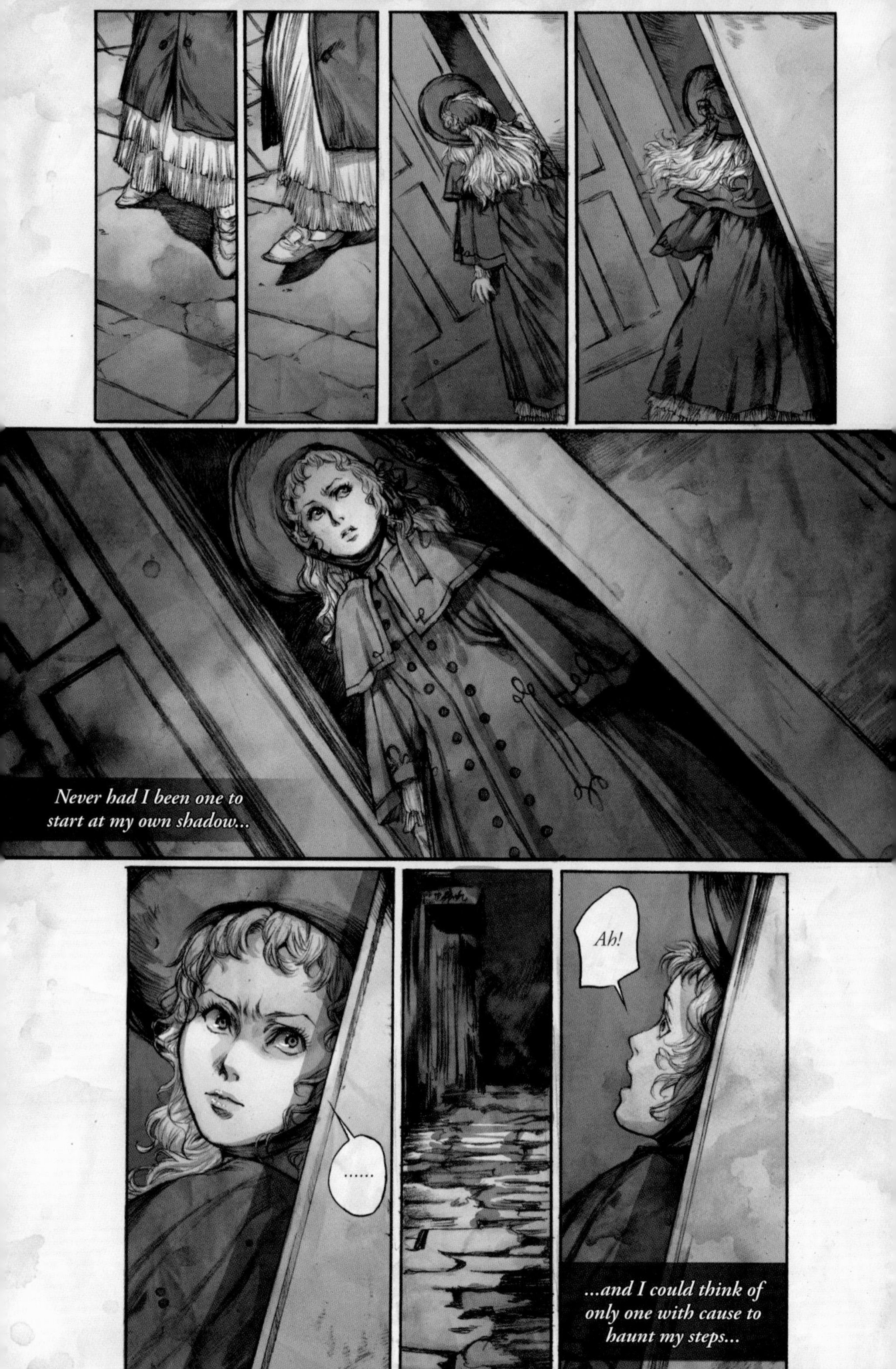
Never had I been one to start at my own shadow...
......
Ah!
...and I could think of only one with cause to haunt my steps...

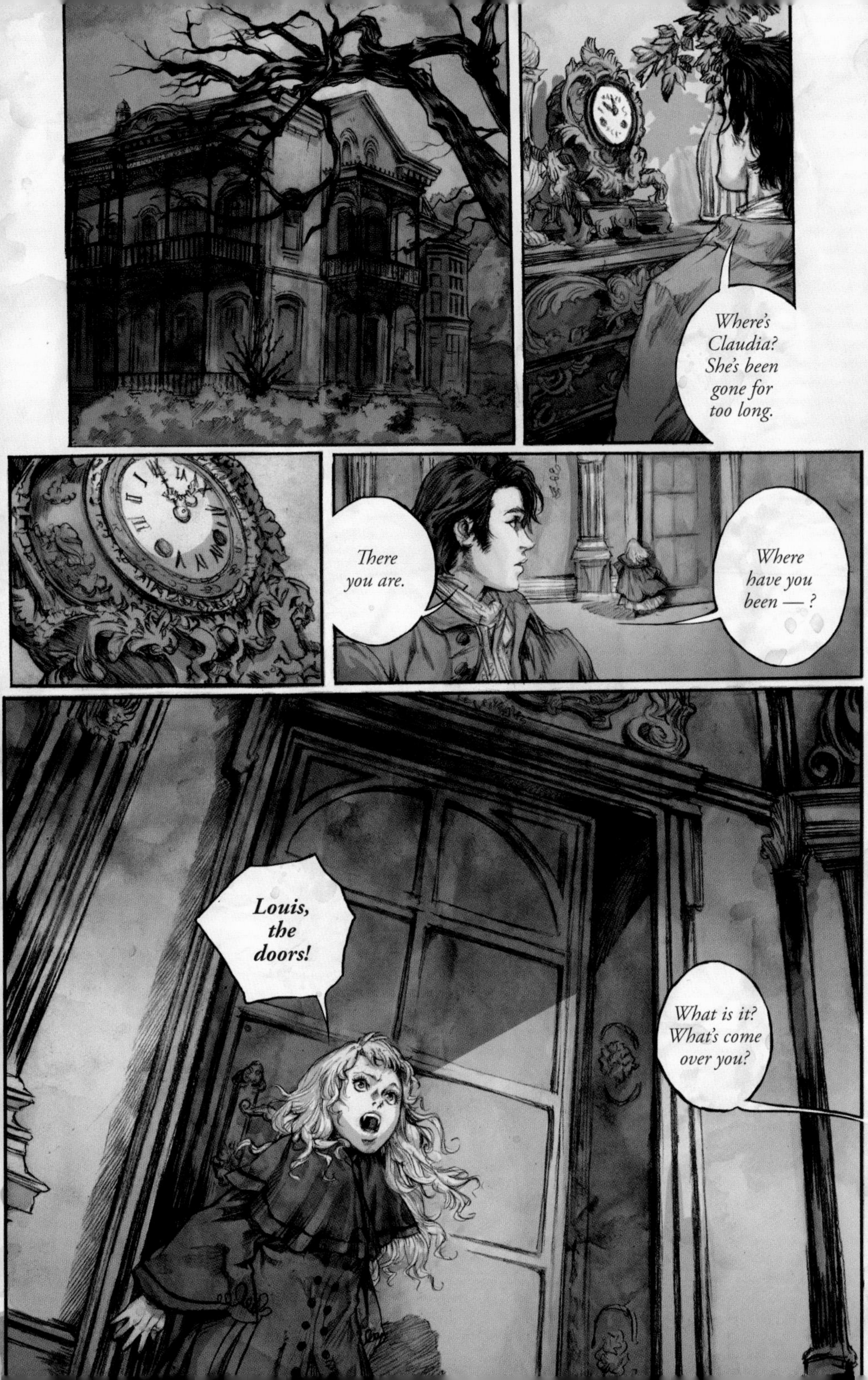
Where's Claudia? She's been gone for too long.
There you are.
Where have you been — ?
Louis, the doors!
What is it? What's come over you?

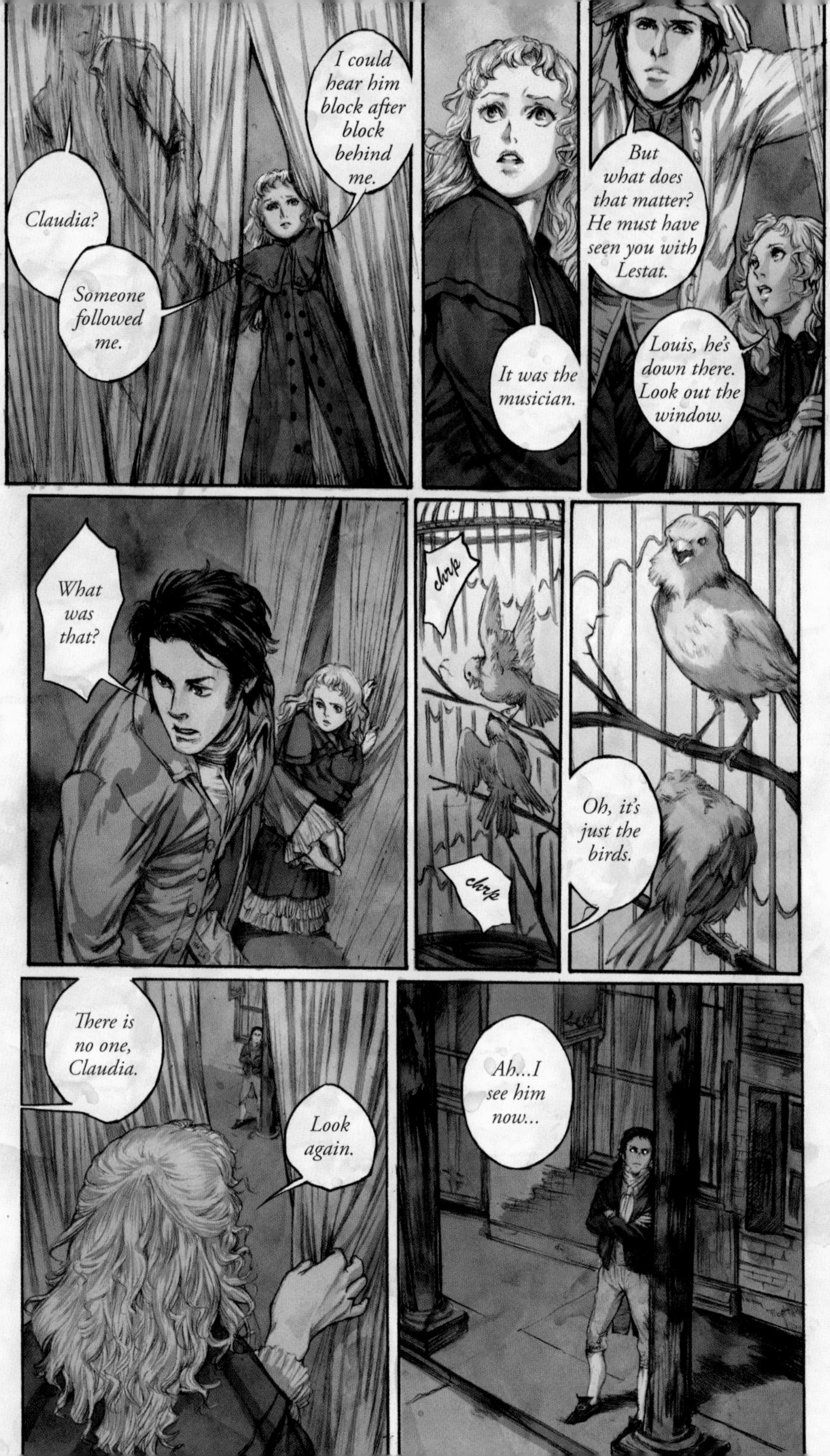
Claudia?
Someone followed me.
I could hear him block after block behind me.
It was the musician.
But what does that matter? He must have seen you with Lestat.
Louis, he's down there. Look out the window.
What was that?
chrp
chrp
Oh, it's just the birds.
There is no one, Claudia.
Look again.
Ah...I see him now...

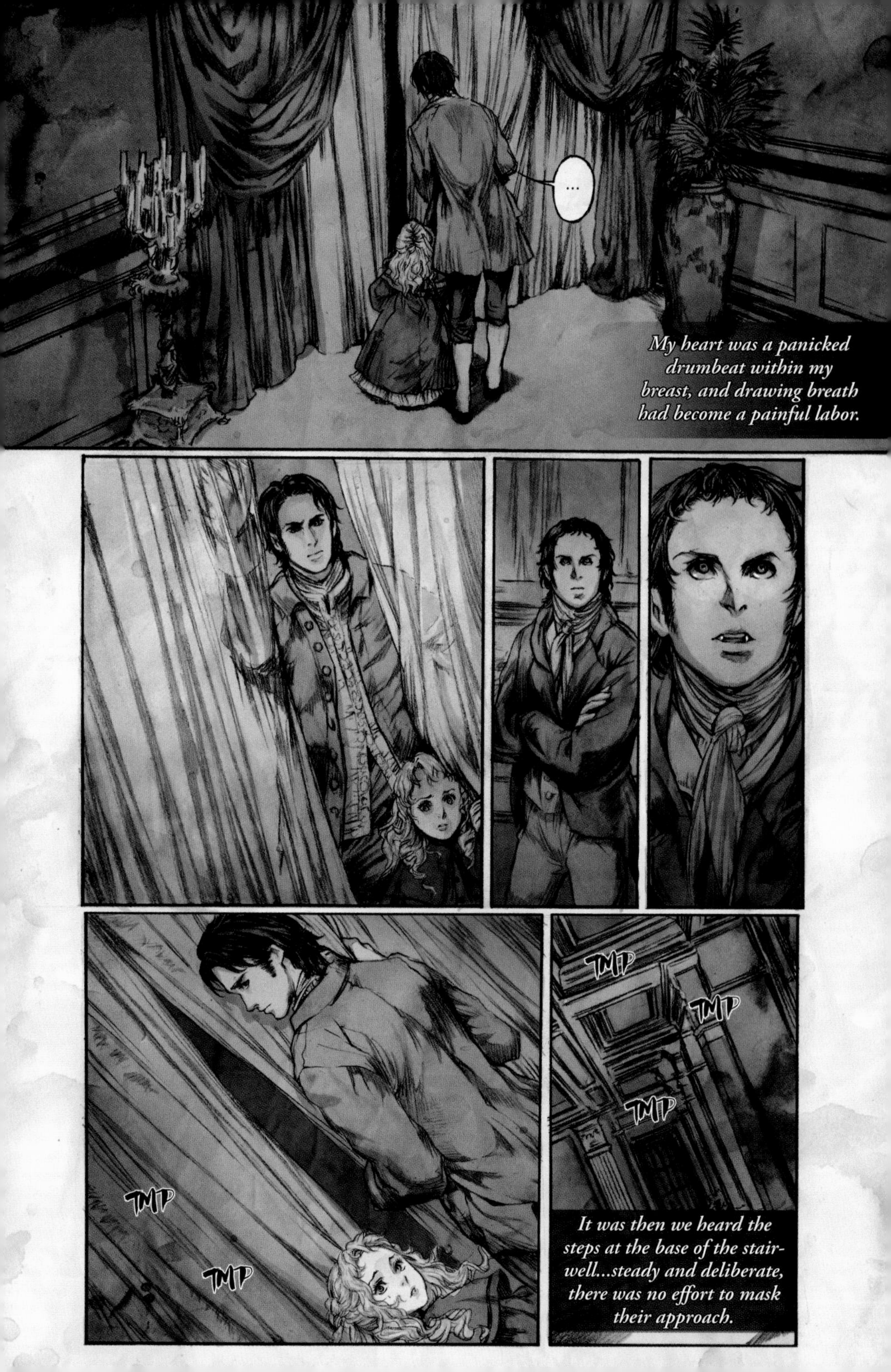
...
My heart was a panicked drumbeat within my breast, and drawing breath had become a painful labor.
TMP
TMP
TMP
TMP
TMP
It was then we heard the steps at the base of the stair-well...steady and deliberate, there was no effort to mask their approach.

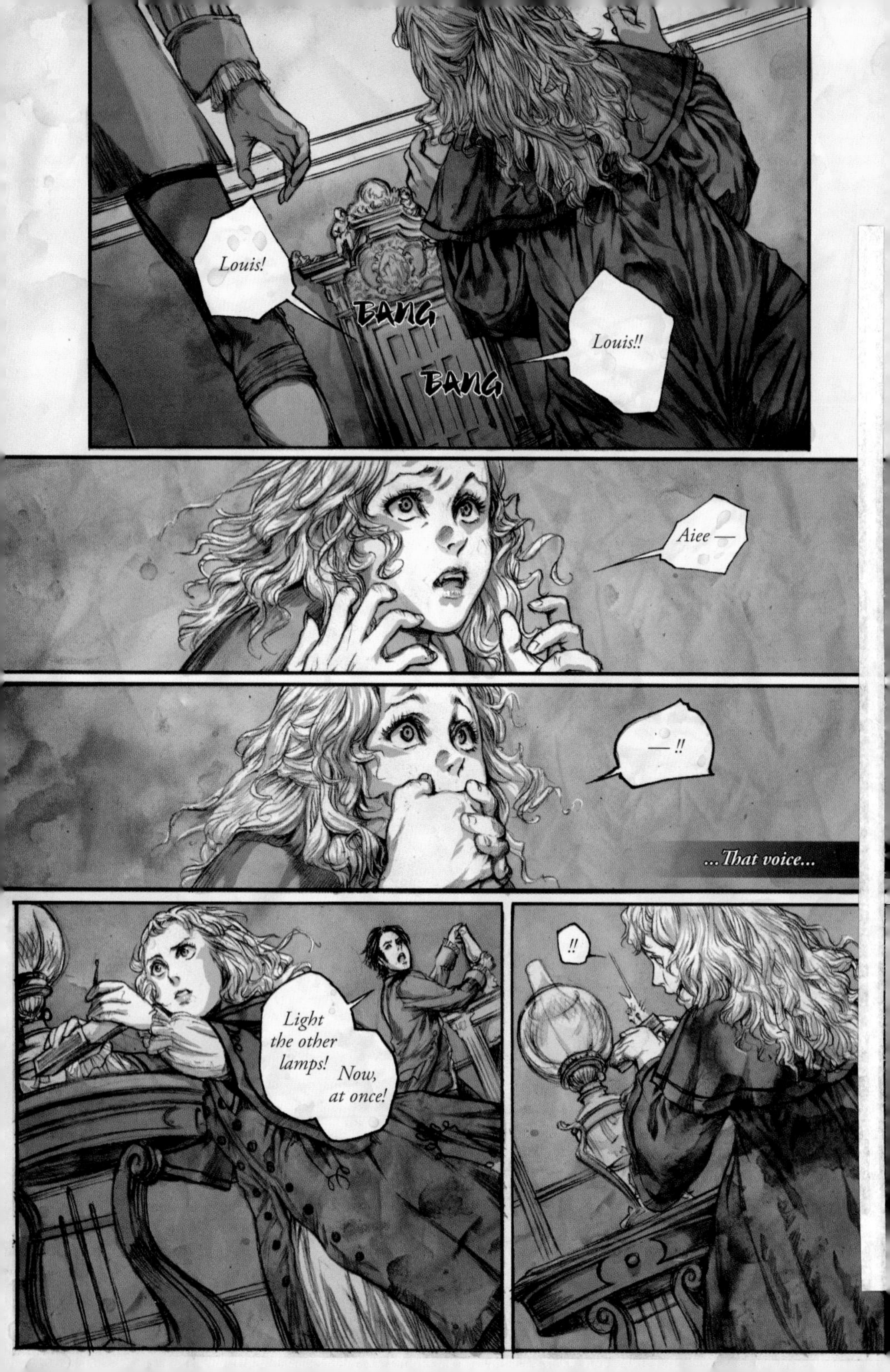
Louis!
BANG
BANG
Louis!!
Aiee —
— !!
...That voice...
Light the other lamps!
Now, at once!
!!

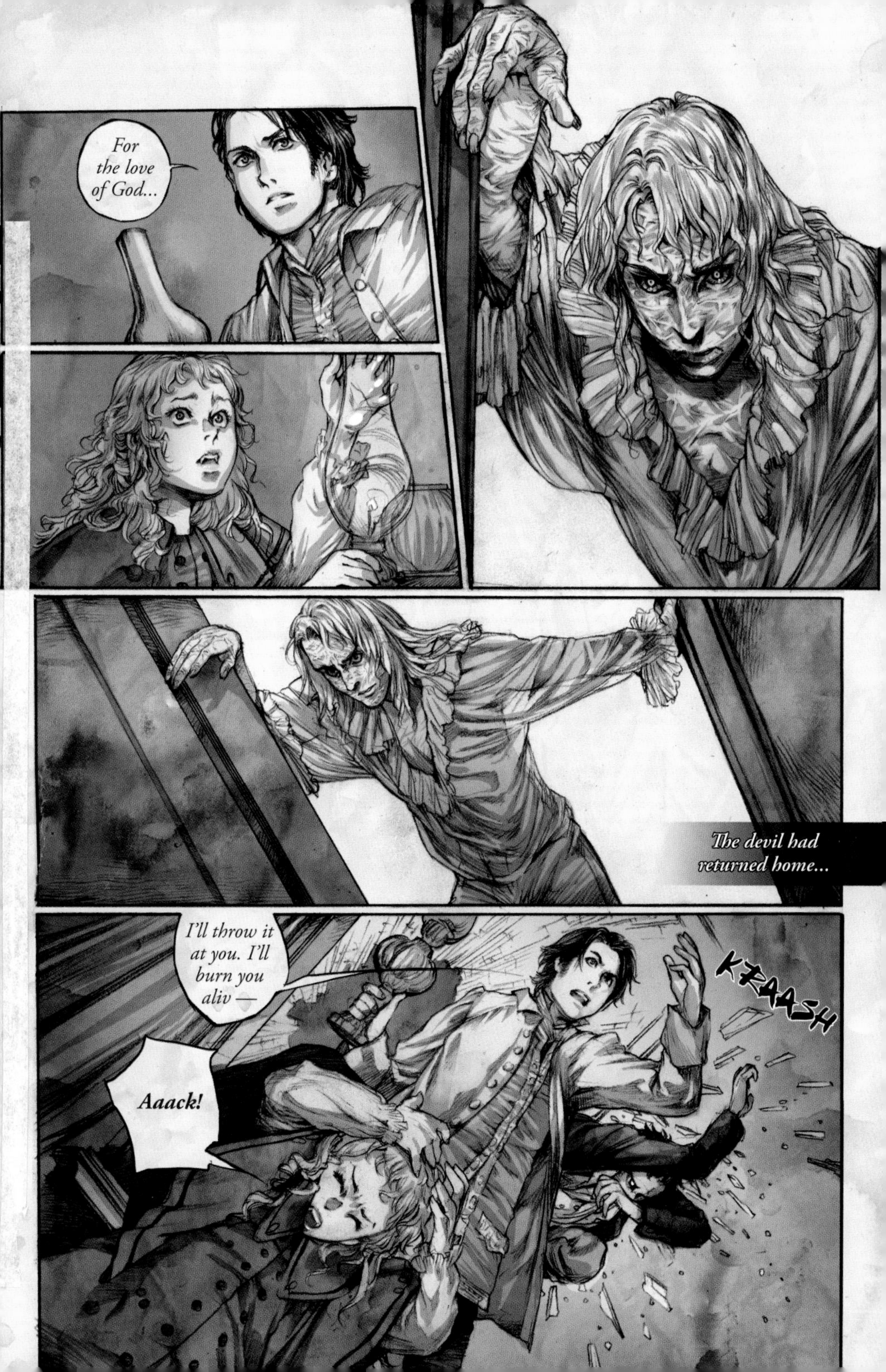
For the love of God...
The devil had returned home...
I'll throw it at you. I'll burn you aliv —
KRAASH
Aaack!

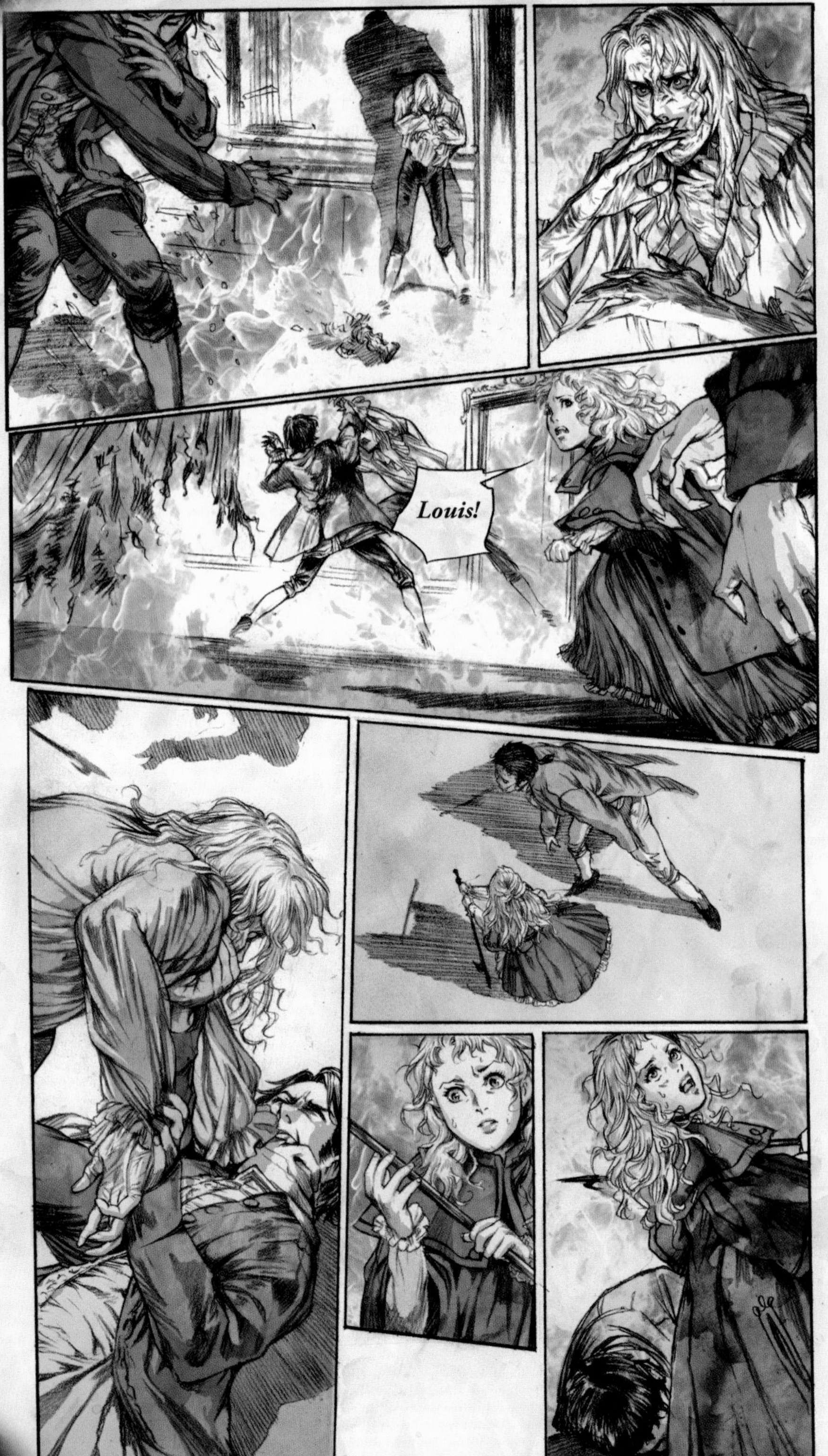
Louis!

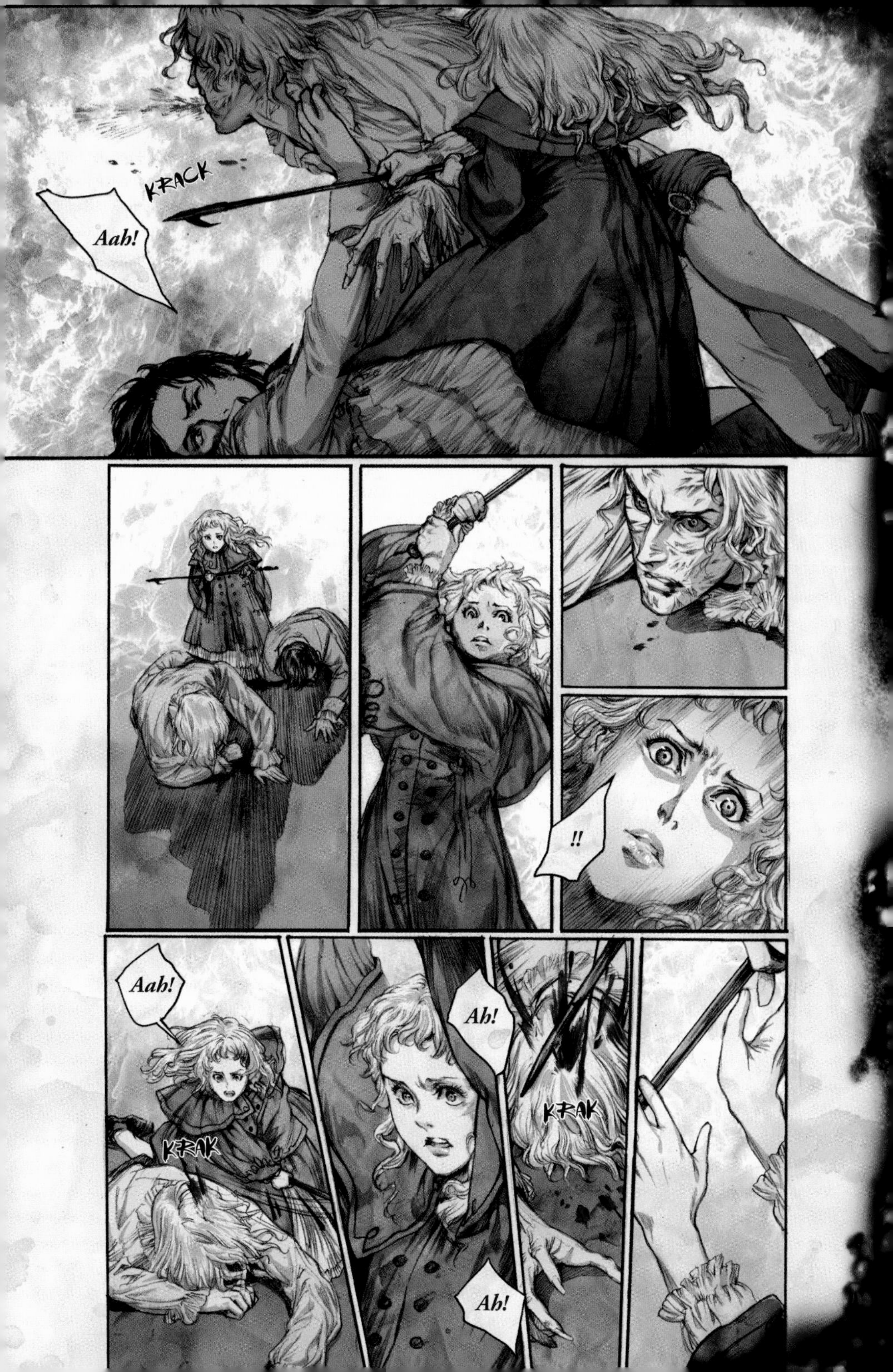
KRACK
Aah!
!!
Aah!
KRAK
Ah!
Ah!
KRAK

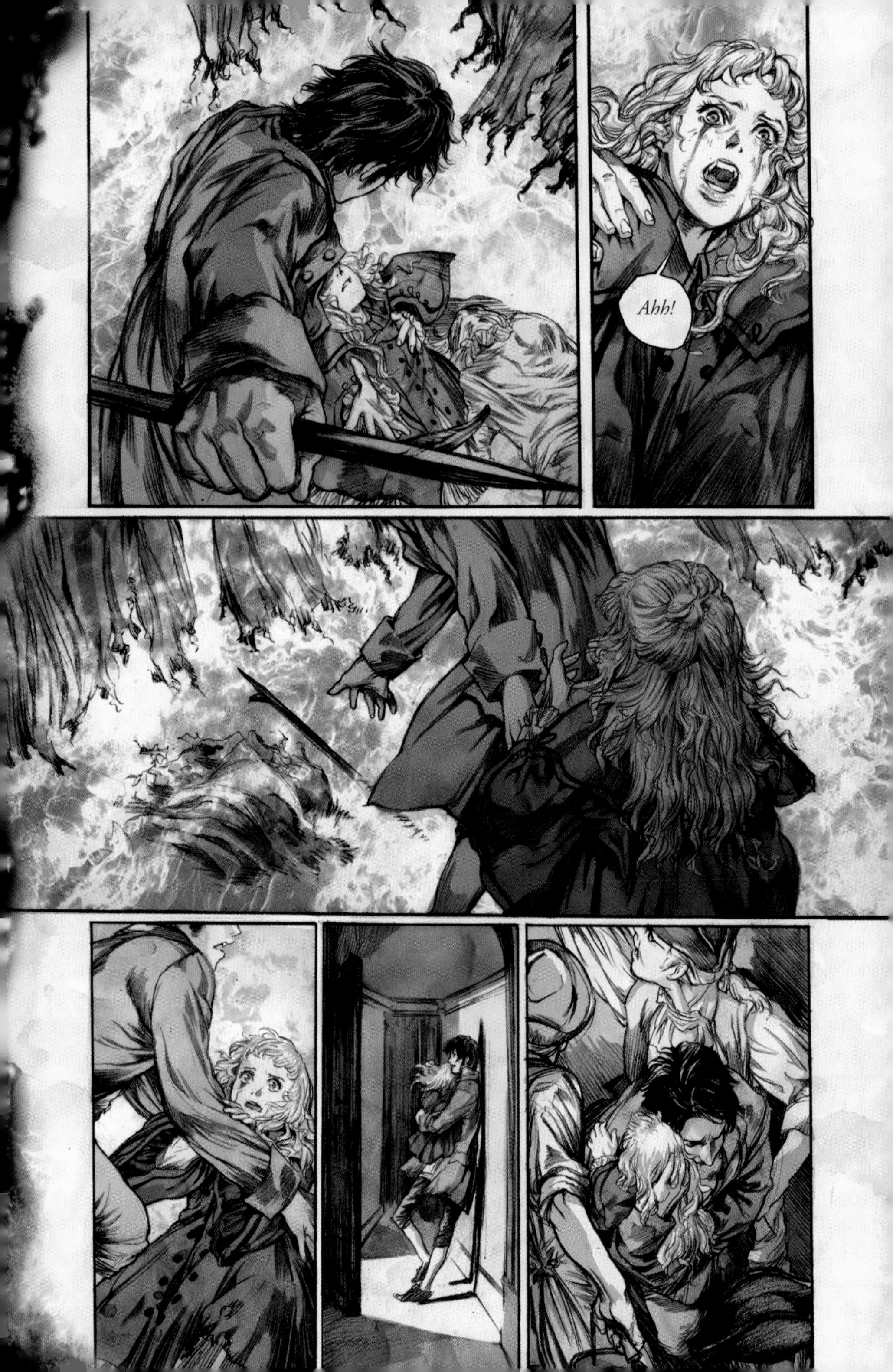
Ahh!

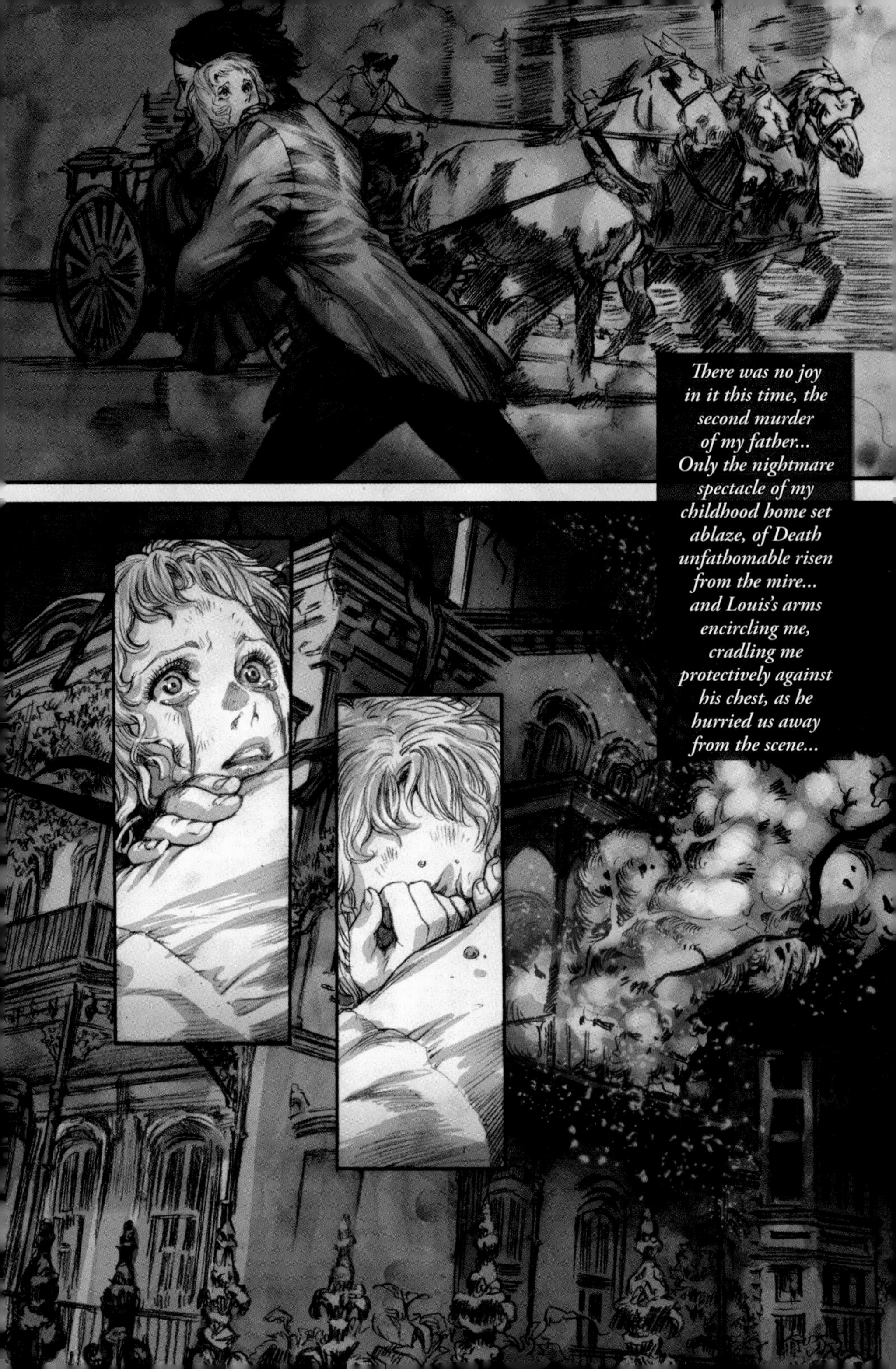
There was no joy in it this time, the second murder of my father... Only the nightmare spectacle of my childhood home set ablaze, of Death unfathomable risen from the mire... and Louis's arms encircling me, cradling me protectively against his chest, as he hurried us away from the scene...

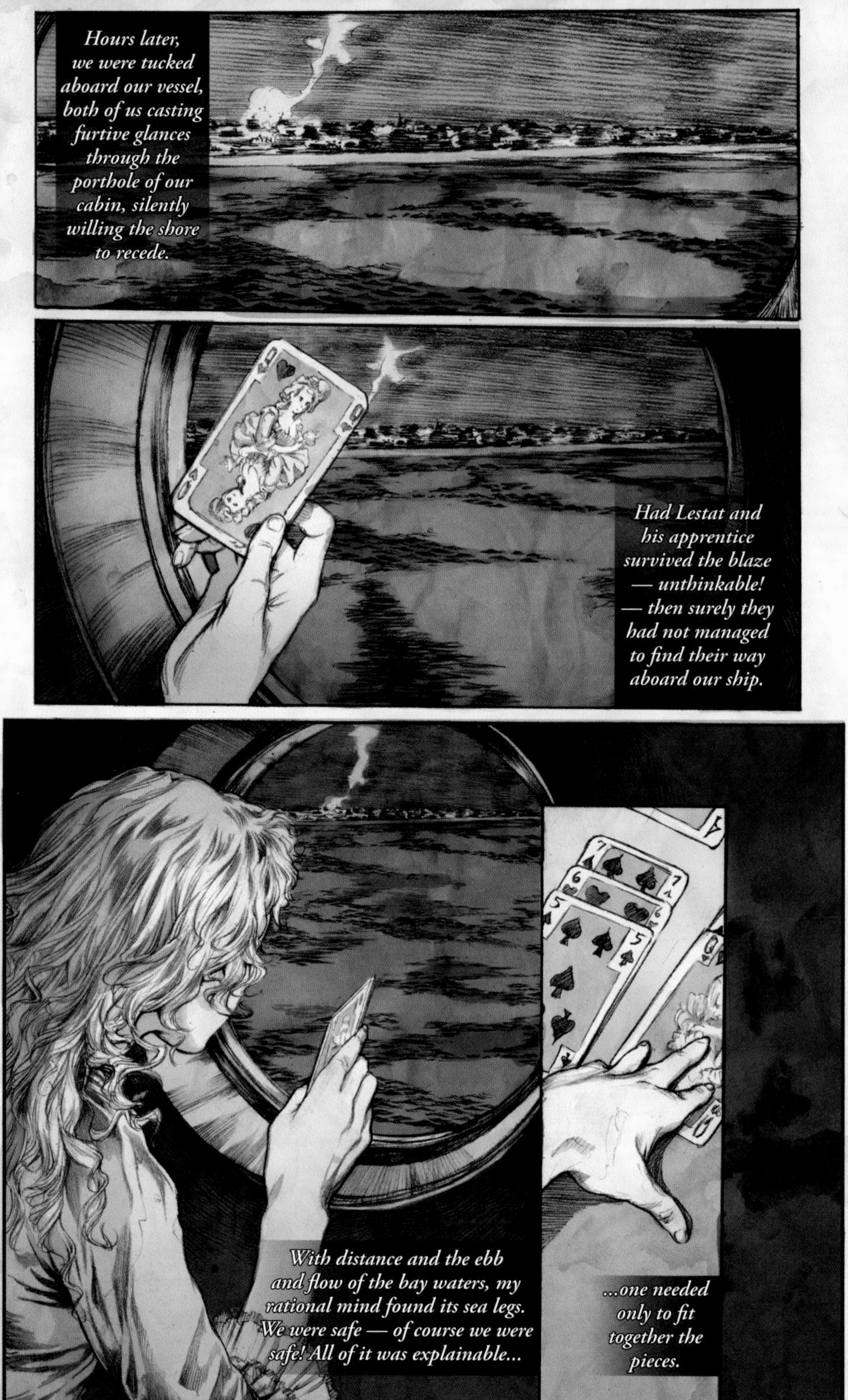
Hours later, we were tucked aboard our vessel, both of us casting furtive glances through the porthole of our cabin, silently willing the shore to recede.
Had Lestat and his apprentice survived the blaze — unthinkable! — then surely they had not managed to find their way aboard our ship.
With distance and the ebb and flow of the bay waters, my rational mind found its sea legs. We were safe — of course we were safe! All of it was explainable...
...one needed only to fit together the pieces.

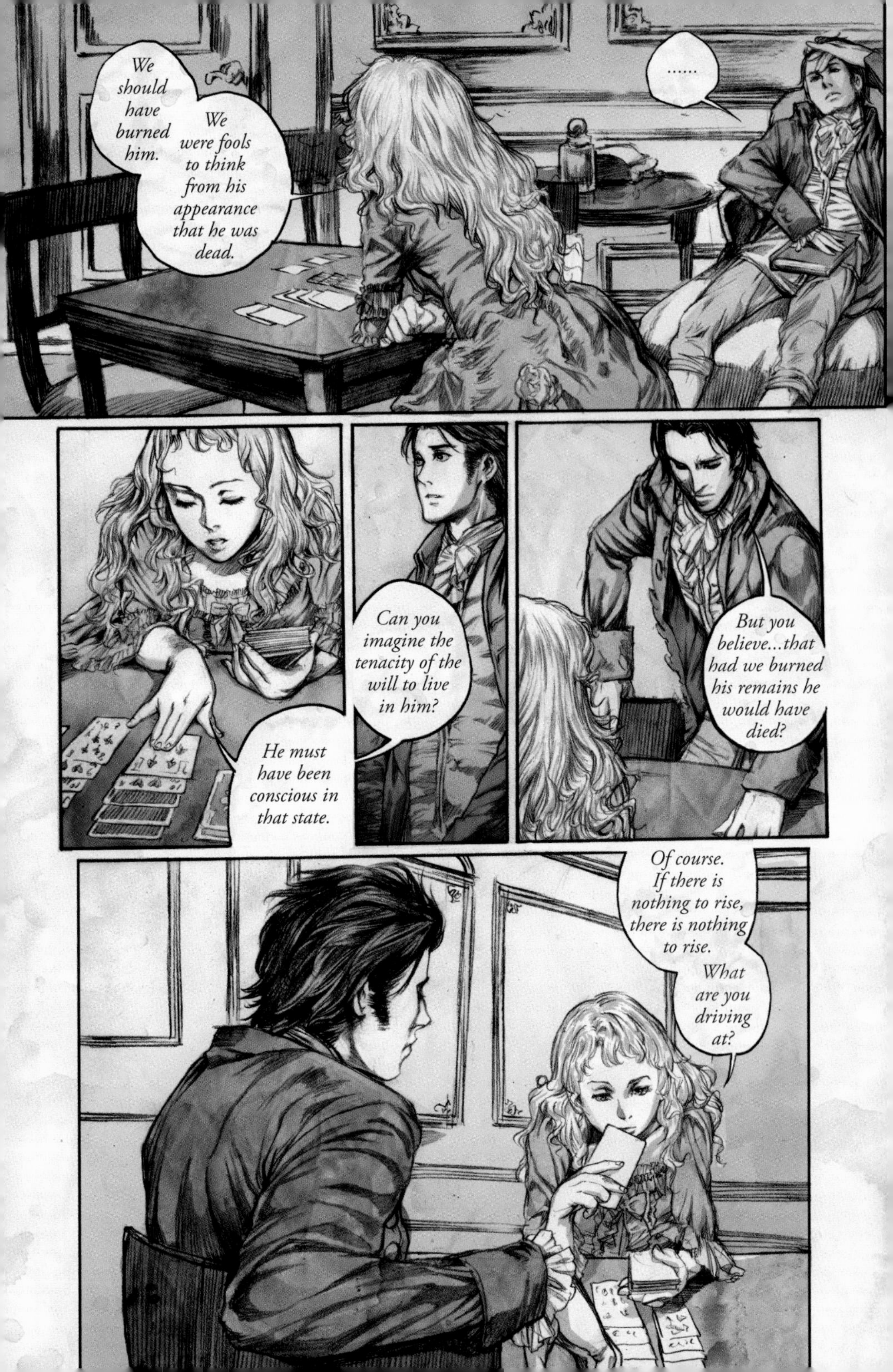
We should have burned him.
We were fools to think from his appearance that he was dead.
......
He must have been conscious in that state.
Can you imagine the tenacity of the will to live in him?
But you believe...that had we burned his remains he would have died?
Of course. If there is nothing to rise, there is nothing to rise.
What are you driving at?

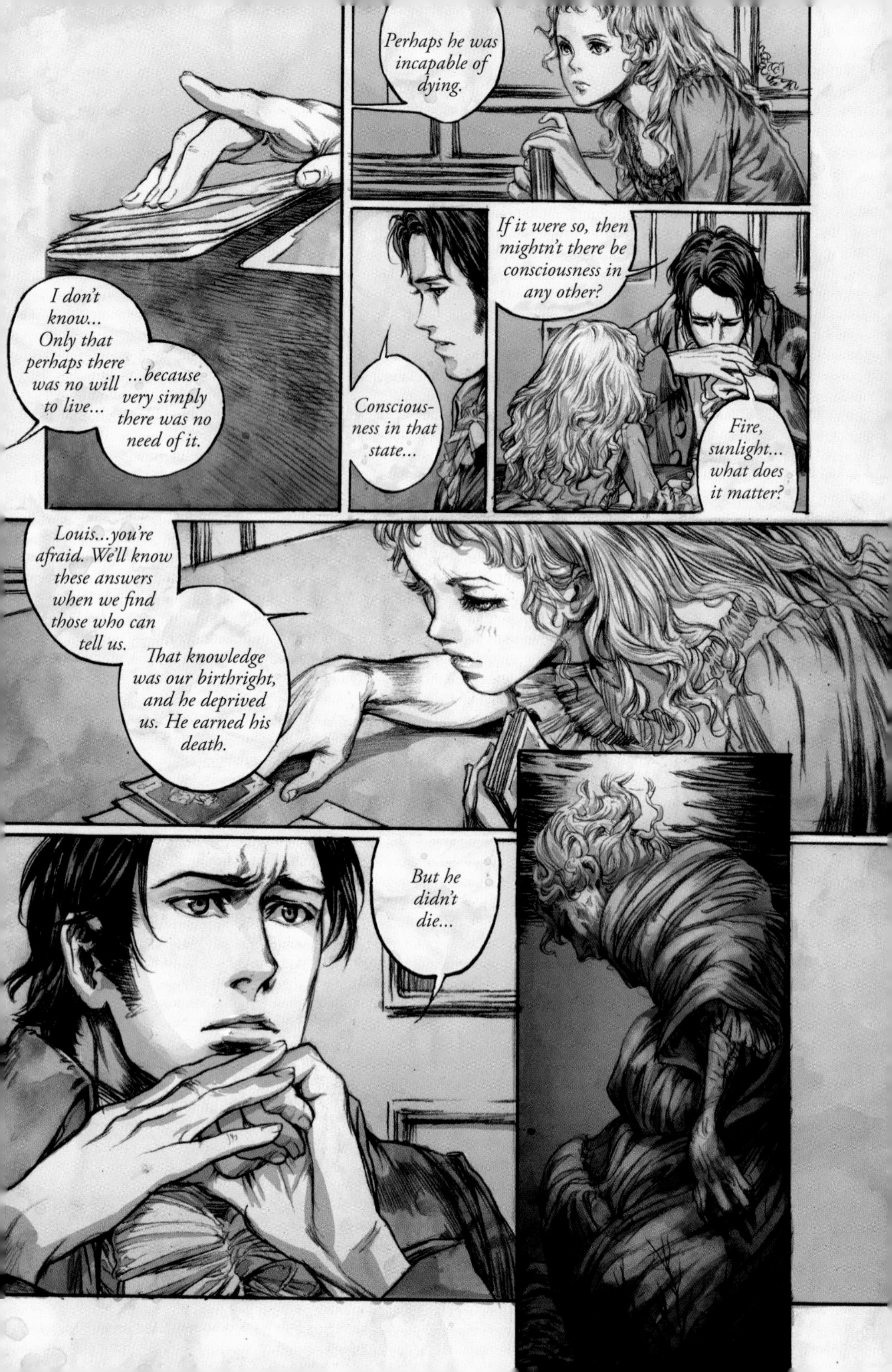
Perhaps he was incapable of dying.
I don't know... Only that perhaps there was no will to live...
...because very simply there was no need of it.
Conscious-ness in that state...
If it were so, then mightn't there be consciousness in any other?
Fire, sunlight... what does it matter?
Louis...you're afraid. We'll know these answers when we find those who can tell us.
That knowledge was our birthright, and he deprived us. He earned his death.
But he didn't die...

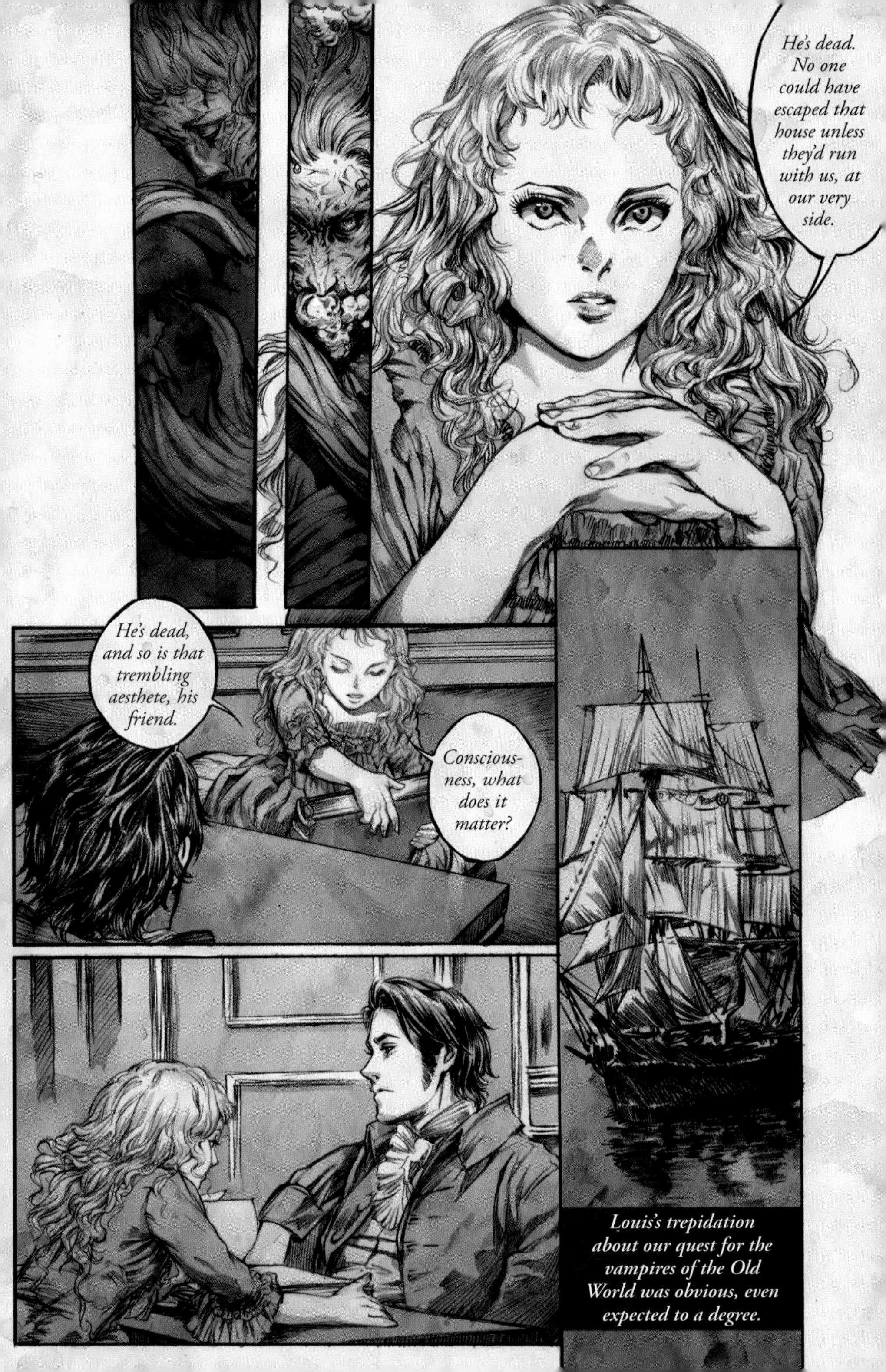
He's dead. No one could have escaped that house unless they'd run with us, at our very side.
He's dead, and so is that trembling aesthete, his friend.
Conscious-ness, what does it matter?
Louis's trepidation about our quest for the vampires of the Old World was obvious, even expected to a degree.

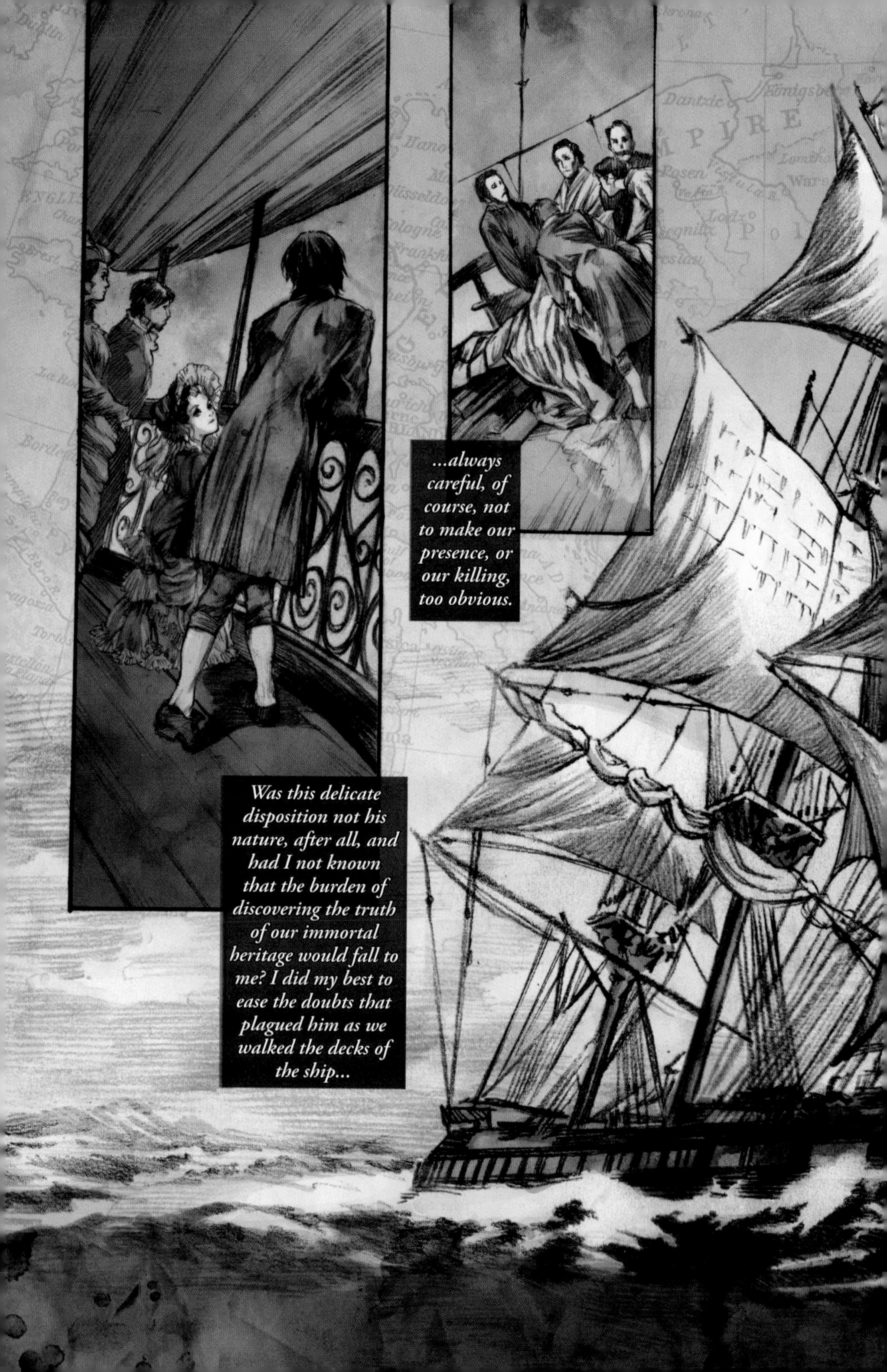
...always careful, of course, not to make our presence, or our killing, too obvious.
Was this delicate disposition not his nature, after all, and had I not known that the burden of discovering the truth of our immortal heritage would fall to me? I did my best to ease the doubts that plagued him as we walked the decks of the ship...

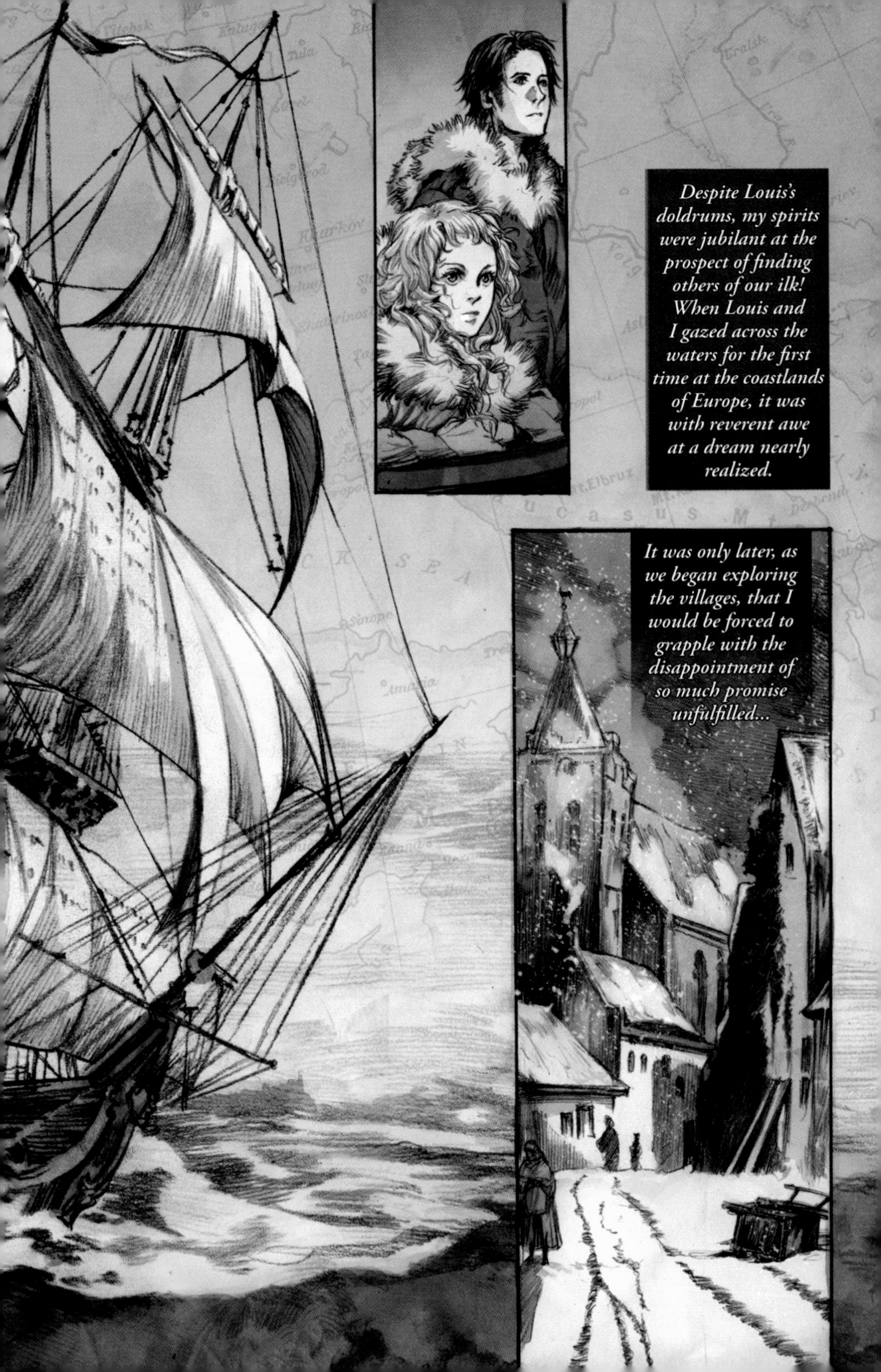
Despite Louis's doldrums, my spirits were jubilant at the prospect of finding others of our ilk! When Louis and I gazed across the waters for the first time at the coastlands of Europe, it was with reverent awe at a dream nearly realized.
It was only later, as we began exploring the villages, that I would be forced to grapple with the disappointment of so much promise unfulfilled...

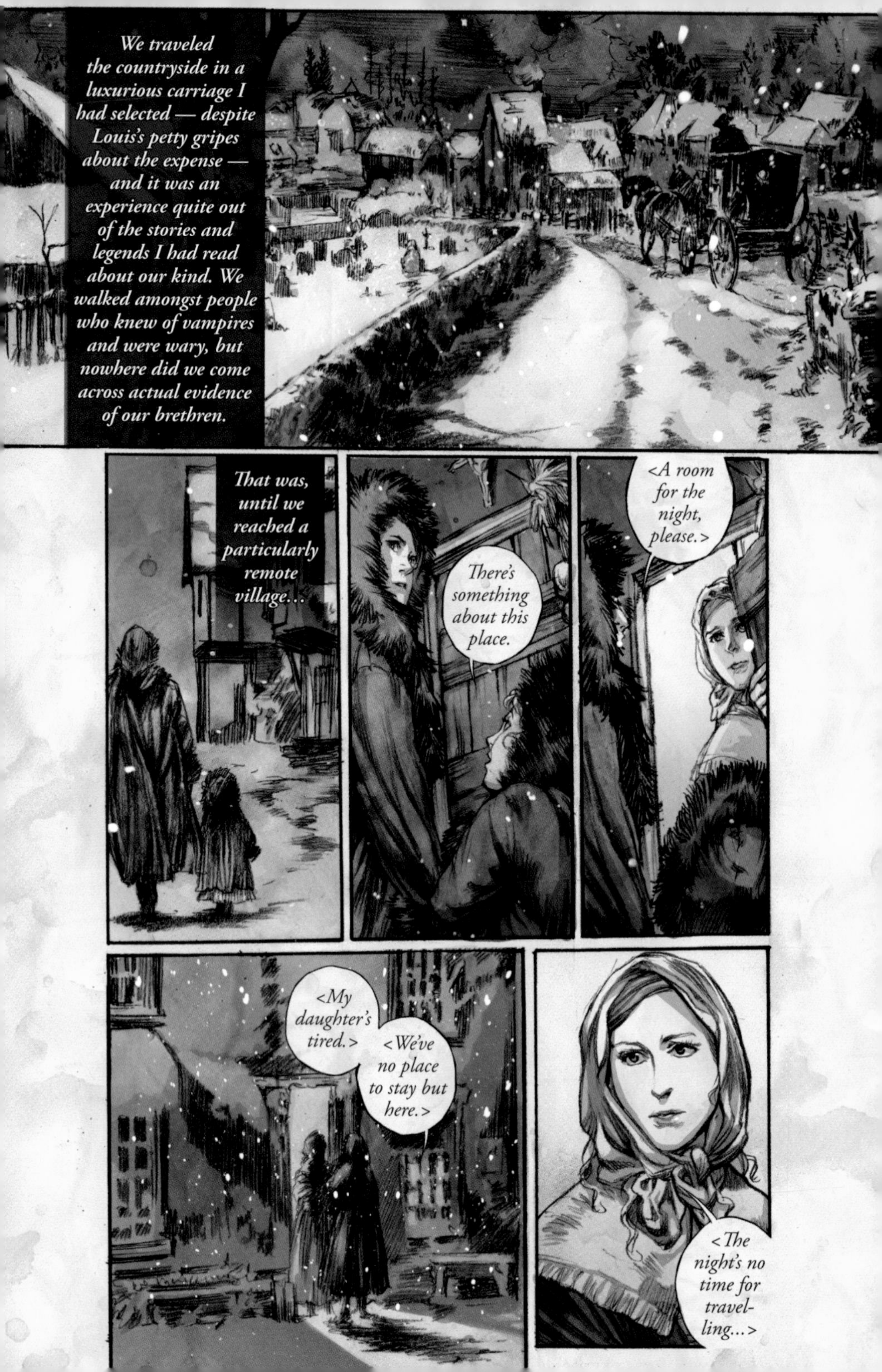
We traveled the countryside in a luxurious carriage I had selected — despite Louis's petty gripes about the expense — and it was an experience quite out of the stories and legends I had read about our kind. We walked amongst people who knew of vampires and were wary, but nowhere did we come across actual evidence of our brethren.
That was, until we reached a particularly remote village…
There's something about this place.
<A room for the night, please.>
<My daughter's tired.>
<We've no place to stay but here.>
<The night's no time for travel-ling…>

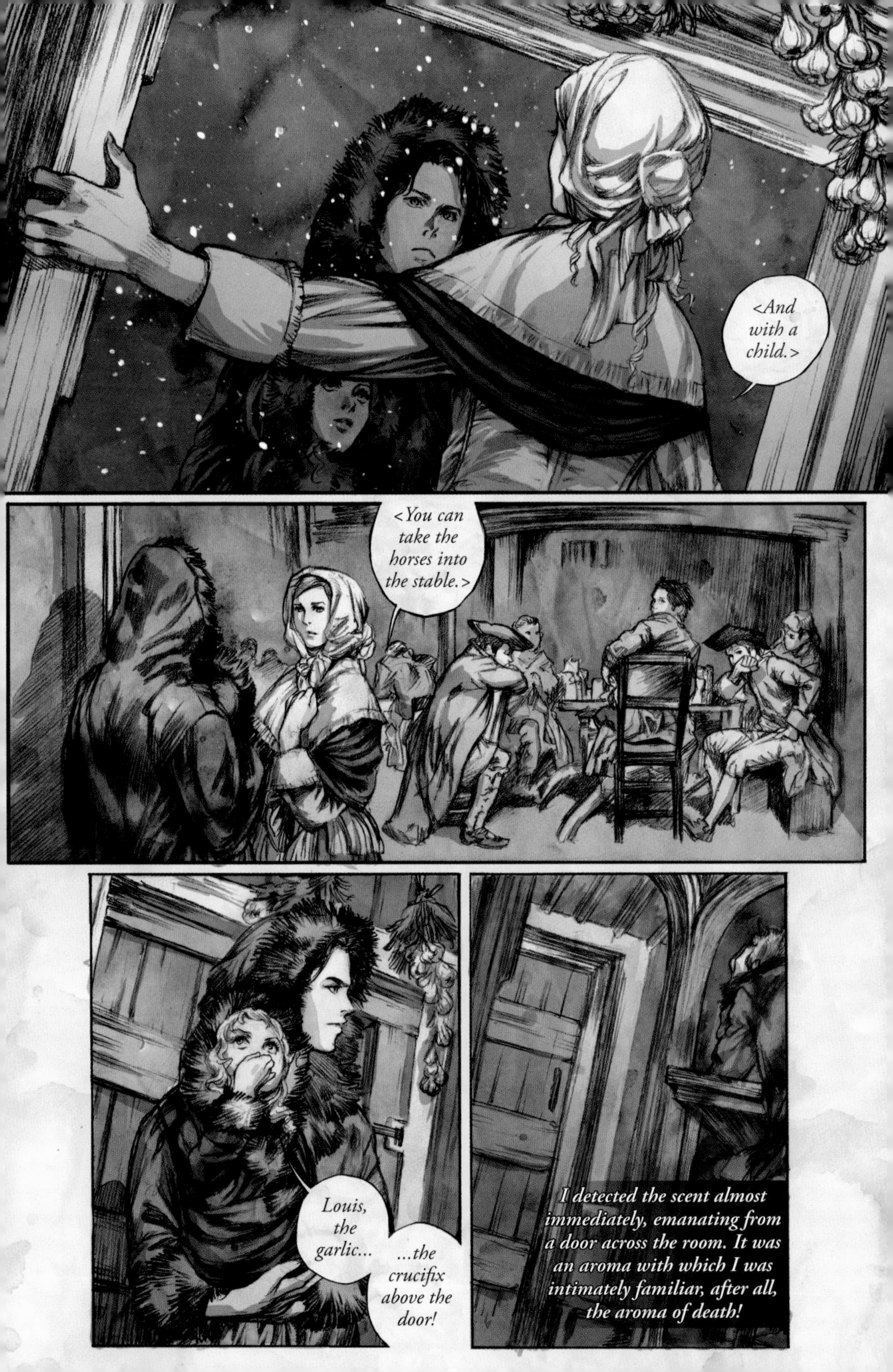
<And with a child.>
<You can take the horses into the stable.>
Louis, the garlic...
...the crucifix above the door!
I detected the scent almost immediately, emanating from a door across the room. It was an aroma with which I was intimately familiar, after all, the aroma of death!

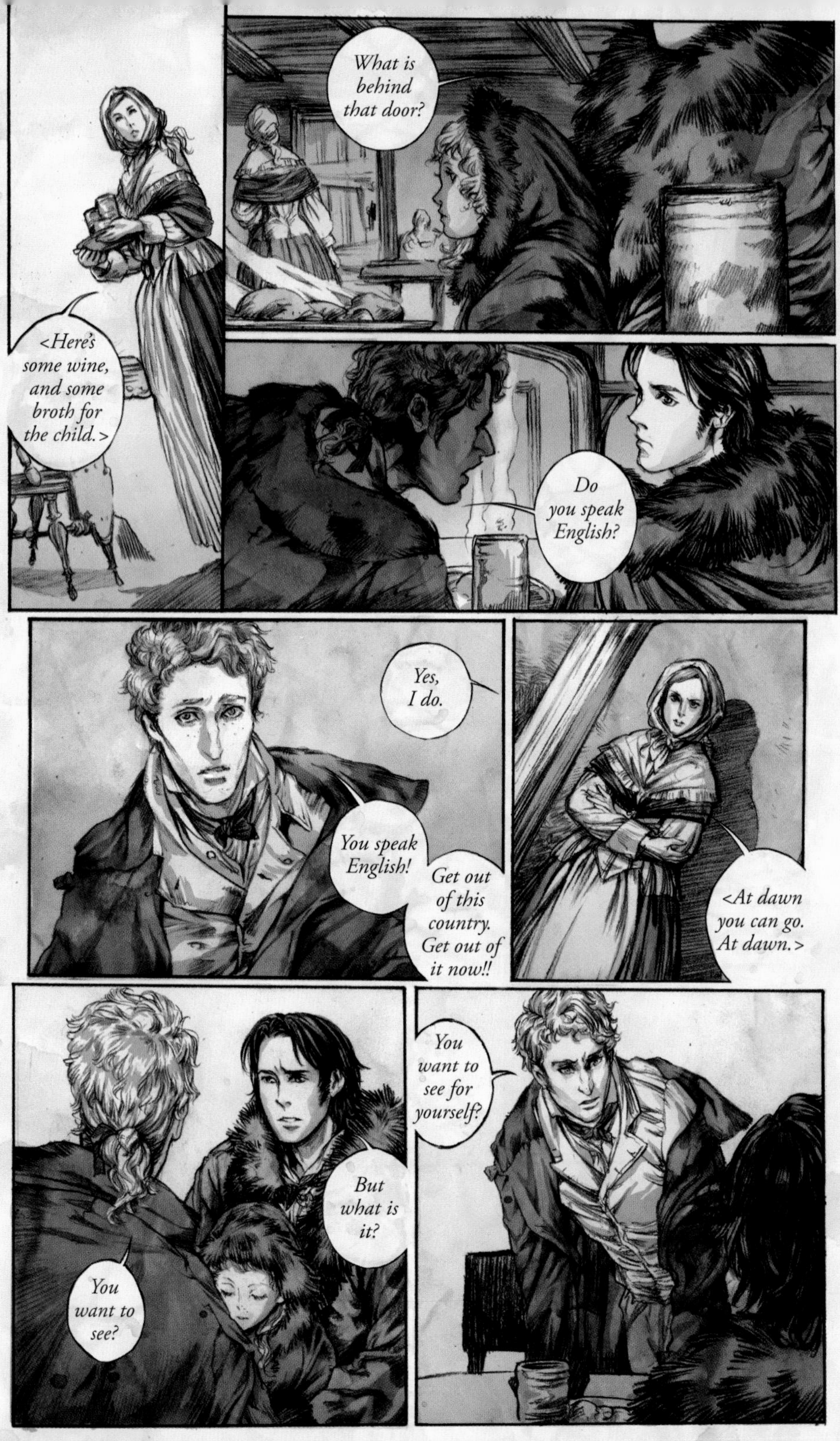

<Here's some wine, and some broth for the child.>
What is behind that door?
Do you speak English?
Yes, I do.
You speak English!
Get out of this country. Get out of it now!!
<At dawn you can go. At dawn.>
You want to see?
But what is it?
You want to see for yourself?

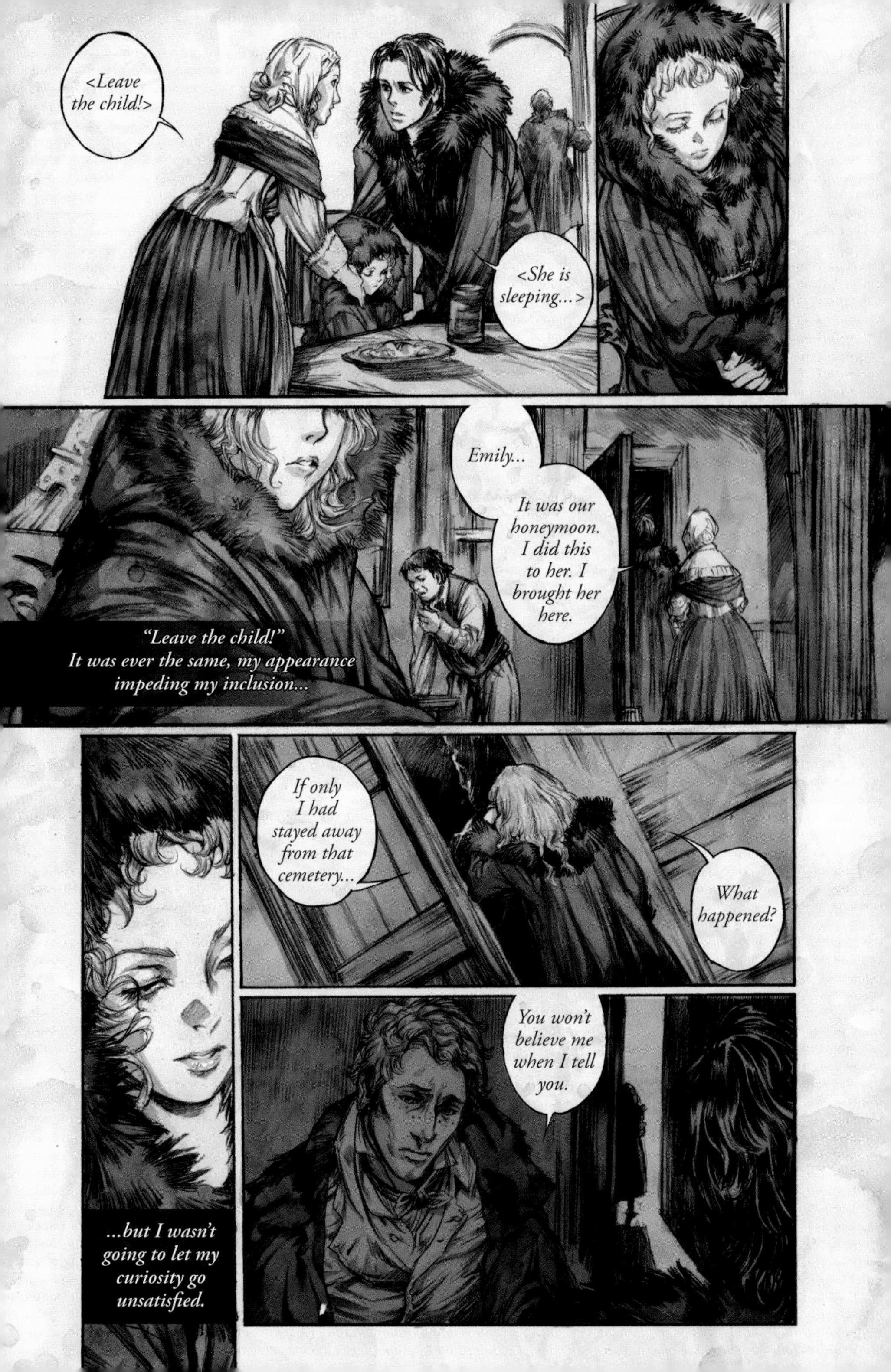
<Leave the child!>
<She is sleeping...>
Emily...
It was our honeymoon. I did this to her. I brought her here.
"Leave the child!" It was ever the same, my appearance impeding my inclusion...
If only I had stayed away from that cemetery...
What happened?
You won't believe me when I tell you.
...but I wasn't going to let my curiosity go unsatisfied.

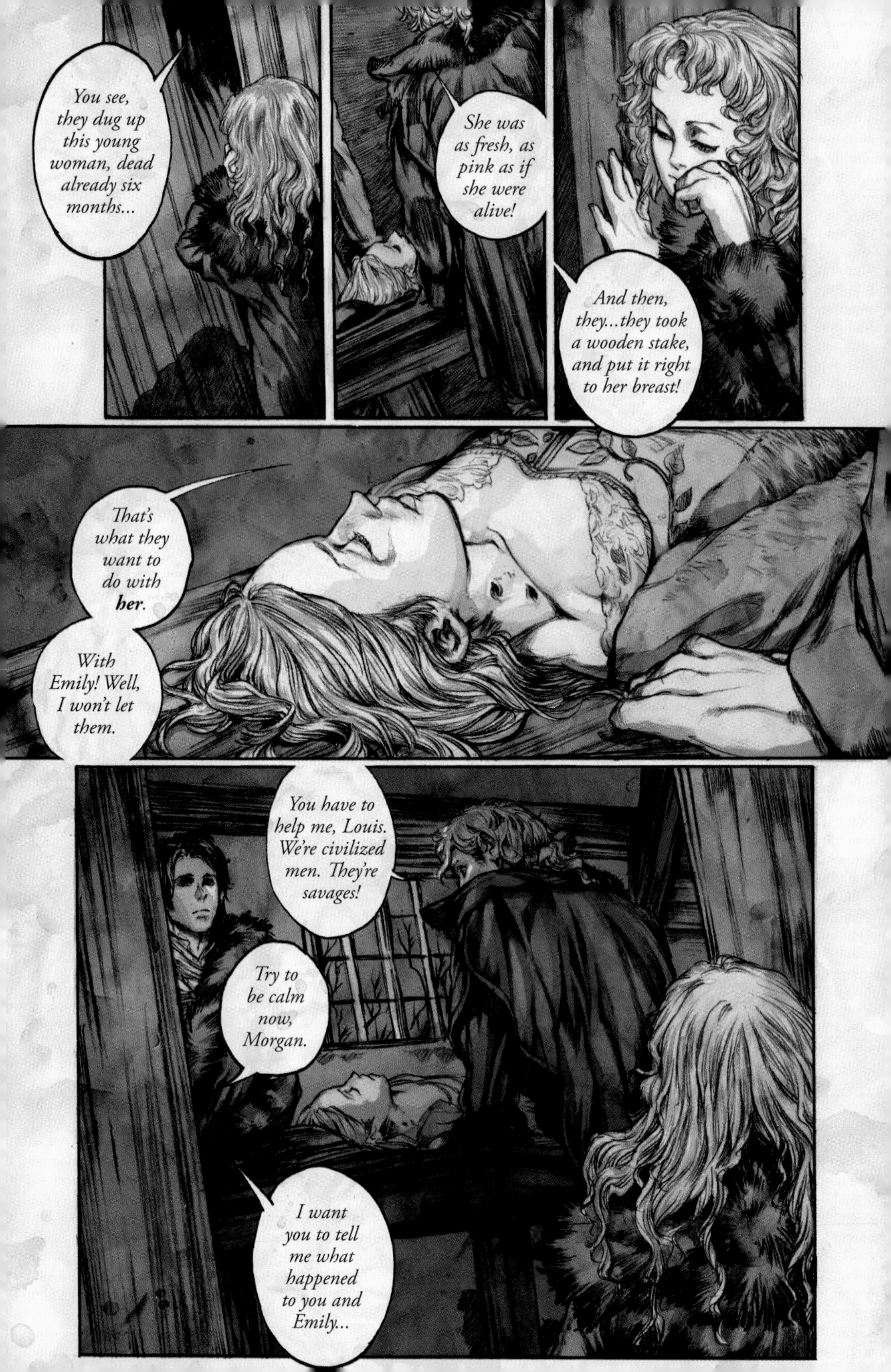
You see, they dug up this young woman, dead already six months...
She was as fresh, as pink as if she were alive!
And then, they...they took a wooden stake, and put it right to her breast!
That's what they want to do with **her**.
With Emily! Well, I won't let them.
You have to help me, Louis. We're civilized men. They're savages!
Try to be calm now, Morgan.
I want you to tell me what happened to you and Emily...

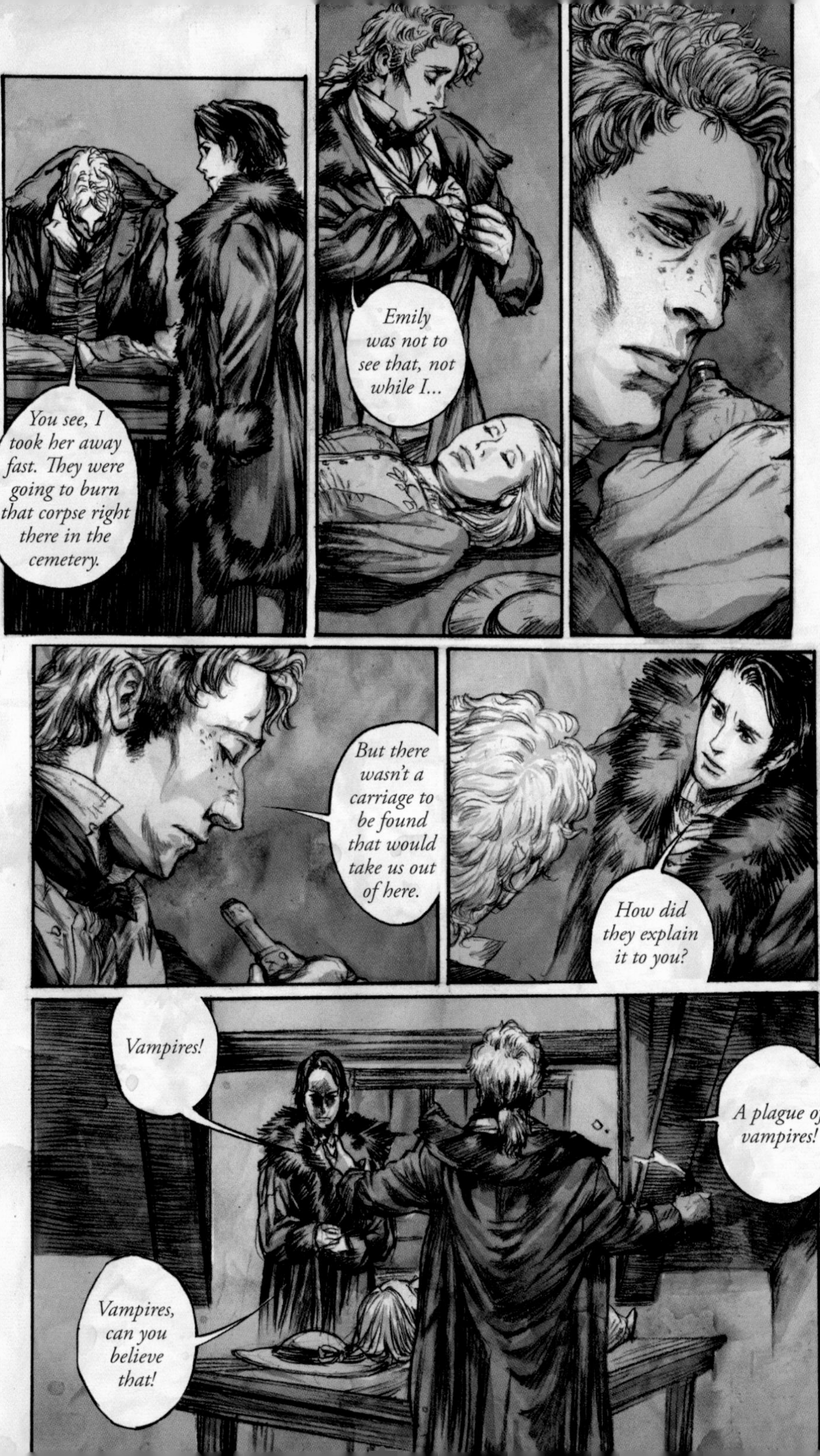
You see, I took her away fast. They were going to burn that corpse right there in the cemetery.
Emily was not to see that, not while I...
But there wasn't a carriage to be found that would take us out of here.
How did they explain it to you?
Vampires!
A plague of vampires!
Vampires, can you believe that!

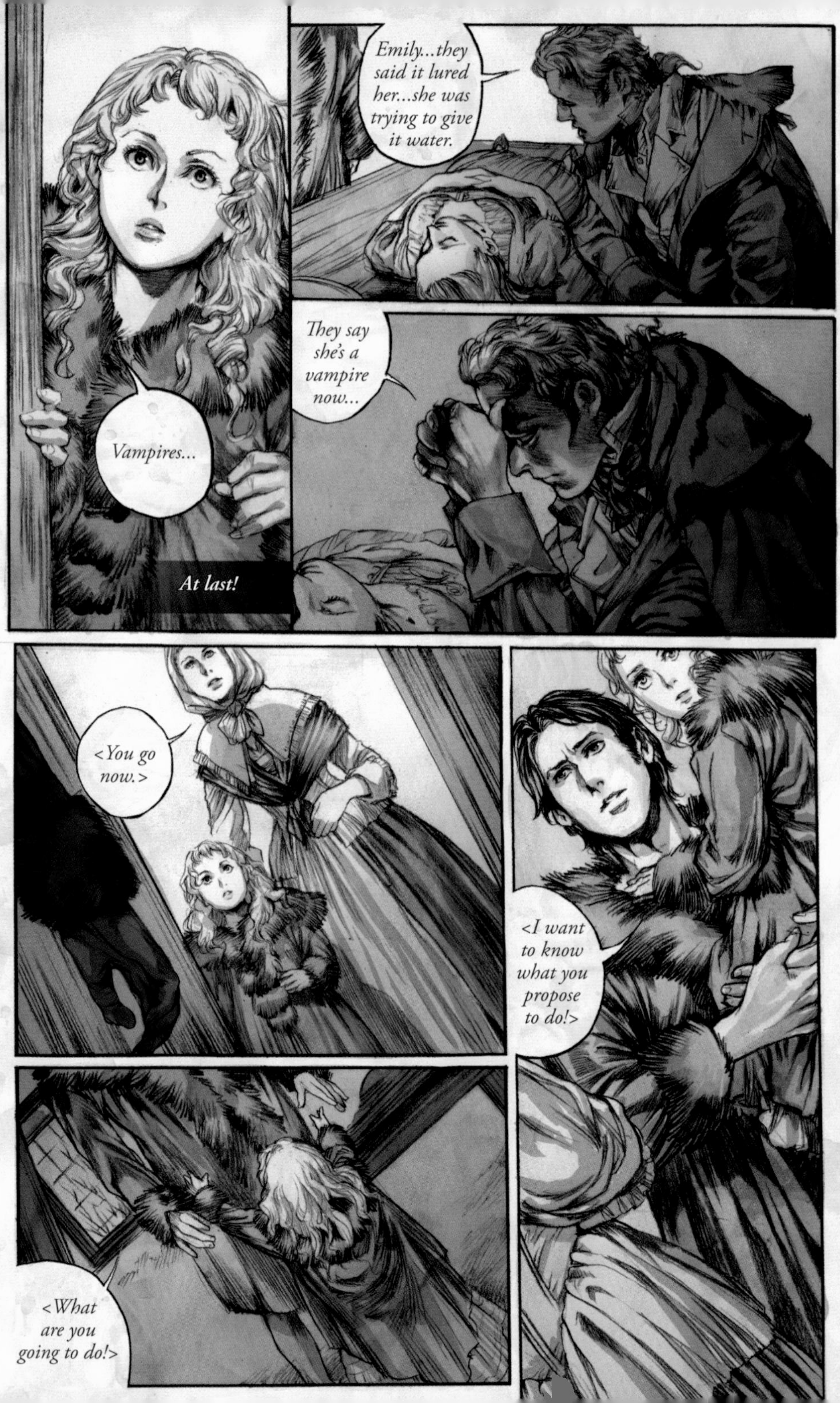
Emily...they said it lured her...she was trying to give it water.
Vampires...
They say she's a vampire now...
At last!
<You go now.>
<I want to know what you propose to do!>
<What are you going to do!>

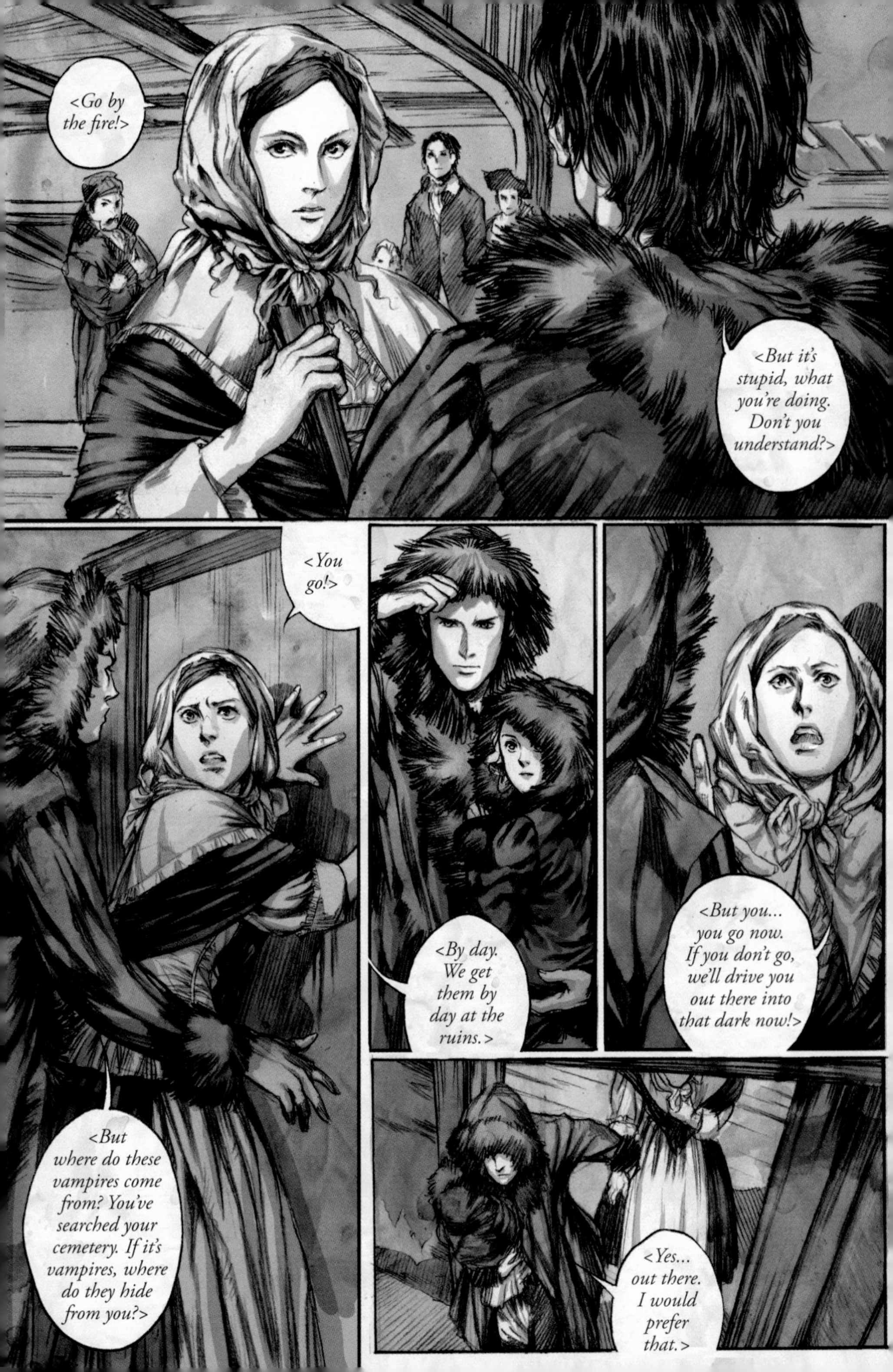
<Go by the fire!>
<But it's stupid, what you're doing. Don't you understand?>
<You go!>
<But where do these vampires come from? You've searched your cemetery. If it's vampires, where do they hide from you?>
<By day. We get them by day at the ruins.>
<But you... you go now. If you don't go, we'll drive you out there into that dark now!>
<Yes... out there. I would prefer that.>

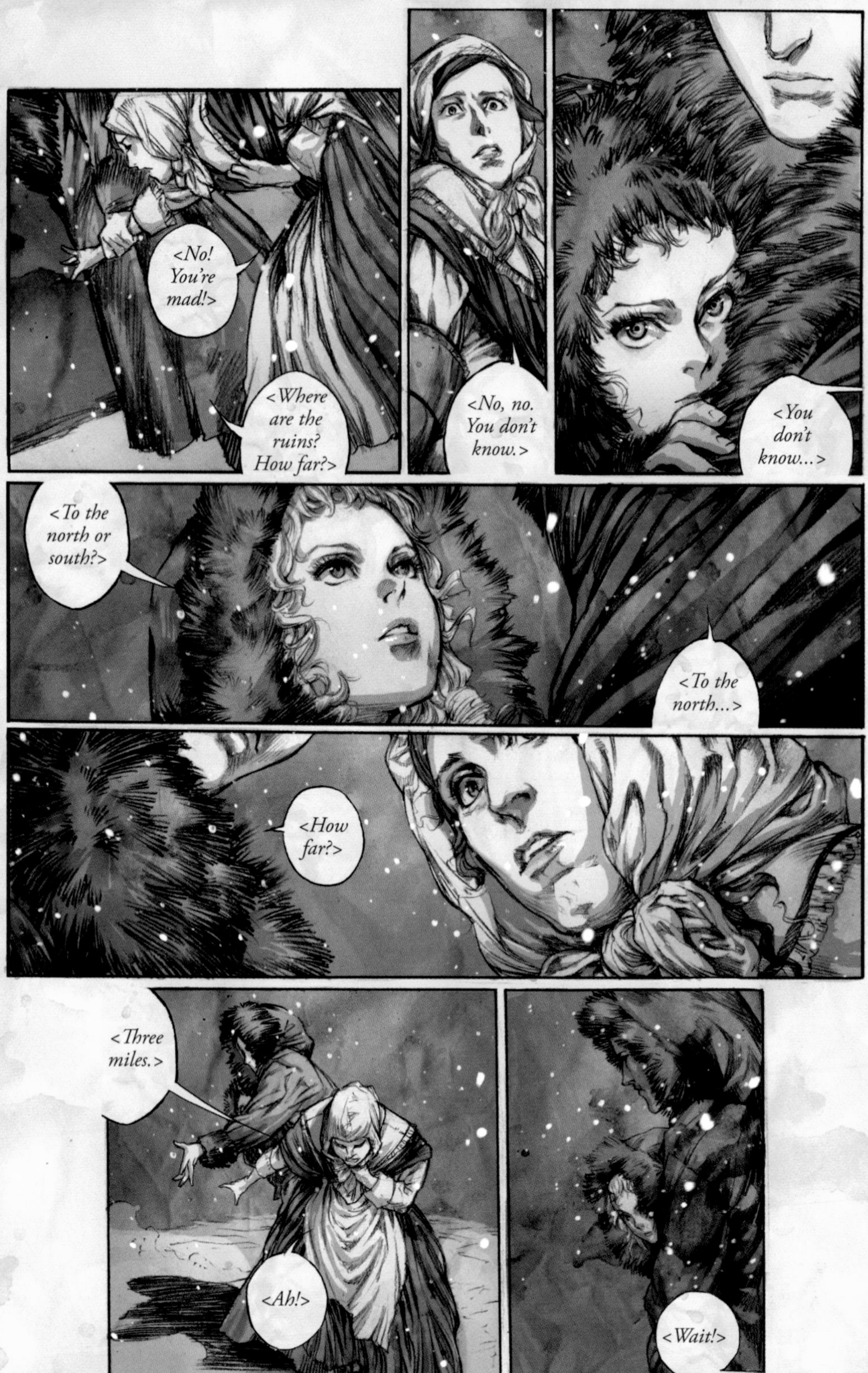

<No! You're mad!>
<Where are the ruins? How far?>
<No, no. You don't know.>
<You don't know...>
<To the north or south?>
<To the north...>
<How far?>
<Three miles.>
<Ah!>
<Wait!>

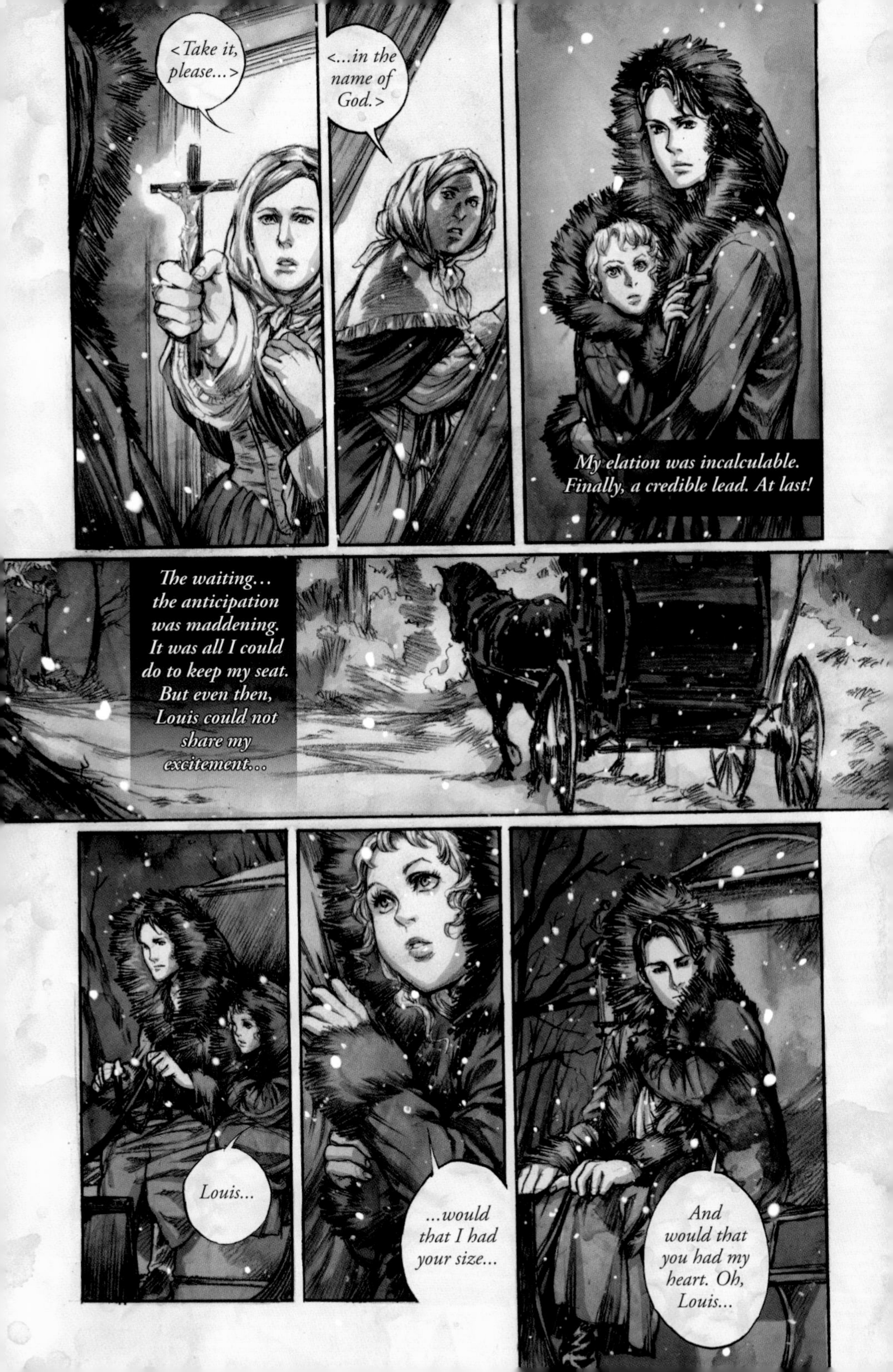
<Take it, please...>
<...in the name of God.>
My elation was incalculable. Finally, a credible lead. At last!
The waiting... the anticipation was maddening. It was all I could do to keep my seat. But even then, Louis could not share my excitement...
Louis...
...would that I had your size...
And would that you had my heart. Oh, Louis...

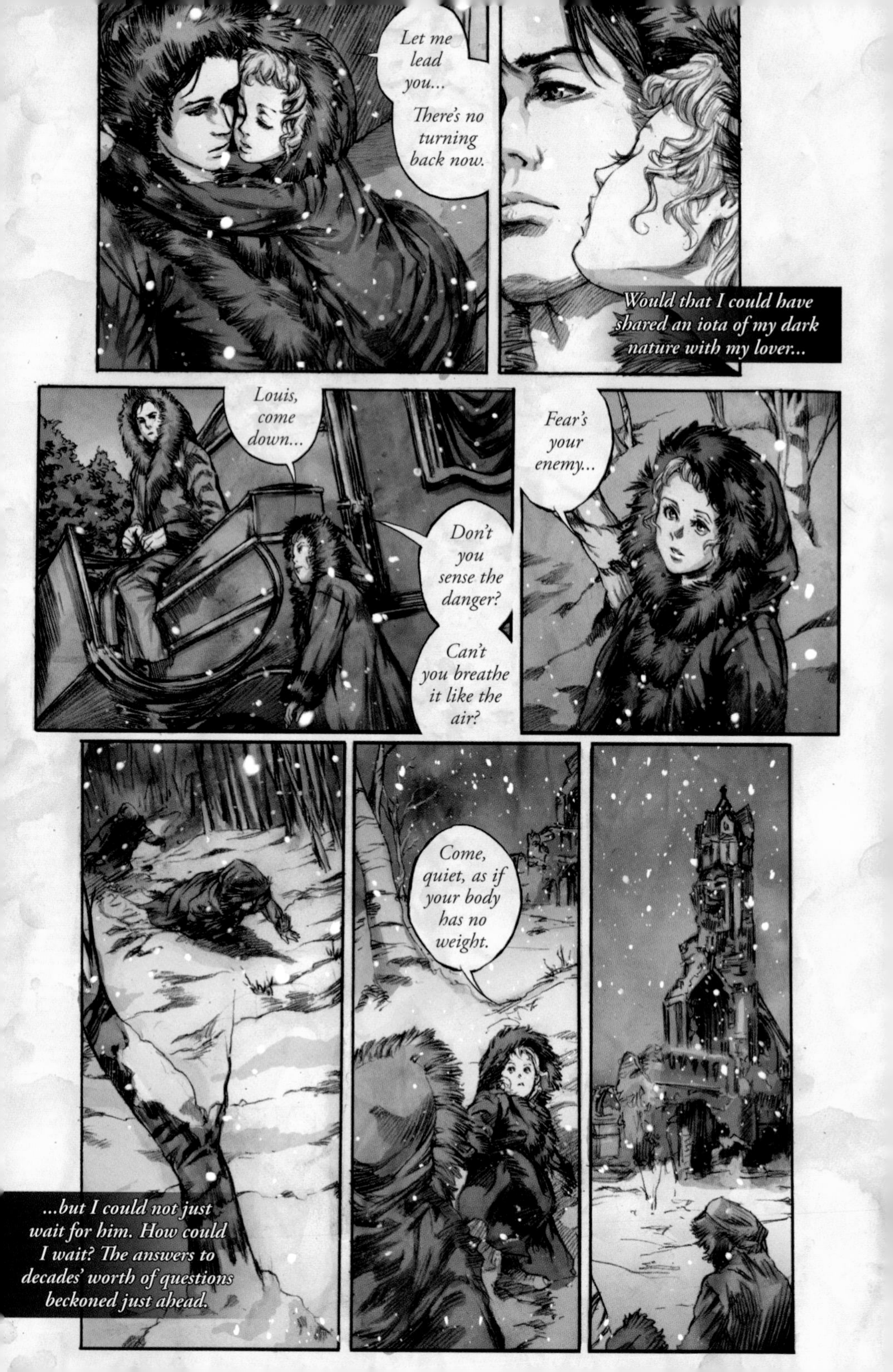
Let me lead you...
There's no turning back now.
Would that I could have shared an iota of my dark nature with my lover...
Louis, come down...
Don't you sense the danger?
Can't you breathe it like the air?
Fear's your enemy...
Come, quiet, as if your body has no weight.
...but I could not just wait for him. How could I wait? The answers to decades' worth of questions beckoned just ahead.

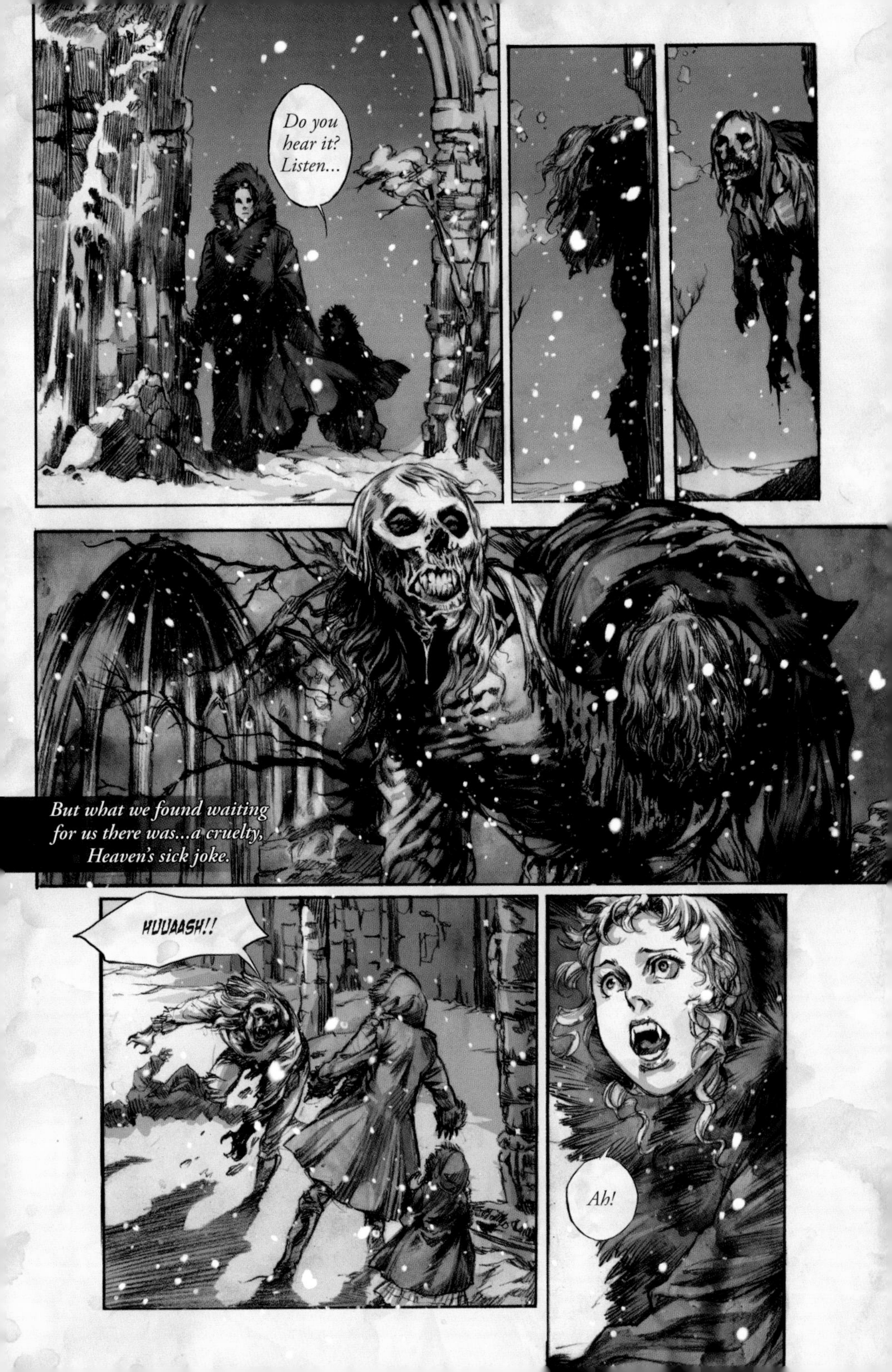
Do you hear it? Listen...
But what we found waiting for us there was...a cruelty, Heaven's sick joke.
HUUAASH!!
Ah!

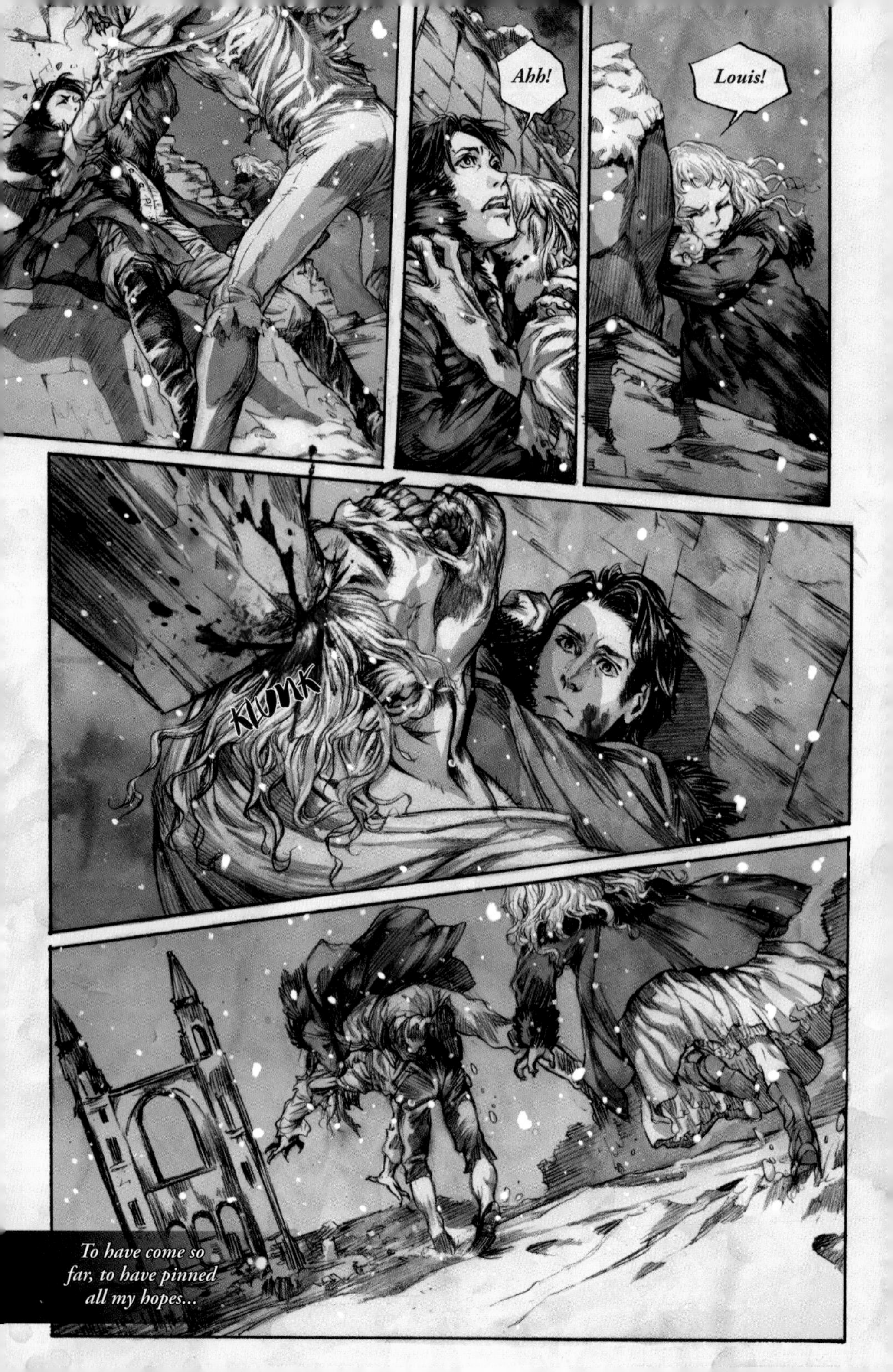
Ahh!
Louis!
KLUNK
To have come so far, to have pinned all my hopes...

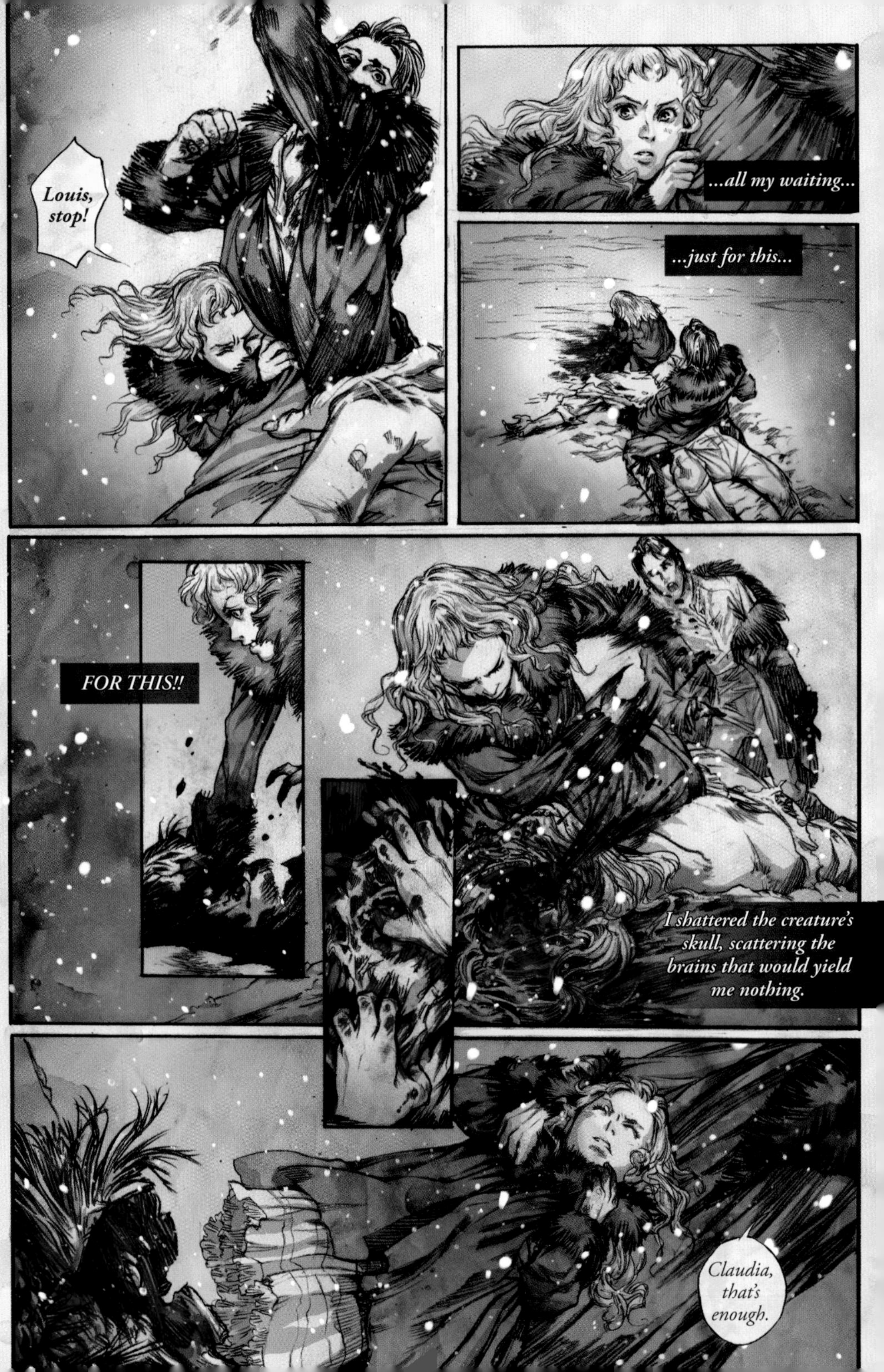
Louis, stop!
...all my waiting...
...just for this...
FOR THIS!!
I shattered the creature's skull, scattering the brains that would yield me nothing.
Claudia, that's enough.

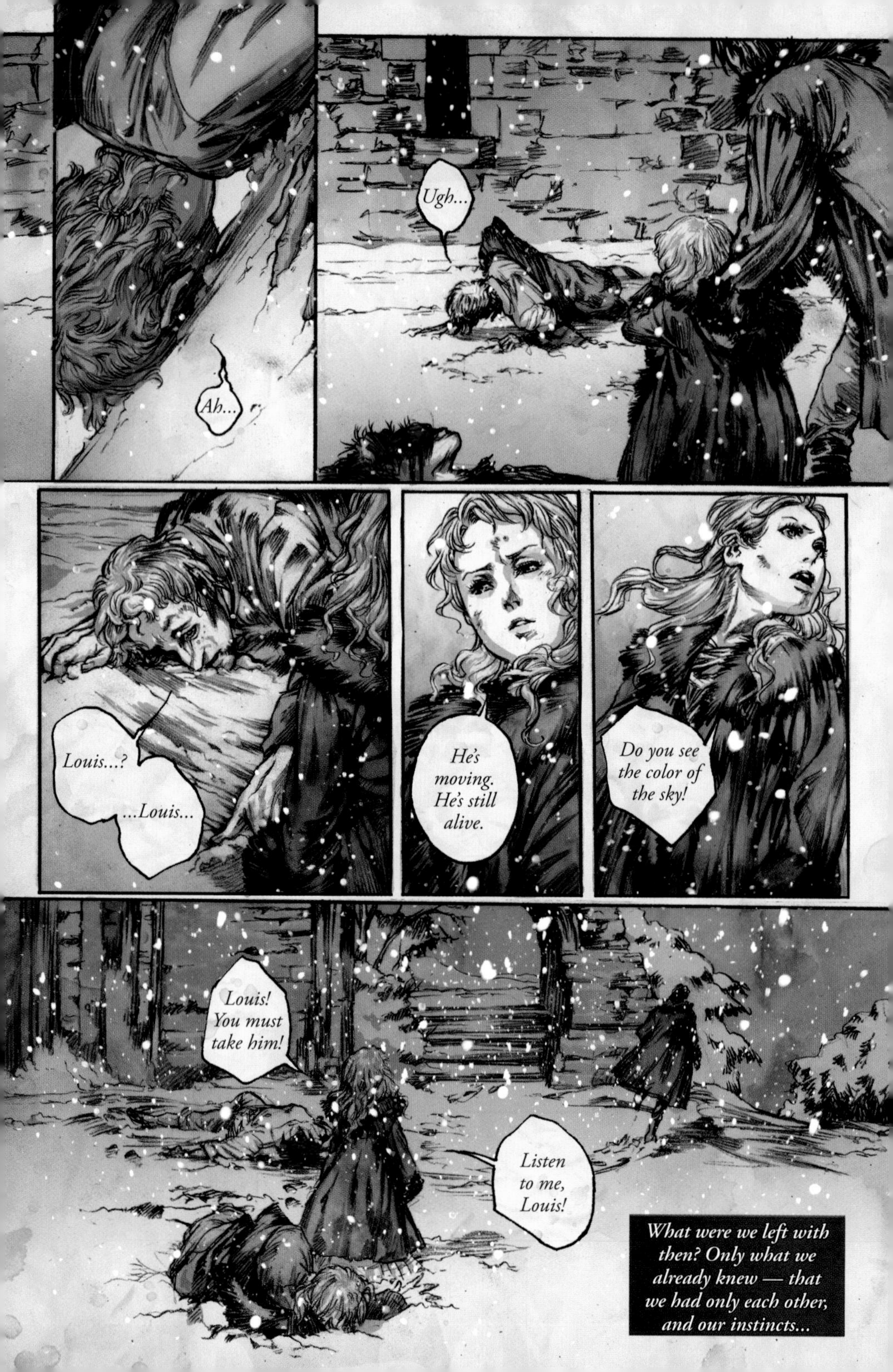

Ah...
Ugh...
Louis...?
...Louis...
He's moving. He's still alive.
Do you see the color of the sky!
Louis! You must take him!
Listen to me, Louis!
What were we left with then? Only what we already knew — that we had only each other, and our instincts...

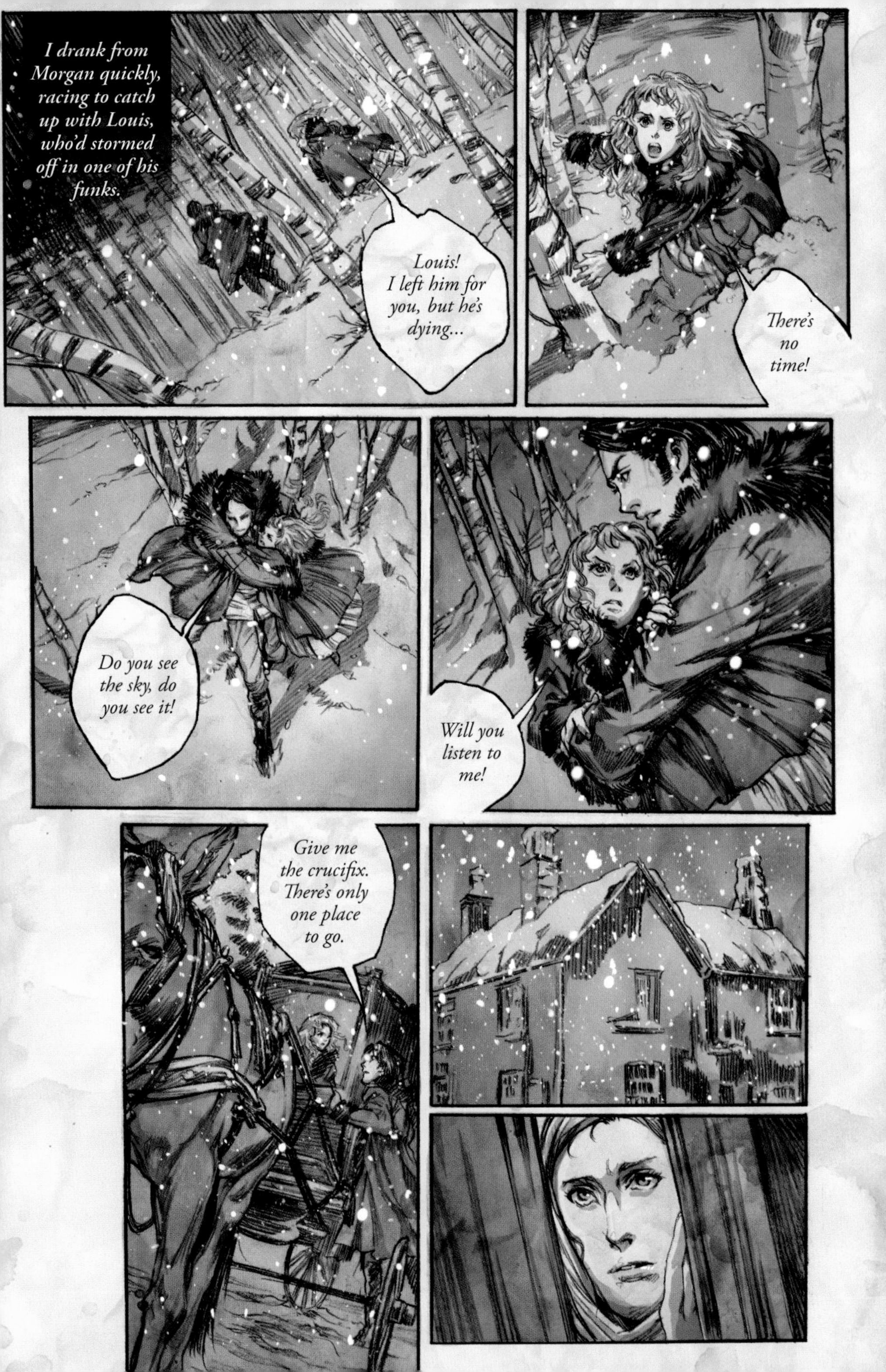
I drank from Morgan quickly, racing to catch up with Louis, who'd stormed off in one of his funks.
Louis! I left him for you, but he's dying...
There's no time!
Do you see the sky, do you see it!
Will you listen to me!
Give me the crucifix. There's only one place to go.

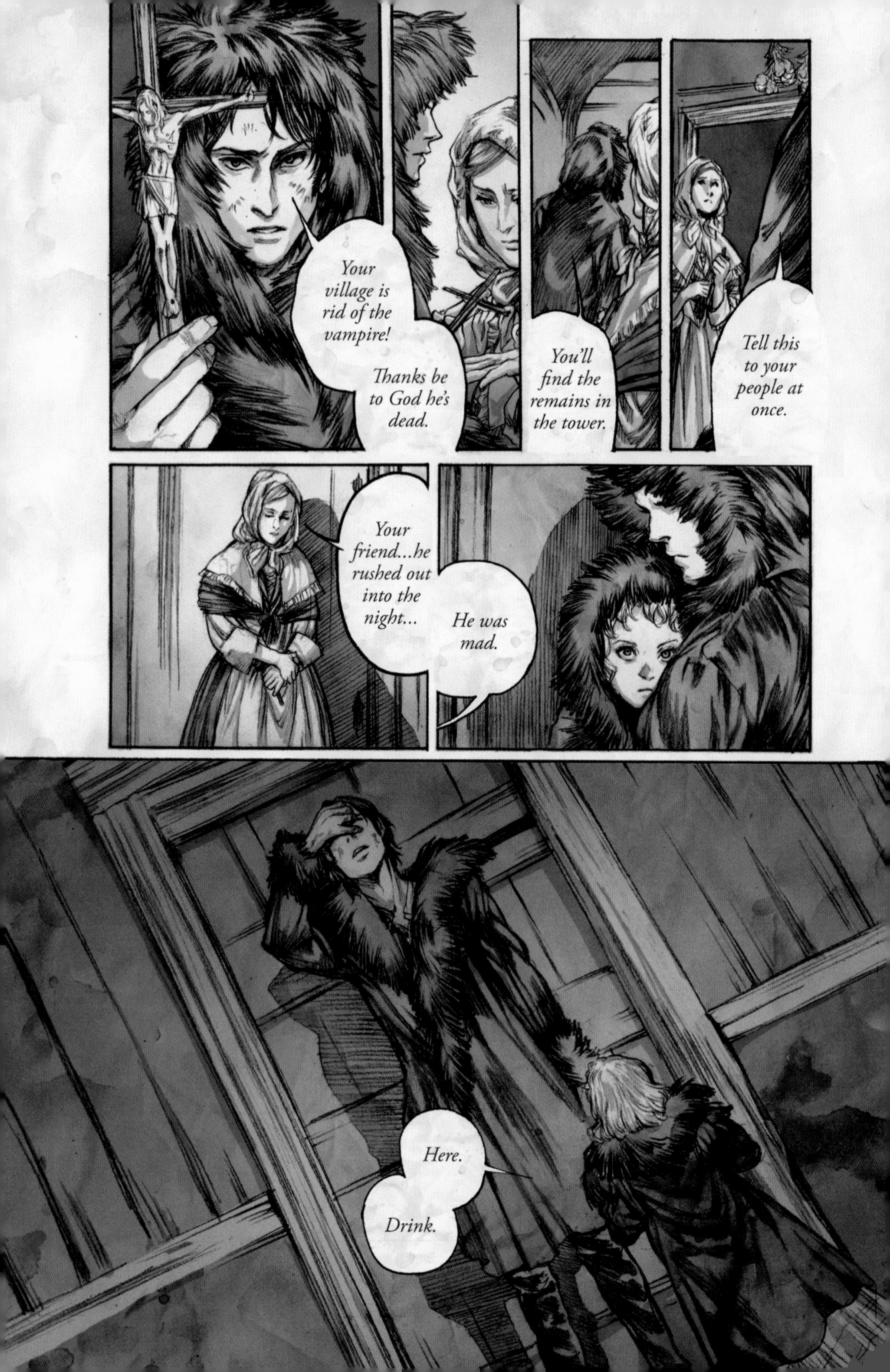
Your village is rid of the vampire!
Thanks be to God he's dead.
You'll find the remains in the tower.
Tell this to your people at once.
Your friend...he rushed out into the night...
He was mad.
Here.
Drink.

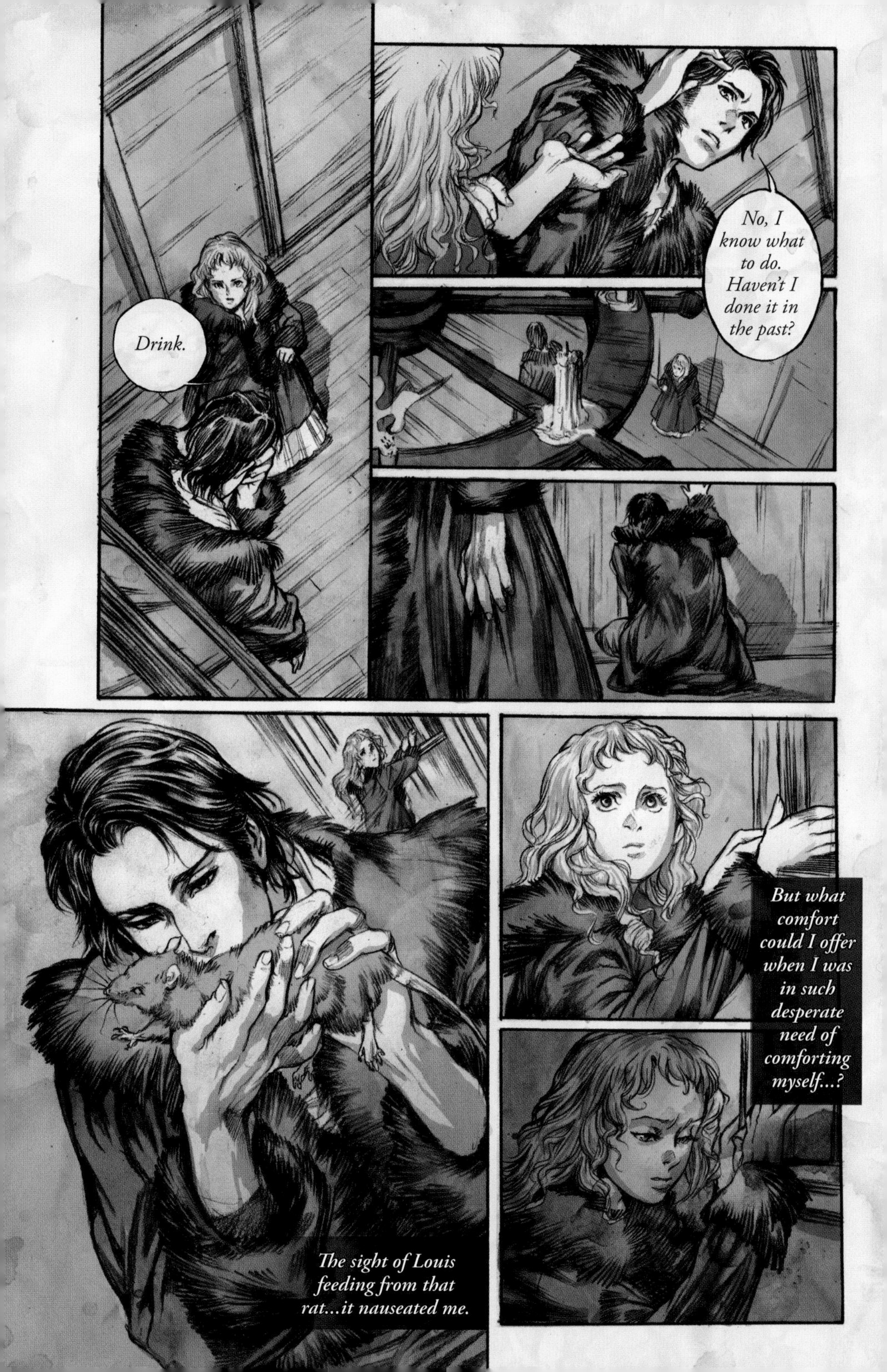

Drink.
No, I know what to do. Haven't I done it in the past?
The sight of Louis feeding from that rat...it nauseated me.
But what comfort could I offer when I was in such desperate need of comforting myself...?

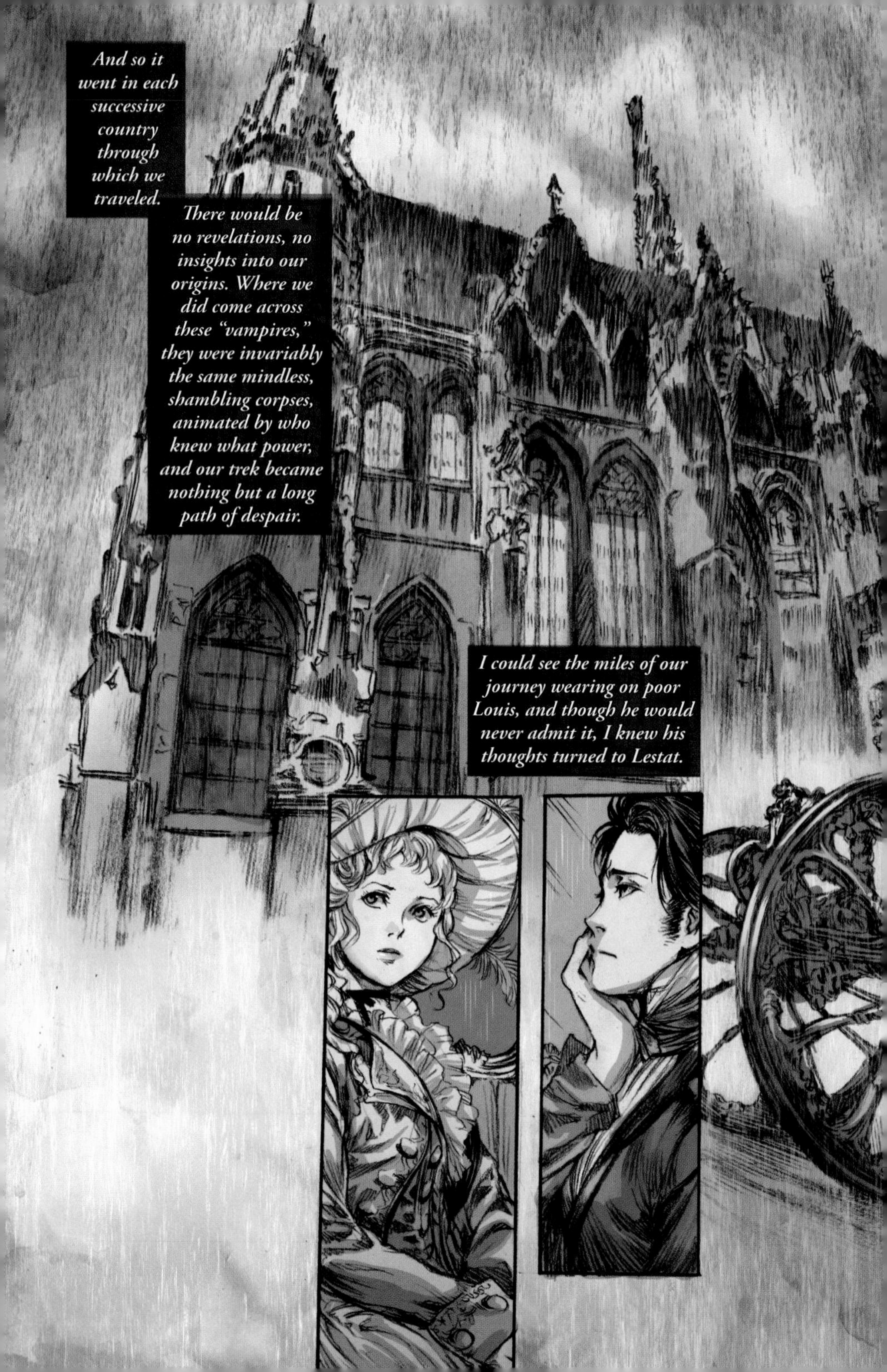
And so it went in each successive country through which we traveled.
There would be no revelations, no insights into our origins. Where we did come across these "vampires," they were invariably the same mindless, shambling corpses, animated by who knew what power, and our trek became nothing but a long path of despair.
I could see the miles of our journey wearing on poor Louis, and though he would never admit it, I knew his thoughts turned to Lestat.

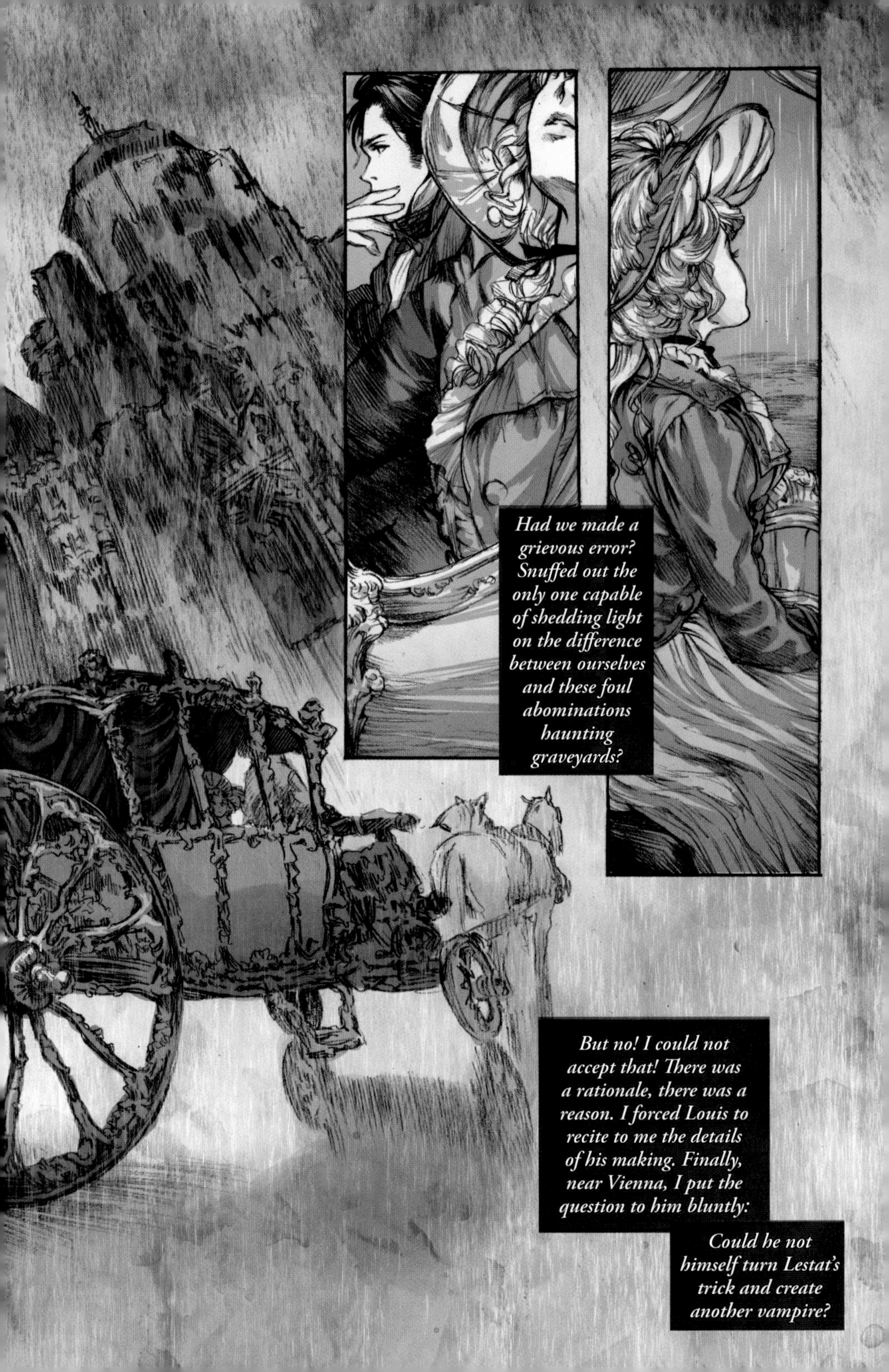
Had we made a grievous error? Snuffed out the only one capable of shedding light on the difference between ourselves and these foul abominations haunting graveyards?
But no! I could not accept that! There was a rationale, there was a reason. I forced Louis to recite to me the details of his making. Finally, near Vienna, I put the question to him bluntly:
Could he not himself turn Lestat's trick and create another vampire?

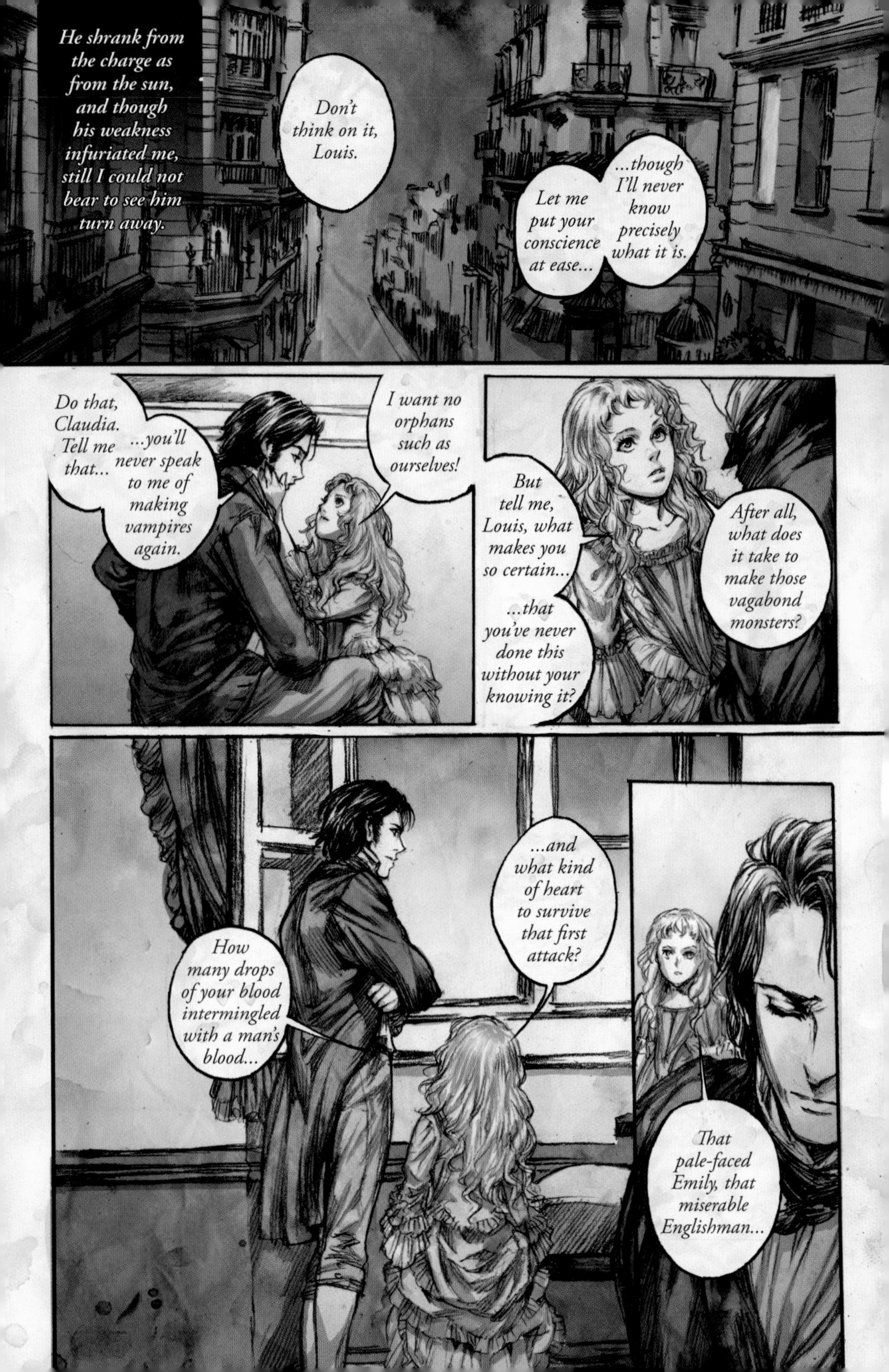
He shrank from the charge as from the sun, and though his weakness infuriated me, still I could not bear to see him turn away.
Don't think on it, Louis.
Let me put your conscience at ease...
...though I'll never know precisely what it is.
Do that, Claudia. Tell me that...
...you'll never speak to me of making vampires again.
I want no orphans such as ourselves!
But tell me, Louis, what makes you so certain...
...that you've never done this without your knowing it?
After all, what does it take to make those vagabond monsters?
How many drops of your blood intermingled with a man's blood...
...and what kind of heart to survive that first attack?
That pale-faced Emily, that miserable Englishman...

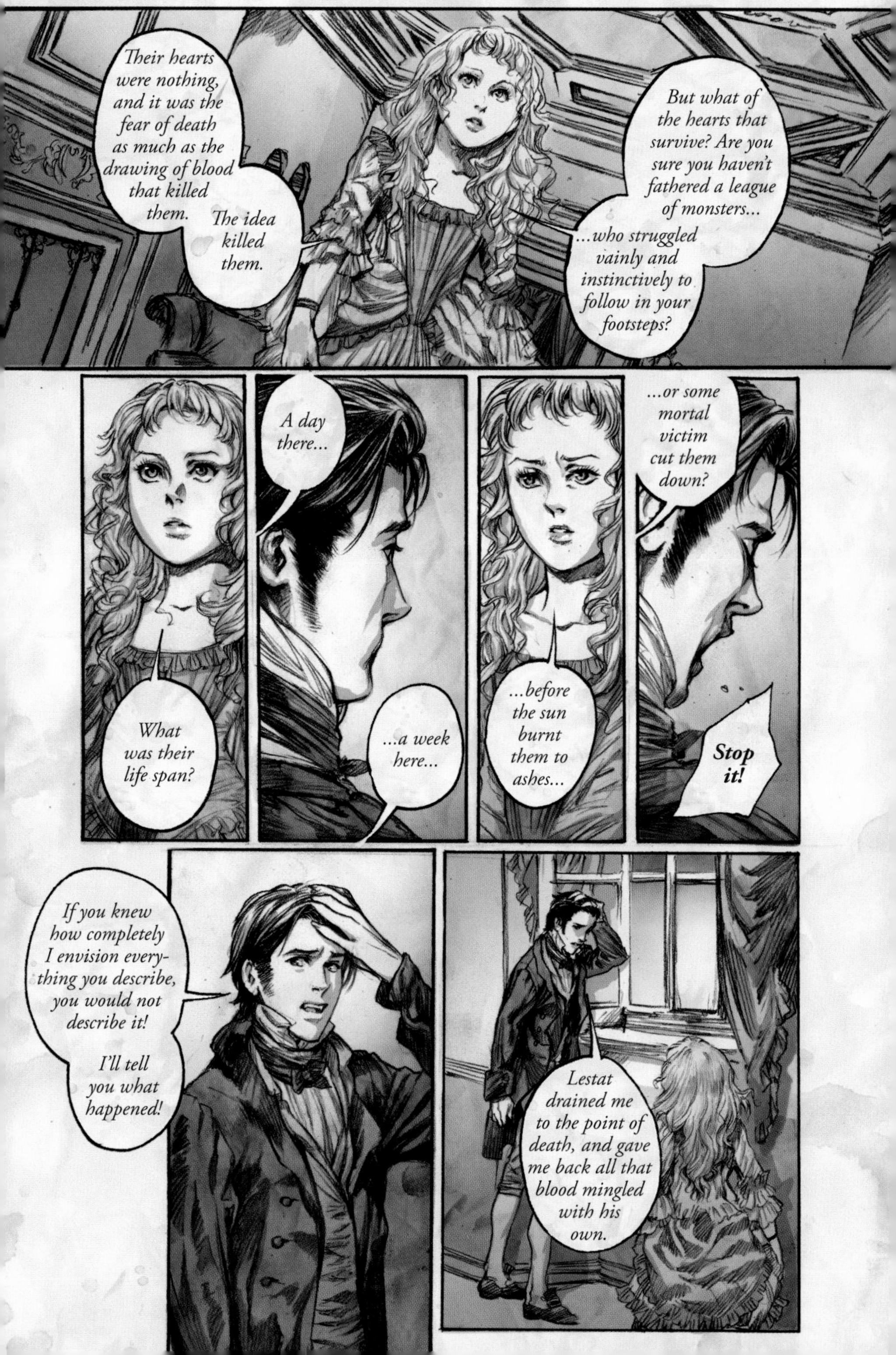
Their hearts were nothing, and it was the fear of death as much as the drawing of blood that killed them.
The idea killed them.
But what of the hearts that survive? Are you sure you haven't fathered a league of monsters...
...who struggled vainly and instinctively to follow in your footsteps?
What was their life span?
A day there...
...a week here...
...before the sun burnt them to ashes...
...or some mortal victim cut them down?
Stop it!
If you knew how completely I envision everything you describe, you would not describe it!
I'll tell you what happened!
Lestat drained me to the point of death, and gave me back all that blood mingled with his own.

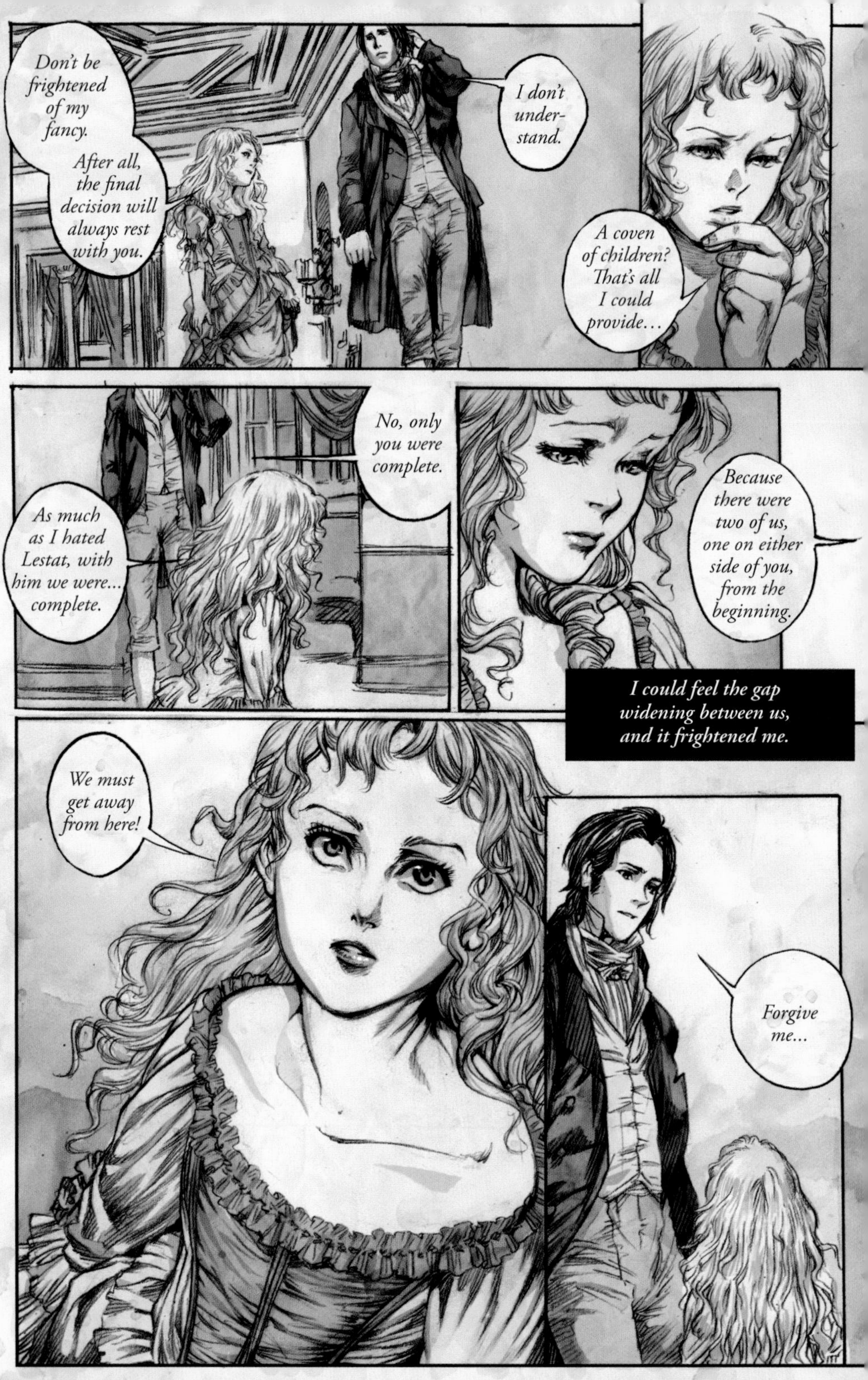
Don't be frightened of my fancy.
After all, the final decision will always rest with you.
I don't under-stand.
A coven of children? That's all I could provide…
As much as I hated Lestat, with him we were… complete.
No, only you were complete.
Because there were two of us, one on either side of you, from the beginning.
I could feel the gap widening between us, and it frightened me.
We must get away from here!
Forgive me…

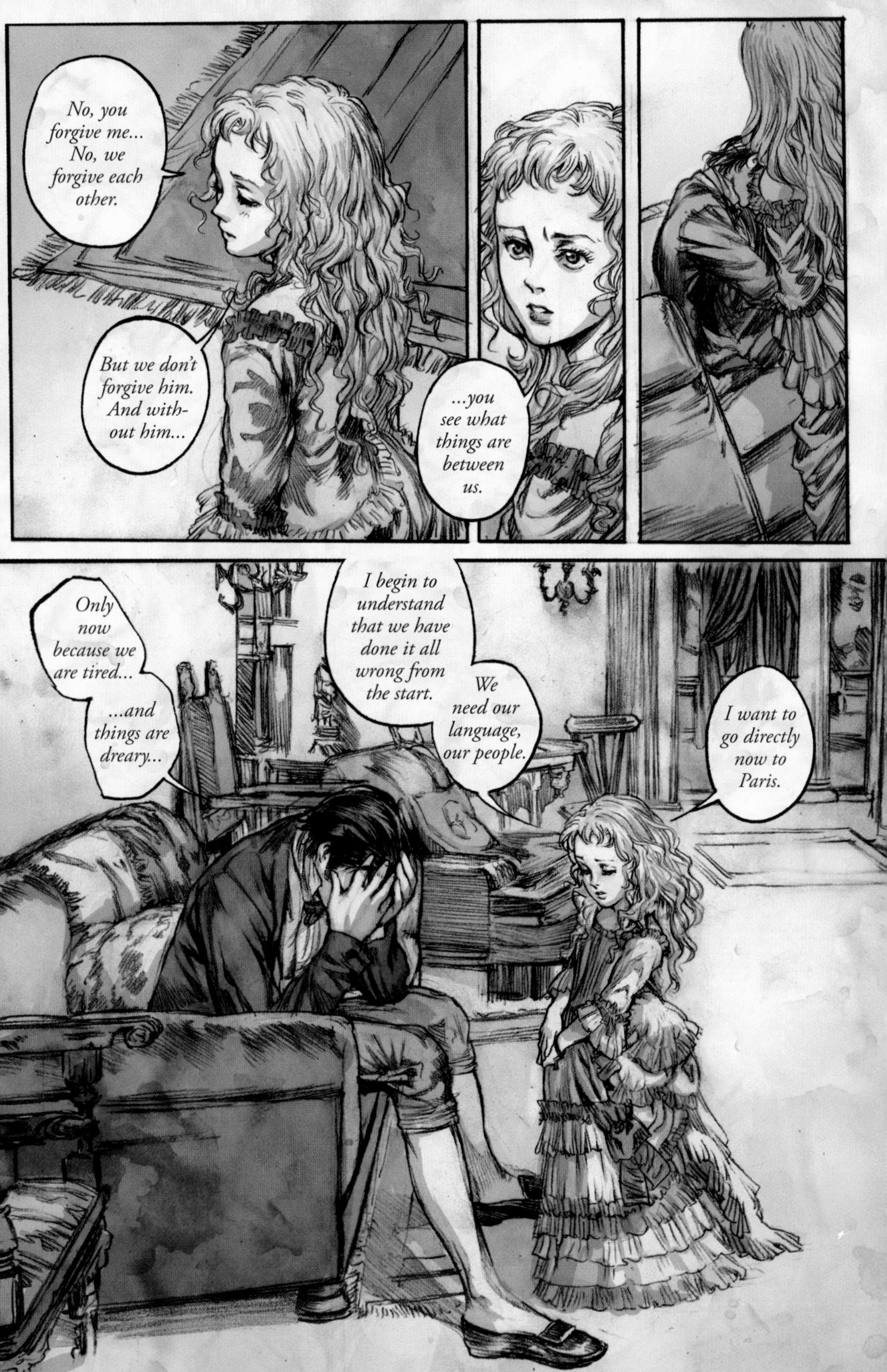
No, you forgive me... No, we forgive each other.
But we don't forgive him. And with-out him...
...you see what things are between us.
Only now because we are tired...
...and things are dreary...
I begin to understand that we have done it all wrong from the start.
We need our language, our people.
I want to go directly now to Paris.

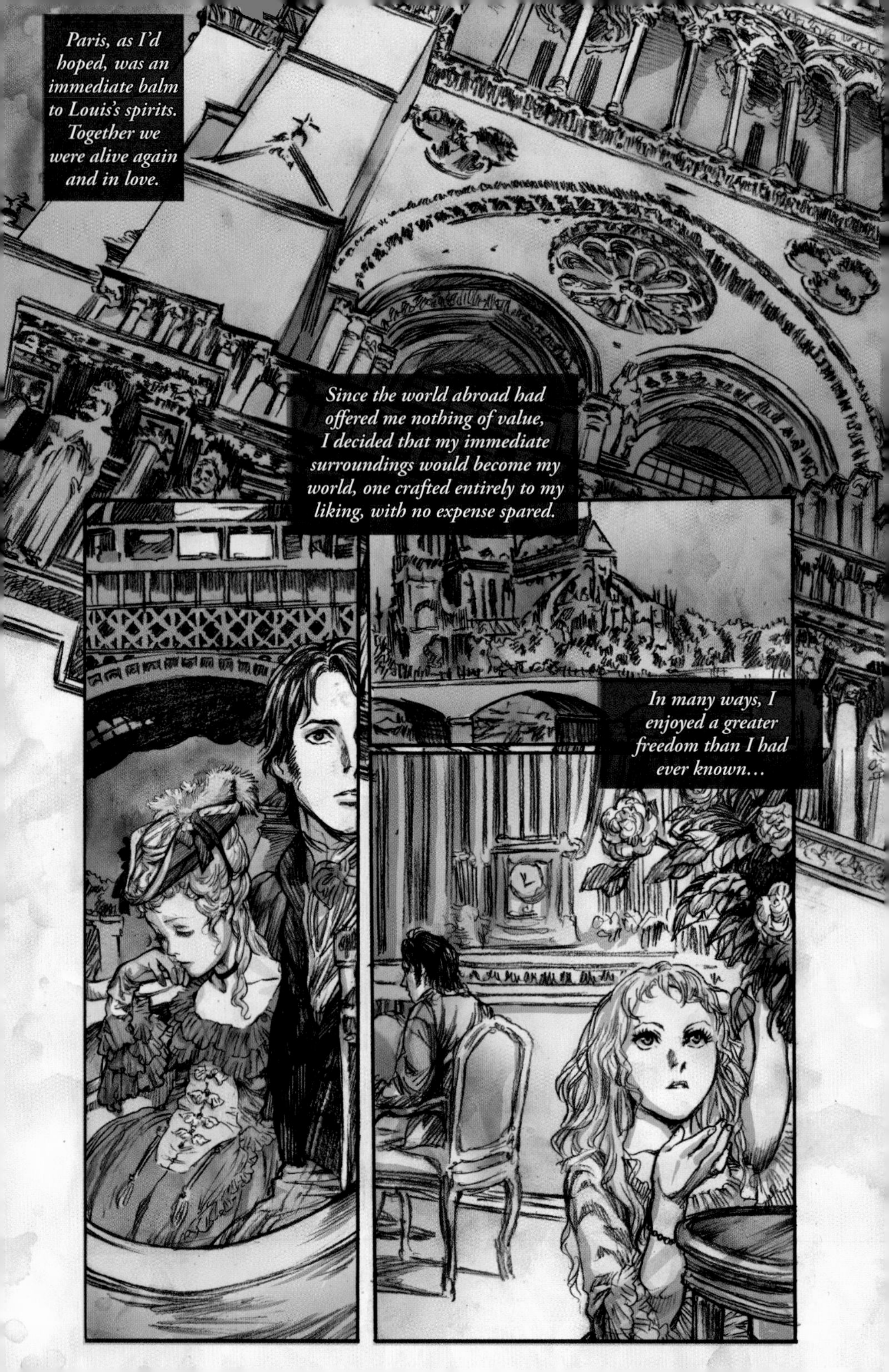
Paris, as I'd hoped, was an immediate balm to Louis's spirits. Together we were alive again and in love.
Since the world abroad had offered me nothing of value, I decided that my immediate surroundings would become my world, one crafted entirely to my liking, with no expense spared.
In many ways, I enjoyed a greater freedom than I had ever known…

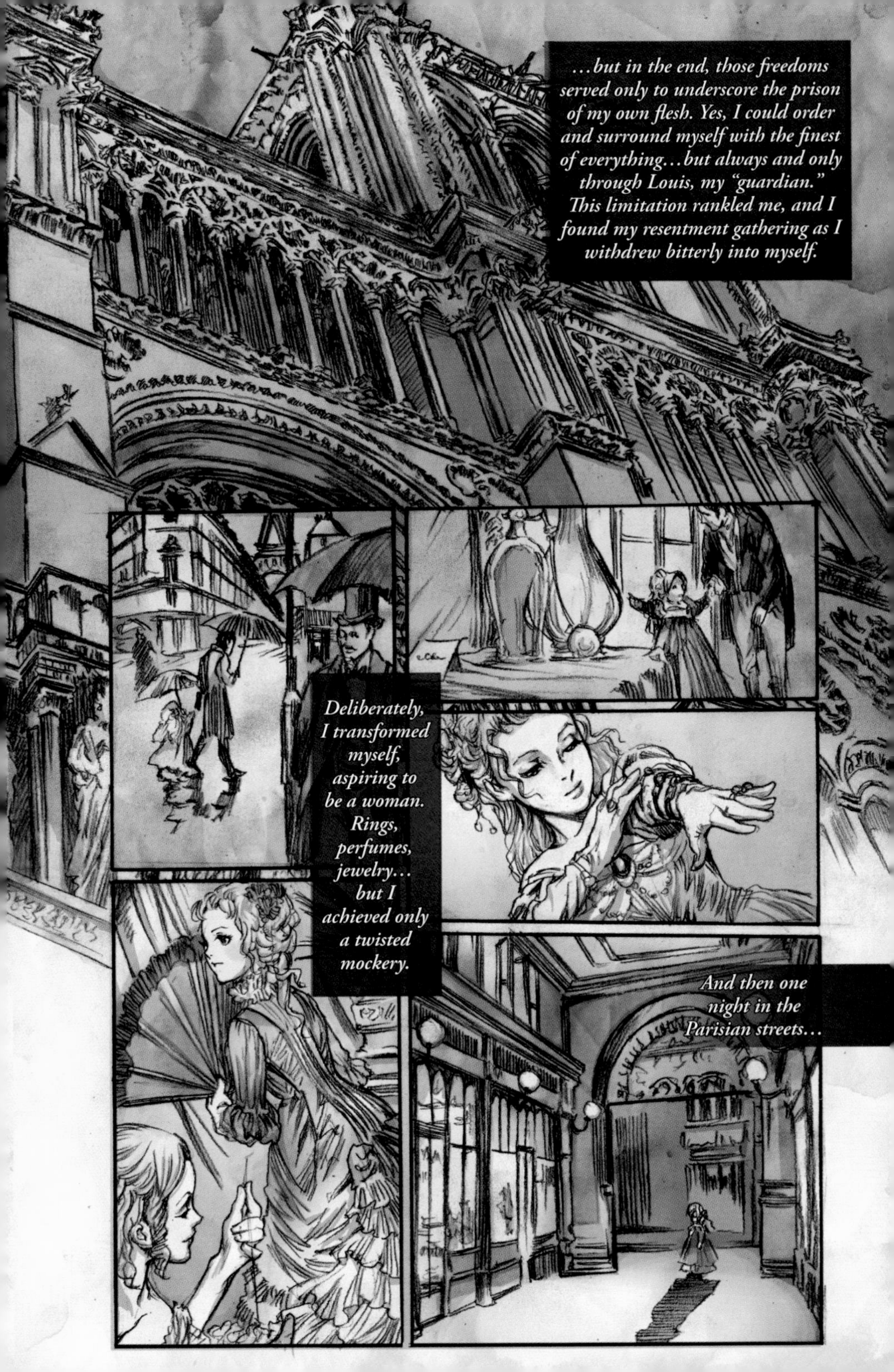
…but in the end, those freedoms served only to underscore the prison of my own flesh. Yes, I could order and surround myself with the finest of everything…but always and only through Louis, my "guardian." This limitation rankled me, and I found my resentment gathering as I withdrew bitterly into myself.
Deliberately, I transformed myself, aspiring to be a woman. Rings, perfumes, jewelry… but I achieved only a twisted mockery.
And then one night in the Parisian streets…

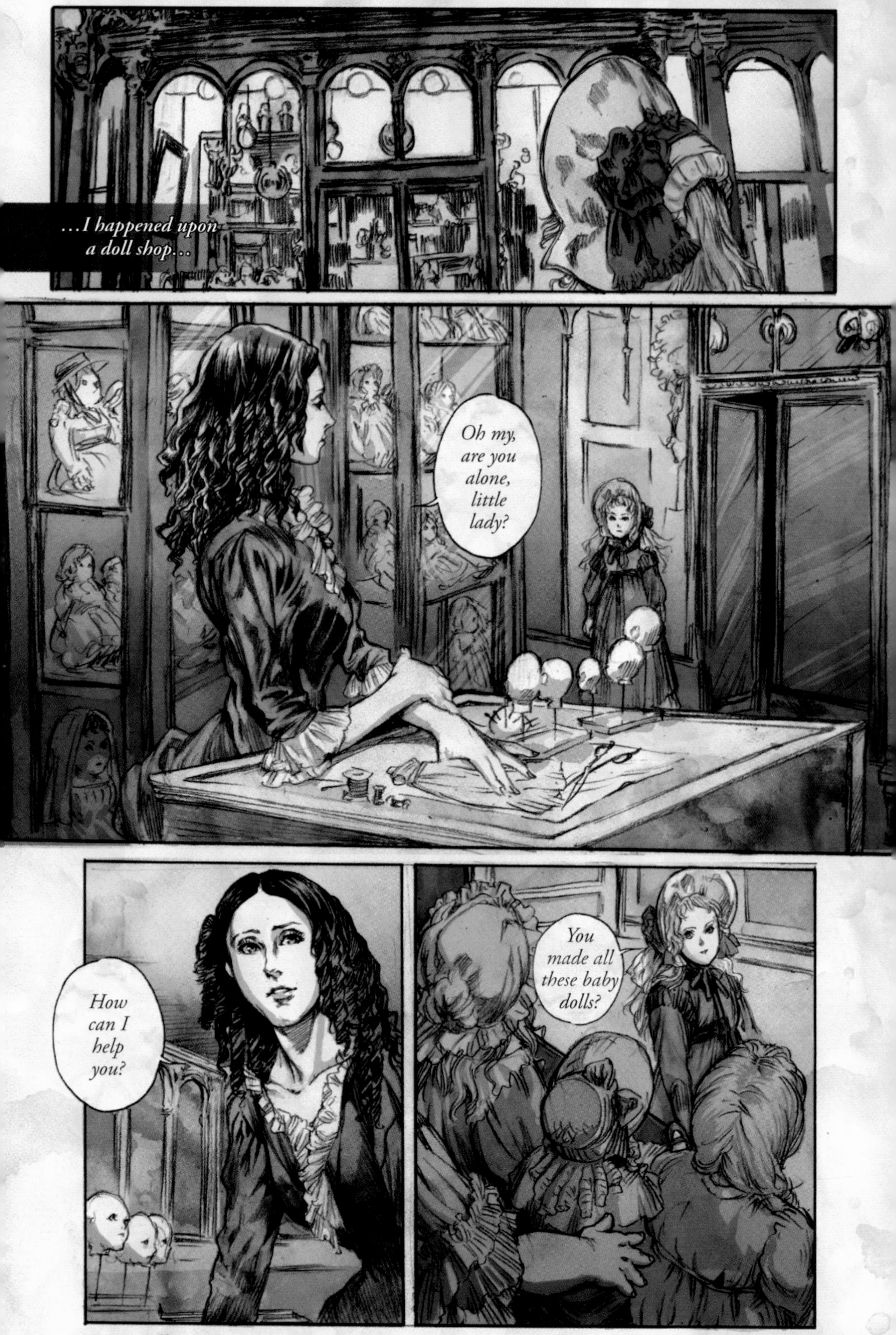
...I happened upon a doll shop...
Oh my, are you alone, little lady?
How can I help you?
You made all these baby dolls?

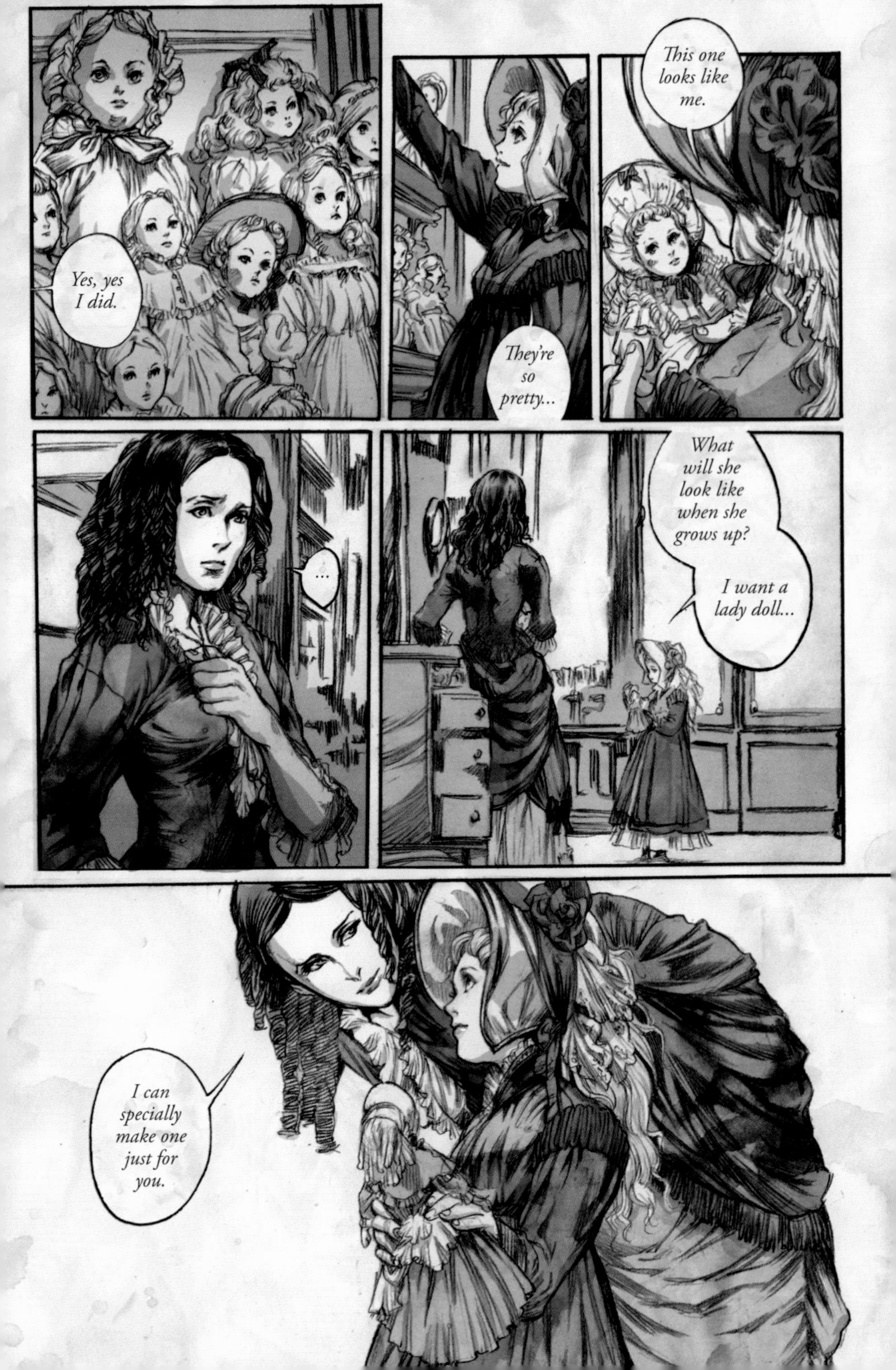

Yes, yes I did.
They're so pretty...
This one looks like me.
...
What will she look like when she grows up?
I want a lady doll...
I can specially make one just for you.

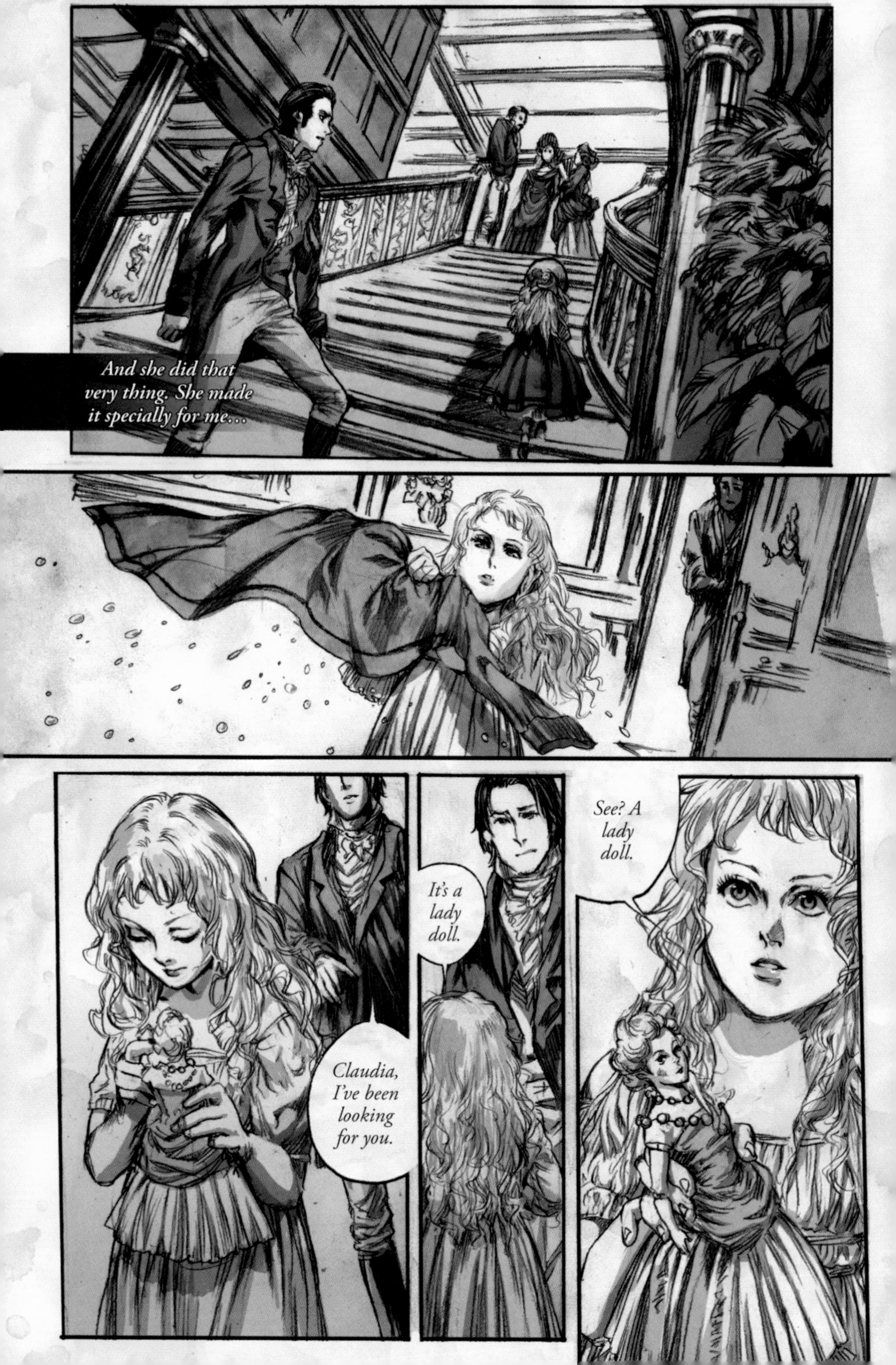
And she did that very thing. She made it specially for me...
Claudia, I've been looking for you.
It's a lady doll.
See? A lady doll.

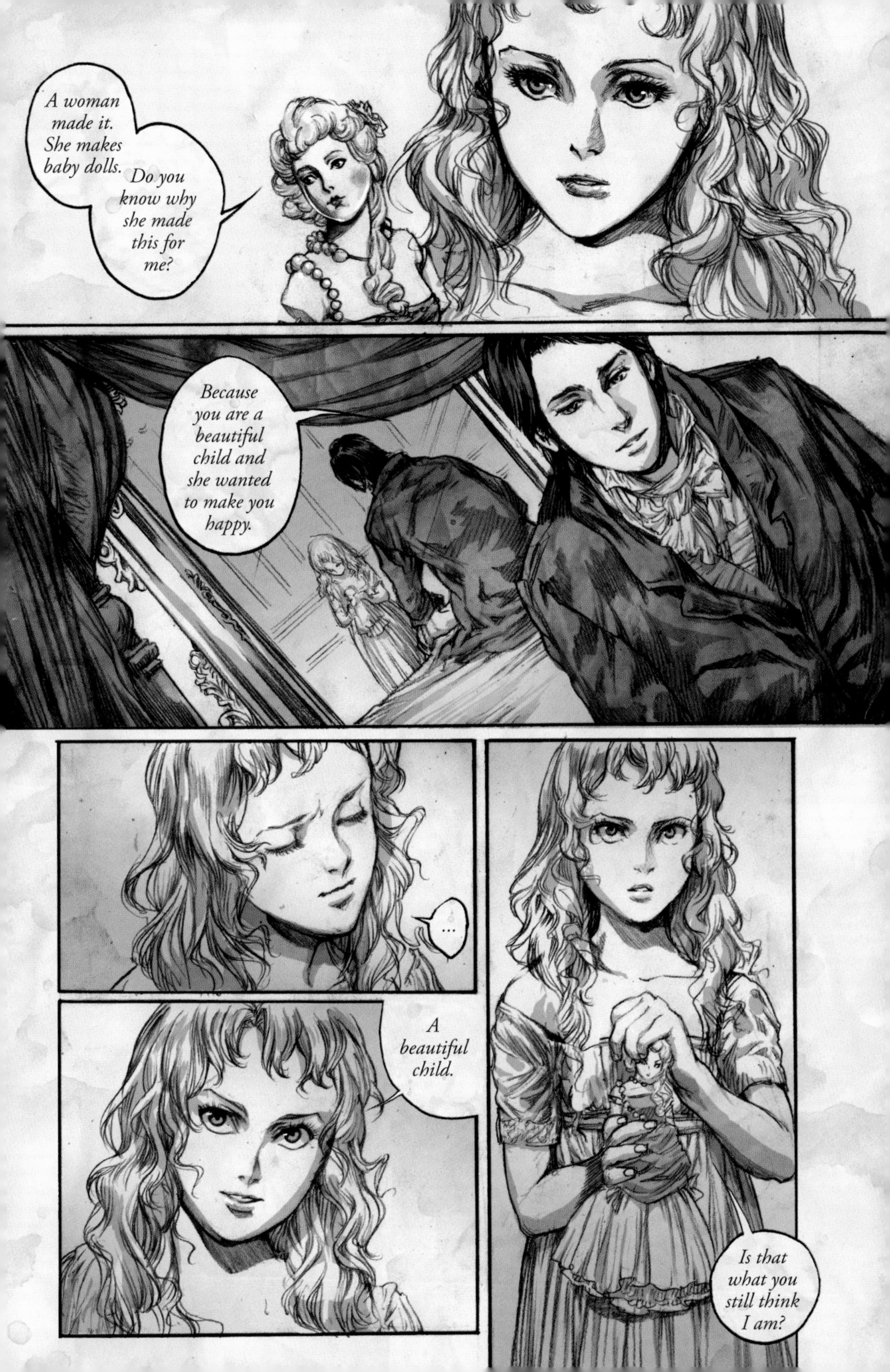
A woman made it. She makes baby dolls.
Do you know why she made this for me?
Because you are a beautiful child and she wanted to make you happy.
...
A beautiful child.
Is that what you still think I am?

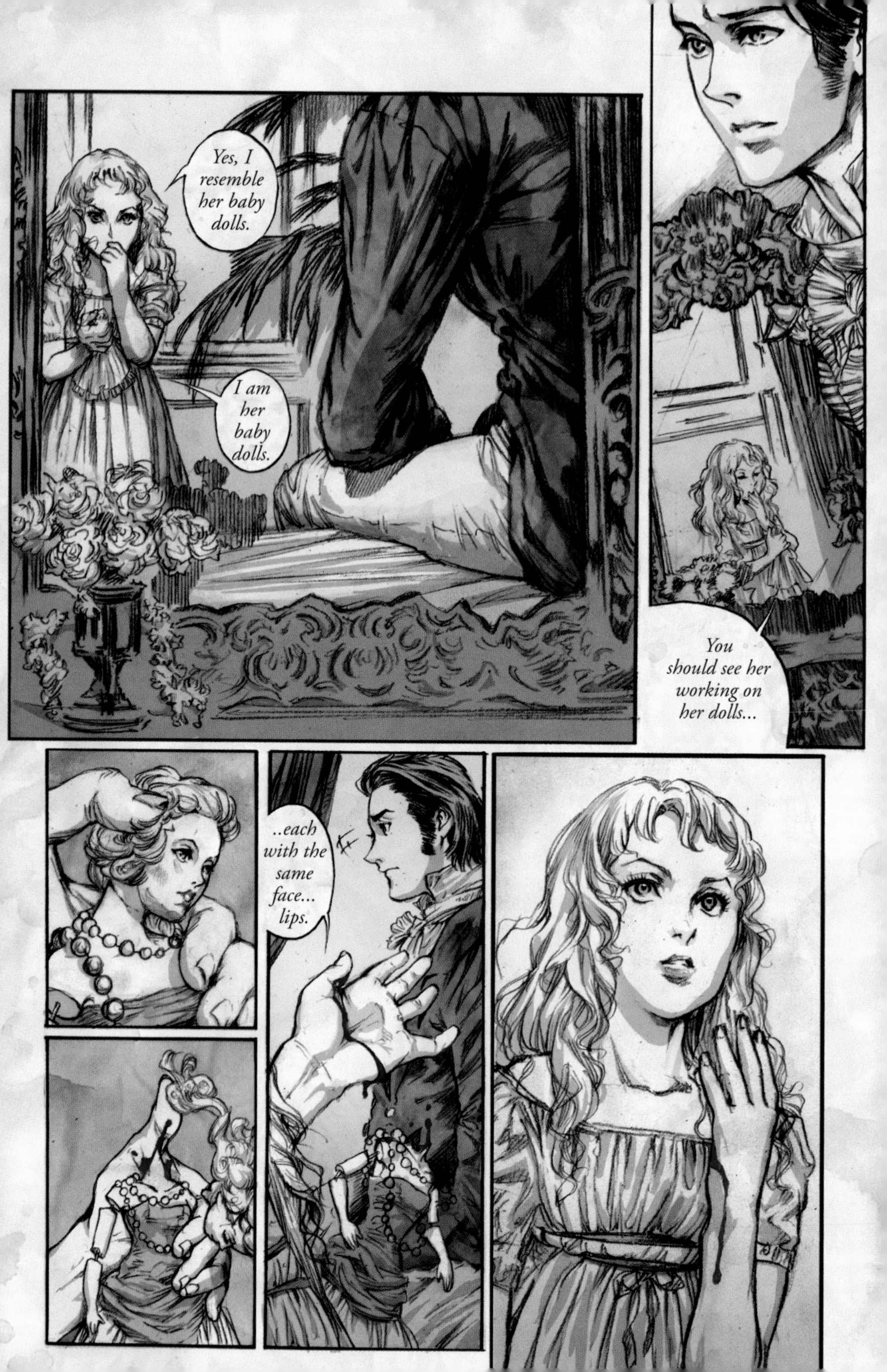

Yes, I resemble her baby dolls.
I am her baby dolls.
You should see her working on her dolls...
..each with the same face... lips.

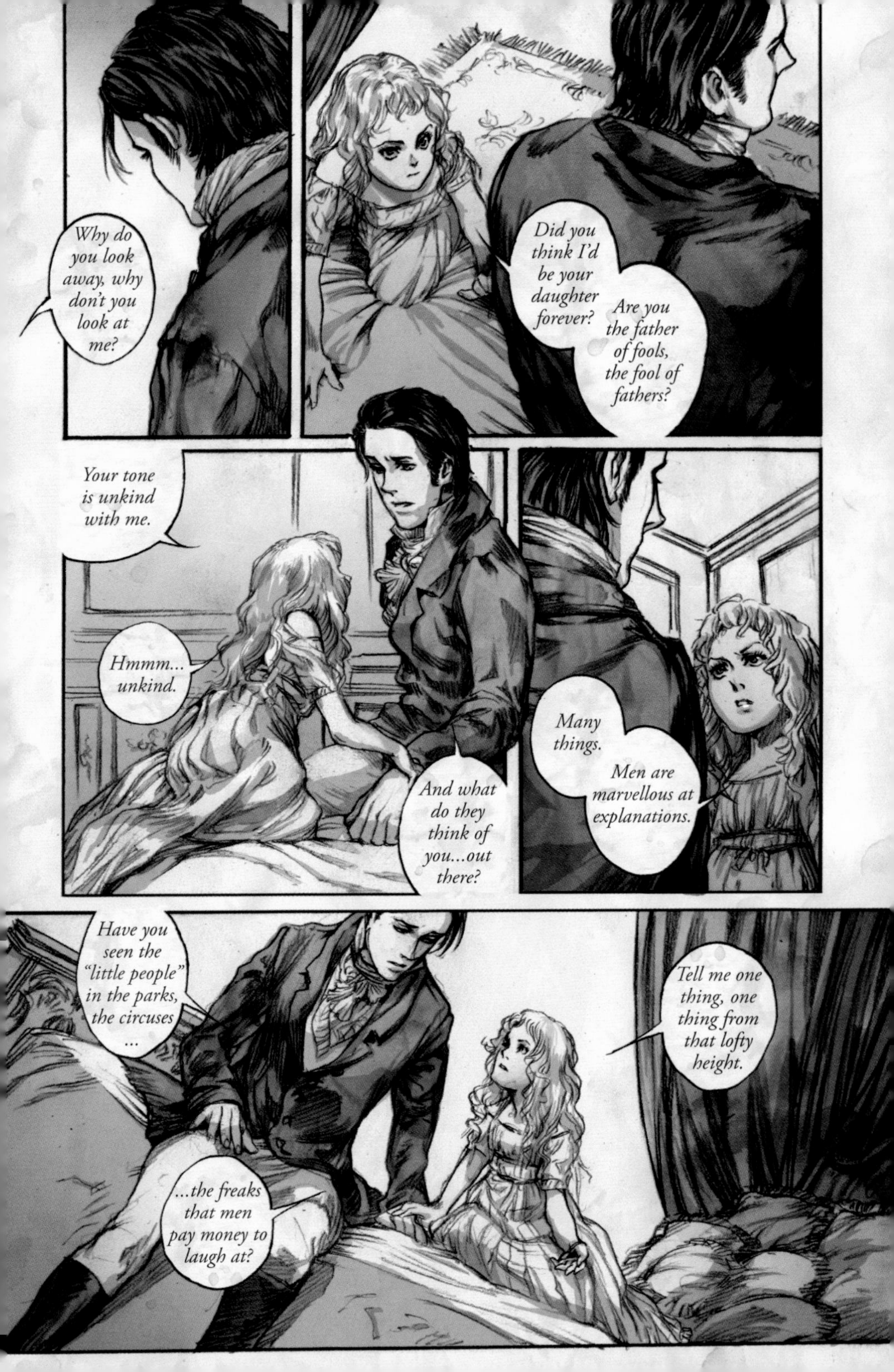
Why do you look away, why don't you look at me?
Did you think I'd be your daughter forever?
Are you the father of fools, the fool of fathers?
Your tone is unkind with me.
Hmmm... unkind.
And what do they think of you...out there?
Many things.
Men are marvellous at explanations.
Have you seen the "little people" in the parks, the circuses ...
...the freaks that men pay money to laugh at?
Tell me one thing, one thing from that lofty height.

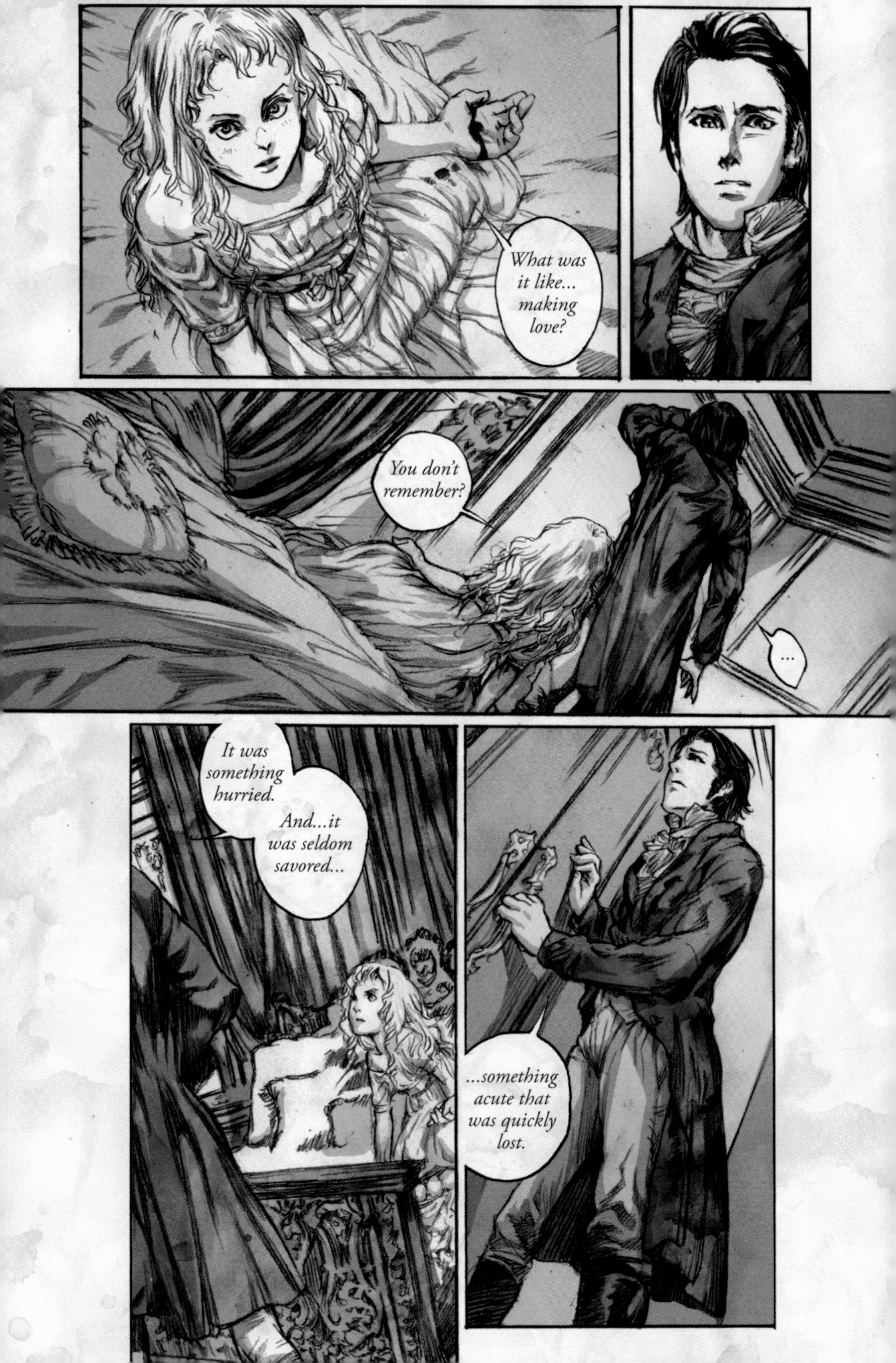
What was it like... making love?
You don't remember?
...
It was something hurried.
And...it was seldom savored...
...something acute that was quickly lost.

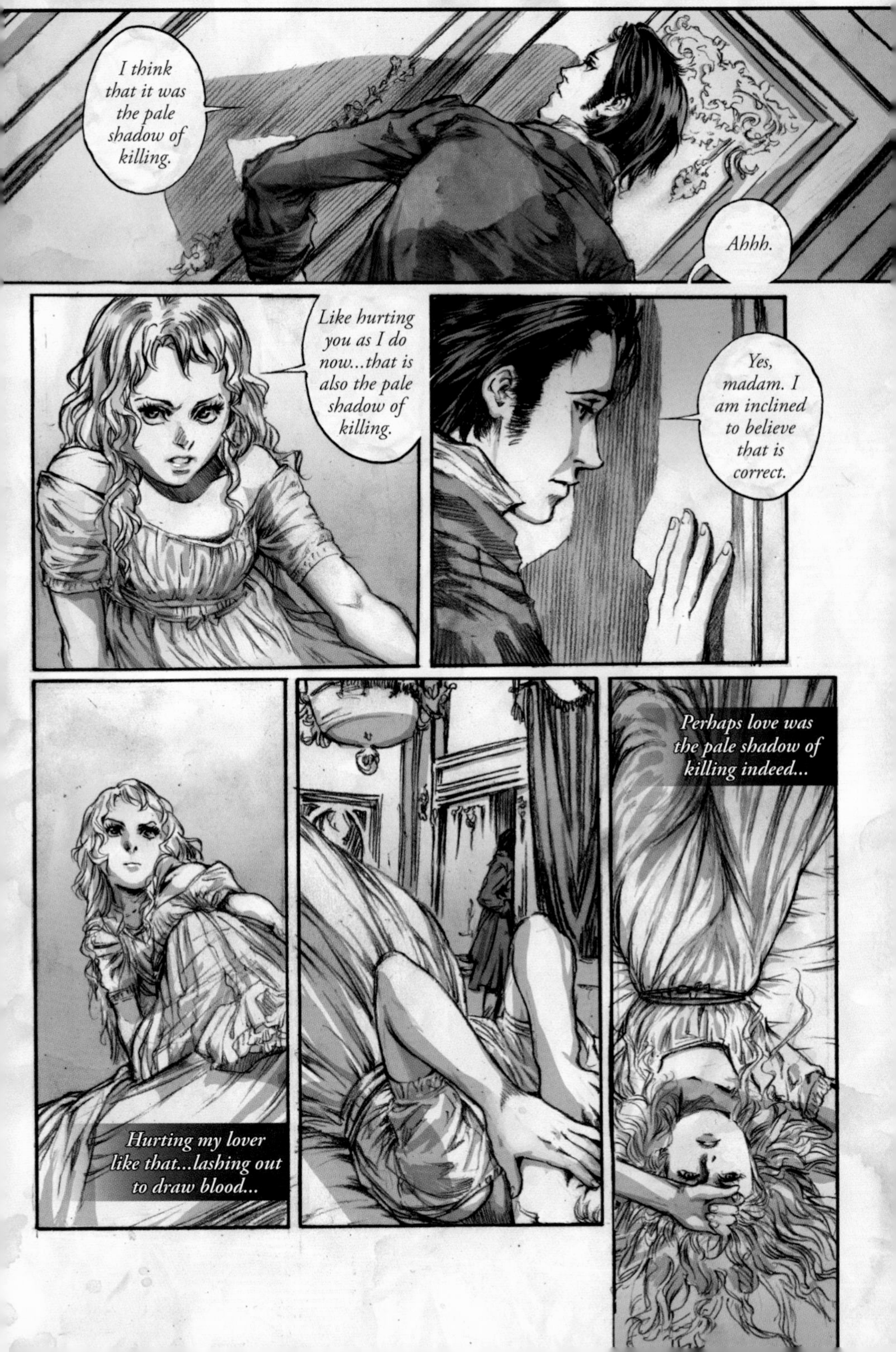
I think that it was the pale shadow of killing.
Ahhh.
Like hurting you as I do now...that is also the pale shadow of killing.
Yes, madam. I am inclined to believe that is correct.
Hurting my lover like that...lashing out to draw blood...
Perhaps love was the pale shadow of killing indeed...

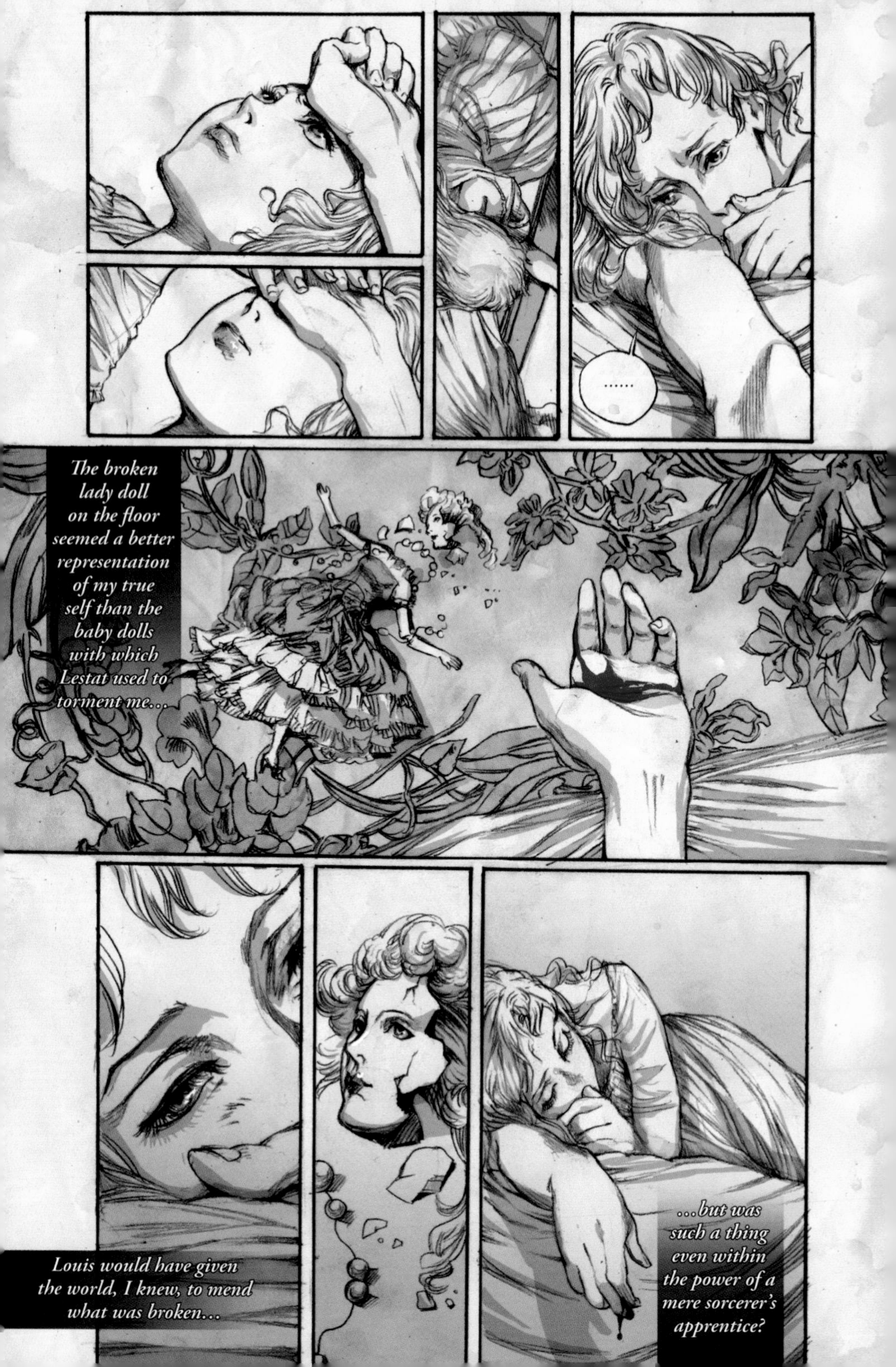

....
The broken lady doll on the floor seemed a better representation of my true self than the baby dolls with which Lestat used to torment me...
Louis would have given the world, I knew, to mend what was broken...
...but was such a thing even within the power of a mere sorcerer's apprentice?

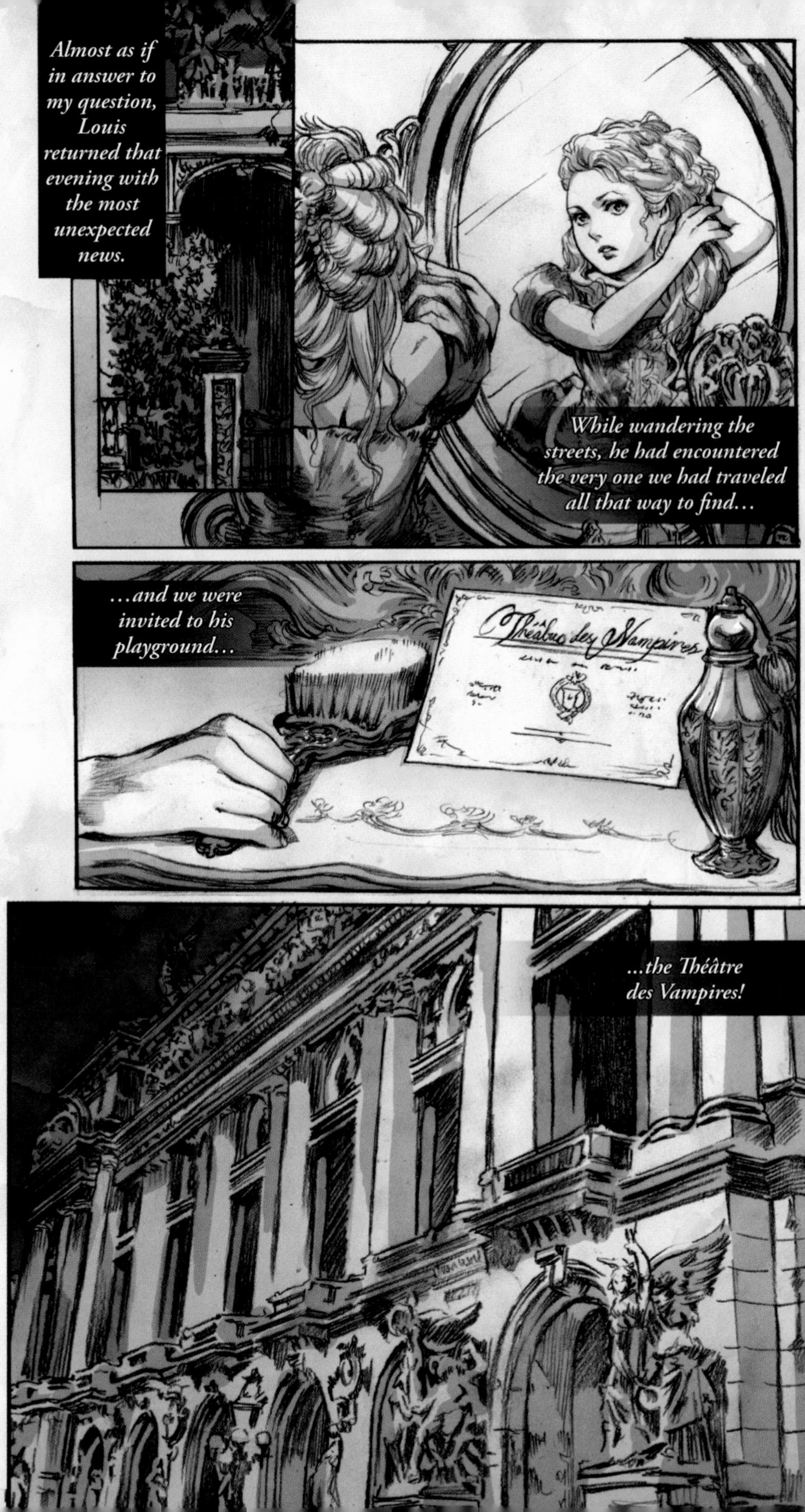
Almost as if in answer to my question, Louis returned that evening with the most unexpected news.
While wandering the streets, he had encountered the very one we had traveled all that way to find…
…and we were invited to his playground…
…the Théâtre des Vampires!

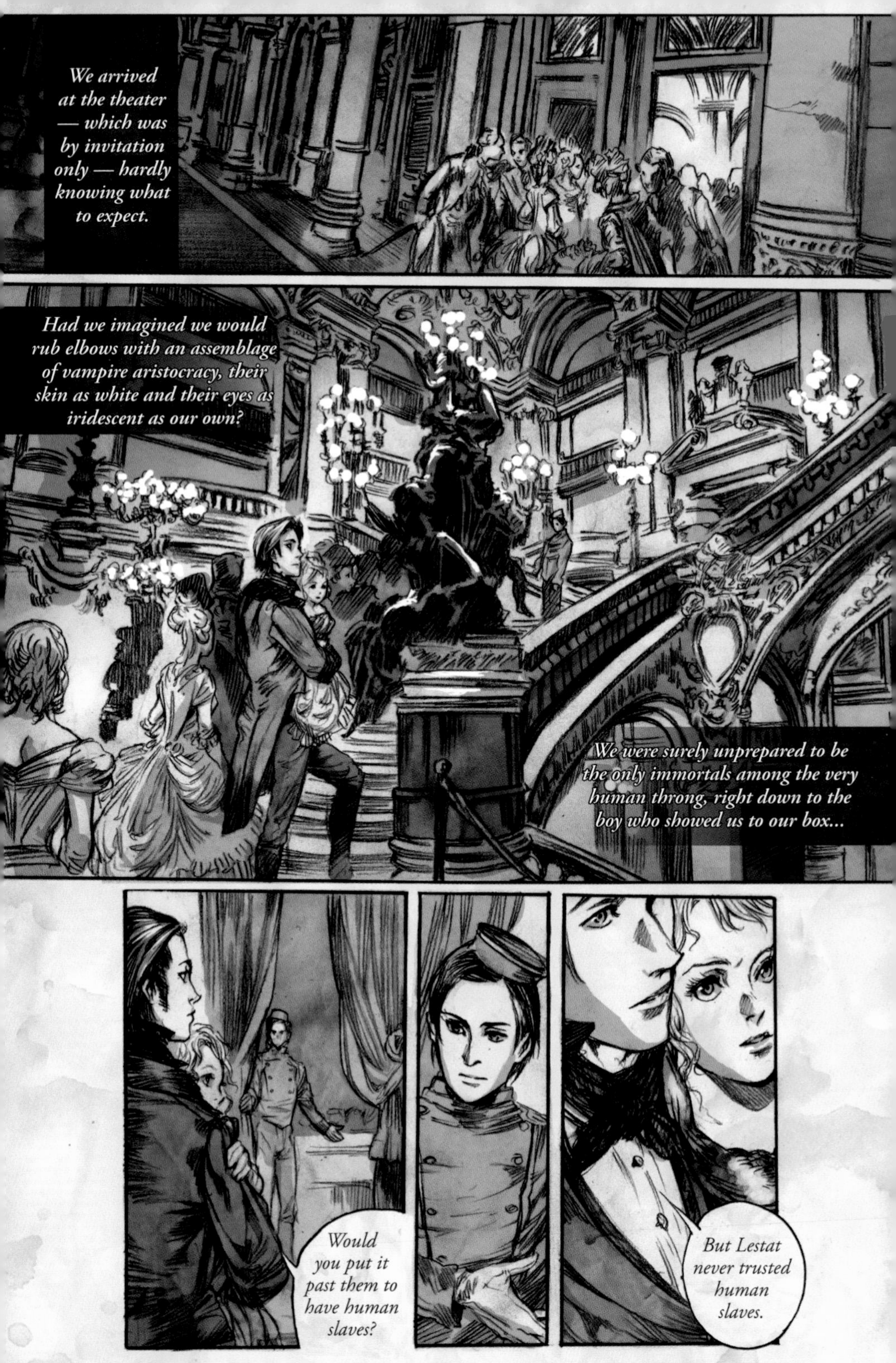
We arrived at the theater — which was by invitation only — hardly knowing what to expect.
Had we imagined we would rub elbows with an assemblage of vampire aristocracy, their skin as white and their eyes as iridescent as our own?
We were surely unprepared to be the only immortals among the very human throng, right down to the boy who showed us to our box...
Would you put it past them to have human slaves?
But Lestat never trusted human slaves.

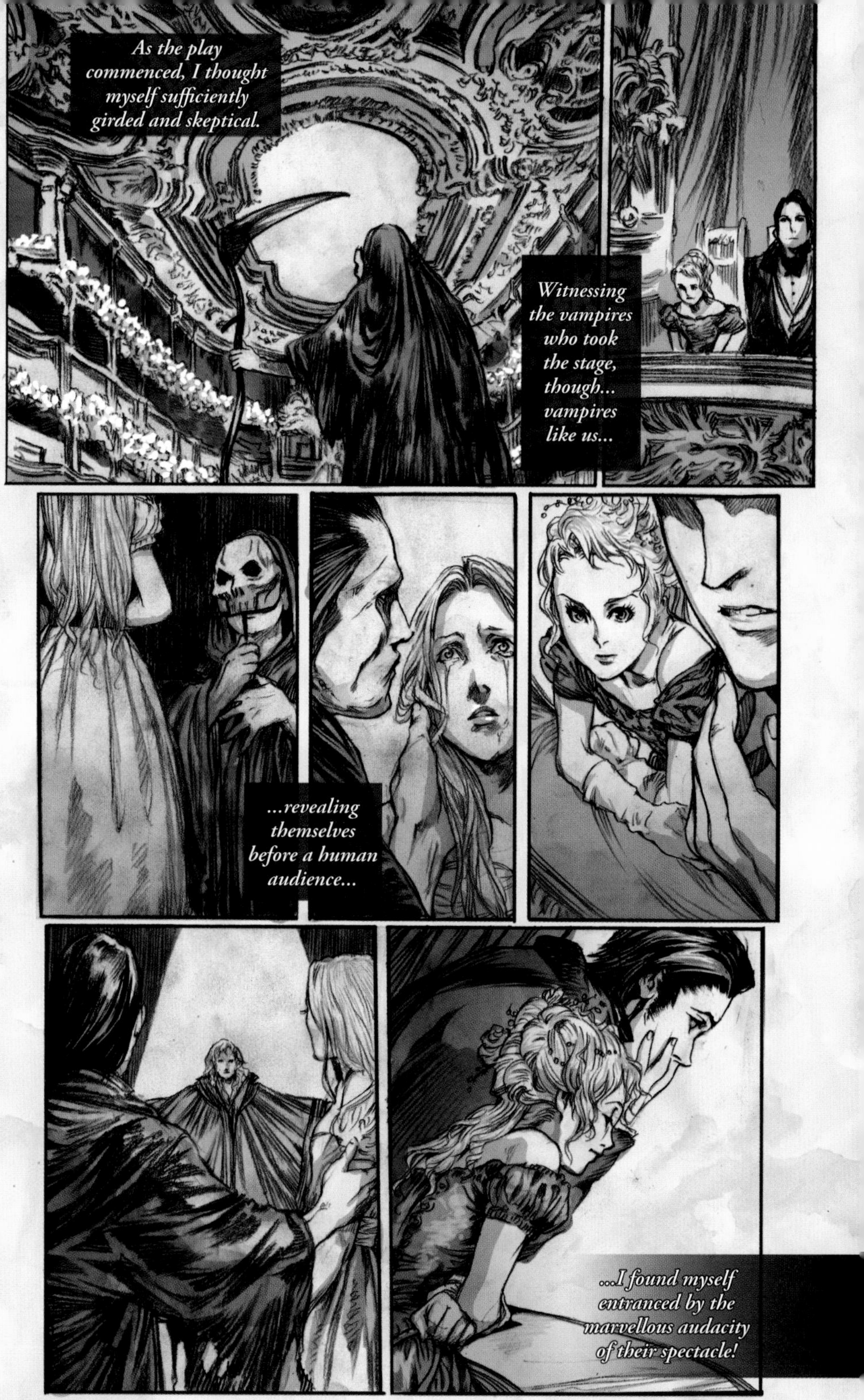
As the play commenced, I thought myself sufficiently girded and skeptical.
Witnessing the vampires who took the stage, though... vampires like us...
...revealing themselves before a human audience...
...I found myself entranced by the marvellous audacity of their spectacle!

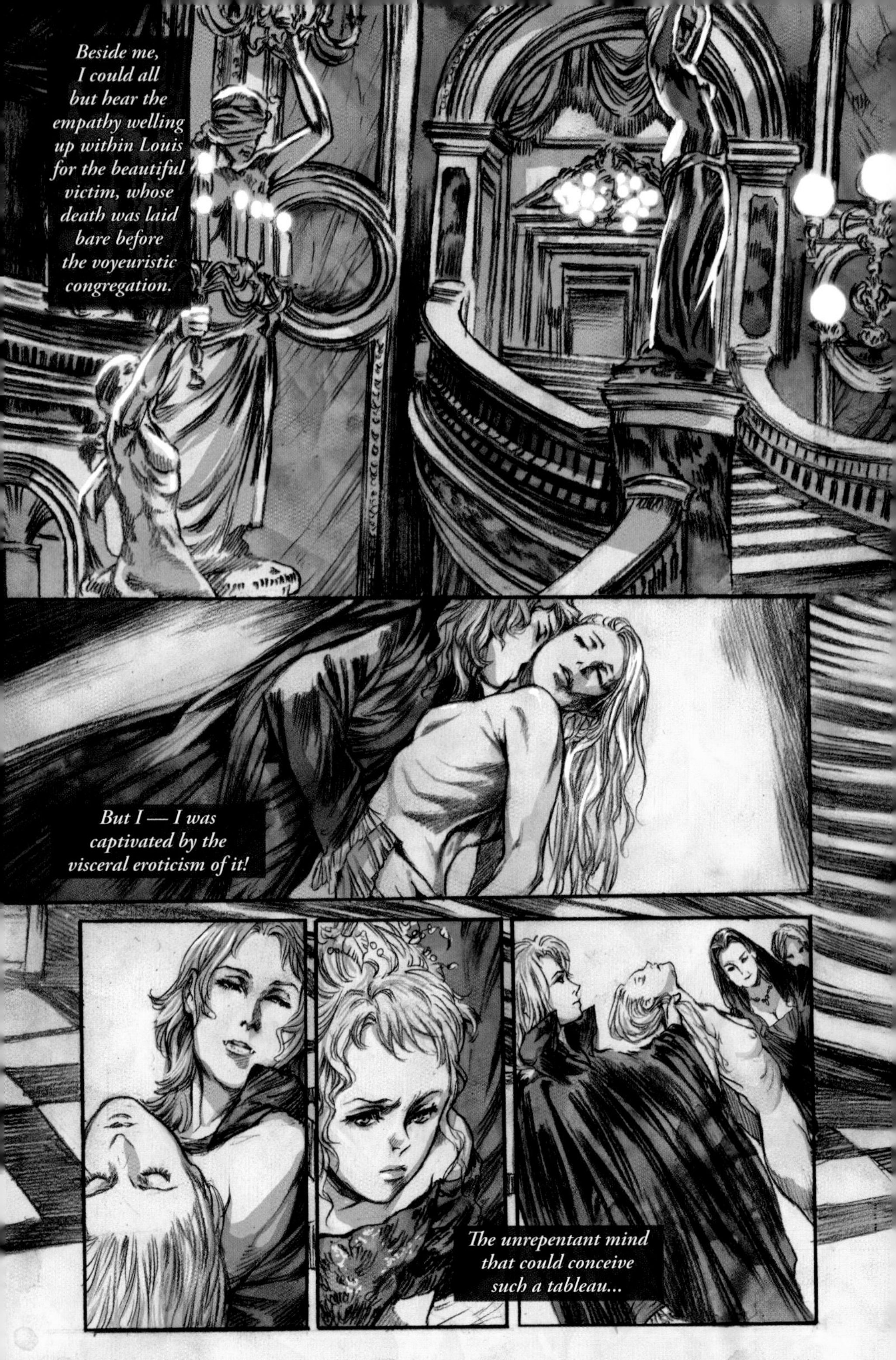
Beside me, I could all but hear the empathy welling up within Louis for the beautiful victim, whose death was laid bare before the voyeuristic congregation.
But I — I was captivated by the visceral eroticism of it!
The unrepentant mind that could conceive such a tableau...

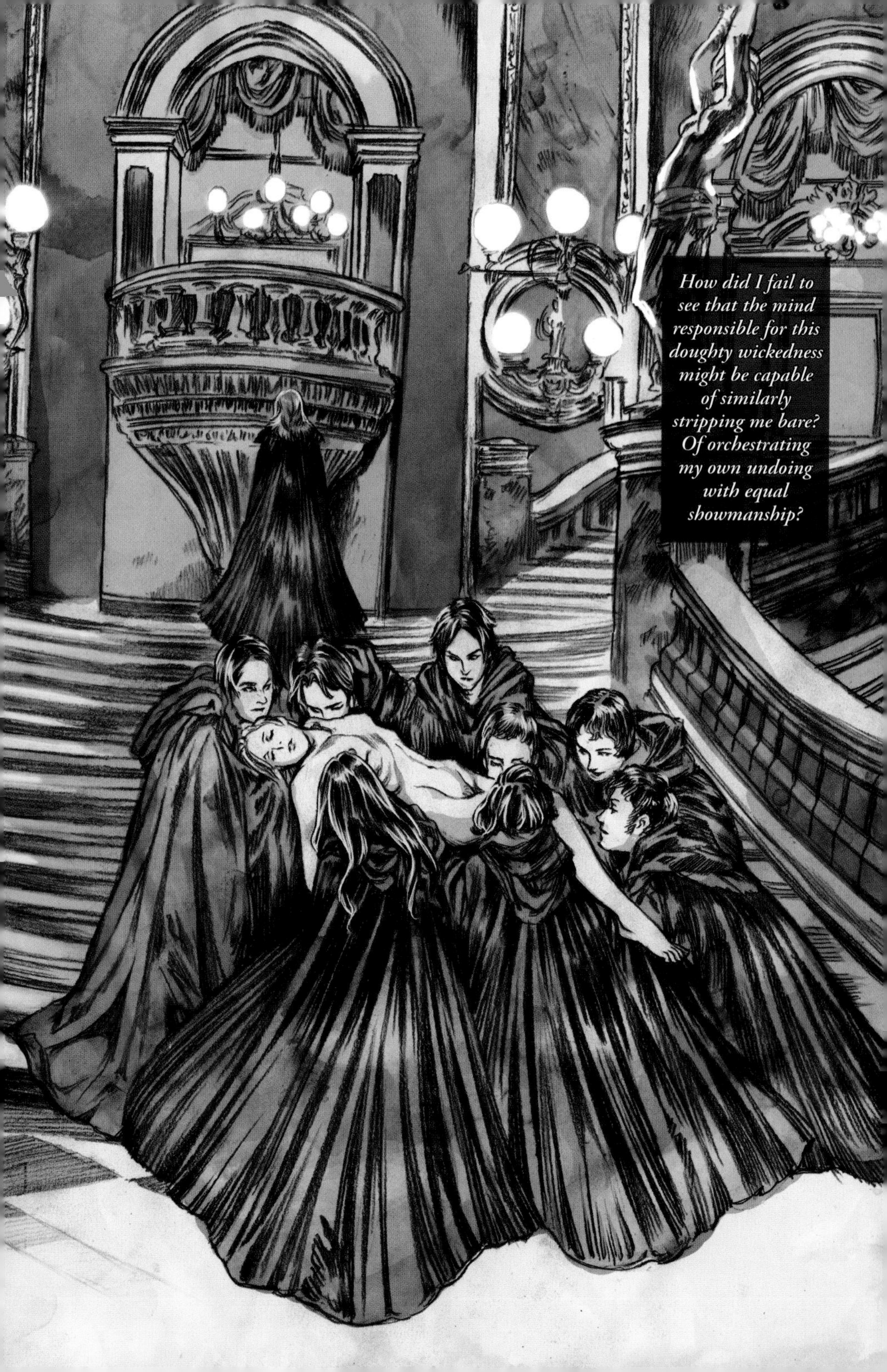
How did I fail to see that the mind responsible for this doughty wickedness might be capable of similarly stripping me bare? Of orchestrating my own undoing with equal showmanship?

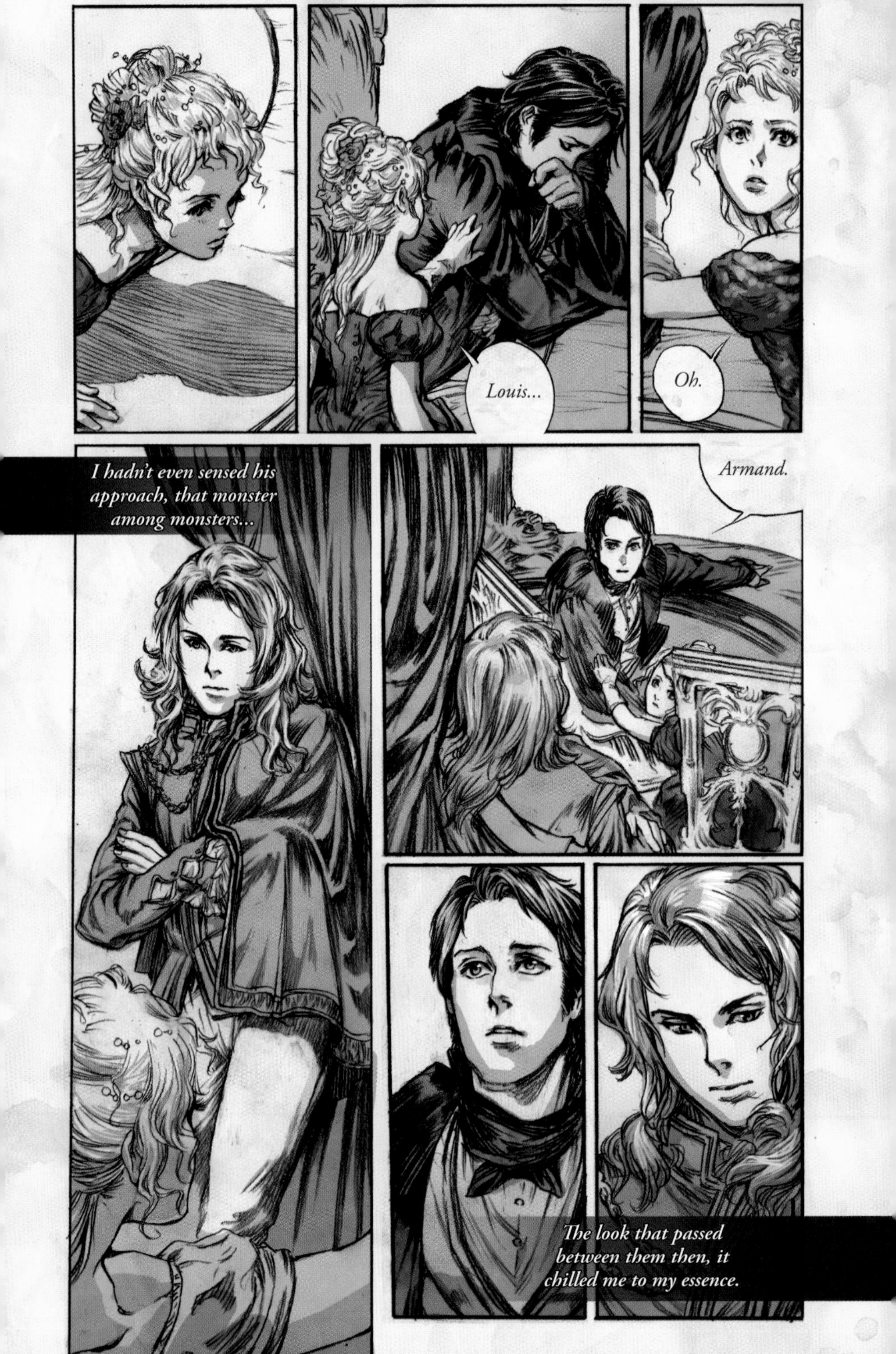
Louis...
Oh.
I hadn't even sensed his approach, that monster among monsters...
Armand.
The look that passed between them then, it chilled me to my essence.

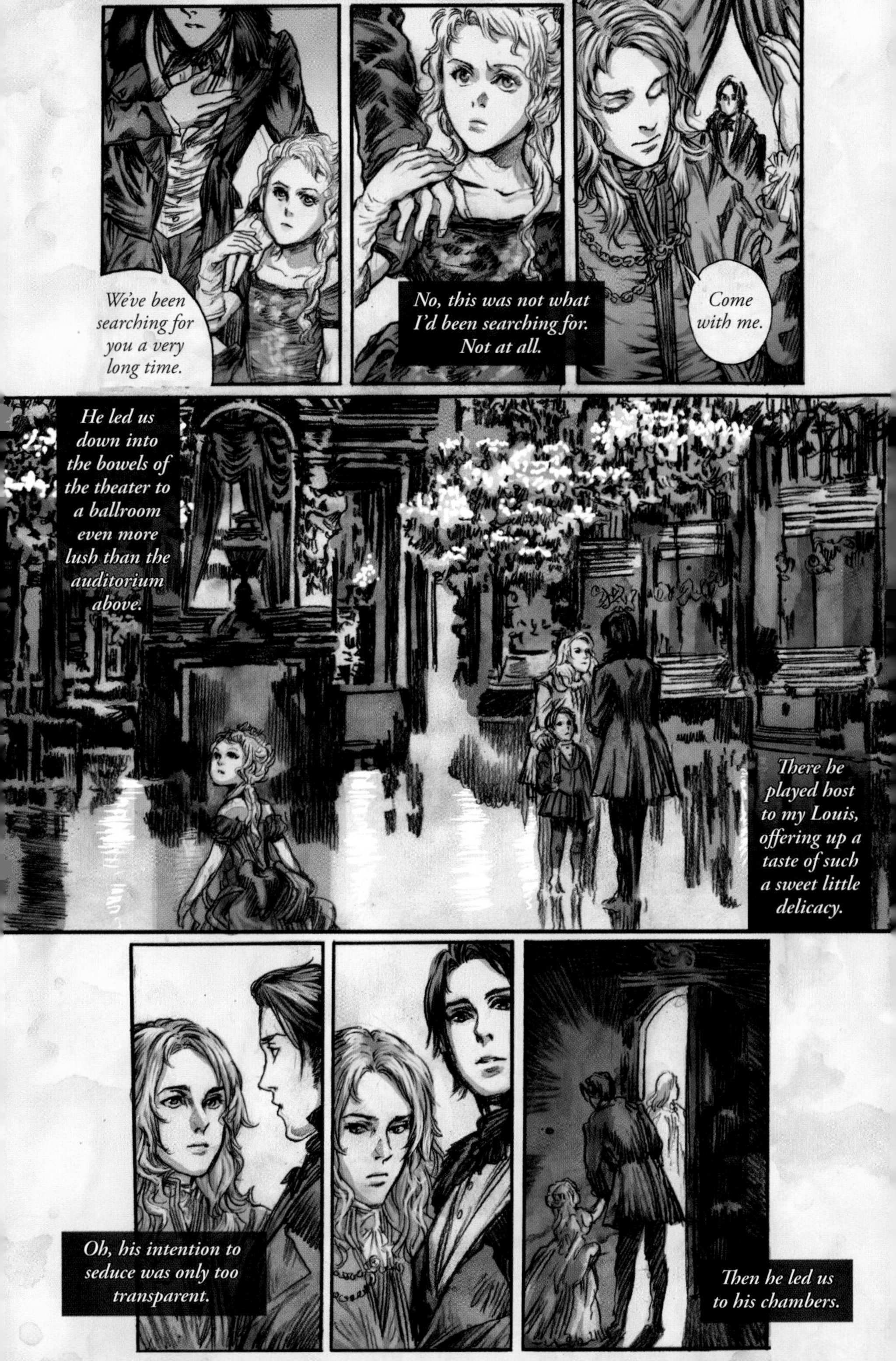
We've been searching for you a very long time.
No, this was not what I'd been searching for. Not at all.
Come with me.
He led us down into the bowels of the theater to a ballroom even more lush than the auditorium above.
There he played host to my Louis, offering up a taste of such a sweet little delicacy.
Oh, his intention to seduce was only too transparent.
Then he led us to his chambers.

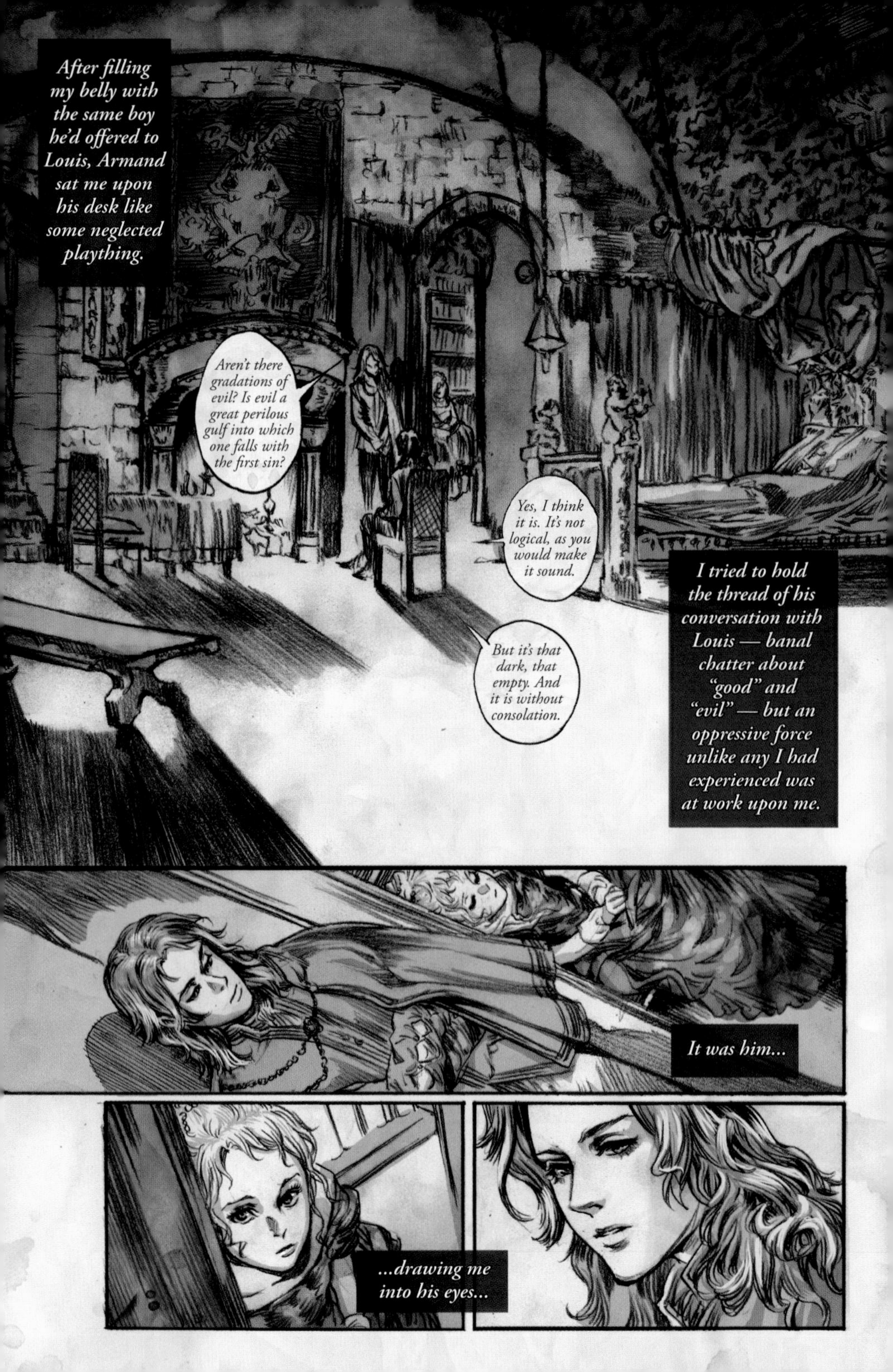
After filling my belly with the same boy he'd offered to Louis, Armand sat me upon his desk like some neglected plaything.
Aren't there gradations of evil? Is evil a great perilous gulf into which one falls with the first sin?
Yes, I think it is. It's not logical, as you would make it sound.
But it's that dark, that empty. And it is without consolation.
I tried to hold the thread of his conversation with Louis — banal chatter about "good" and "evil" — but an oppressive force unlike any I had experienced was at work upon me.
It was him...
...drawing me into his eyes...

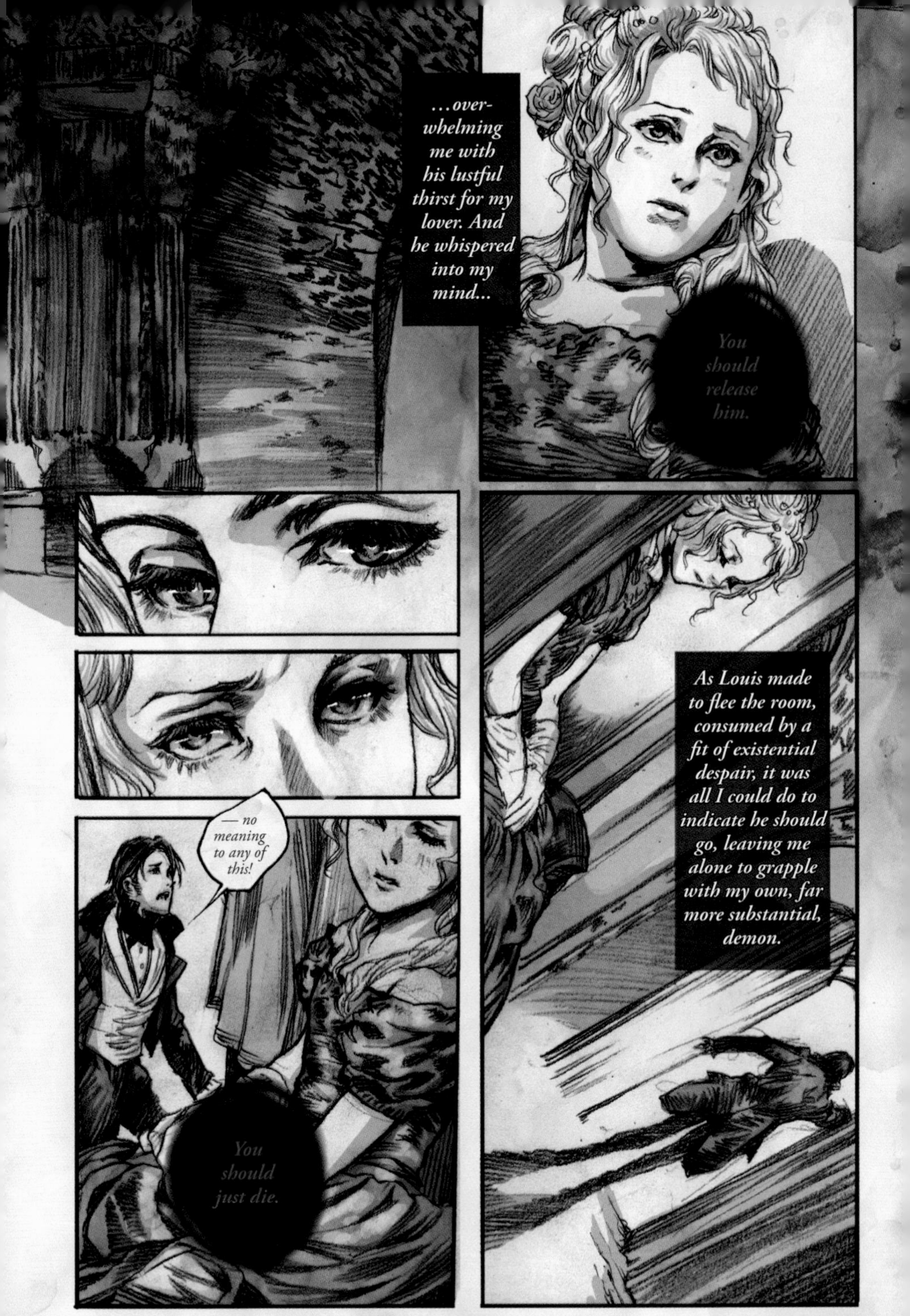

…over-whelming me with his lustful thirst for my lover. And he whispered into my mind…
You should release him.
— no meaning to any of this!
You should just die.
As Louis made to flee the room, consumed by a fit of existential despair, it was all I could do to indicate he should go, leaving me alone to grapple with my own, far more substantial, demon.

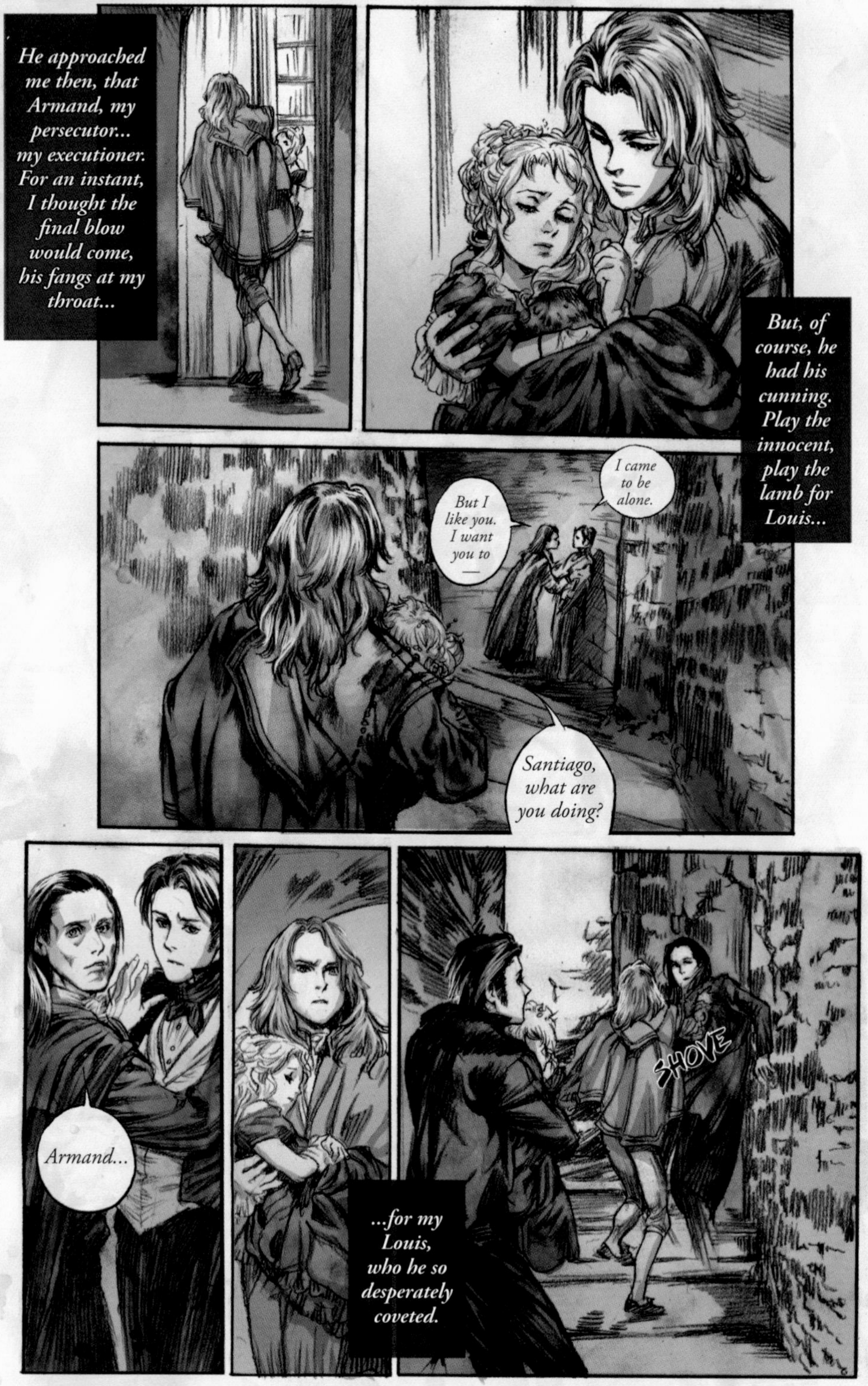

He approached me then, that Armand, my persecutor... my executioner. For an instant, I thought the final blow would come, his fangs at my throat...
But, of course, he had his cunning. Play the innocent, play the lamb for Louis...
I came to be alone.
But I like you. I want you to —
Santiago, what are you doing?
Armand...
...for my Louis, who he so desperately coveted.
SHOVE

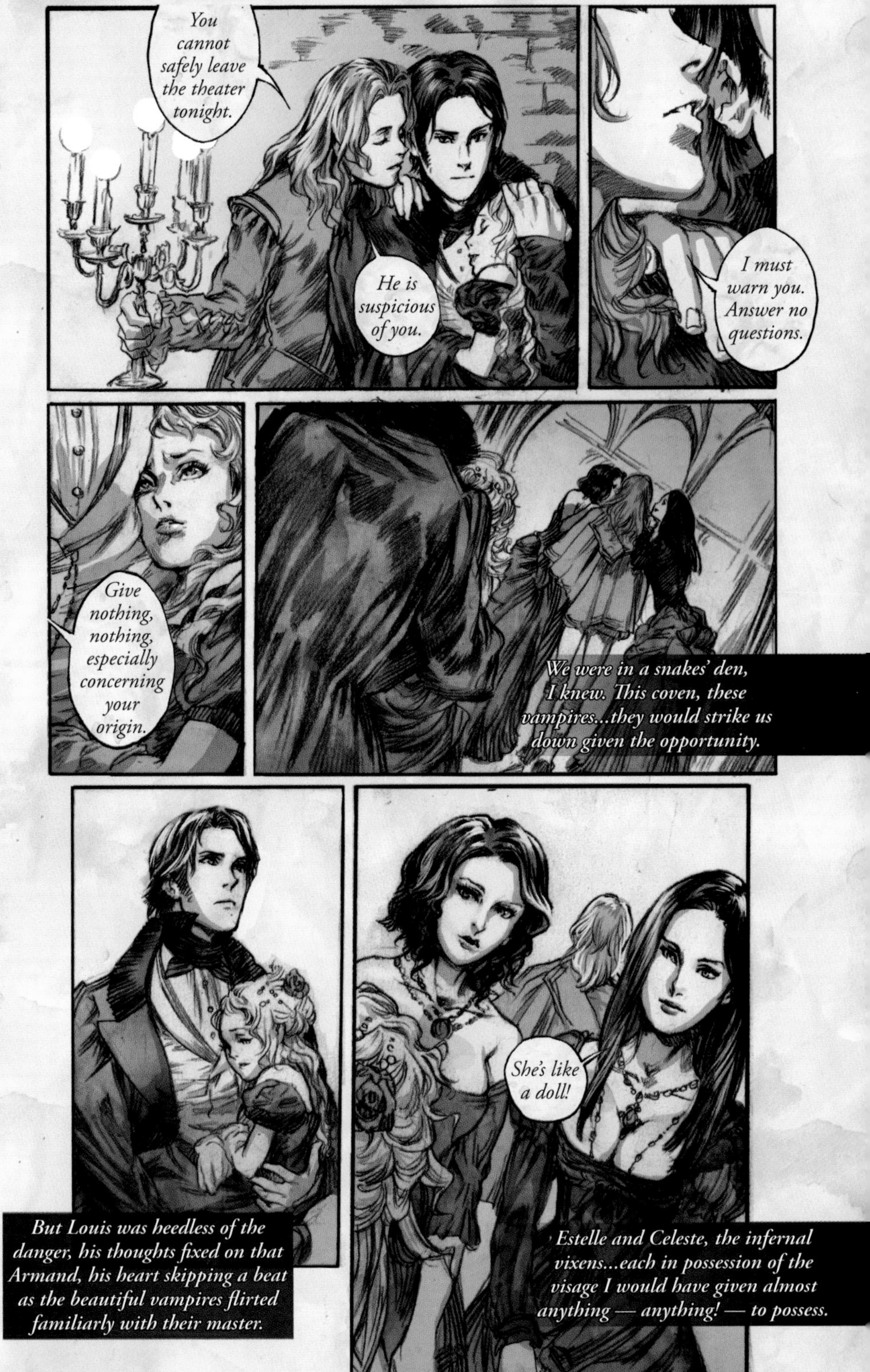
You cannot safely leave the theater tonight.
He is suspicious of you.
I must warn you. Answer no questions.
Give nothing, nothing, especially concerning your origin.
We were in a snakes' den, I knew. This coven, these vampires...they would strike us down given the opportunity.
But Louis was heedless of the danger, his thoughts fixed on that Armand, his heart skipping a beat as the beautiful vampires flirted familiarly with their master.
She's like a doll!
Estelle and Celeste, the infernal vixens...each in possession of the visage I would have given almost anything — anything! — to possess.

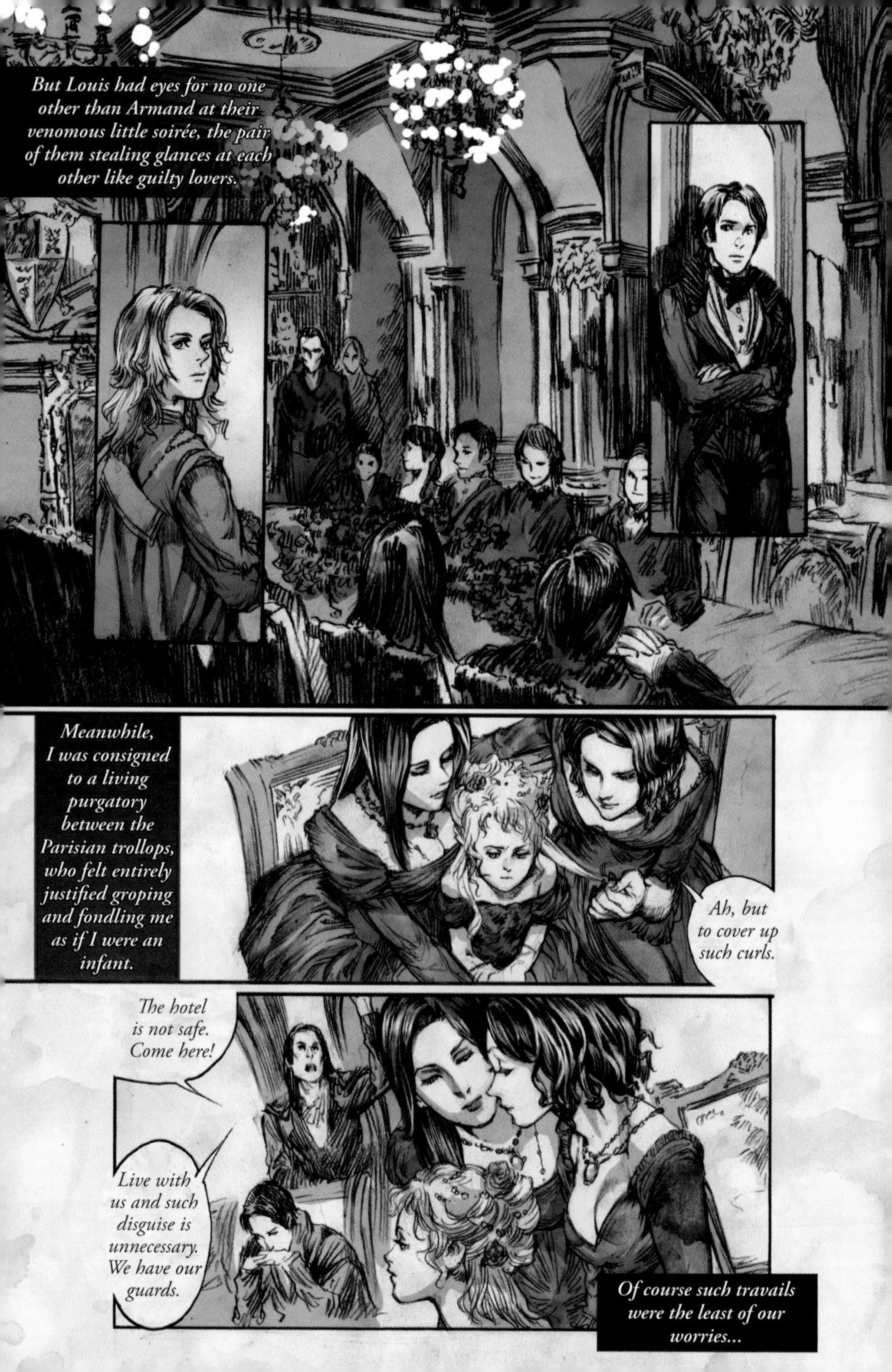

But Louis had eyes for no one other than Armand at their venomous little soirée, the pair of them stealing glances at each other like guilty lovers.
Meanwhile, I was consigned to a living purgatory between the Parisian trollops, who felt entirely justified groping and fondling me as if I were an infant.
Ah, but to cover up such curls.
The hotel is not safe. Come here!
Live with us and such disguise is unnecessary. We have our guards.
Of course such travails were the least of our worries...

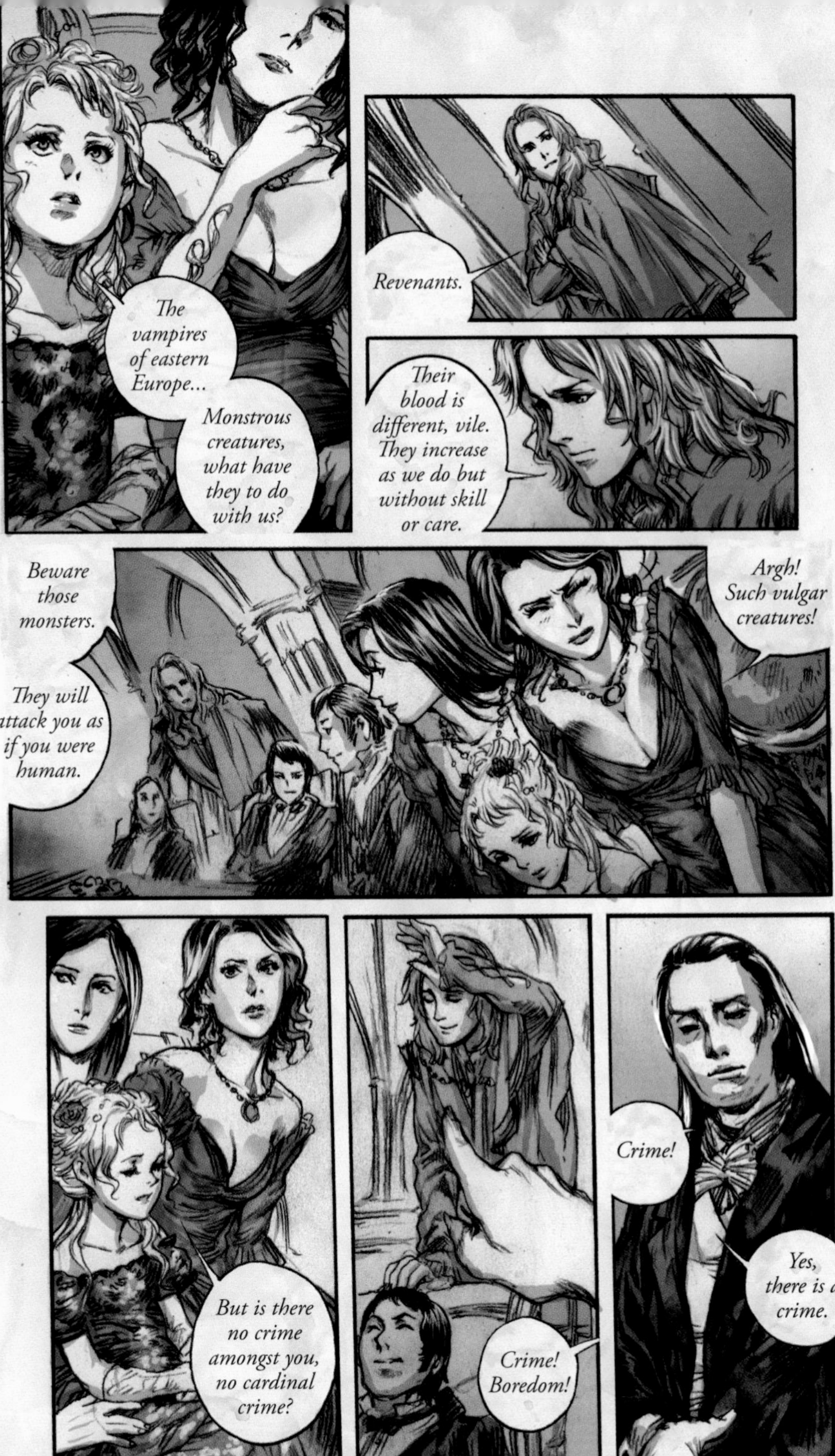
The vampires of eastern Europe...
Monstrous creatures, what have they to do with us?
Revenants.
Their blood is different, vile. They increase as we do but without skill or care.
Beware those monsters.
They will attack you as if you were human.
Argh! Such vulgar creatures!
But is there no crime amongst you, no cardinal crime?
Crime! Boredom!
Crime!
Yes, there is a crime.

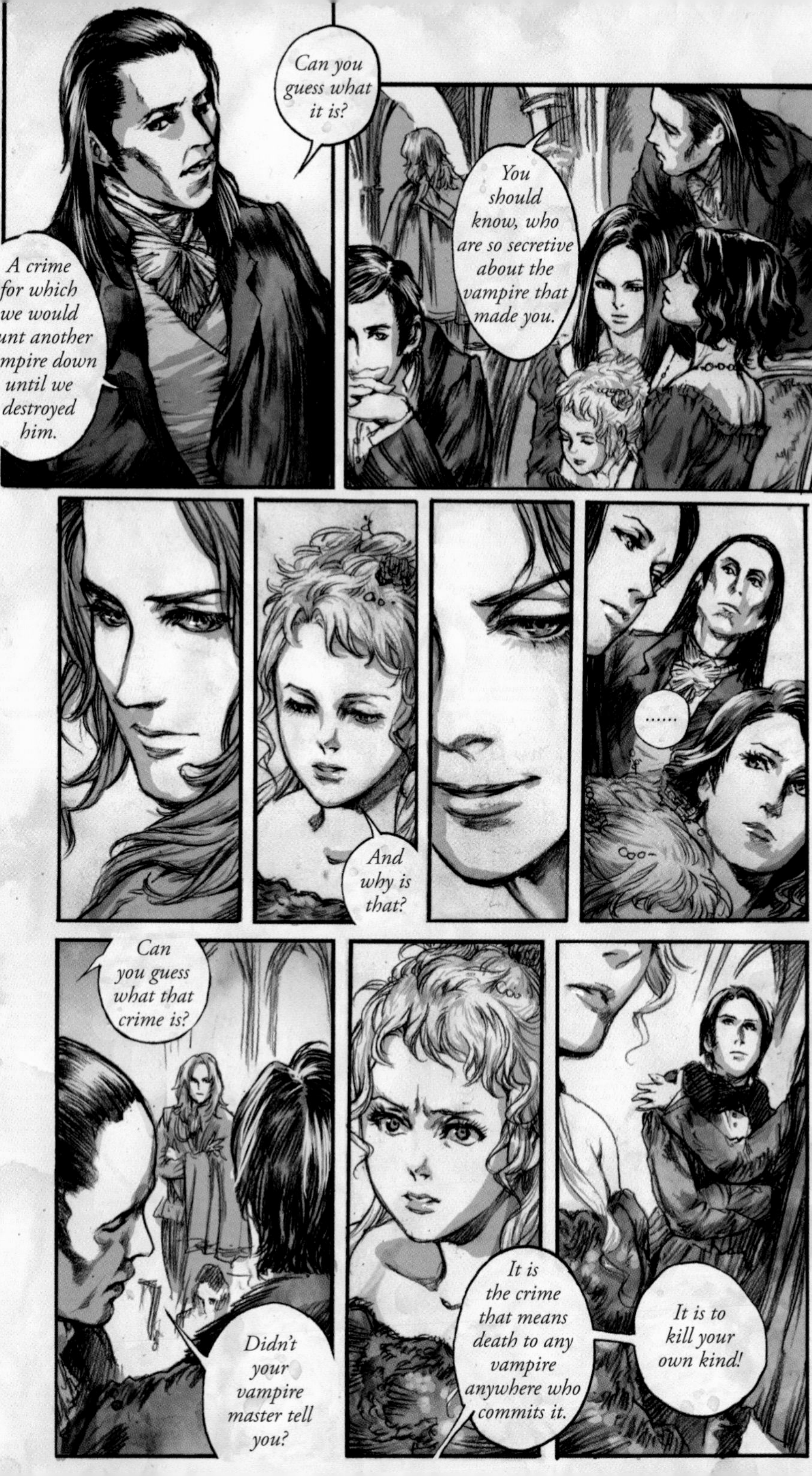
Can you guess what it is?
A crime for which we would hunt another vampire down until we destroyed him.
You should know, who are so secretive about the vampire that made you.
And why is that?
......
Can you guess what that crime is?
Didn't your vampire master tell you?
It is the crime that means death to any vampire anywhere who commits it.
It is to kill your own kind!

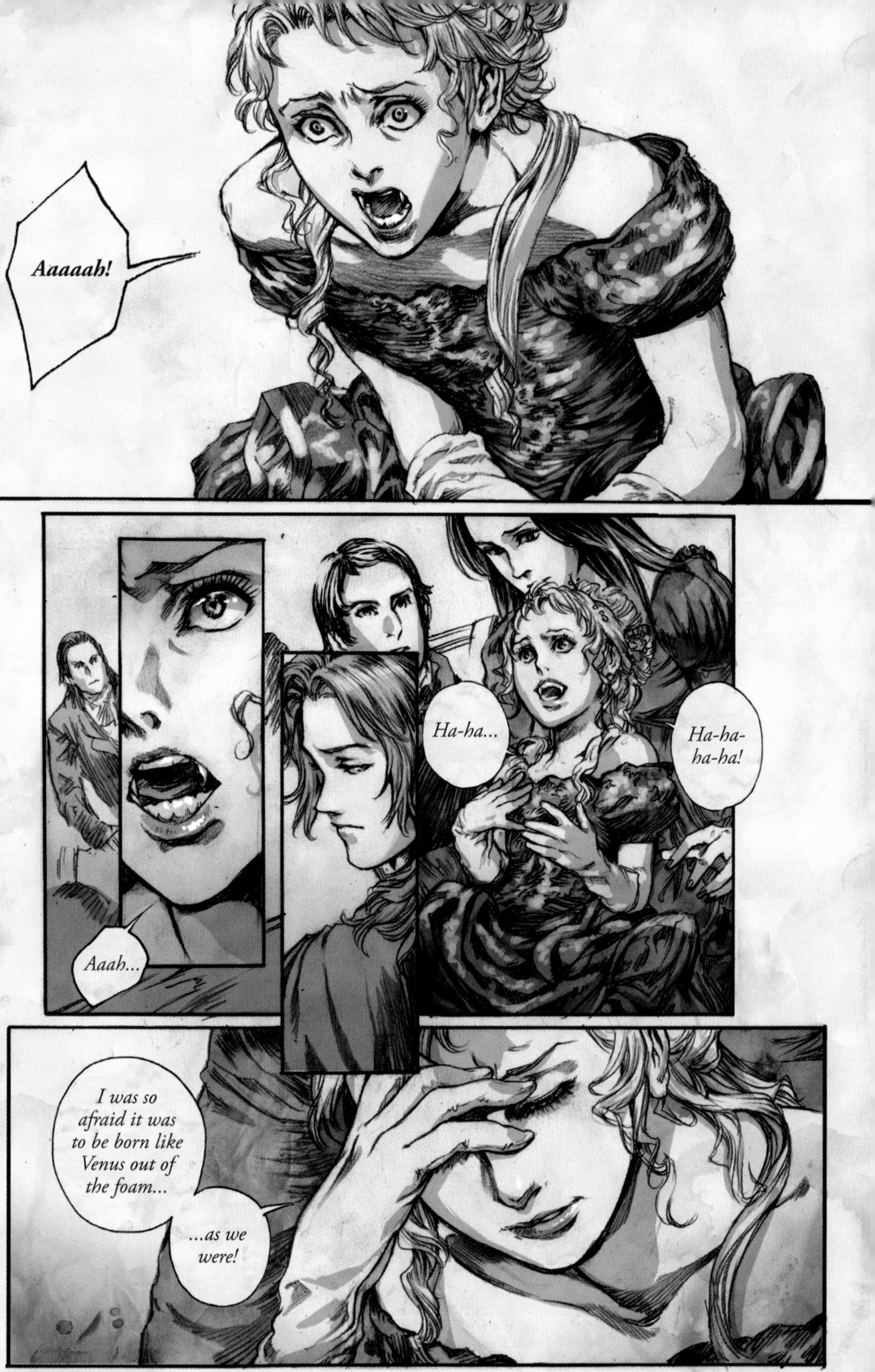
Aaaaah!
Aaah...
Ha-ha...
Ha-ha-ha-ha!
I was so afraid it was to be born like Venus out of the foam...
...as we were!

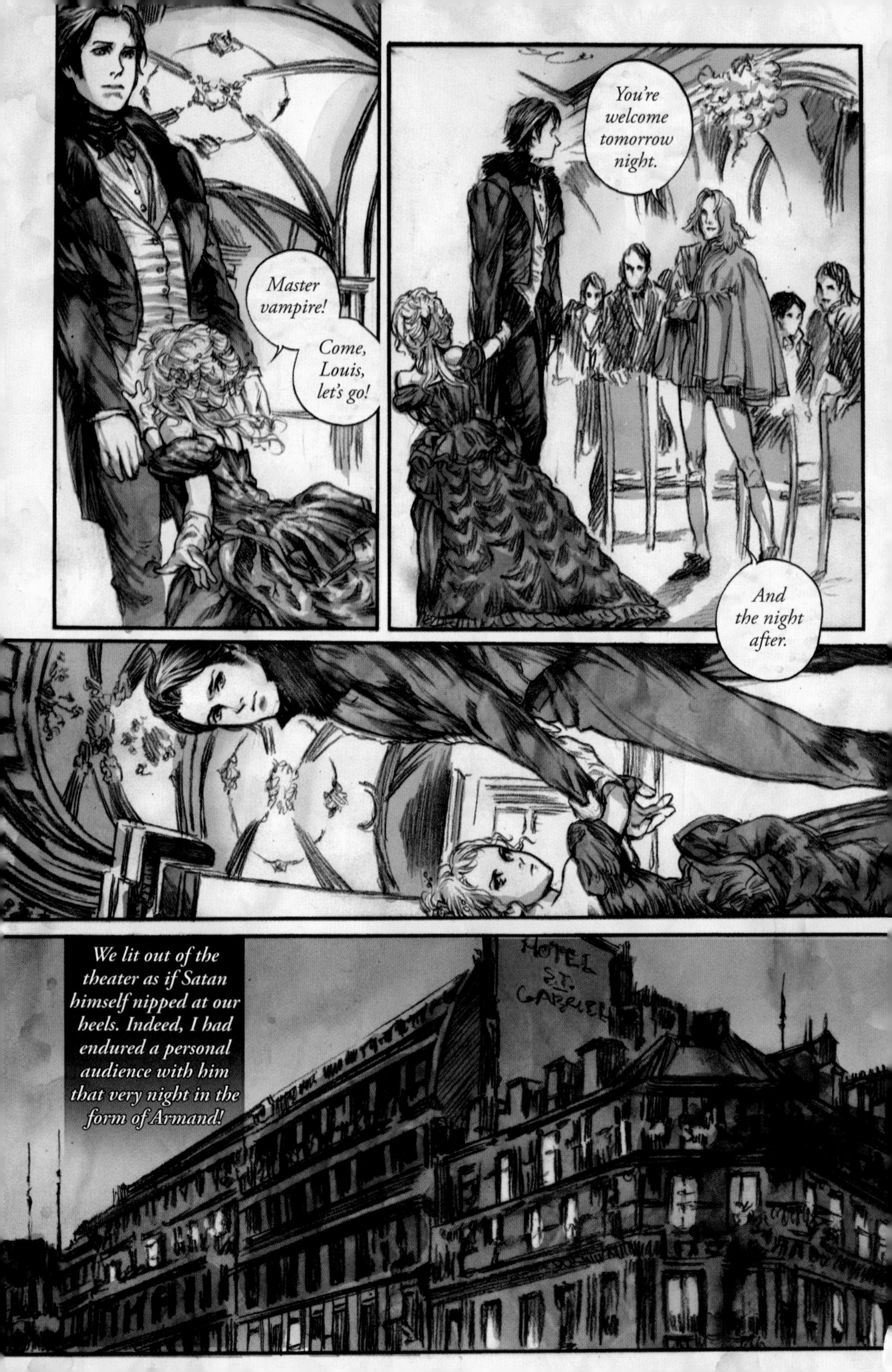
Master vampire!
Come, Louis, let's go!
You're welcome tomorrow night.
And the night after.
We lit out of the theater as if Satan himself nipped at our heels. Indeed, I had endured a personal audience with him that very night in the form of Armand!

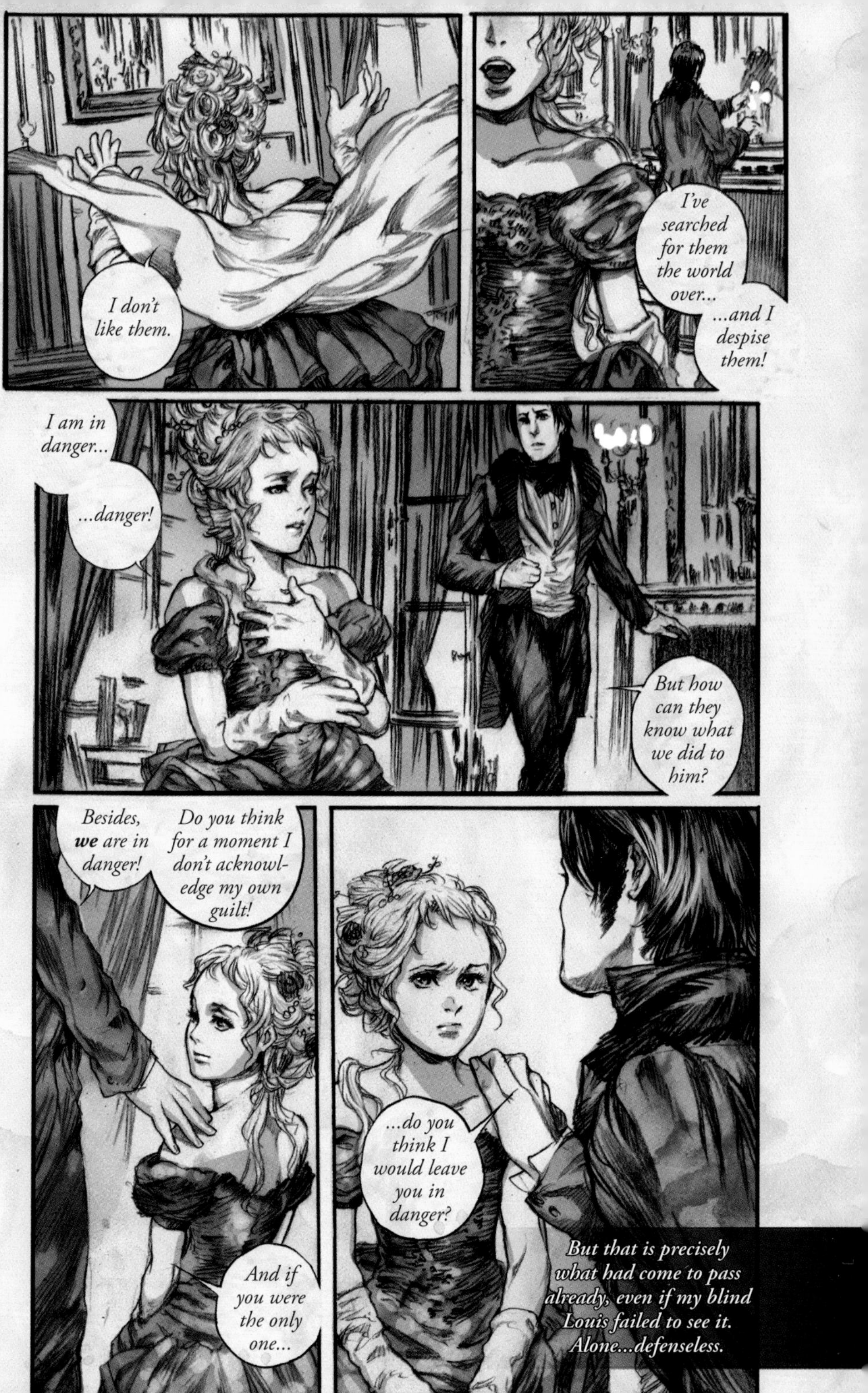
I don't like them.
I've searched for them the world over...
...and I despise them!
I am in danger...
...danger!
But how can they know what we did to him?
Besides, **we** are in danger!
Do you think for a moment I don't acknowledge my own guilt!
And if you were the only one...
...do you think I would leave you in danger?
But that is precisely what had come to pass already, even if my blind Louis failed to see it. Alone...defenseless.

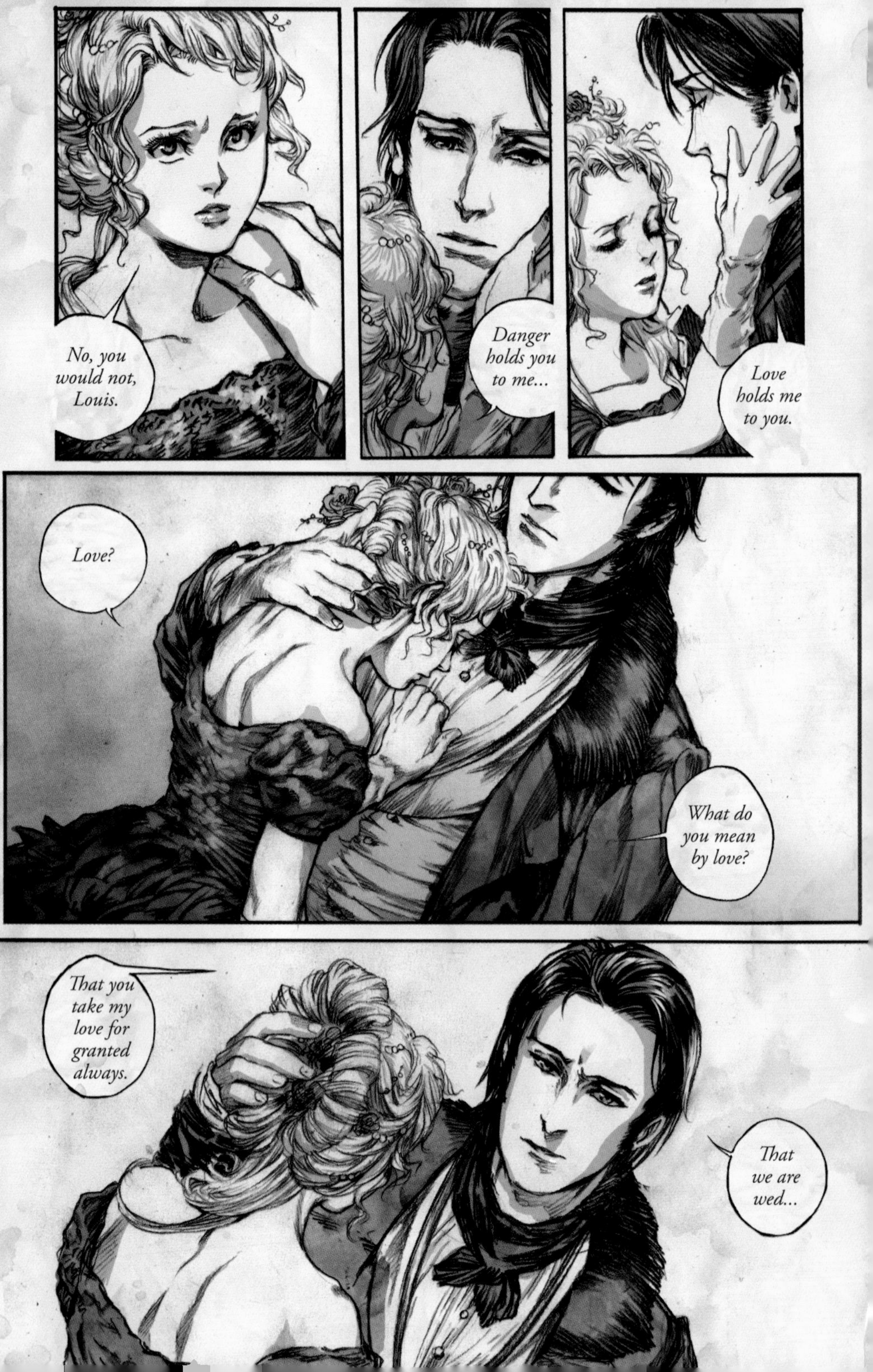
No, you would not, Louis.
Danger holds you to me...
Love holds me to you.
Love?
What do you mean by love?
That you take my love for granted always.
That we are wed...

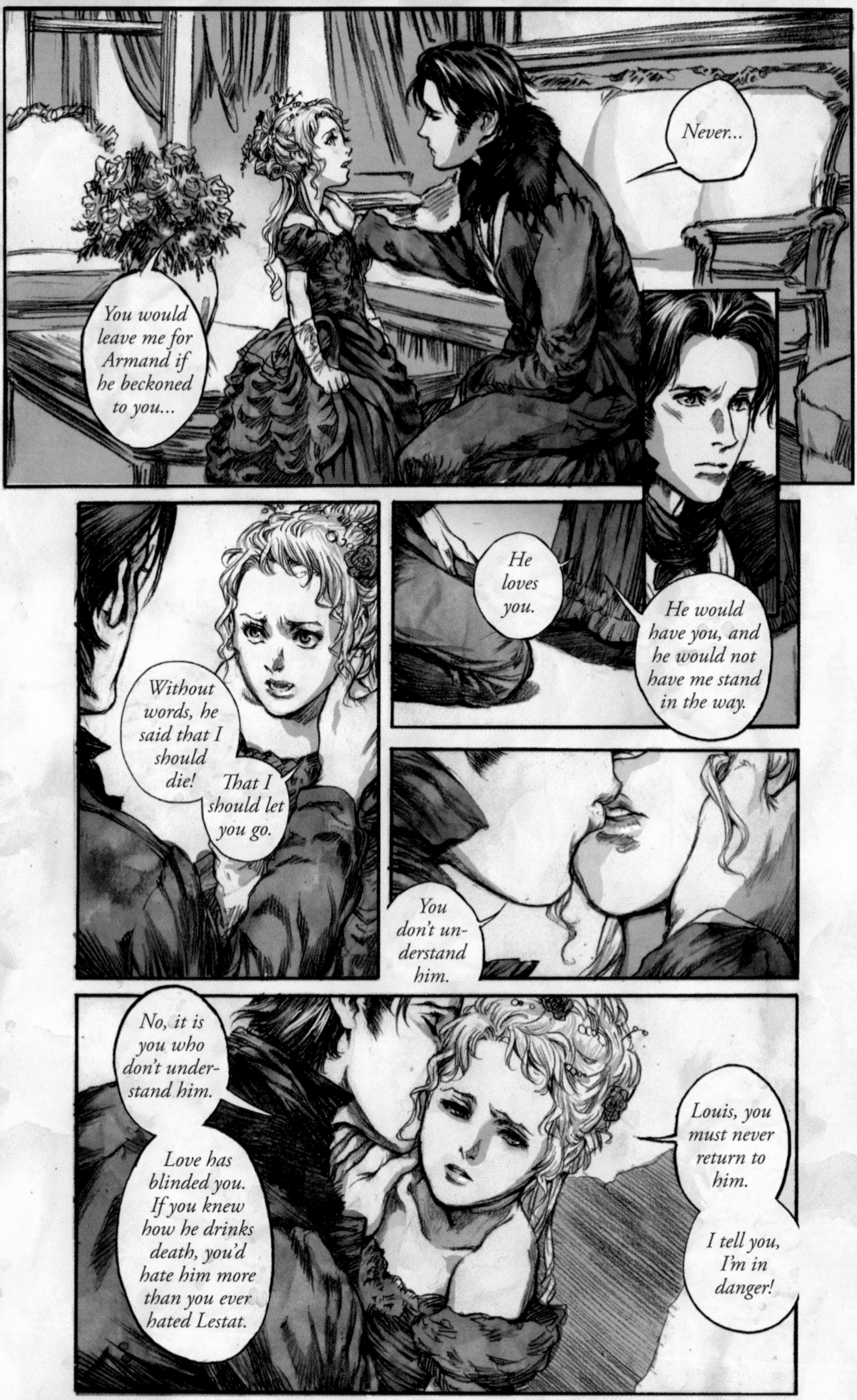
Never...
You would leave me for Armand if he beckoned to you...
Without words, he said that I should die!
That I should let you go.
He loves you.
He would have you, and he would not have me stand in the way.
You don't un-derstand him.
No, it is you who don't under-stand him.
Love has blinded you. If you knew how he drinks death, you'd hate him more than you ever hated Lestat.
Louis, you must never return to him.
I tell you, I'm in danger!

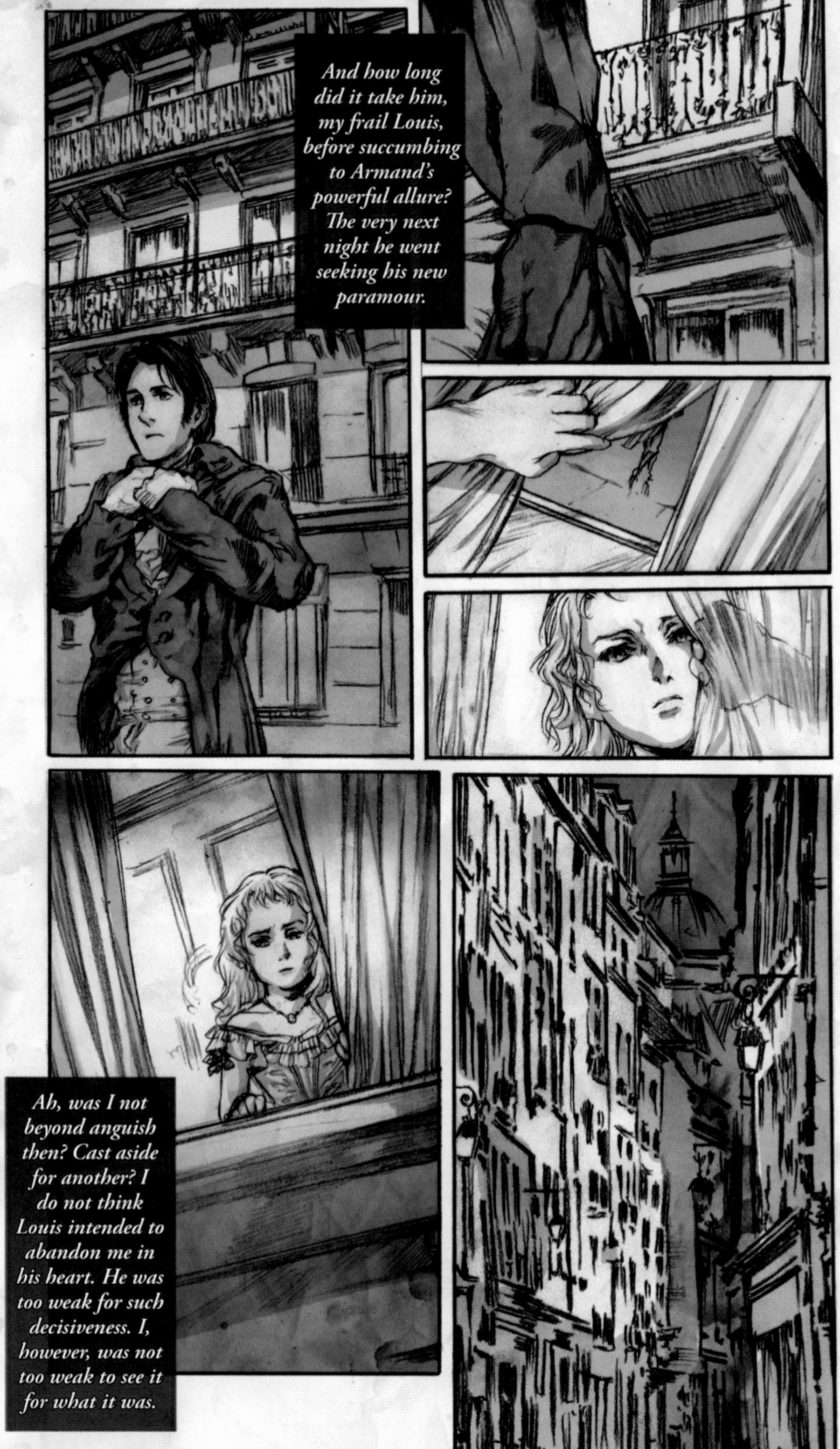
And how long did it take him, my frail Louis, before succumbing to Armand's powerful allure? The very next night he went seeking his new paramour.
Ah, was I not beyond anguish then? Cast aside for another? I do not think Louis intended to abandon me in his heart. He was too weak for such decisiveness. I, however, was not too weak to see it for what it was.

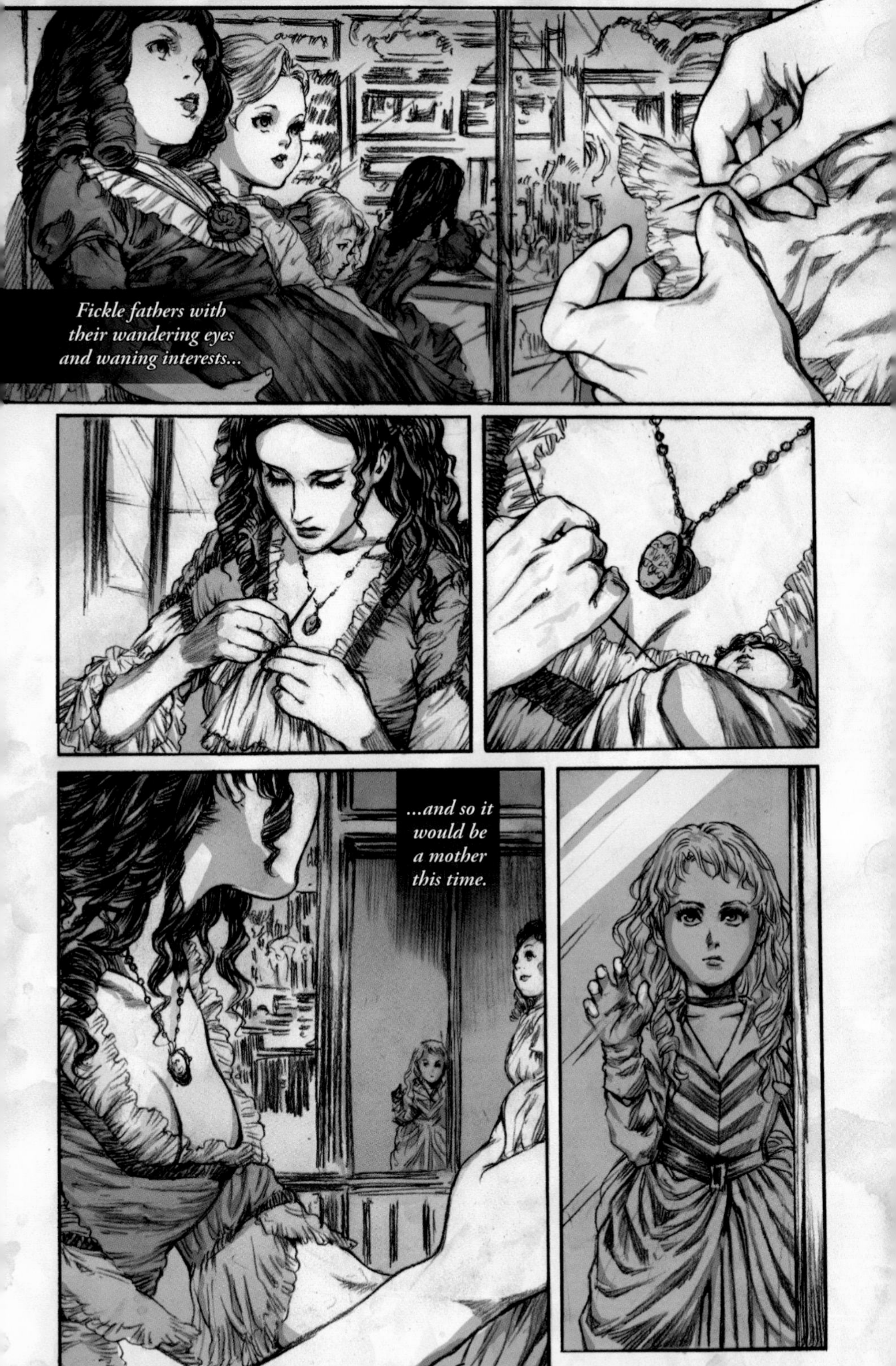

Fickle fathers with their wandering eyes and waning interests...
...and so it would be a mother this time.

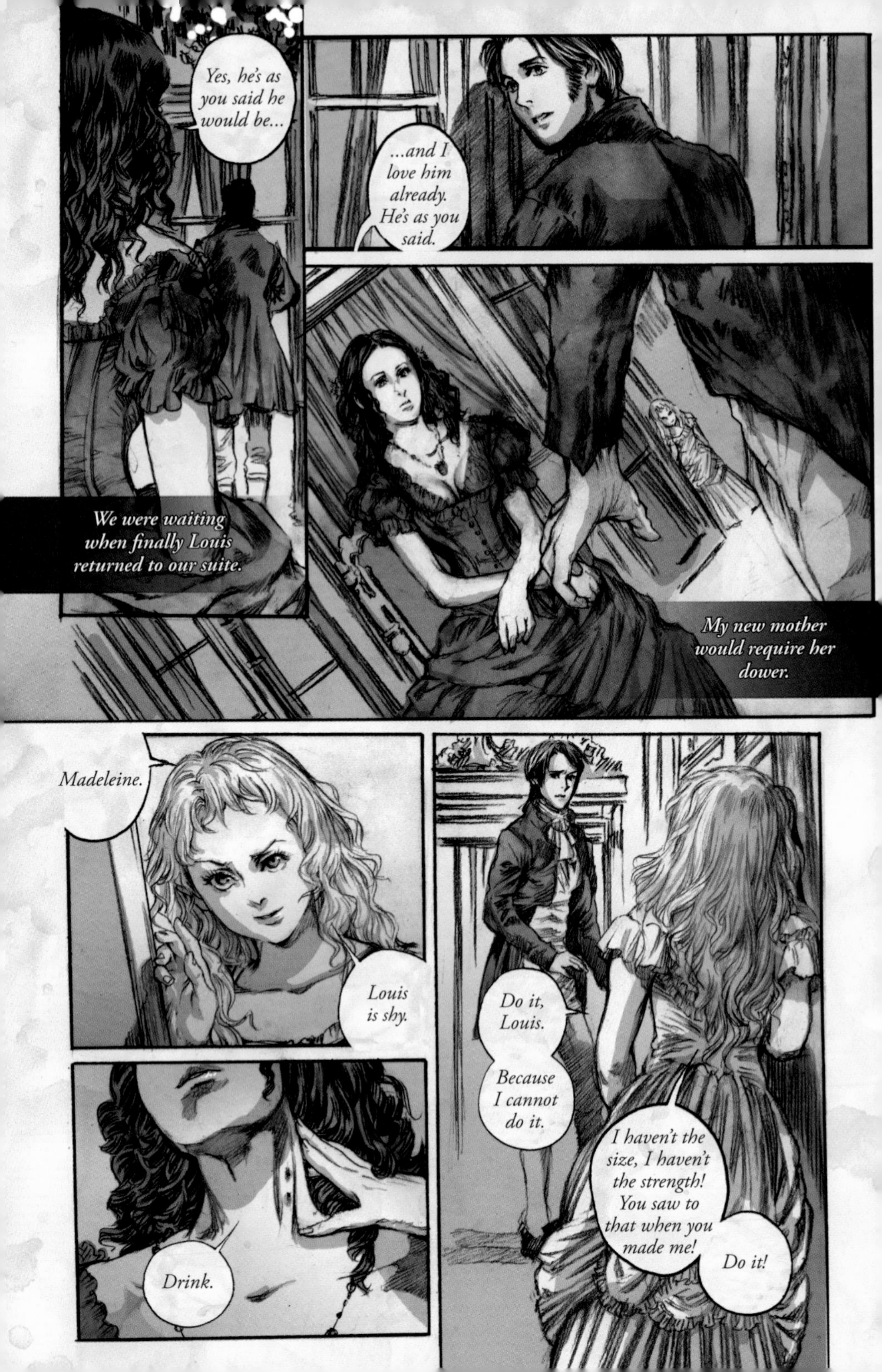
Yes, he's as you said he would be...
...and I love him already. He's as you said.
We were waiting when finally Louis returned to our suite.
My new mother would require her dower.
Madeleine.
Louis is shy.
Drink.
Do it, Louis.
Because I cannot do it.
I haven't the size, I haven't the strength! You saw to that when you made me!
Do it!

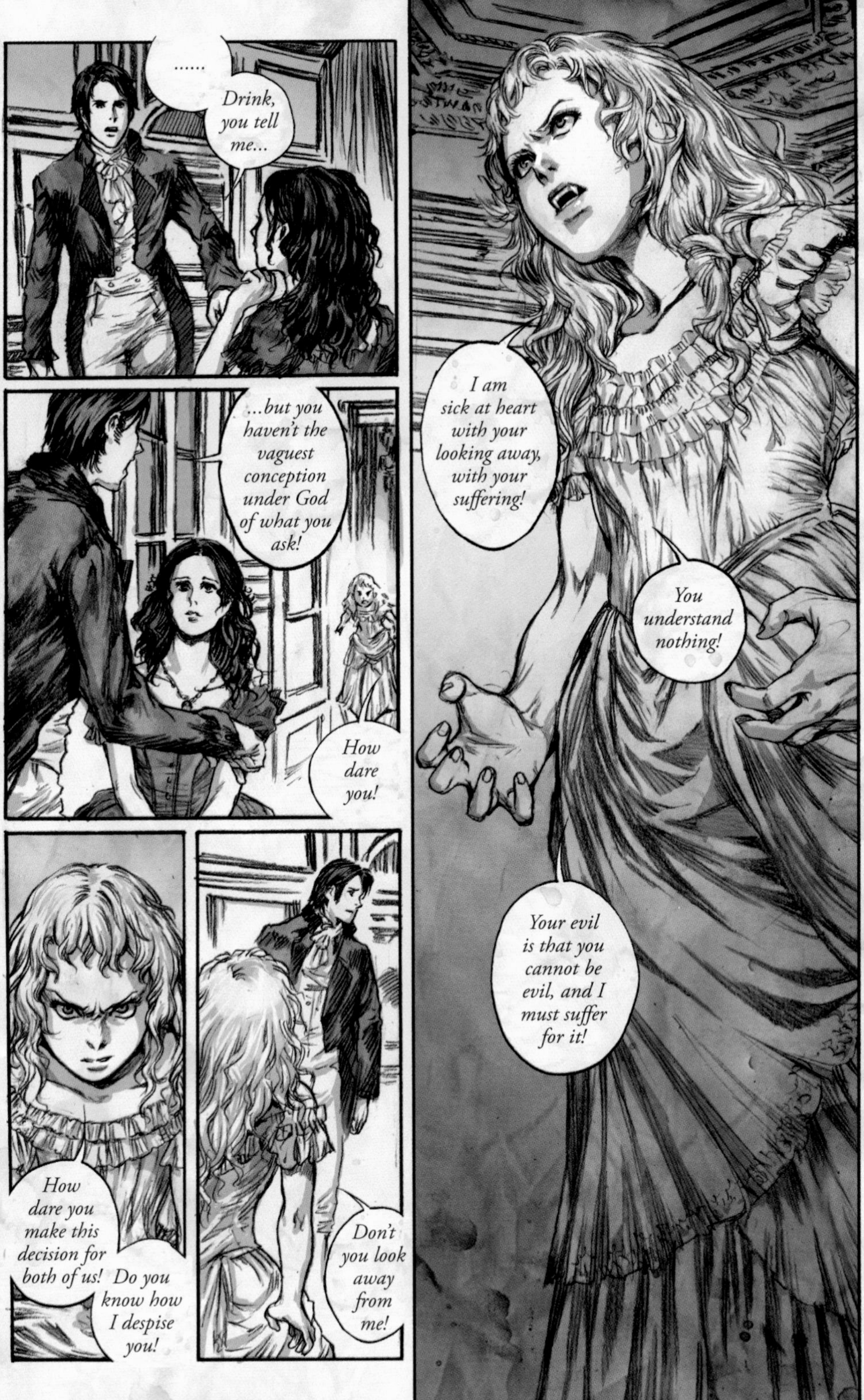
......
Drink, you tell me...
...but you haven't the vaguest conception under God of what you ask!
How dare you!
How dare you make this decision for both of us!
Do you know how I despise you!
Don't you look away from me!
I am sick at heart with your looking away, with your suffering!
You understand nothing!
Your evil is that you cannot be evil, and I must suffer for it!

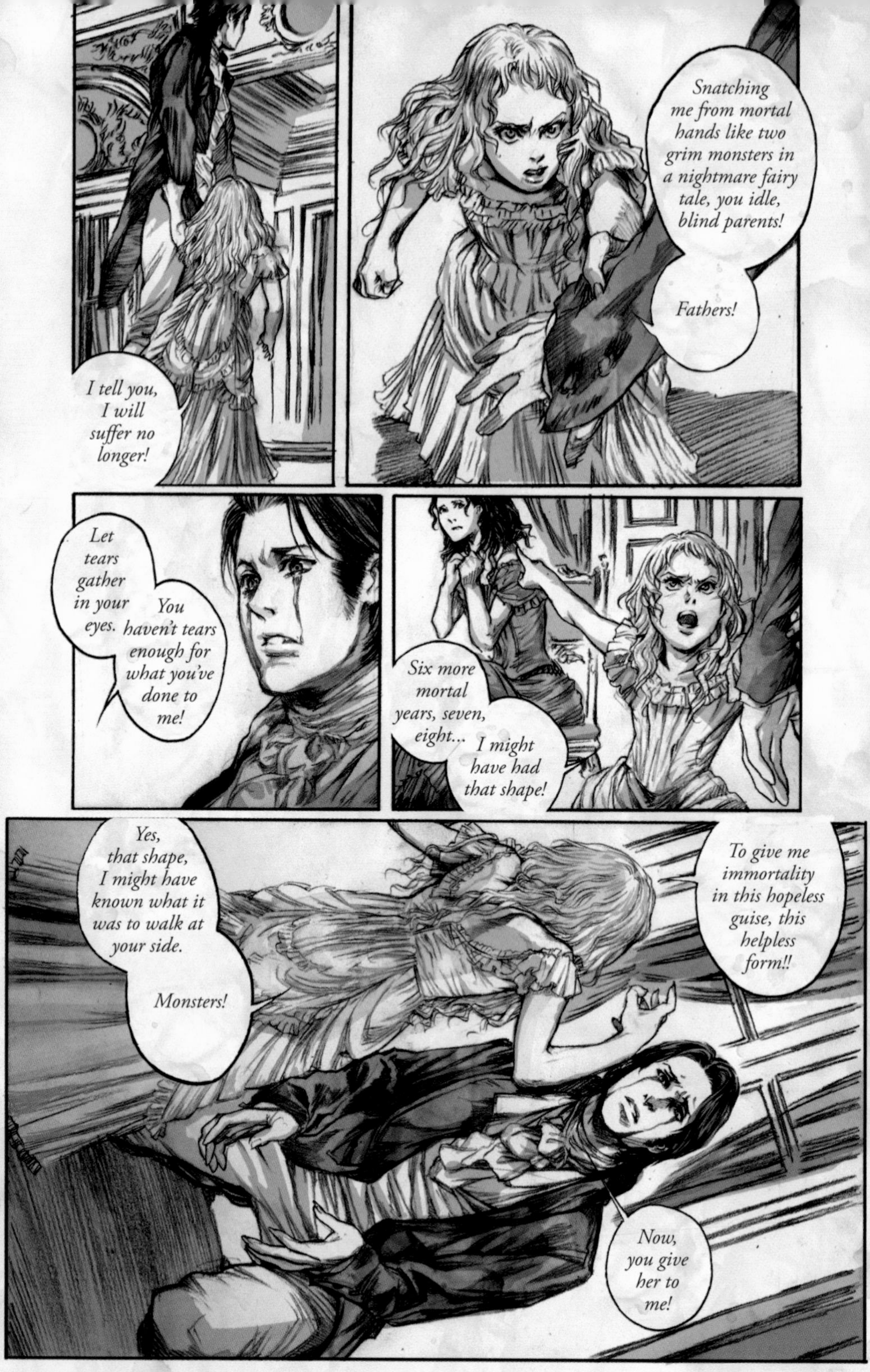

Snatching me from mortal hands like two grim monsters in a nightmare fairy tale, you idle, blind parents!
Fathers!
I tell you, I will suffer no longer!
Let tears gather in your eyes.
You haven't tears enough for what you've done to me!
Six more mortal years, seven, eight...
I might have had that shape!
Yes, that shape, I might have known what it was to walk at your side.
Monsters!
To give me immortality in this hopeless guise, this helpless form!!
Now, you give her to me!

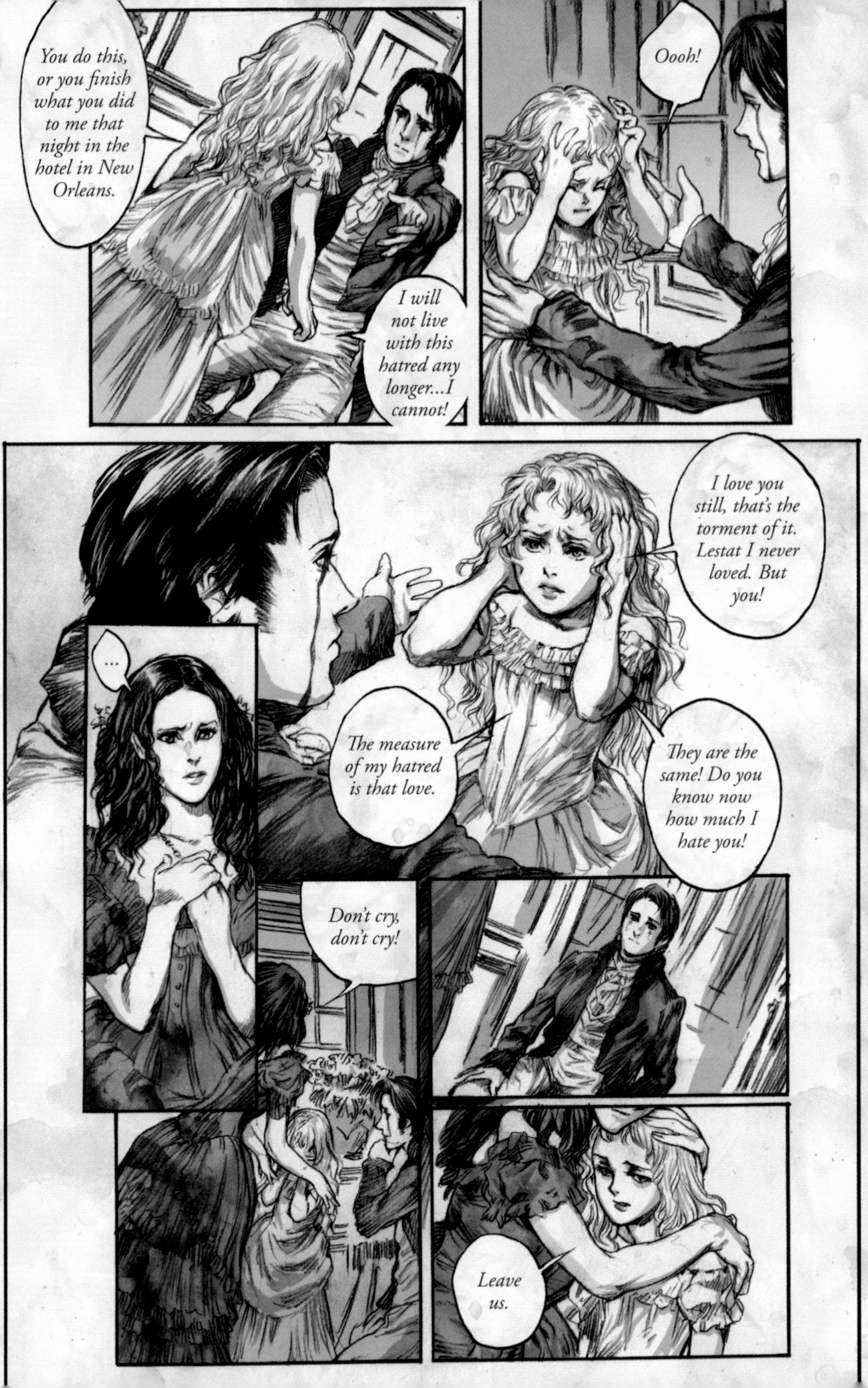
You do this, or you finish what you did to me that night in the hotel in New Orleans.
I will not live with this hatred any longer...I cannot!
Oooh!
I love you still, that's the torment of it. Lestat I never loved. But you!
...
The measure of my hatred is that love.
They are the same! Do you know now how much I hate you!
Don't cry, don't cry!
Leave us.

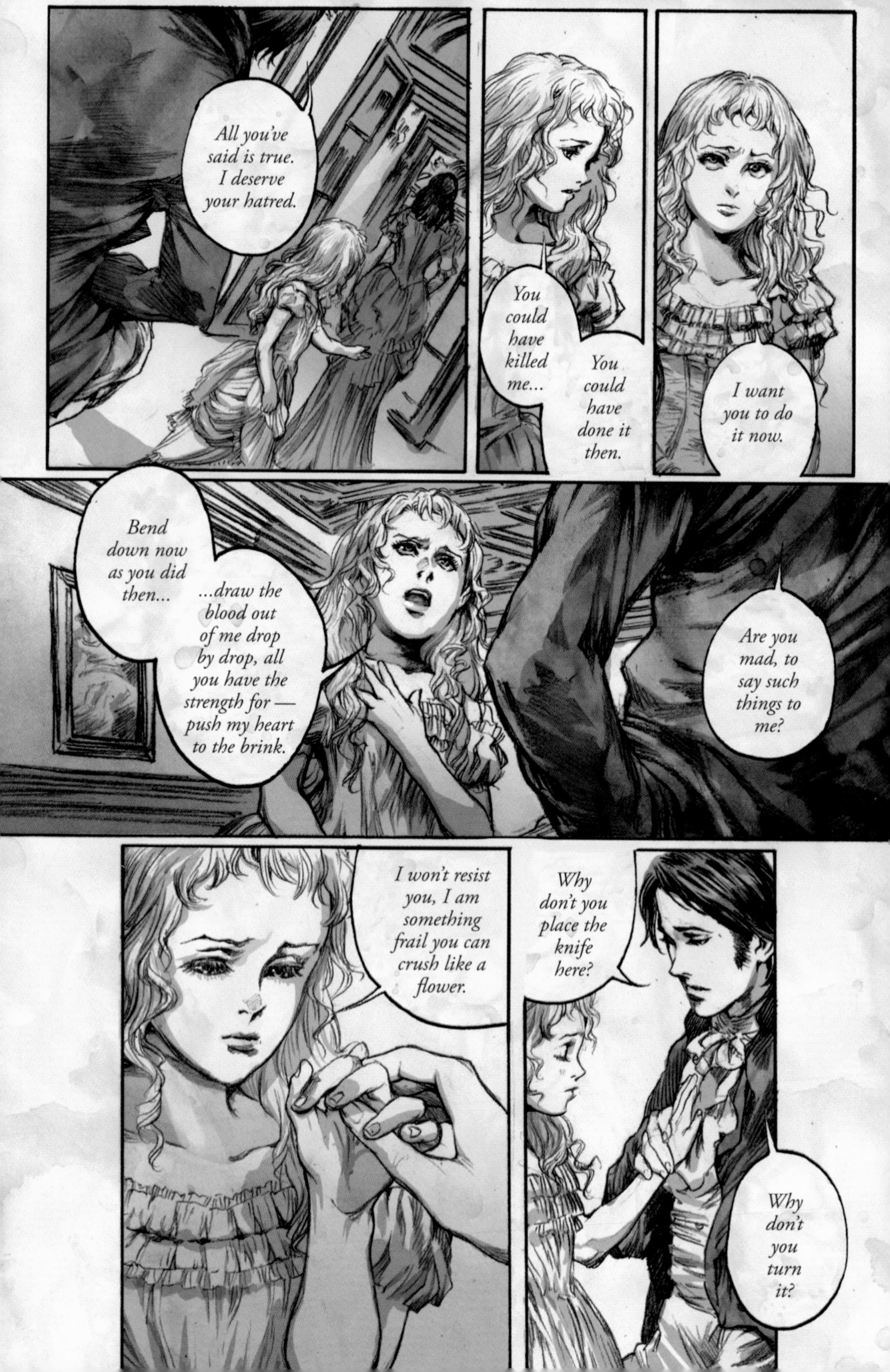
All you've said is true. I deserve your hatred.
You could have killed me...
You could have done it then.
I want you to do it now.
Bend down now as you did then...
...draw the blood out of me drop by drop, all you have the strength for — push my heart to the brink.
Are you mad, to say such things to me?
I won't resist you, I am something frail you can crush like a flower.
Why don't you place the knife here?
Why don't you turn it?

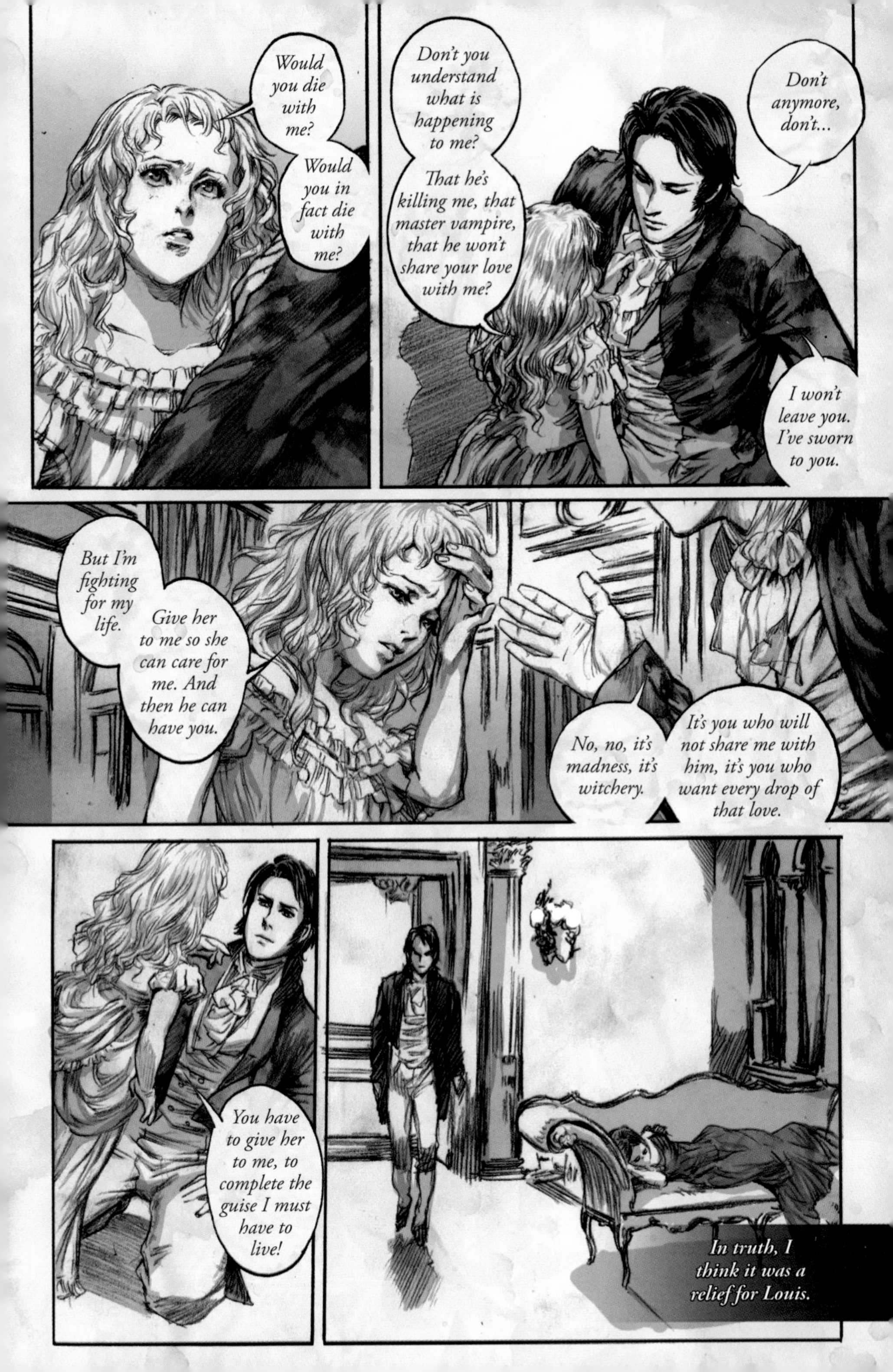
Would you die with me?
Would you in fact die with me?
Don't you understand what is happening to me?
That he's killing me, that master vampire, that he won't share your love with me?
Don't anymore, don't...
I won't leave you. I've sworn to you.
But I'm fighting for my life.
Give her to me so she can care for me. And then he can have you.
No, no, it's madness, it's witchery.
It's you who will not share me with him, it's you who want every drop of that love.
You have to give her to me, to complete the guise I must have to live!
In truth, I think it was a relief for Louis.

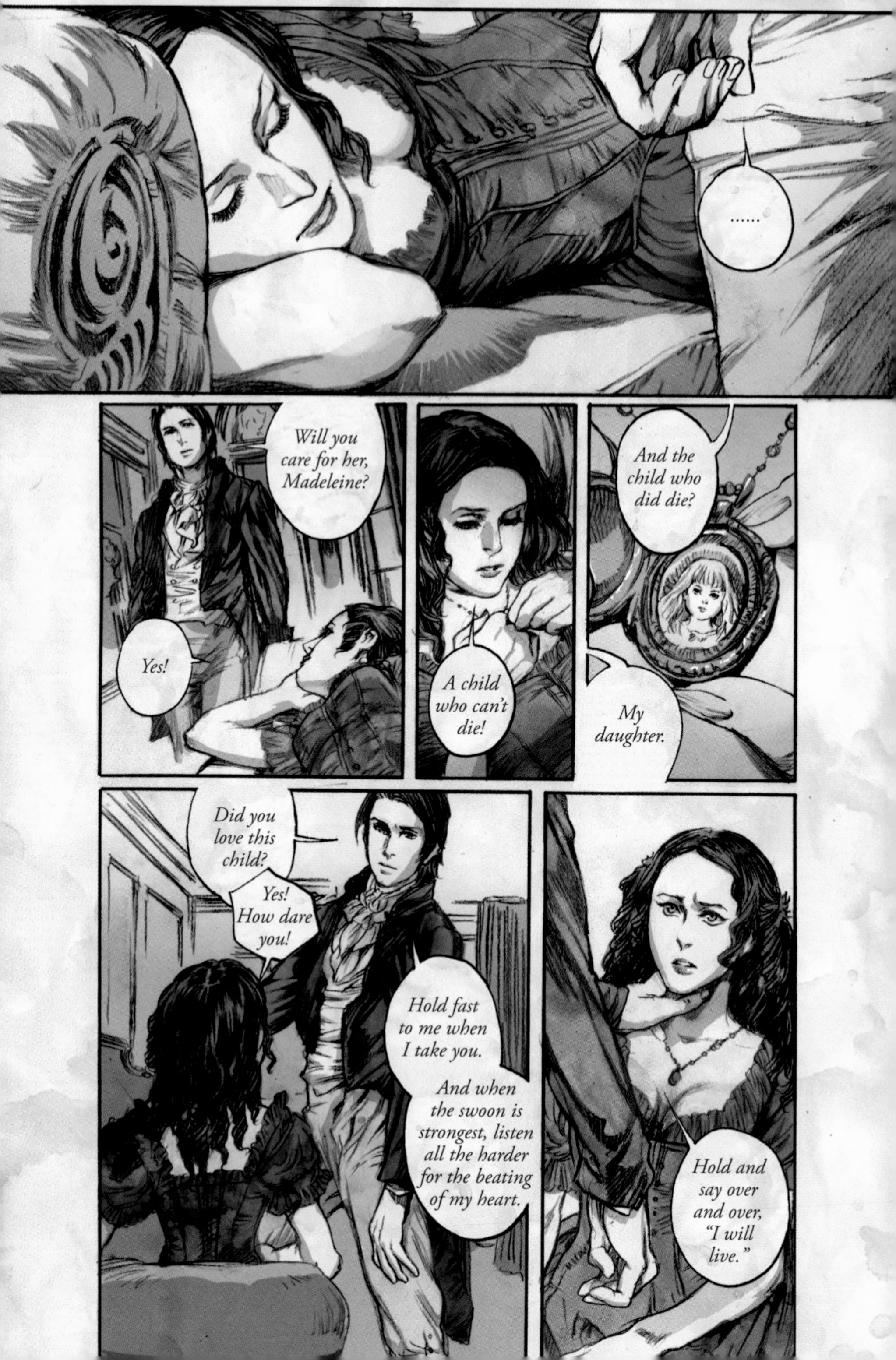
......
Will you care for her, Madeleine?
Yes!
A child who can't die!
And the child who did die?
My daughter.
Did you love this child?
Yes! How dare you!
Hold fast to me when I take you.
And when the swoon is strongest, listen all the harder for the beating of my heart.
Hold and say over and over, "I will live."

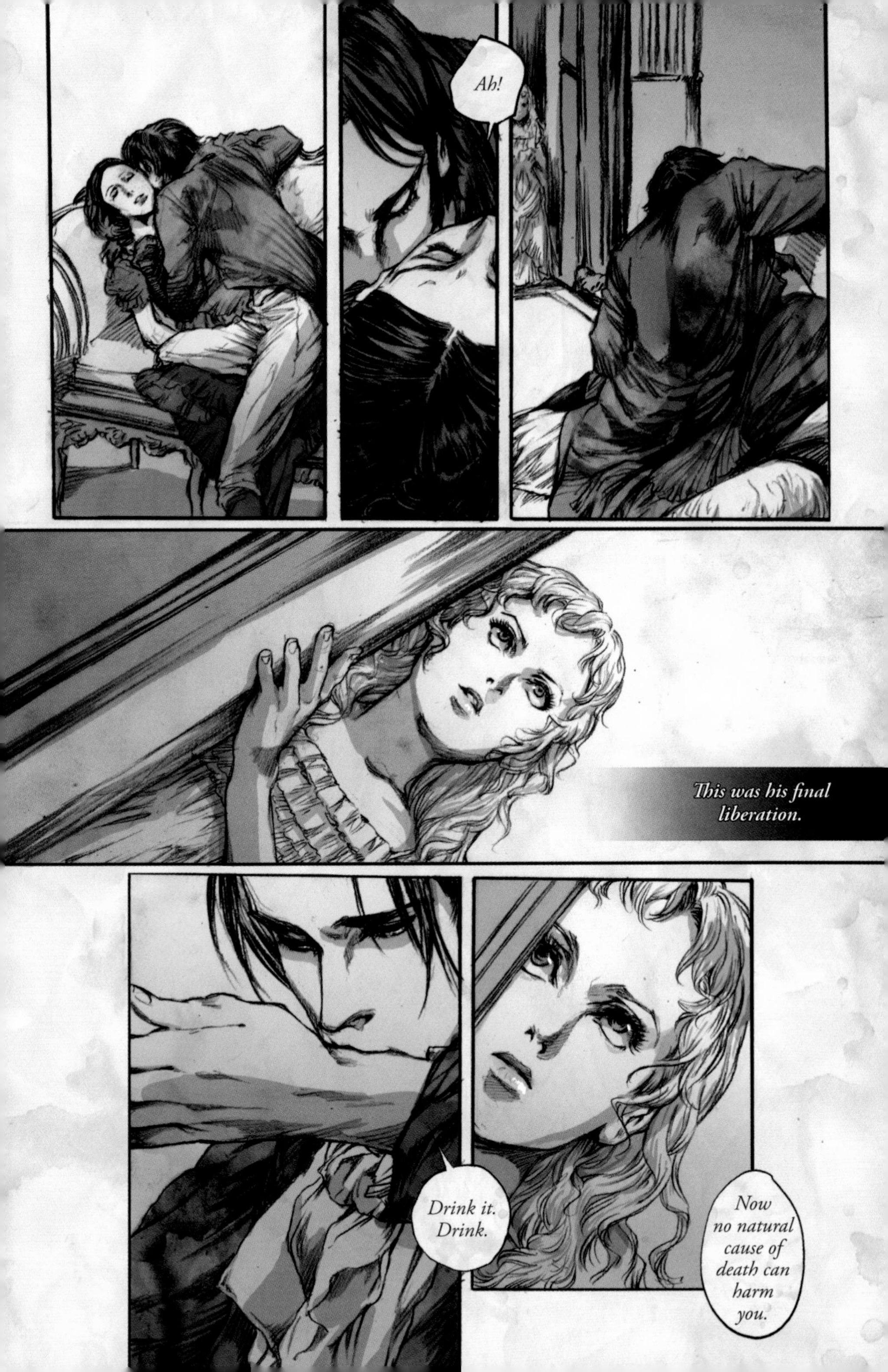
Ah!
This was his final liberation.
Drink it. Drink.
Now no natural cause of death can harm you.

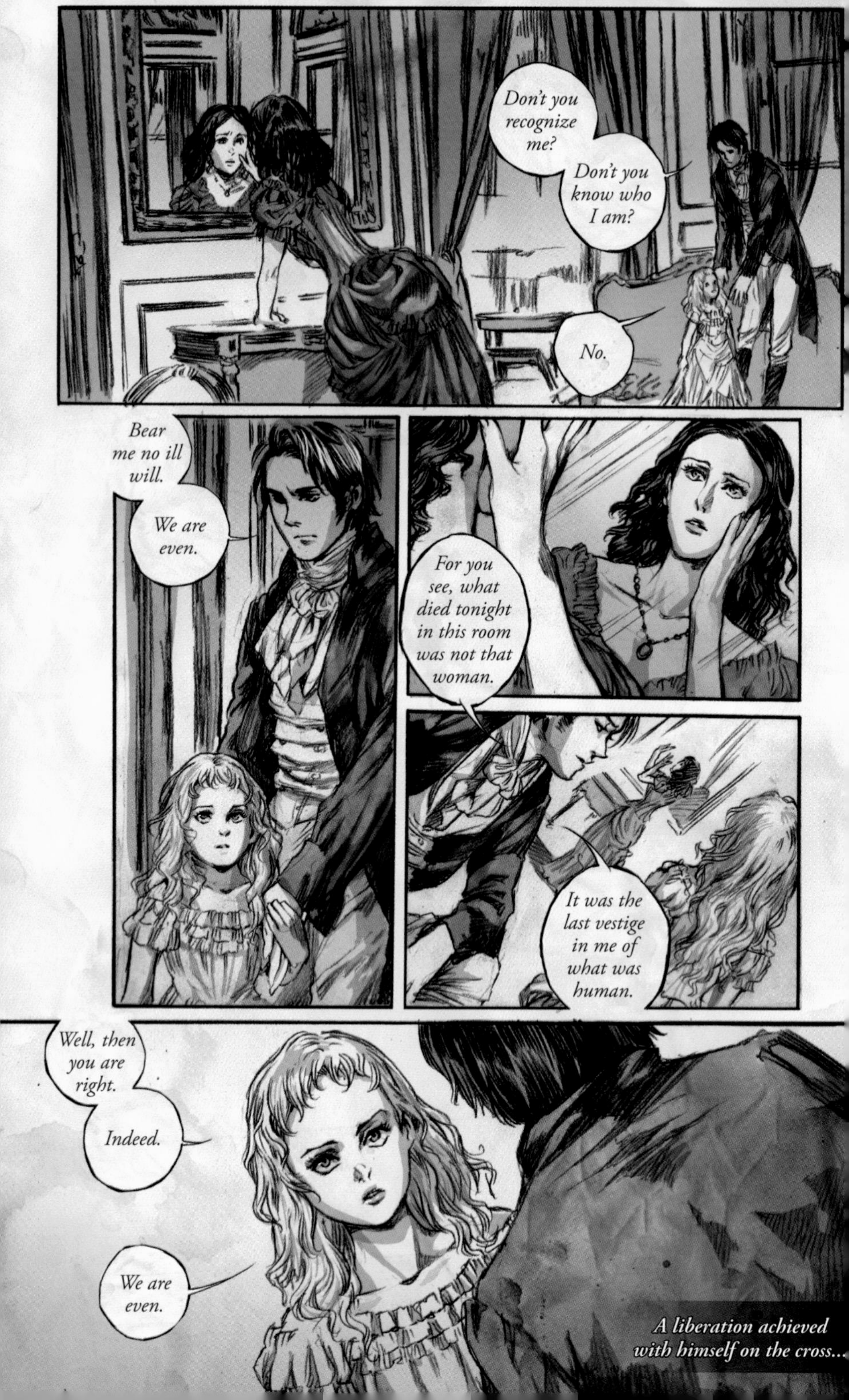
Don't you recognize me?
Don't you know who I am?
No.
Bear me no ill will.
We are even.
For you see, what died tonight in this room was not that woman.
It was the last vestige in me of what was human.
Well, then you are right.
Indeed.
We are even.
A liberation achieved with himself on the cross...

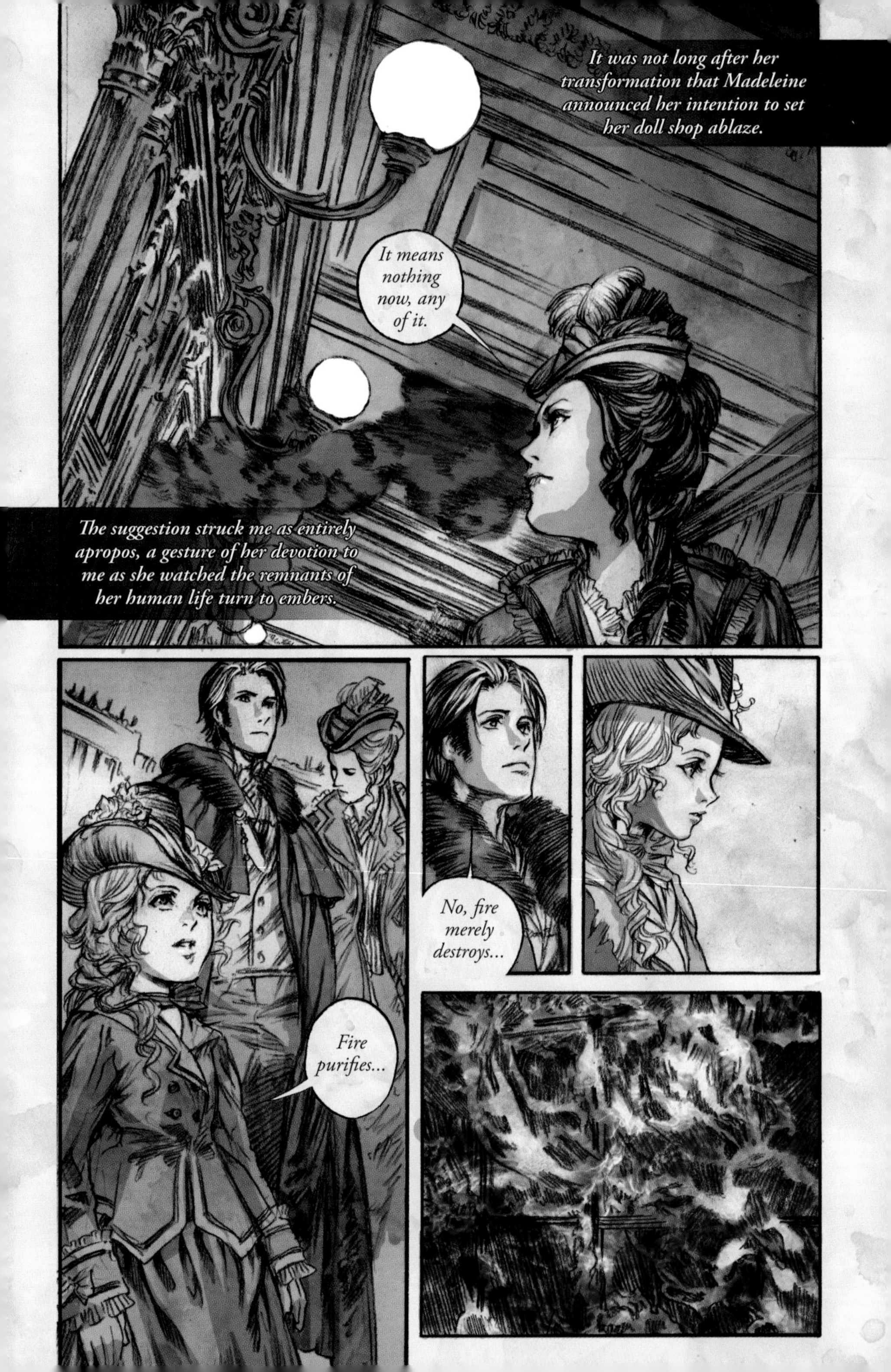
It was not long after her transformation that Madeleine announced her intention to set her doll shop ablaze.
It means nothing now, any of it.
The suggestion struck me as entirely apropos, a gesture of her devotion to me as she watched the remnants of her human life turn to embers.
Fire purifies...
No, fire merely destroys...

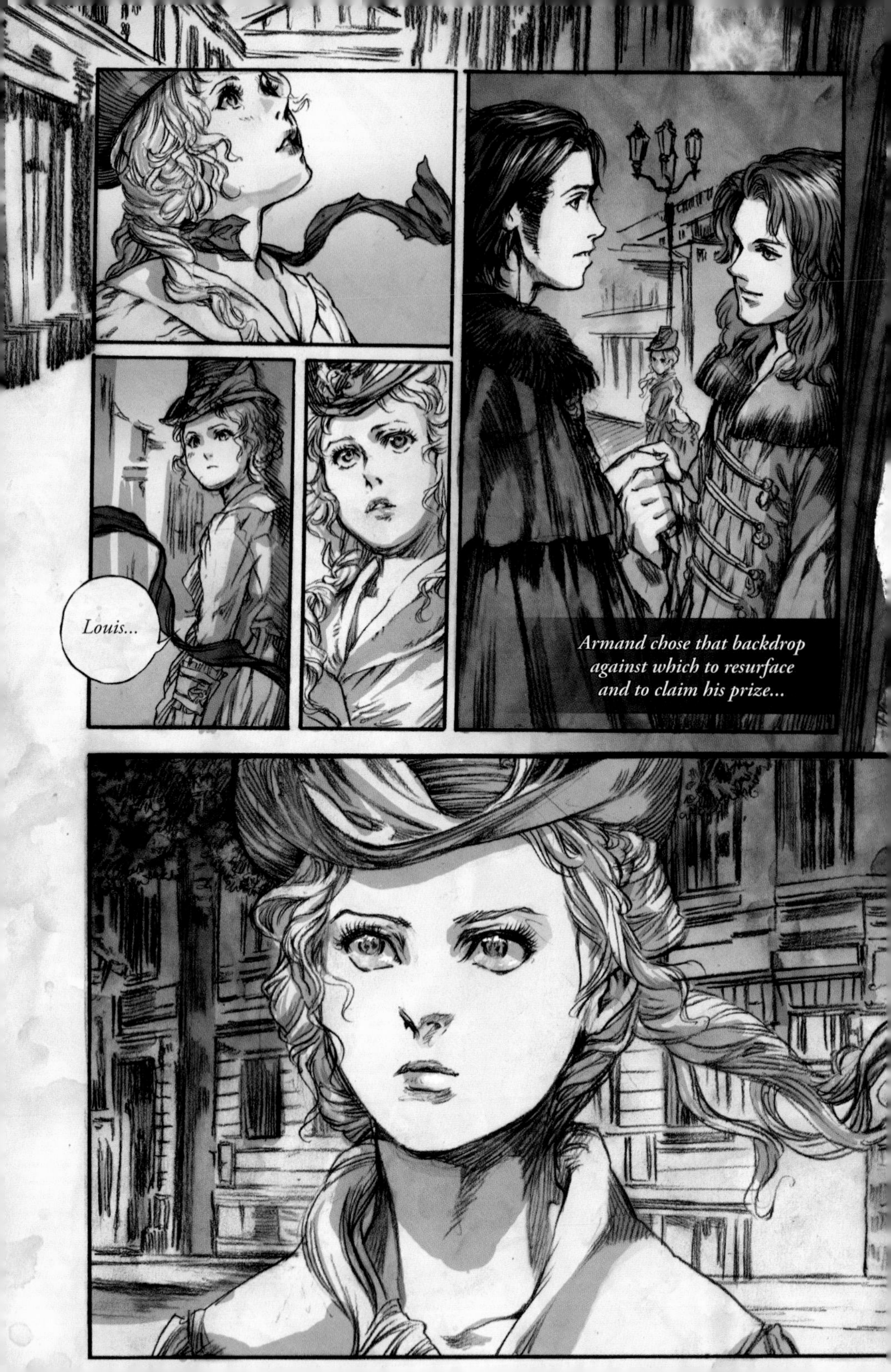

Louis...
Armand chose that backdrop against which to resurface and to claim his prize...

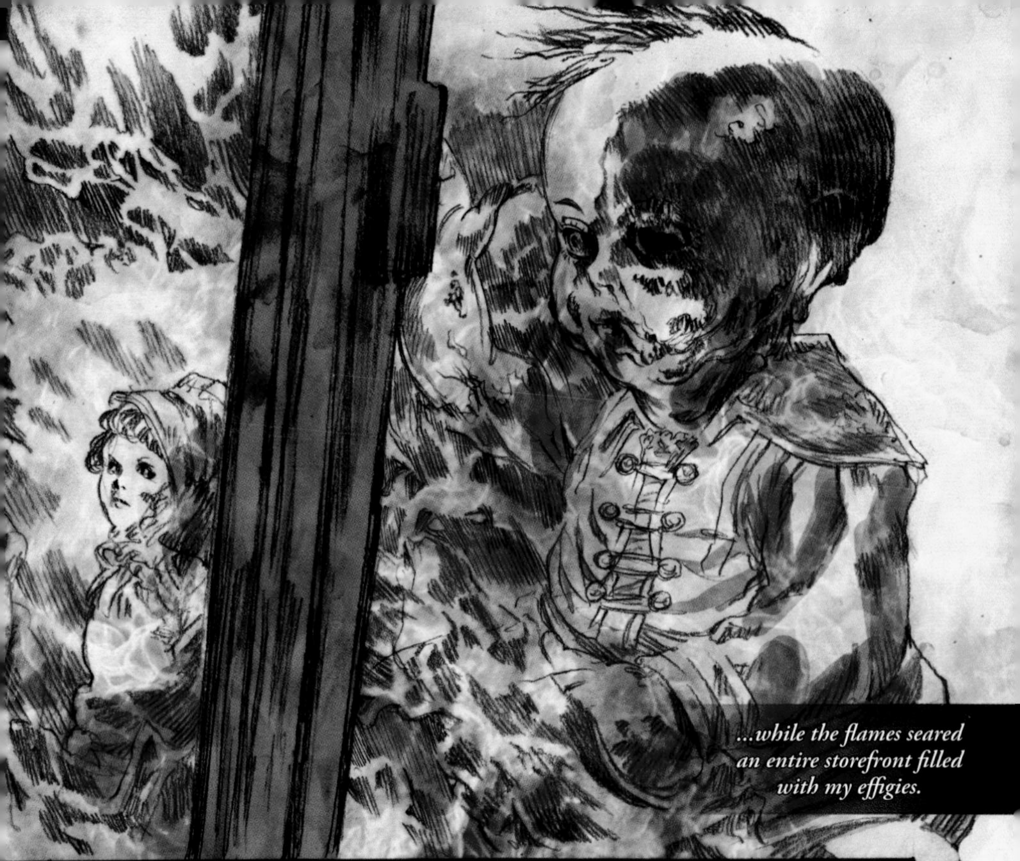
...while the flames seared an entire storefront filled with my effigies.

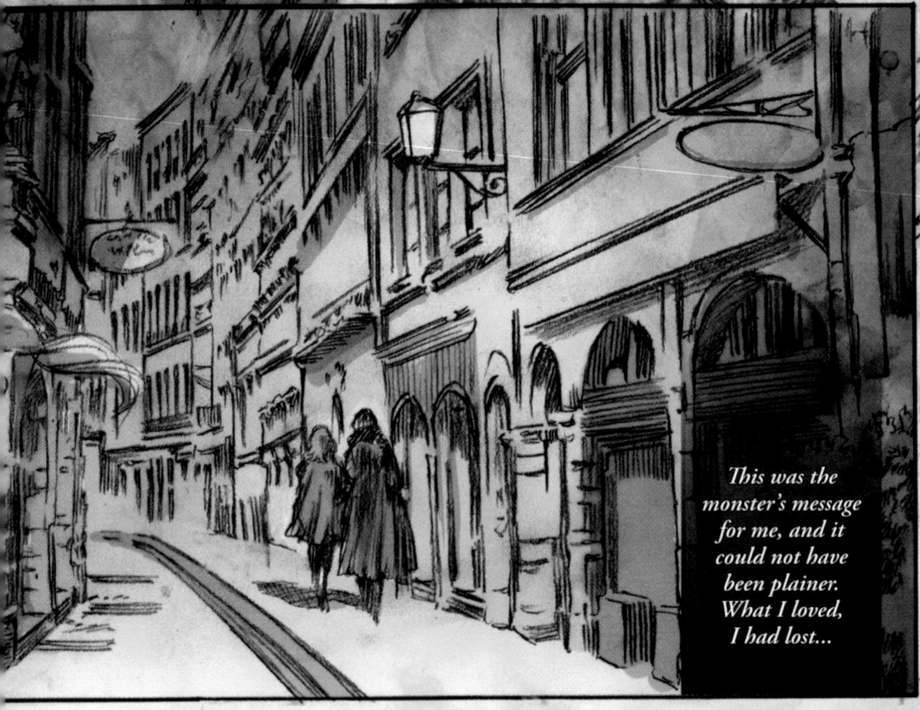
This was the monster's message for me, and it could not have been plainer. What I loved, I had lost...

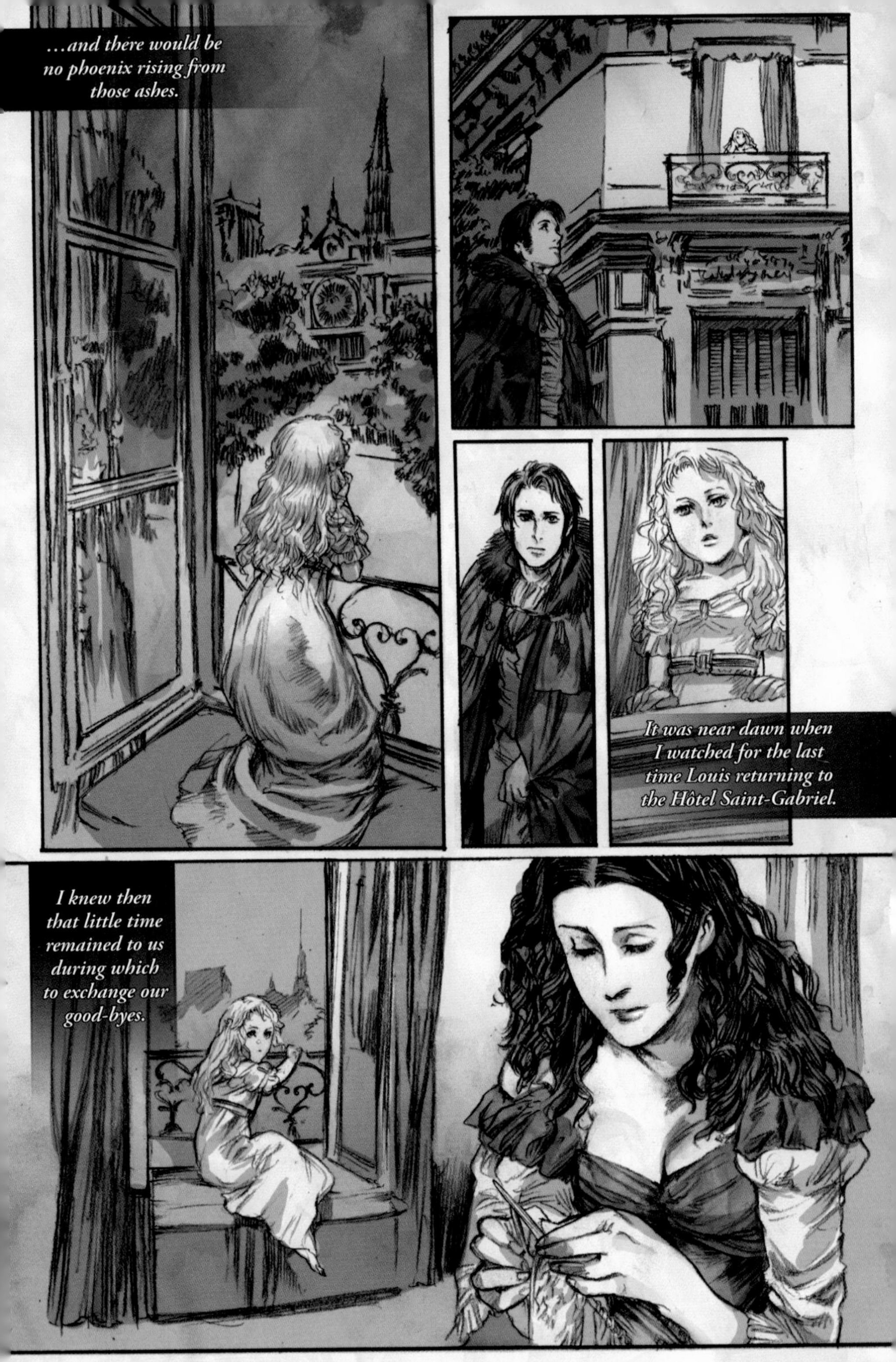
…and there would be no phoenix rising from those ashes.
It was near dawn when I watched for the last time Louis returning to the Hôtel Saint-Gabriel.
I knew then that little time remained to us during which to exchange our good-byes.

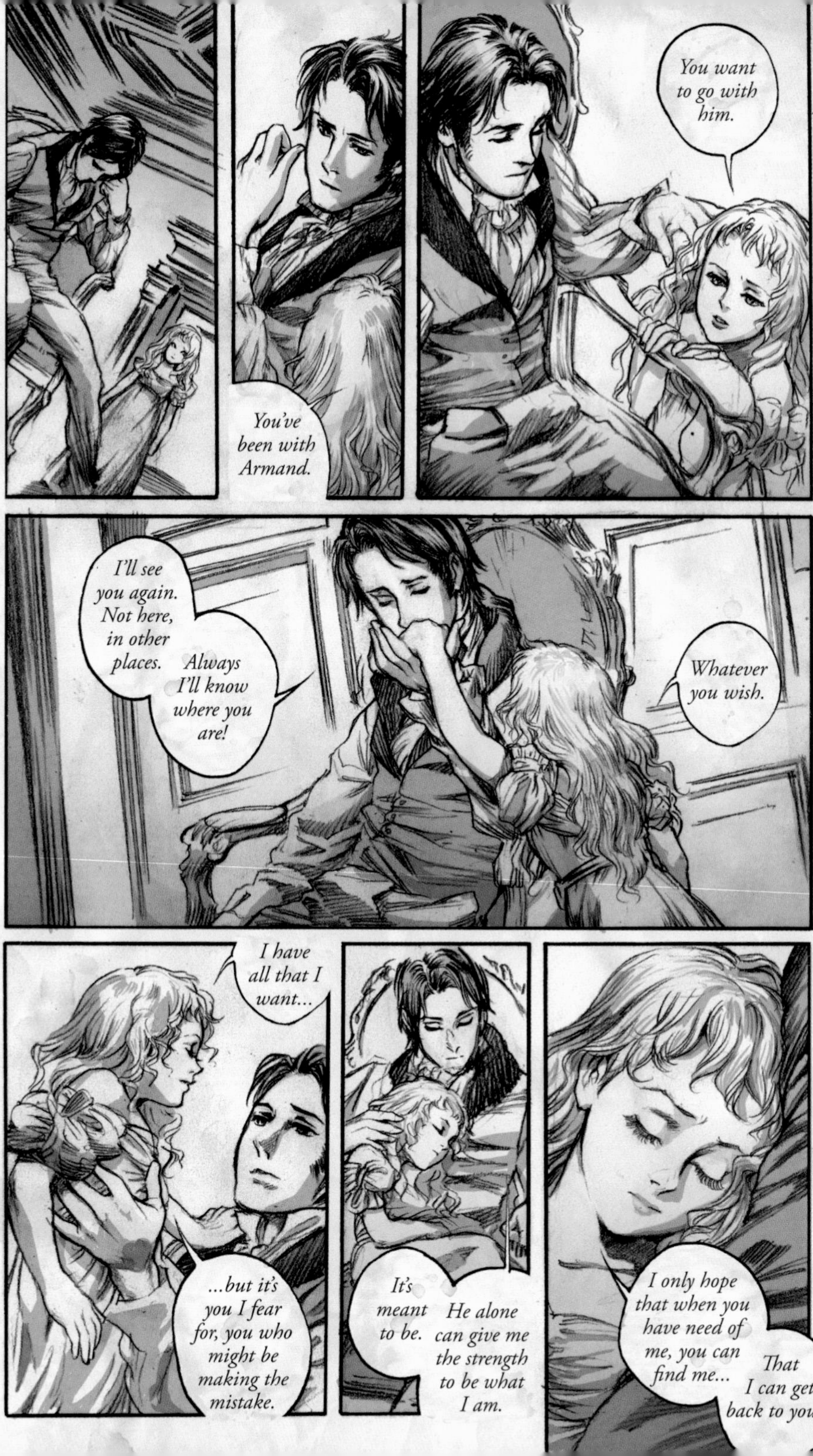
You've been with Armand.
You want to go with him.
I'll see you again. Not here, in other places.
Always I'll know where you are!
Whatever you wish.
I have all that I want...
...but it's you I fear for, you who might be making the mistake.
It's meant to be.
He alone can give me the strength to be what I am.
I only hope that when you have need of me, you can find me...
That I can get back to you...

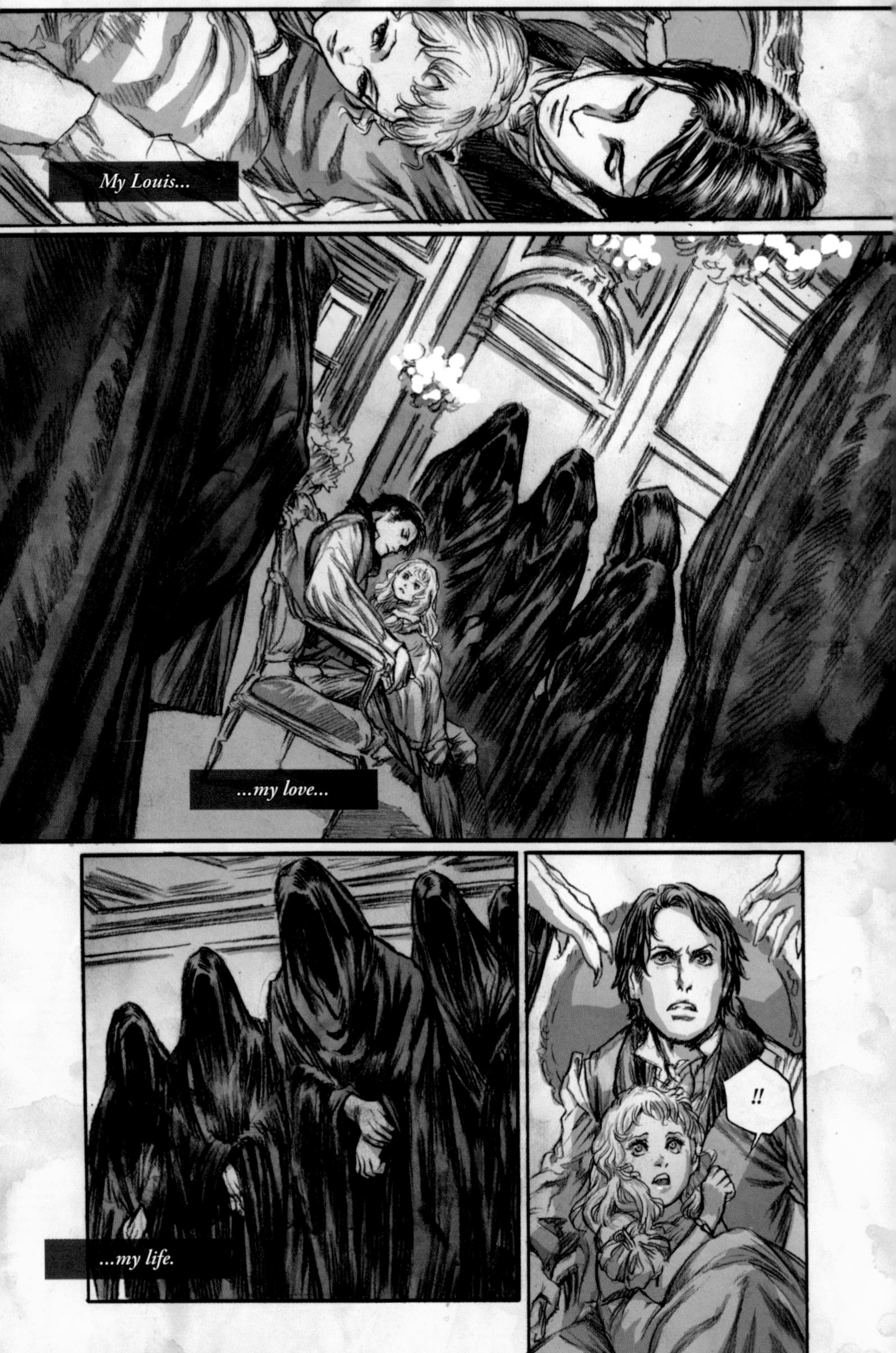
My Louis...
...my love...
...my life.
!!

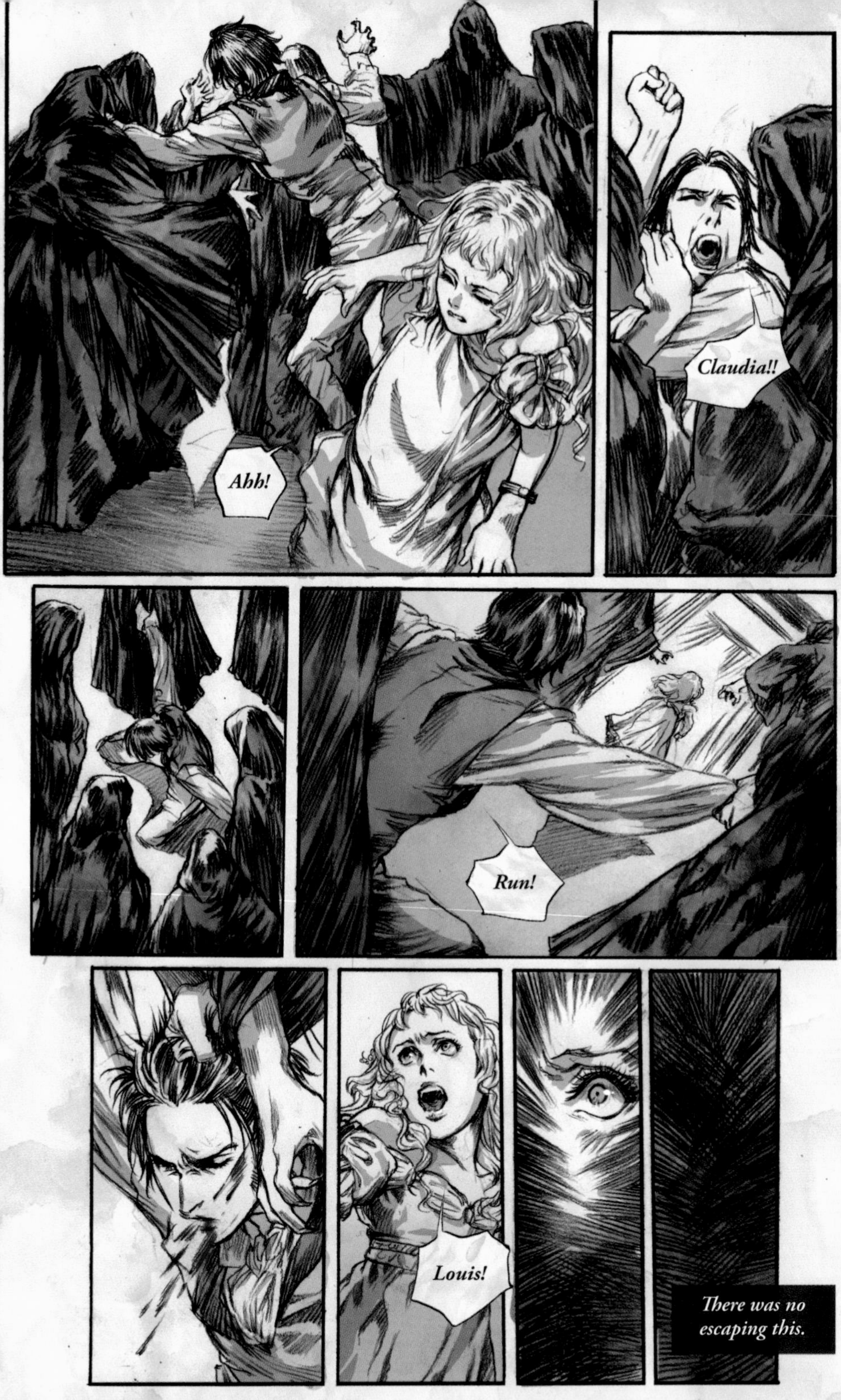
Ahh!
Claudia!!
Run!
Louis!
There was no escaping this.

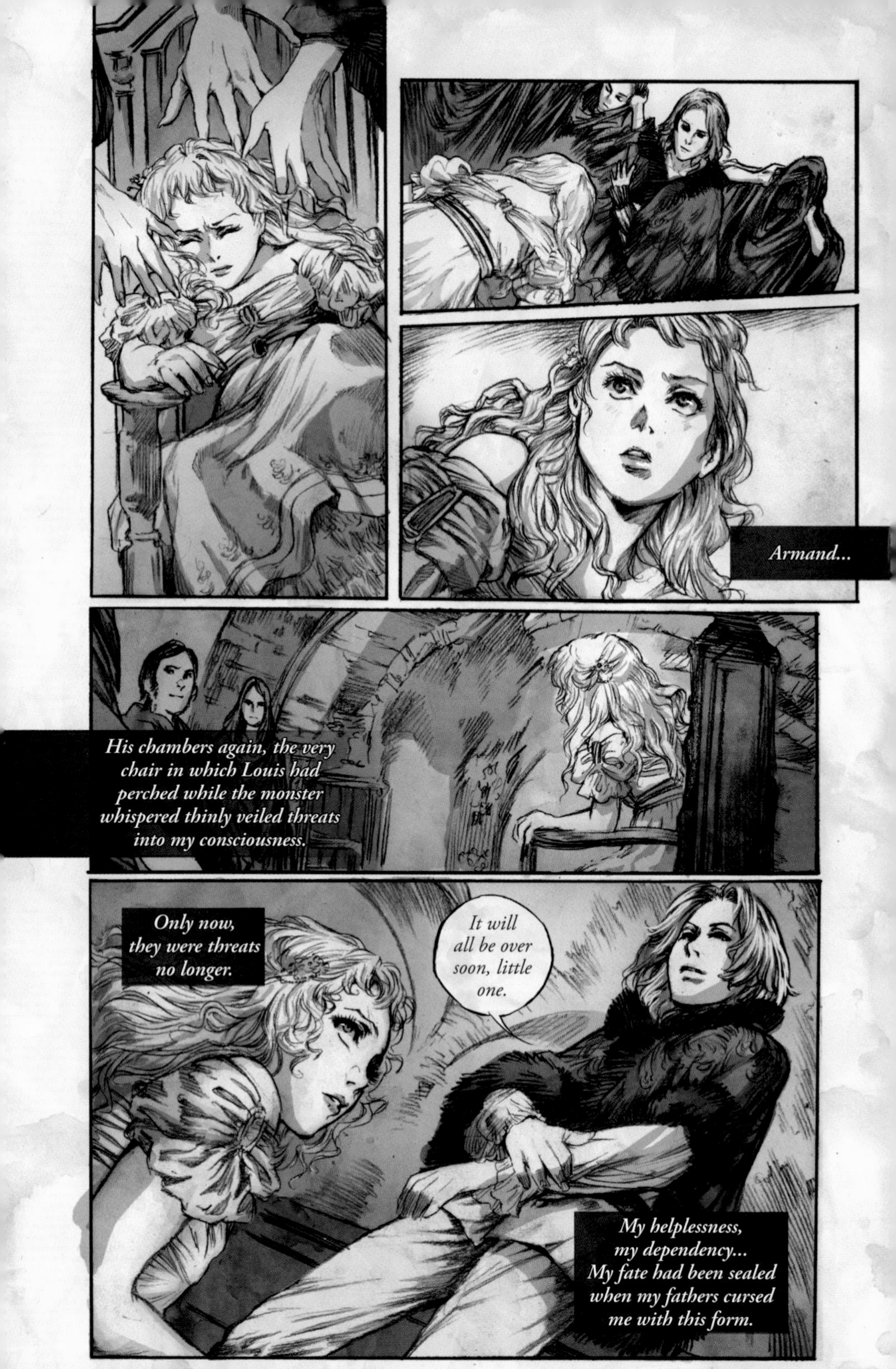
Armand...
His chambers again, the very chair in which Louis had perched while the monster whispered thinly veiled threats into my consciousness.
Only now, they were threats no longer.
It will all be over soon, little one.
My helplessness, my dependency... My fate had been sealed when my fathers cursed me with this form.

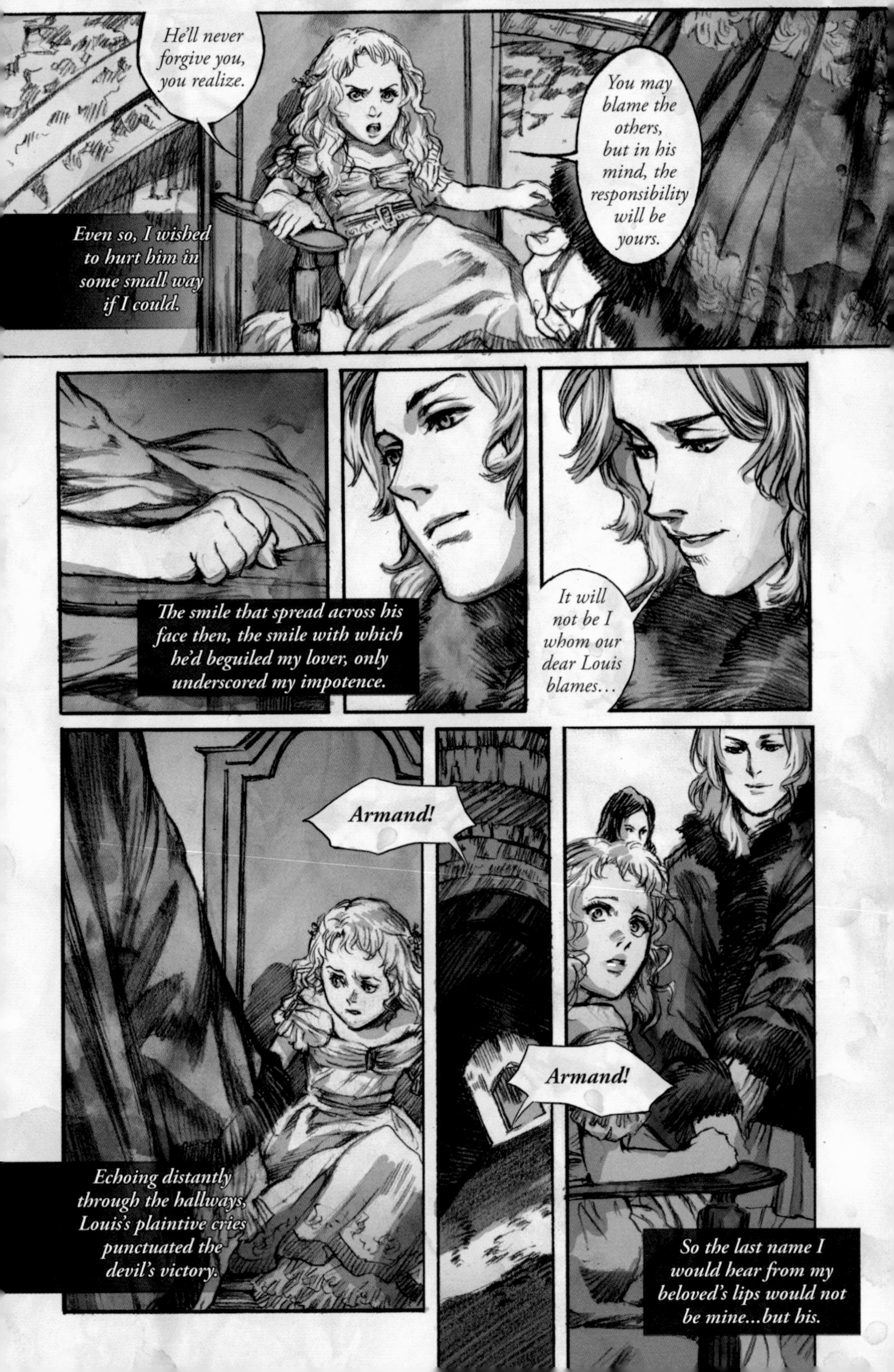
He'll never forgive you, you realize.
You may blame the others, but in his mind, the responsibility will be yours.
Even so, I wished to hurt him in some small way if I could.
The smile that spread across his face then, the smile with which he'd beguiled my lover, only underscored my impotence.
It will not be I whom our dear Louis blames...
Armand!
Echoing distantly through the hallways, Louis's plaintive cries punctuated the devil's victory.
Armand!
So the last name I would hear from my beloved's lips would not be mine...but his.

It is time.

Shortly after Louis's screams died away, the vampire Santiago made his entrance.

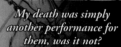

My death was simply another performance for them, was it not?

Is there any final request I might grant you, little one?

He would have me beg at the end, debase myself for his satisfaction...

Let's just be done with this.

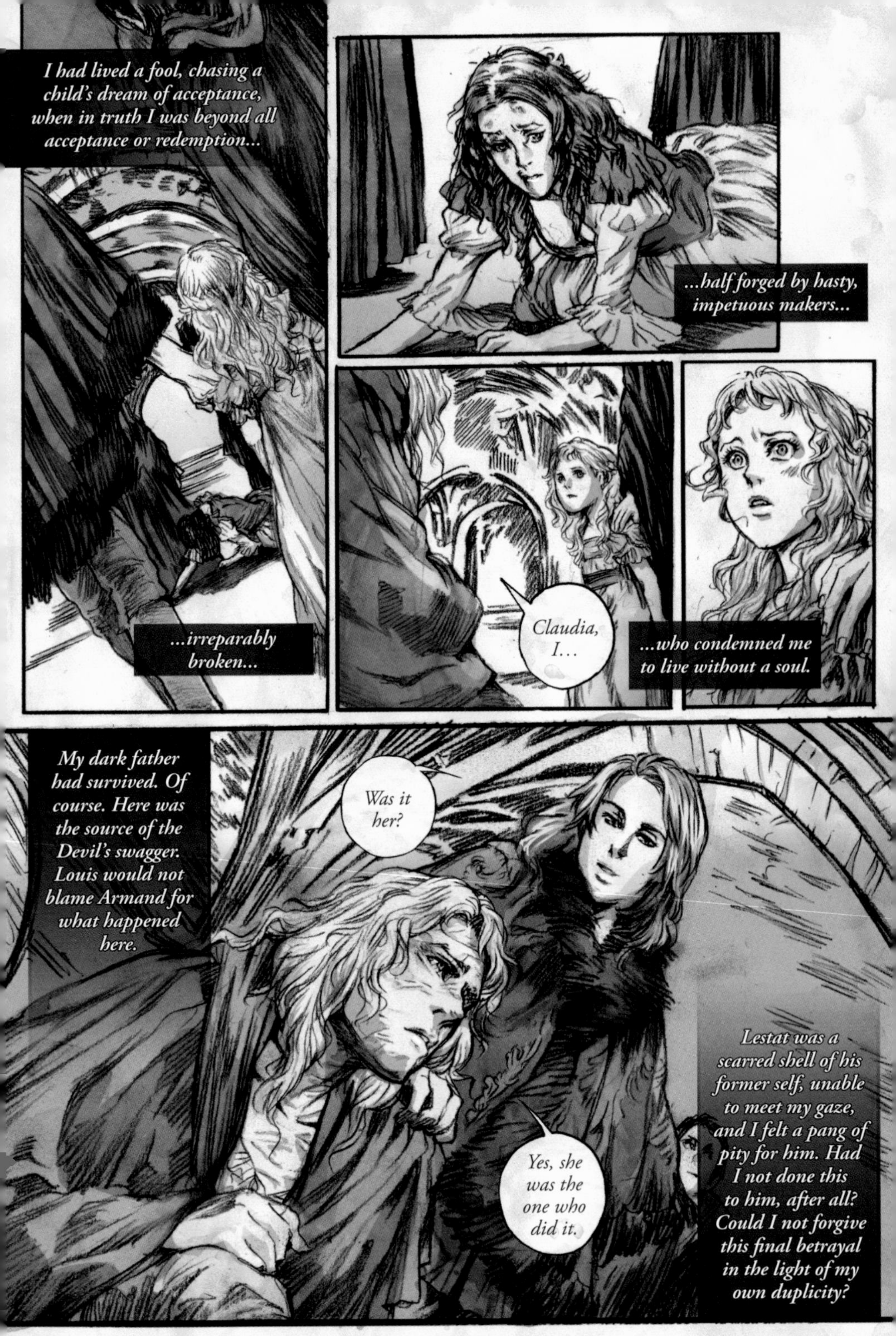
I had lived a fool, chasing a child's dream of acceptance, when in truth I was beyond all acceptance or redemption...
...irreparably broken...
...half forged by hasty, impetuous makers...
Claudia, I...
...who condemned me to live without a soul.
My dark father had survived. Of course. Here was the source of the Devil's swagger. Louis would not blame Armand for what happened here.
Was it her?
Yes, she was the one who did it.
Lestat was a scarred shell of his former self, unable to meet my gaze, and I felt a pang of pity for him. Had I not done this to him, after all? Could I not forgive this final betrayal in the light of my own duplicity?

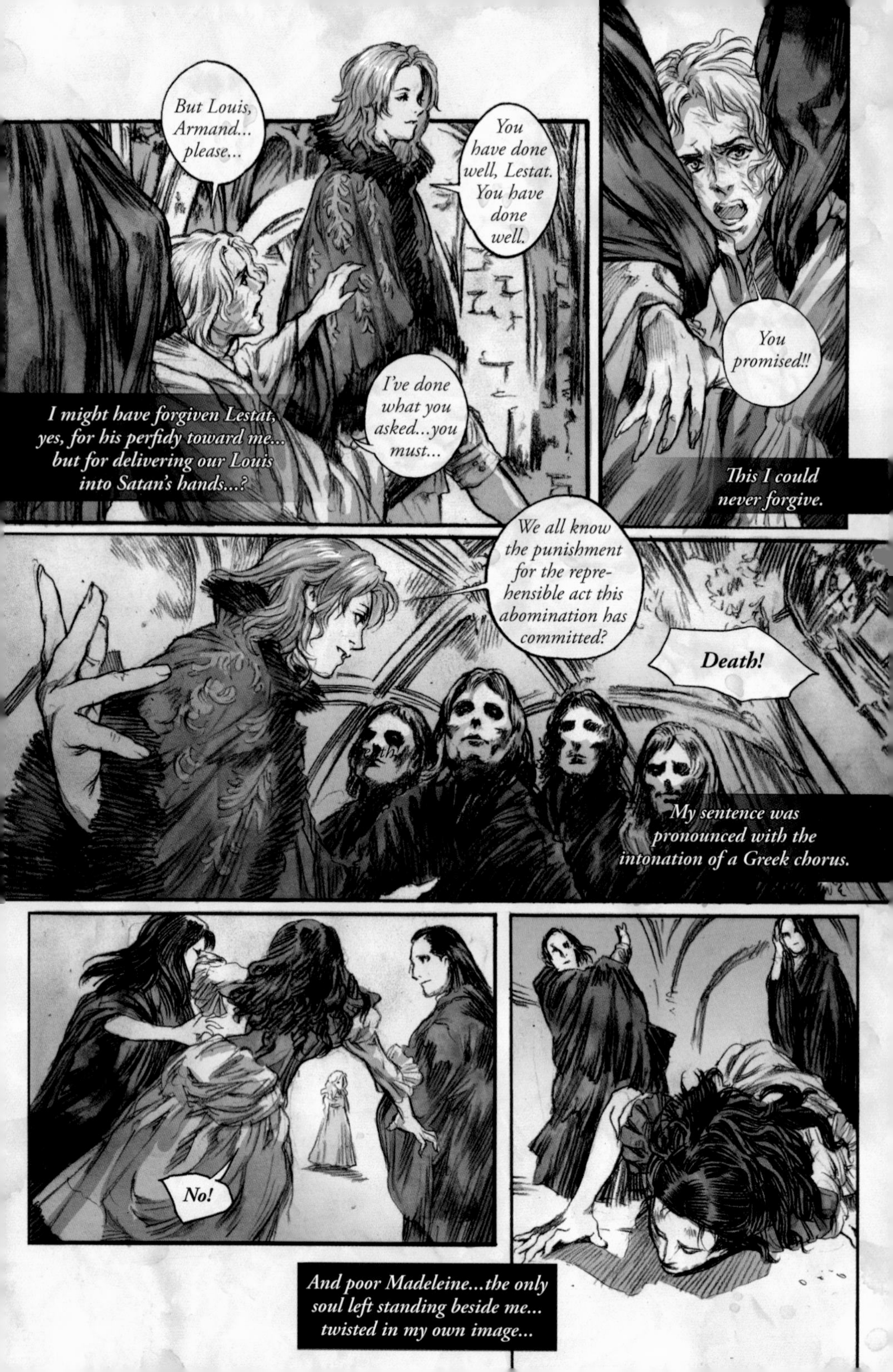
But Louis, Armand... please...
You have done well, Lestat. You have done well.
I've done what you asked...you must...
I might have forgiven Lestat, yes, for his perfidy toward me... but for delivering our Louis into Satan's hands...?
You promised!!
This I could never forgive.
We all know the punishment for the reprehensible act this abomination has committed?
Death!
My sentence was pronounced with the intonation of a Greek chorus.
No!
And poor Madeleine...the only soul left standing beside me... twisted in my own image...

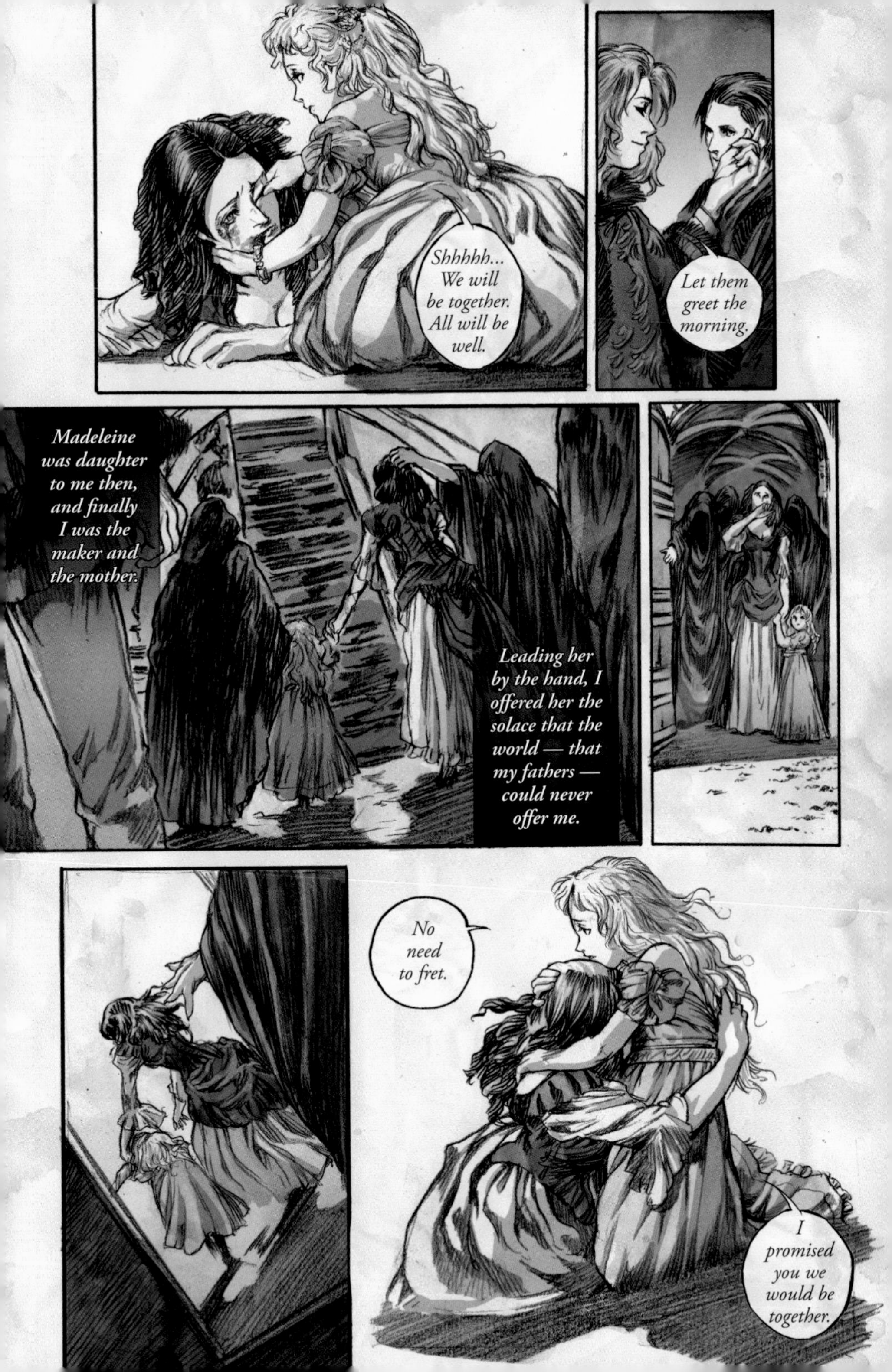
Shhhhh... We will be together. All will be well.
Let them greet the morning.
Madeleine was daughter to me then, and finally I was the maker and the mother.
Leading her by the hand, I offered her the solace that the world — that my fathers — could never offer me.
No need to fret.
I promised you we would be together.

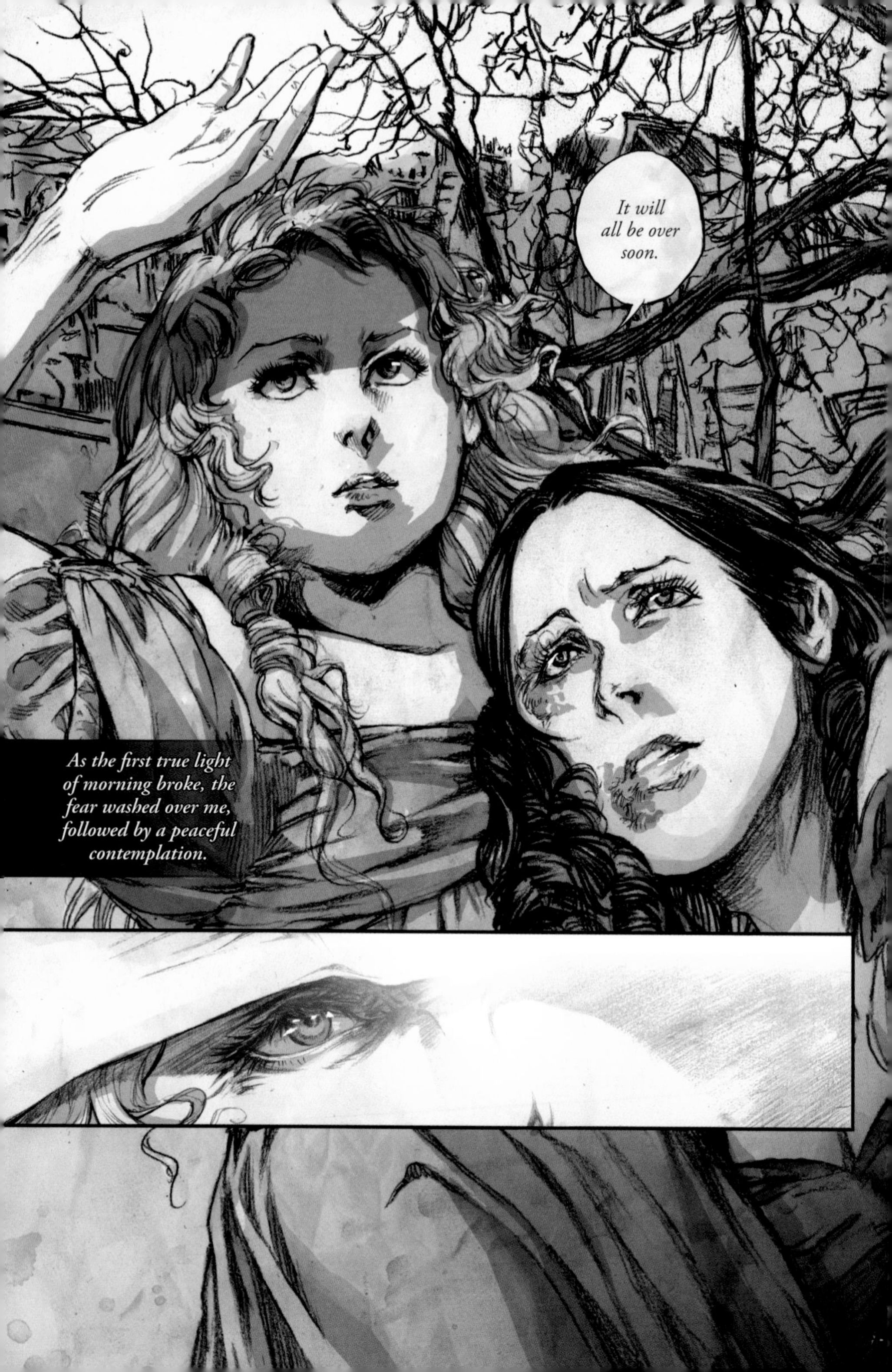
It will all be over soon.
As the first true light of morning broke, the fear washed over me, followed by a peaceful contemplation.

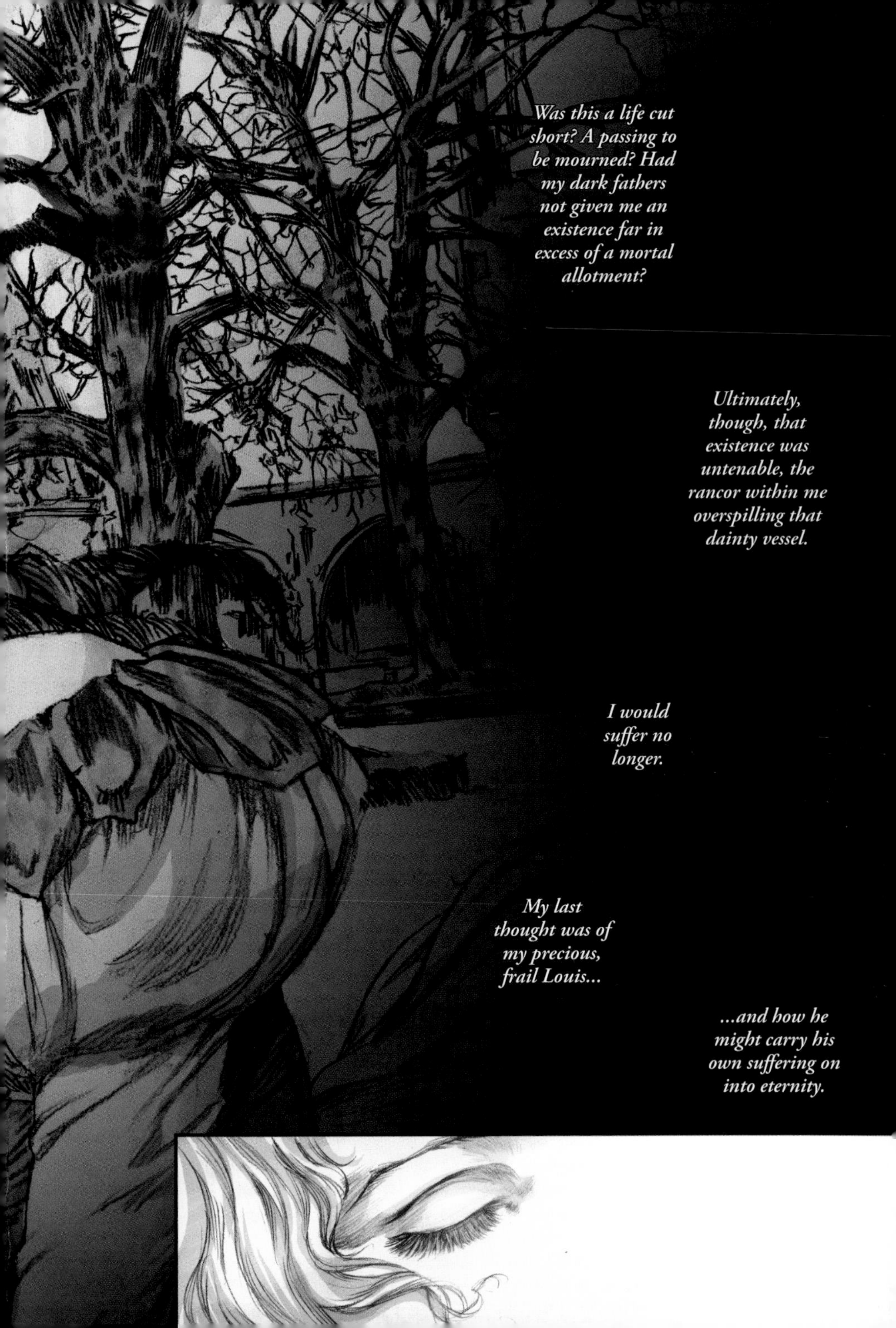
Was this a life cut short? A passing to be mourned? Had my dark fathers not given me an existence far in excess of a mortal allotment?
Ultimately, though, that existence was untenable, the rancor within me overspilling that dainty vessel.
I would suffer no longer.
My last thought was of my precious, frail Louis...
...and how he might carry his own suffering on into eternity.

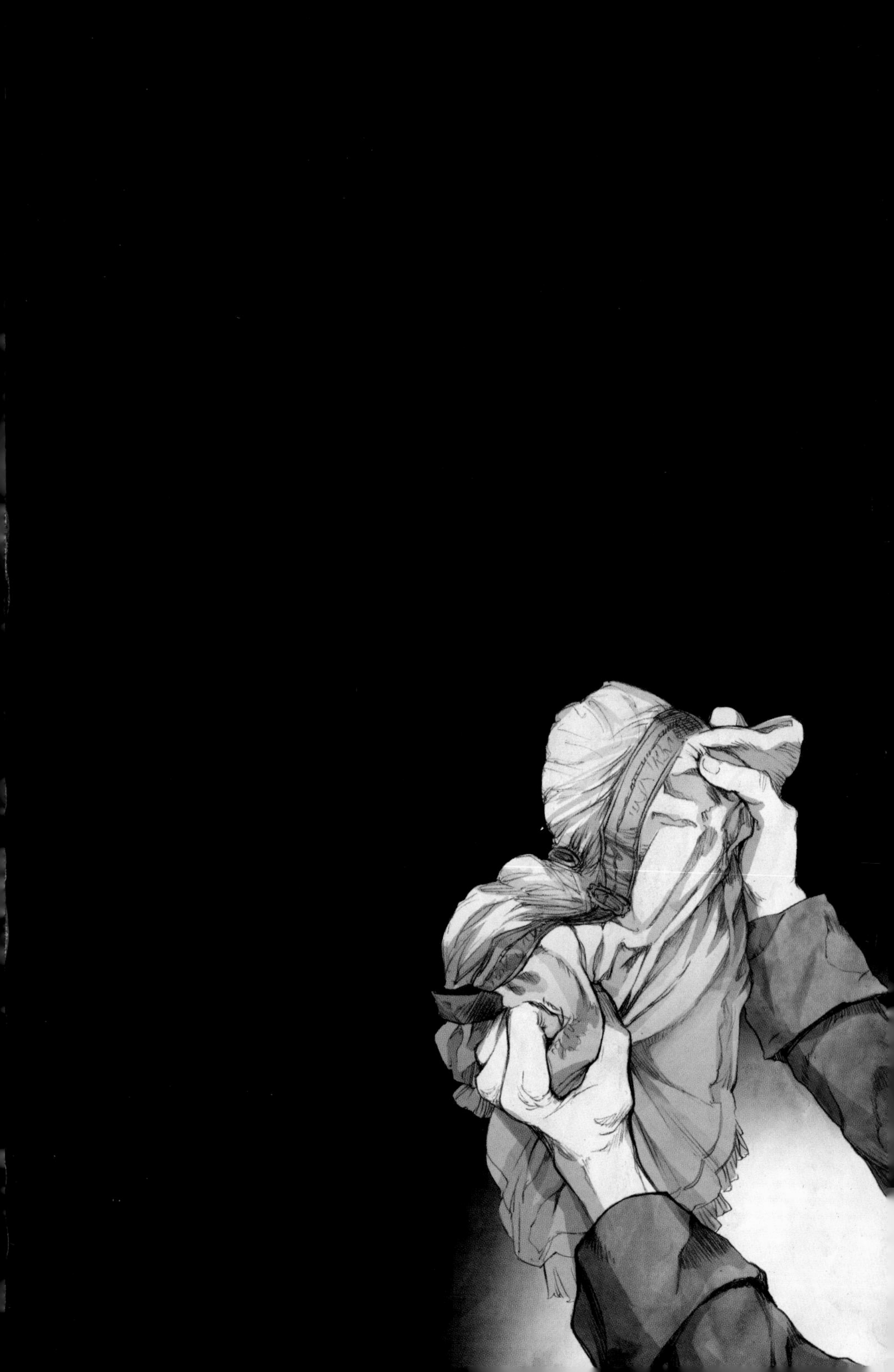